Books by Emily Carmichael

LAWLESS
VISIONS OF THE HEART
TOUCH OF FIRE
OUTCAST

Published by
WARNER BOOKS

OUTCAST

EMILY CARMICHAEL

WARNER BOOKS

A Time Warner Company

Cover design by Diane Luger
Cover photograph by Herman Estevez
Inset photo by Comstock/Jack Elness
Hand lettering by Carl Dellacroce

Warner Books, Inc.
1271 Avenue of the Americas
New York, NY 10020

W A Time Warner Company

ISBN 0-446-36411-8

Printed in the United States of America

Prologue

Virginia City, Montana
July, 1887

A good old-fashioned hanging was an entertainment that the citizens of Virginia City, Montana, hadn't seen in twenty years or more—not since the rowdy vigilante days of the 1860s. Consequently, a good-sized crowd turned out to see Gabriel William Danaher O'Connell dangle from a tree limb. The spectacle promised to liven up a dull, hot Sunday afternoon.

Will O'Connell, however, could have done without this particular entertainment. Hands bound behind his back and a hemp noose chafing at his neck, he sat astride his horse and stared out at the milling crowd. The world had gone mad, and even his Irish imagination couldn't stretch far enough to comprehend how the peaceful life he had made for himself had suddenly twisted and thrust him into this nightmare. On a day such as this one, he should have been mending harness, fixing fence, working with the spring foals, or pulling a white-faced heifer out of a brush tangle. What demented turn of fate had him facing an ugly death with a rope around his neck?

Angry protests ached in his throat, but Will bit them back. He refused to lose control before this damnable crowd. The mass of faces stared and gaped, eager to hear the crack of his neck and see the final twitching of his body. They had no right to enjoy his death; they had no right to kill him so casually. But the spectators weren't interested in the truth of what had happened. They didn't care that he had a family that needed his protection. Will O'Connell lived outside the bounds of what "decent" people considered proper; therefore he was wicked. When a leading citizen accused him of murder and mayhem, a trial wasn't necessary—only a hanging.

Will scanned the mob, bringing faces into focus one by one. Miss Samantha Edgar, the schoolteacher, looked faintly disapproving both of the crowd and its victim. He had spoken to her only once—the day she had refused to admit Katy and Ellen to her school. John Miller, the blacksmith, had a mile-wide grin on his broad face. This was probably the most fun he'd had in years. Mecham Tully, the storekeeper, looked properly solemn, but of the people Will had done business with in the nine years he'd raised cattle and horses on his ranch outside Virginia City, he didn't see one willing to speak for him. The only friend who might defend him was not here. Old Widow Casey thought anyone who hailed from the Emerald Isle was, if not good, at least redeemable. Katy and Ellen would be safe with her, bless her heart.

"This here hangin' will come to order while the charges are read!"

At Marshal Kale's shout, the crowd grew expectantly silent.

"Will O'Connell has been found guilty of murderin' Buck Candliss, one of Virginia City's most upstanding citizens, and shootin' Buck's brother Ace in the leg. Poor man'll be a gimp for the rest of his days."

Will smiled grimly. He'd shot the bastards, all right, but his only crime was that his aim hadn't been as true with Ace as it had with Buck. Buck's demise was the only part of this grim situation that gave Will any comfort.

The marshal cleared his throat officiously. "Will O'Connell has also been found guilty of killing the Blackfoot squaw who was living with him, a woman by the name of Many Horses Woman."

The name sliced through Will's heart, and he closed his eyes as if that could block some of the pain. Minnie, he'd called her. For eleven years she'd been his wife, but to these people a Blackfoot marriage ceremony was merely a heathen ritual—and Minnie was just a squaw. He could see her soft brown eyes, her wide smile, the glossy black hair that fell to her waist. But in his last memory of her that hair had been scarlet with blood, the brown eyes hard and glassy as they had stared sightlessly at the rafters of their home, and the wide mouth slack and lifeless. He could smell the sharp odor of gun smoke and the metallic scent of blood as if they still surrounded him. Anger swelled his chest until he thought it would burst.

"This bein' a crime so hei . . . heinous that it calls for instant action on the part of the good people of Virginia City, and havin' the reliable word of Mr. Ace Candliss as to the true events . . . uh"—

Will opened his eyes as the marshal squinted at the speech Candliss had written for him. The time was growing close. He could feel his gut tighten in anticipation.

—"uh . . . and seein' that Judge Parker is out of town for two weeks, I . . . uh . . . duly authorize this hangin' in the interest of the town's peace." He nodded his head with satisfaction.

The marshal checked that the hanging rope was secured properly to the branch above Will's head, and out of the corner of his eye Will saw a deputy move behind his horse in preparation for slapping its rump. His bowels tightened. He didn't want to die. He didn't want to strangle at the end of a rope until the breath had left his body.

Time seemed to slow. The words of his Blackfoot friend Crooked Stick played through his mind. "The man who is not afraid of death is a fool. The man who cannot control his fear is a coward." He would not be a coward. He would not let this goddamned mob feed on his fear.

Anger was the answer. Will focused his gaze on Ace Candliss, standing at the front of the crowd with his crutches and bandaged thigh. He saw his own anger and hatred reflected in the man's eyes.

The marshal's voice broke into his concentration. "Will. Do you have any last words?"

"I've said what I had to say, and you didn't listen."

The marshal cleared his throat. "Well, let's get on with it."

The deputy's slap on the horse's hindquarters coincided almost exactly with the crack of a rifle shot. The horse lunged forward just as the rope parted. Stunned by his sudden release, blood thundering madly in his ears, Will dug his heels into the horse's sides and galloped straight into the gawking crowd. Spectators fled to either side in a wave of screams and curses. Will had always thought the luck of the Irish was just a fable, but now he muttered a quick prayer to Saint Patrick to keep it coming.

"Pa! Here!" A pint-sized girl mounted on a rawboned Appaloosa galloped from an alleyway. As she rode, she struggled to stuff a rifle into the saddle boot. "This way, Pa!"

"Katy! Dammit! What the . . . ?"

"This way!"

They galloped toward the hills west of town. A swift glance over his shoulder told Will that the chase was on. The marshal and at least three other men were mounting up. Then trees hid the town from view.

Katy's horse slid to a stop so fast that Will's almost slammed into it on the narrow trail. She pulled a knife from her belt and sawed at the ropes that bound Will's hands.

"Leave the noose," he told her. "I can deal with it later. You get out of here."

Katy ignored him. "Ellen! Ellen, come out!"

"Oh God! Not Ellen too!"

The brush at the side of the trail rustled. Hesitantly, an almost perfect duplicate of Katy led her horse onto the trail.

"Well, mount up!" Katy ordered. "You think we have all day?"

"Both of you get out of here!" Will gave his daughters a scowl that should have sent them running for cover. The girls, both black-haired and green-eyed with elfin pointed chins and a dimple denting each left cheek, stared back. "Go back to Widow Casey's. And stay there!"

"No time," Katy chirped confidently. "We're going with you."

"The hell you are!"

But Katy was already galloping ahead. "I know a way out of this," she shouted over her shoulder, then grinned. "You gonna stay here all day?"

Will cursed again, but he followed. There was nothing else he could do. Falling in behind him, Ellen declared, "This was Katy's idea."

"That's what I figured."

They galloped steadily for ten minutes, and all that time Will heard the sounds of pursuit grow closer. The hills were too open to hide them, and with the girls along he couldn't even stand and make a fight of it. They paused to look back along the trail.

"Katy, take Ellen and circle back to town. I'm going to have to fight my way out of this."

"No, Pa. I know a way. Come on."

Will cursed the day Minnie gave him daughters and cursed himself for teaching them to think like men. The country was growing rougher, and the posse was in sight and closing fast. Katy urged her horse into a stream that wound down a brush-clogged gulch.

"This way, Pa. I've been scouting around since you've been in jail. Widow Casey thought I was upstairs moping like Ellen, but I figured Ma wouldn't want us to sit around doing something useless like crying when you were fixing to get your neck stretched."

The gulch grew narrower. There would be no escape if it ended in a box canyon. The hoofbeats of the posse were plain to hear now.

"This is it. Come on."

The gulch ended in a ten-foot waterfall. The pool below might be just deep enough to break the fall of a man and horse. Will saw his way out of the hangman's noose. He doubted fat Marshal Kale or any of his makeshift posse wanted him badly enough to risk the jump. Katy threw him a smug look.

Ellen peered over the edge. "Katy! You can't mean it!"

"It's not that high."

"It's impossible!"

Will interrupted their debate. "You girls go back to town with the posse. The marshal's not a man to take out his temper on ten-year-olds. I'll be back for you when I can."

"Sure, Pa."

They were better off with Widow Casey than with him, even if Katy did run wild rings around the lady. The widow was rich and she loved the girls. She would protect them. When Will had found a way to deal with Ace Candliss, he could be with his family again.

If he thought about it any more, Will knew, he wouldn't be able to leave them. He steeled himself and dug his heels into the horse's flanks. Startled, the mare lurched forward, and Will's stomach crowded his throat as the world seemed to drop and leave them behind. The fall felt longer than it had looked. They hit with a painful slap. The water wrenched Will out of the saddle, then swallowed him. Through the murk he could see the churning of the horse's hooves as he pushed off the pool's bottom and stroked for the surface. He emerged and cleared his eyes just in time to see Ellen jump.

"Goddammit!" He dove for her as she went under. She surfaced sputtering accusations.

"Katy jabbed my horse with a stick!"

"Get out of the way!" Katy called from above. "Here I come!"

A string of Irish curses ran through Will's head as he pulled his daughters from the churning murk. All three horses awaited them, snorting and dripping, when he hauled the girls onto the bank.

"Told you I knew a way out!" Katy grinned at him.

"How do you like that?"

"I don't like it," Marshal Kale snapped at his deputy. "If Ace Candliss expects me to break my neck goin' after that devil, then he's got another think comin'."

The rest of the posse reined in their horses at the lip of the falls and stared down at the Irishman and his two half-breed brats leading their horses away from the stream.

"If that don't beat all," Abe Harper muttered.

"It beats me." Kale turned his horse back the way they had come. "From now on Candliss can do his own dirty work."

Chapter 1

Elkhorn, Montana
November 1889

*W*ell, Margaret, I just don't know what advice to give you, dear. It is a vexing problem indeed. Who would think one would have to consider such a delicate social issue in an out-of-the-way place like Elkhorn? I mean to say, one knows how to deal with unrefined miners and prospectors and gamblers and the loose women who inhabit this town, but just how does one react to a woman like Olivia Baron?"

Margaret Norton pursed her lips and gave her friend an exasperated look. "That's what I was asking you, Cornelia. What do I do about Olivia Baron?"

Henry Shriner forestalled any answer by appearing from the back room of his general mercantile and giving the two matrons a smile. "Good afternoon, Mrs. Norton, Mrs. Stanwick. Can I help you ladies with anything?"

"Ah, yes, Henry." Margaret opened her reticule and extracted a piece of paper. "I have a list to be filled. If your boy could bring it around later this afternoon, please. My people need to start preparations for the musicale and tea I'm giving tomorrow evening. I do hope you and your dear wife received my invitation."

"Penelope's looking forward to the event. Unfortunately, I have a meeting to attend at Fraternity Hall."

"Well, of course, you can't miss your Masonic meeting."

Margaret cast a glance askance at Cornelia. Men were so unrefined. Imagine choosing a rowdy, smoky meeting in Fraternity Hall to the up-lifting diversion offered at her musicale, where her cousin Edgar from Pennsylvania would entertain them with pieces on the piccolo and flute. Neither would Henry Shriner understand the issue of Olivia Baron, which is why Margaret delayed further discussion of the problem until the man turned his attention elsewhere.

Cornelia was more interested in shopping, however. "I heard you have a new shipment of bonnets, Mr. Shriner."

"Yes indeed, Mrs. Stanwick. A fine lot of hats this time. Just in from Helena. You'll find them two aisles over from yard goods, in front of the shovels. Excuse me, ladies. If you need anything else, just ask. I'll be sure that these items are delivered on time, Mrs. Norton." He turned to greet a man who had just entered the store accompanied by a blast of cold air from the open door.

Margaret clutched her coat more snugly about her and frowned at her companion. "Cornelia! You can't look at hats until you help me decide what to do about Olivia Baron."

"I told you, dear. I've no idea what you should do."

"She's the guest of one of the town's leading families. If I don't invite her, I might offend Mrs. Talbot. Then I would be in a pickle indeed."

"Yes, you would."

"But if I do invite her, no one will pay proper attention to the music or credit the refreshments. They'll all be gawking at her."

"Yes, that's true. It's quite a dilemma. Look here." Cornelia picked up a bottle from a display. "Hoofland's Entirely Vegetable German Bitters. Do you think this would help my stomach?"

"Cornelia, you're not paying attention," Margaret chided. "I simply do not understand why a woman would take up a profession such as medi-cine. I honestly do not. It's not as if Miss Baron weren't born with advan-tages. No indeed. Mrs. Talbot told me herself that the woman's family is prominent in banking in New York. And she's quite passable looking, in a plain sort of way. I'm sure she could have found a husband had she put her energy into cultivating her femininity instead of pursuing subjects that should be left to men. It's unnatural! That's what it is!"

"I'm sure you're quite right, Margaret. You usually are, after all."

"If she weren't a dear friend of Amy Talbot's, I wouldn't give her the time of day, I assure you. But I suppose I must invite her for tomorrow evening. Mrs. Talbot would be upset if I didn't, and I wouldn't want to upset Mrs. Talbot in her delicate condition."

"I think I will buy this tonic. Lydia Pinkham's is simply not as settling as it once was."

Margaret sighed. "You do that, dear. But come along, now. I really must get back to the house. Mr. Shriner!" She raised her voice to snatch the storekeeper's attention from his other customer. "You will have those goods delivered this afternoon, won't you?"

"Yes, Mrs. Norton. You can be sure that I will."

"Very well. Come, Cornelia. The afternoon is wasting."

"But the bonnets!"

"You can look at them later, dear. Really! There's so much to be done."

From behind the yard-goods display, Amy Talbot flinched as the door shut behind the two matrons. "Olivia, I'm so embarrassed. I do apologize for those two old biddies. Certainly we will not go to their stupid musicale tomorrow evening."

"Oh posh." Rachel Olivia Baron smiled. "I'm not twigged a bit, Amy, so don't let it bother you."

"But what they said! It's horrible, and I'm ashamed of them and the whole town that's treated you like some sort of zoo exhibit ever since you came to Elkhorn. It makes me furious, is what it does! You were kind enough to come all the way from New York to help a friend, and I would expect people to credit your generosity and dedication and kindness. Instead, they mince around you as though you were some kind of freak. Their attitude really gets my dander up, I tell you."

"You get your dander up much too easily." Olivia smiled again. "I've grown used to being the center of ladies' gossip. If they didn't treat me as such an item I'm sure I'd feel quite neglected."

"You're much too good-natured. The idea of Margaret Norton saying such things makes me . . . makes me . . ."

"Makes your stomach churn and your head hurt. Yes, I know. Really, Amy, such a temper is not good for the child you carry."

Amy instantly looked abashed.

Olivia chuckled at her friend's prompt reaction. The sure way to get Amy to comply with any suggestion was to invoke the good of her unborn child. After having lost two babies, she would do anything to bear her husband a live, healthy child—even persuade the most trusted friend of her girlhood to delay a hard-won medical appointment at the New England Hospital for Women and Children and make a journey to the backside of nowhere to attend her. "Chin up, dear. I'm not foretelling disaster. Just try to keep your emotions a little more serene."

Amy pouted prettily. "That's easy for you to say. You're always in perfect control of yourself. How can you fail to be upset when you're treated like a sideshow creature?"

"People have been telling me I'm an unnatural female since I was ten and decided to become a physician. Even my father thought I was bound for calamity, bless his heart. He read to me from the writings of Dr. E. H. Clarke and even had me memorize the most vivid portions of his warnings. I can still quote the foolish diatribe: 'Higher education for women produces monstrous brains and puny bodies, abnormally active cerebration and abnormally weak digestion, flowing thought and constipated bowels.' Dr. Clarke really became quite tiresome on the subject."

"Oh, dear. Your father truly made you read such things?"

Olivia smiled without rancor. "That and more, bless him! I've endured the outlook of almost every friend and relation on the subject, as well as professors of medicine and fellow physicians. Women are too limited in intellect to comprehend the complexities of medicine, they lack courage and judgment, are nervous, excitable, and subject to uncontrolled hysteria."

"What nonsense!"

"Of course it is. But one becomes accustomed to such attitudes, you see, and simply goes on to accomplish one's goal. Allowing other people to upset you with their prejudices is quite pointless."

"Well, I'm certainly glad that Sylvester is not so narrow-minded. He was really delighted when I suggested inviting you here."

"Sylvester would be delighted to provide anything you desire. You could ask for a monkey from Africa to attend you and he would move the earth to humor you."

Amy smiled. "Perhaps. But I'm sure he considers you more qualified to attend me than a monkey."

Privately, Olivia doubted that.

"Speaking of Sylvester, Amy, we did promise to meet for hot chocolate in twenty minutes. If you want to look at fabric for nursery curtains, we'd better start looking."

"Yes." Amy sighed. "I simply got sidetracked by those two old dragons. Now, where is Mr. Shriner when I need him? Goodness only knows where he put aside that bolt of calico he promised me."

While Amy went in search of the storekeeper, Olivia wandered the aisles and enjoyed the mixed aromas that seemed to fill such stores whether they were in crowded New York City or the wilds of the Montana West—the warm scent of leather, the sugary odor of the open candy bins, the tang of tobacco and fresh-cut wood. In one corner, a nickel-plated stove added a bite of wood smoke and radiated a meager warmth that just managed to soften the November cold—until someone came through the door and brought with him a gust of cold air.

The mercantile stocked everything from ladies' fripperies to gold pans, cooking utensils to picks and shovels. Wall shelves were crowded with canned goods—evaporated milk, fruits, and meats. Barrels held candies and some rather sorry-looking vegetables that had been hauled by wagon from warmer climes, and behind the cash register was stacked a display of patent medicines to cure every ailment of the human condition, arranged neatly in alphabetical order from August Flower Bitters to Whitcomb's Remedy. Olivia scowled at the colorful bottles and the extravagant claims splashed across their labels. In her practice in New York she'd seen what these highly alcoholic and sometimes narcotic tonics could do to the naive men and women who depended on them for "nerves," stomach disorders, or general malaise.

"We have quite a complete stock of medicines, Dr. Baron." Henry Shriner gestured proudly to the pyramid of bottles.

"Indeed you have, Mr. Shriner. But I would hesitate to use the term 'medicines' for such remedies, sir. They do much more harm than good."

The storekeeper seemed taken aback by the level look she gave him. Many men, Olivia had found, were intimidated by a woman who dared to look them straight in the eyes—perhaps because they were so unaccustomed to it.

He cleared his throat awkwardly. "Well, now, Dr. Cahill and old Doc Traleigh both send patients in all the time to pick up one or another of these. Those doctors don't seem to agree with you, ma'am."

In the storekeeper's voice was the kind of condescension Olivia had grown accustomed to. She merely smiled. "Could you direct me to Mrs. Talbot? We seem to have become separated."

"Mrs. Talbot is in the back room looking at a bolt of calico. Would you like me to show you?"

"No, thank you. I'll just wander until she's done. You can tell her I'll be over by your new shipment of hats."

"I'll do that, Miss . . . uh . . . Doctor Baron."

Olivia could not resist looking at the hats. A passion for hats was one of the few feminine indulgences she allowed herself. When a woman chose to lead a life of science, study, dedication, and work, she needed to grant herself some small pleasures.

Even with the vaunted new shipment from Helena, the selection of hats in Mr. Shriner's general mercantile was nothing like the assortment Olivia would have found in New York. Still, after trying on several styles and critically evaluating them in the small oval looking glass on the pineboard wall, she decided a little straw bonnet that perched forward on her head was most becoming in a quiet sort of way. The hat reminded her of a fashion she'd seen in Paris, except that the Parisian women tilted their hats saucily forward and added false hair to increase the volume of their own tresses. Olivia was not sure that she achieved quite the desired effect with the hat atop her plain, severely parted coiffure.

Footsteps behind her indicated Amy's return. Olivia supposed she should ask her friend's opinion before buying the hat; Amy really did have a better eye for fashion than Olivia did.

"Do you think this is a bit too saucy, Amy? It's impractical, I suppose. Still, it is pretty, isn't it?"

"It looks like a hat I saw on a prospector's mule up the street."

That rich baritone certainly did not belong to Amy! Olivia whirled, her face burning, and had to tilt up her head to meet green eyes deep-set in a sun-browned face. "I beg your pardon!"

Her frosty tone simply made the man smile, and, unlike most men, he met her straightforward gaze without flinching. "You seemed to want an opinion, and since no one else is around at the moment, I thought mine might do. After all, don't ladies buy these useless little hats to impress men?"

"Certainly not! We buy them to decently cover our hair and keep the sun from our faces."

"Well, in that case, you won't want to buy that one. There's plenty of your hair left to see, and I can guarantee you'll have a burned face if you depend on that thing to ward off the sun."

"I didn't ask your opinion, sir."

"Well, now, I thought you did."

"I heard your footsteps and thought you were my friend Mrs. Talbot."

"Last time I looked I was certainly not Mrs. Talbot. Gabriel Danaher at your service, madam."

His voice was colored by just a hint of Irish brogue, so subtle as to be scarcely discernible, but it gave his words a lilting cockiness that Olivia found most irritating. Awareness of his own swarthy good looks no doubt added to his arrogance. Emerald-green eyes shone with jewel-like clarity against bronzed skin. Black hair, glossy and thick, curled in an unkempt mane to his shoulders. A faint scar cut his jawline and added a certain rakishness to his strong, pleasant face. Tall and broad-shouldered, the man had the sort of bearing that suggested he owned a room simply by virtue of being in it. It was a trait that seemed reserved by nature to men alone, and it never failed to impress the ladies.

Olivia, however, was not impressed. She had found that men who fancied themselves charming or handsome were frequently so confident of their reception that they forgot the necessity of manners.

"And you are . . ." he prompted with a smile.

"Not someone of your acquaintance. I do not have the habit of making conversation with men to whom I have not been introduced."

"I thought I just introduced myself."

The amused crinkle around his eyes grew more pronounced as Olivia tightened her lips in firm disapproval. The rogue was teasing her, a novel experience. During her twenty-six years Olivia had been scolded, lectured, and occasionally wooed, but seldom teased. She found it most annoying, and her usual good nature fled before a sudden urge to put the insolent Mr. Danaher in his place.

Olivia drew herself up to her full three inches over five feet. "I fear I cannot credit you with being a reliable sponsor for your character, Mr. Danaher. A gentleman does not engage a lady in personal conversation unless they are acquaintances of long standing; he does not answer questions intended for another; he does not continue to force his presence"—she swept him with a scathing glance—"his *dusty* presence, on a lady who has tactfully indicated an unwillingness for further acquaintance."

"Tactful?"

Olivia flushed. "Yes. Tactful. But when tact doesn't work, Mr. Danaher, I do have an arsenal of stronger words."

"I'll just bet you do."

The most annoying thing about this conversation was that Mr. Danaher did not seem at all annoyed. The amused crinkle had not left his eyes, and his lips—which were rather too thin and most probably an indication of a lack of character, Olivia noted with satisfaction, continued to curve upward in a smile.

"I would appreciate it, sir, if you would take yourself to another section of the store. I cannot think that you have any great interest in ladies' hats, and since our conversation is finished . . ."

"Olivia! My goodness!" Amy appeared around the corner of the yard-goods shelves. "Is this man bothering you? Should I call Mr. Shriner?"

"I'm perfectly capable of taking care of myself, Amy. No harm has been done."

The irritating man nodded politely toward Amy. "Mrs. Talbot."

Amy spared him a cold glance before pointedly ignoring him. "Are you sure you're all right?" she queried Olivia.

"Of course I am."

"Nice to make your acquaintance, Miss Olivia."

Olivia detected a hint of triumph in the man's smile before he turned and left. He had discovered her name despite her refusal to give it to him, though why it should matter to him Olivia couldn't guess. No doubt he was simply enjoying getting his own way.

"I'm so sorry, Olivia. Sometimes I do long for New York, where riffraff like that wouldn't be allowed in the same shop with ladies. Towns like Elkhorn are such hodgepodge conglomerations of crude and refined. The whole West is like that. There is absolutely no protection from all sorts of unpleasant people."

Olivia still stared after Gabriel Danaher, who had moved out of earshot and was examining a rack of mining hardware. "Who is that perturbing man?"

"His name is Gabriel Danaher, and he's trash. Sylvester told me once that I should cross to the other side of the street if I ever should see him in town. Mary Kate Loudon told me he lives in the mountains with two Indian floozies. Two women! Can you imagine?" She giggled. "Sylvester would scold me if he knew I'd been listening to such things. He thinks a lady shouldn't be contaminated by knowing about such goings-on. But anyway, Mr. Danaher has a mine in the mountains and comes to town very rarely. And one never sees his harem, though Mary Kate vows she saw them once."

"Yes, well . . ." Olivia brushed a speck of imaginary dust from her skirt. "Two women. That's extraordinary. I've heard that Indians sometimes have more than one wife."

"Oh, they couldn't be his wives, Olivia. After all, he is a white man."

"Well! If a white man can live in such a union with an Indian woman, he certainly should be able to marry her."

Amy smiled and shook her head. "I'm sure that type of man doesn't worry about what he *should* do. If he's like half the prospectors around here, he's wanted by the law for some piece of mischief somewhere."

Olivia gestured as if to wipe the subject from their conversation. It was nothing, after all, and she shouldn't be wasting her time wondering about some strange man. "Speaking of Sylvester. I'm sure we're late for our appointment with him."

"He won't mind. I'm late for almost everything. The calico Mr. Shriner set aside for me is so bright and cheerful. I told him to deliver it to the house this afternoon. I can hardly wait to start on the nursery curtains.

You'll adore the print—little yellow buttercups and bright-green leaves . . ."

Olivia smiled affectionately and followed Amy out the door in the wake of her chatter. But she couldn't resist one backward glance into the store. Gabriel Danaher was still watching her. She hastily turned her face away and hurried after Amy.

Gabe Danaher, in other places and other times known as Will O'Connell, stared out the window of the mercantile at the two women strolling down the dusty boardwalk. His mouth twitched in an unintentional smile. Olivia. The name fit the woman. It sounded like someone's prim, scolding grandmother. She didn't look old enough to be a grandmother, but she certainly had the primness and the scolding down pat.

Henry Shriner emerged from the back room. "Find that blasting powder you wanted, Gabe?"

"Did I ever."

"Beg pardon?"

"Yeah, Henry. Right by the ammunition, like you said it was." He lifted the heavy box and carried it to the counter. "How much?"

While Henry entered the sale and proudly bragged about the new machine he'd just purchased from the National Cash Register Company, Gabe glanced out the window once again. The ladies were out of sight. What had moved him to spar with that skinny little gray mouse of a woman? He was a man who kept to himself—a habit that had become a necessity in the last two years—and he certainly didn't make a practice of pushing himself on reluctant women. Maybe it was because she had looked so ridiculous in that hat. Or maybe his interest had been piqued because her dark garb and severely scraped-back hair wasn't quite in tune with the youthful flush of her skin and the obvious delight she took in such a useless frippery.

"Will that be all today, Gabe?" Henry followed Gabe's gaze out the window. "Something going on out there?"

"What? Oh. Nothing. Just woolgathering."

"Is that all?"

"No. I need flour, bacon, beans, salt, saleratus—" Gabe fished in his shirt pocket for a list. "And throw in a couple of those red ribbons."

Henry scanned the wrinkled piece of paper. "You going to be in town long?"

"Leaving tonight."

"If you come by later, I'll have this ready in some gunnysacks you can sling over your saddle."

"Good idea." He glanced out the window again. "Think I'll head out and buy myself a drink."

"That'll take the November cold outta your bones."

Gabe wandered down the dusty street to the Silver Pick Saloon. Like its neighbor the Masonic Fraternity Hall, it was one of the very few buildings in Elkhorn, Montana, that was not false-fronted. Both had good milled lumber on all four walls, not just on a fancied-up front that hid a crude log building. Inside the saloon, a plank floor was covered with straw to soak up spills of grease, liquor, and expectorations too poorly aimed to reach a spittoon.

Gabe sat down facing the door with the wall to his back. A girl came to his table and flipped her skirt in his direction.

"Drink?"

"Whiskey."

"Bottle?"

"A glass'll be enough." Gabe seldom drank, having seen his father drink himself to death before his mother packed up her children and dragged them aboard a boat that sailed from Ireland to New York. But right now he felt in need of a whiskey.

The girl slanted him a smile. "Comin' right up." A missing front tooth made the smile more comic than inviting, but her eyes were warm and friendly. Despite the fact that she smelled of sweat and her neck seemed to have a permanent dirt line, she could give the frosty-mannered Olivia a lesson in down-home friendliness. "Anything else, mister?"

"Not right now, thanks."

"Whatever you say, but keep me in mind."

There he went thinking about the woman from the mercantile again. Funny the way her eyes had seemed so much younger than her face, or maybe it was simply her stiff manner that had added years to her appearance. She could have been anywhere from early twenties to late thirties. Not that it mattered. He didn't know why she had caught his attention in the first place.

He chuckled and tilted his chair back against the wall. His mother, a gently reared and delicate woman who had remained a lady despite the poverty she had ended in, had once assured him that the soul knew its mate; and when he met the good Irish girl who was meant for him, he would not be able to keep his eyes or attention from her. It had been that way with Minnie. He believed his mother would have approved of Many Horses Woman even though the Blackfoot girl had been about as far from Irish as a person could get.

Gabe felt the black mood come upon him as it always did when he thought of his wife. Better to think of the indignant little package of blasting powder that had tried to take his head off at Shriner's. A man would have to be awfully hard up to look in that woman's direction; and if he did, God and Saint Patrick help the poor sod.

"Here's your whiskey, love." The bargirl gave him another gap-toothed smile; but when he responded with no more than a nod, she left. For lack of anything more interesting to watch, Gabe followed the swaying of her skirt through the crowded saloon, until a loud curse caught his attention.

"Goddamned shithead greenhorn! Whadda ya mean ya ain't got enough money?"

"I . . . I . . ."

At a table by the bar, a young fresh-faced lad, whose clothes and clean new boots marked him as recently arrived from more civilized parts, stammered his excuses.

"I had enough until the last bet, and I thought sure I'd win this hand. God! What are the chances of you having a royal flush!"

Judging from how the man had been dealing, the chances of his having a royal flush were very good indeed, Gabe observed.

"Ya don't make bets with Dan Kyle that ya can't keep, greenhorn."

The youngster fumbled in his vest pocket. "I . . . I have a watch. A good one. You can have it."

"A watch." Dan Kyle mimicked the boy's pleading tone for the benefit of the other patrons, who were watching with avid interest. "I can have his goddamned watch!" He swung a lethal gaze on his victim. "Ain't near enough."

The boy pushed his chair back and stood. "I got my horse."

"Ain't enough."

"He's worth fifty at least."

"You bet two hundred."

"You'll get it!"

"I'll get it outta your hide, boy."

Gabe believed in keeping to himself—usually—but he also had a weak spot for an underdog. That weakness had landed him in trouble before this, and Gabe figured it was going to get him in trouble now. The green-horn was young and stupid, but his tormentor was a cheat and a sonofa-bitch. It wasn't hard to choose sides.

"Why don't you pick on someone who knows how to fight as dirty as you play cards, Kyle?" Gabe kept his voice conversational, but all eyes immediately swung toward his table.

Kyle's eyes narrowed. "A mick, ain't ya?"

Gabe raised his glass in acknowledgment.

"You sayin' I was cheatin'?"

"You weren't cheating very well, but you were cheating."

"That's an invite to a fight, mick."

Everyone in the room drew a collective breath of anticipation. Gabe sighed. This was the way it always turned out. One of these days he was going to learn to mind his own business. "I guess I don't have anything better to do right now." He stood and rolled back his sleeves.

The whole saloon shouted encouragement as Kyle lunged. There was nothing like a good brawl to liven up the afternoon. Before a half minute had passed, every man there had chosen sides and had dived into the fun. No sense in letting a low-down cheat and a cheeky mick hog it all.

Chapter 2

I'm full enough to burst."

Sylvester Talbot regarded his wife fondly as she polished off the last of her dried apricot pie. "Was it good?"

Amy sighed. "Wonderful." She glanced apologetically at Olivia, who sipped her tea in silent disapproval. "I know I promised to have only the hot chocolate, but the pie looked simply too delicious."

"Your appetite burgeons right along with your middle."

Amy blushed, and Sylvester looked rather shocked.

"Really, Amy. You must try to save your appetite for food that will add to your strength, not burden you with extra weight."

"Yes, dear Olivia. I know. When I'm hungry I think with my stomach instead of my brain."

"The delivery will be much easier if you can cultivate muscle instead of fat. Besides, if you eat like this until the baby comes in February, you'll be bigger than a cow."

Olivia noted that Sylvester's face was tinged with pink, and his stiff, tight collar looked to be in danger of bursting. She knew that her frank conversation distressed him; he was a man who believed that women should be delicate in manners and speech. But Amy, bless her heart, was in dire need of someone who would refuse to pamper her. Sylvester was so anxious about the pregnancy that he treated her as though she were a piece of fragile china.

Sylvester cleared his throat awkwardly. "Are you ladies sure that I shouldn't fetch the buggy so you can ride to the house?"

"Don't be ridiculous, Sylvester. Your house isn't more than half a mile at most. Both Amy and I can use the exercise."

Sylvester looked dubious.

"Really, Sylvester. Amy is not sick. She's as healthy as you or I. Cosseting her will only make these last months more difficult."

"Oh, I don't want to be cosseted," Amy declared. "All I want is to have a healthy baby."

"Bravo! Now, shall we be on our way? It'll soon be dark."

Amy cast a furtive longing glance at the meager leavings on her plate.

"Amy!" Olivia chided.

"I'm coming. I'm coming."

The sun was low as the trio emerged from the Grand Hotel onto Elkhorn's main street. Olivia clutched her coat tightly against the chill and thought once again that she'd never seen a place so desolate. The barrenness was accentuated by the evergreen beauty of the mountains rising above them. The valley of Elkhorn Creek had once been as green and beautiful, but man's lust for gold and silver had denuded the surrounding hills of their natural pine forest. The logs had been needed to construct the big mill that squatted on the creek like some ugly troll, to build the hotels, saloons, bawdy houses, mercantiles, and miners' shacks, the Masonic Fraternity Hall, the Miner's Union Hall, the barbershop, the candy store, jewelry store, and schoolhouse. Now that the land around Elkhorn was stripped of trees, the woodcutters traveled even farther into the mountains to cut cordwood to burn in stoves and fireplaces during the winter that was almost upon them.

"I wish we would get some rain to settle the dust." Amy covered her mouth as a wagon rattled by and raised a choking storm in its wake.

"We'll get it soon enough, and it'll be snow, not rain, my dear." Sylvester looked up at the metallic blue sky. "You've not been through a Montana winter before. Believe me, when spring comes, that blue sky up there will look mighty good." He smiled reassuringly. "Of course, you and our child will be warm and cozy all winter long in our snug house."

"Yes, Sylvester."

Olivia sighed.

The Talbots' home was situated at the lower end of town, close to the mill of which Sylvester was a managing partner and major investor. The walk from the Grand Hotel was downhill through town. The air was brisk and crystal-clear; Olivia felt a glow of invigoration as they walked past Ford's Candy Store, the Elkhorn Trading Company, and the schoolhouse.

Her New York lungs were finally becoming accustomed to the thin mountain air. Halfway through town she stopped before a small structure that only two weeks ago had been a shack. Now the little building had curtains at its new glass windows and a fresh coat of paint.

Sylvester and Amy, who'd been trailing a bit behind Olivia, stopped beside her.

"It looks very fine," Amy offered.

"Yes, it does. And the sign Mr. Rivers painted is just what was needed." Olivia thanked Sylvester with a smile. "It was very kind of you to arrange a medical office for me, Sylvester."

"It was the least I could do," he said expansively. "Your friendship is very precious to Amy, and you've been generous enough to come all the way from New York to be with her during this trying time. Since you'll be visiting for several months, and Amy has told me how you like to be active, the least I could do was to arrange proper facilities to enable you to pursue your interests."

Amy chimed in enthusiastically. "I'm sure you'll have a whole herd of patients once the people of Elkhorn find out what a truly fine doctoress you are."

Sylvester smiled condescendingly at his wife. "Now, Amy. Remember that there are already two physicians in Elkhorn."

Amy raised a brow. "I doubt either one of them has studied in Paris at the École de Medicine as Olivia has!"

Olivia smiled. Even when she and Amy were girls together at the fashionable Miss Tatterhorn's Academy for Young Ladies, Amy had been vehement in defending her; and those protective instincts had been called upon quite often, for Olivia had often ignored her art and music to study the science and mathematics books she had been sent by her friend and idol, Dr. Mary Putnam—now Dr. Mary Putnam Jacobi since her marriage to a German pediatrician. Her ambition to be a physician had made her unpopular both with her teachers and her fellow students. "I doubt Elkhorn's doctors were required to travel to Paris for their post-graduate clinical study, Amy. Many fine teaching hospitals are available in this country where men can get their clinical training; but only a few institutions accept women physicians, and they only accept a limited number. That is the only reason I studied in Paris."

"Oh piffle! You went to Paris because Miss Tatterhorn forced you to learn French!"

Both women laughed, and Sylvester regarded them with a pucker of disapproval in his brows.

"Amy dear, I don't believe such uncontrolled high spirits are beneficial to your condition."

"Oh, Sylvester! Really. Now that Olivia is here, I'm sure that everything will be all right."

He smiled rather weakly at Olivia as they walked on. "I'm sure Olivia is a fine doctoress, Amy. But I would feel more comfortable if we could . . . perhaps . . . have a man's . . . or rather . . . another doctor's view as well."

Amy's high spirits seemed to drain from her. "I don't want a man examining me, Sylvester."

"Of course you don't, my sweet. You are a delicate woman of great sensibility. But Dr. Cahill is a fine physician."

"Not nearly as fine as Olivia!"

Olivia didn't hesitate to step into what promised to become a row. "Sylvester's right, Amy. It's always a good idea to get more than one opinion. I'm not at all offended by Sylvester wanting to consult with Dr. Cahill. In light of the difficulties and sad endings of your first two pregnancies, no resource should be ignored to ensure this one ends happily."

"There! You see? Even Olivia thinks it's a good idea."

"Olivia is simply being generous."

Sylvester sighed in exasperation.

Dusk gathered quickly as they walked along the street, and as daylight faded, Elkhorn's fourteen saloons grew brighter and noisier. Just ahead, the Silver Pick Saloon seemed to be having a particularly volatile night. Brash piano music poured out the doors and windows accompanied by thumps, crashes, and the sound of splintering furniture.

Sylvester took Amy and Olivia by the arm and guided them to the opposite side of the street as they neared the Silver Pick. "I should have fetched the buggy. Amy shouldn't be exposed to this sort of rowdiness."

Olivia gave the bar a wary look. "The street was very quiet when Amy and I left Mr. Shriner's mercantile."

"This happens almost every night," Sylvester told her. "Montana isn't as civilized as New York, Olivia. Fighting and drinking themselves into a stupor are the favorite pastimes of miners and prospectors."

"Believe me, Sylvester, New York has its— Oh my!"

A body catapulted out the saloon door and somersaulted onto the street. Another flew backward onto the boardwalk and stumbled rear-first into the watering trough. As that man came up sputtering and cursing, a third fellow sailed out a window amid a tinkling explosion of glass. He staggered to his feet, swayed a few steps forward, and collapsed onto the boardwalk with his head hanging down into the dirt of the street.

Almost without thinking, Olivia hurried toward the three. The first had risen to his feet by the time she reached him.

"Are you all right?"

The man gave her a bloody grin. "Yes, ma'am. Thank'ee." He dusted himself off and charged back through the saloon door.

The second climbed out of the watering trough and brushed Olivia's concern aside as he wrung water from the tails of his shirt. The lake around his soggy boots grew as he stood and stared at the saloon door.

"Are you sure you don't want at least a dry blanket?"

He gave her a disgusted look, growled a few unintelligible words, and walked away, every step squishing as he plodded down the street.

The third man lay where he had fallen. As Olivia knelt beside him, Sylvester reached her side.

"What do you think you're doing?"

She could scarcely hear his indignant demand over the noise of the brawl still crashing and thumping to the enthusiastic accompaniment of piano music.

"This man is hurt!" she shouted over the turmoil.

"This is no place for you!"

"I'm a doctor, Sylvester!"

He tried to pull her away, but she ignored him. The man on the board-walk moaned and lifted his head out of the dirt, then collapsed again. Fresh blood glistened on his hair, and one cheek was already swelling and discolored. Olivia looked for broken bones or spinal injuries that might keep her from moving him. Finding none, she turned him onto his back and lifted his head onto the walkway.

"Gabriel Danaher." In the dim light and with his face covered with dirt and bruises, Olivia had not until now recognized the man who had been so insolent in Shriner's store.

"How do *you* know him?" Sylvester demanded.

"I met him this afternoon at Shriner's."

"Well, he's certainly no one you should be seen with, and he doesn't merit your concern. Gabe Danaher is riffraff, and if he ends up lying in the dirt of the street, it's evidence of his nature seeking its true level. Now come away before you upset Amy."

"Take Amy home, Sylvester. I'll be along presently."

"Olivia!"

Olivia didn't have time to convince Sylvester that the slums of New York, where she had run a women's charity clinic three nights a week for the past year, were far more dangerous than a street outside a rowdy saloon in Elkhorn. Nor would he understand that as a doctor she felt obligated to help a man who was injured. In his opinion, she was just a woman, after all; and for her, medicine must be only an avocation, not a sacred profession.

"Take Amy home!" she said more firmly. "Then you may return and continue your scolding if you wish."

She heard his disgusted grunt as he left, but it scarcely registered, for the door of the saloon opened and the glow of lamplight fell on her patient's abused face. He certainly didn't look like the same man who had been so cocky in the mercantile—the one with the hint of Irish lilt in his voice and Irish mischief in his smile. Clearly Gabriel Danaher didn't limit his troublemaking to giving unwanted critiques of ladies' hats, and this time he'd riled someone who had retaliated with fists instead of words.

His eyelids twitched, then opened. He squinted up at her with an unbelieving look on his face. "You?"

"Mr. Danaher. It seems that I'm not the only one who finds you irritating."

He grunted, then flinched. "You've got a hell of a punch." His voice grated with the dust lodged in his throat.

"I didn't hit you, Mr. Danaher. You appear to have offended someone with a temper more volatile than mine."

"Uh?"

"You were fighting." Holding his head still with her fingers grasping his chin, she lifted one of his eyelids. "Hmm. I need better light."

"All I did was . . . was say the hat was . . . was . . ." He trailed off into senseless muttering.

A change in noise level suddenly came to Olivia's notice. She looked up to discover she had gained an audience. A ring of grinning faces, most of which bore cuts and bruises, looked down at her, and as she watched, more staring eyes appeared above the saloon's swinging doors. Apparently the men in the Silver Pick considered the scene on the boardwalk more entertaining than their brawl.

"Can I get two of you gentlemen to carry this man to my surgery, please?"

They looked at her uncertainly.

"I'm a doctor. This man is injured. I have a clinic just down the street."

"Oh yeah!" a gravelly voice commented. "Heard we had a *doctoress* in town."

A few of the men chuckled.

"This man's injuries are not a laughing matter."

"You don't wanna dirty your hands with him, ma'am." A burly, bearded fellow who looked as though he hadn't touched soap for months offered this advice. "He's trash. Injun-lover. Irish, too."

Olivia was losing patience.

"You!" With the look that had intimidated more than one man who thought to brush her demands aside, she speared one tall young fellow. "Help me get him to my surgery."

"Uh . . . well . . ."

"Hell, ma'am!" a husky older man interrupted the boy's stammering. "We don't mind knockin' a man about in a fair fight, but it seems carryin' things a bit far to deliver a fellow up to a lady doc!"

A few chortles from the others echoed agreement.

Olivia noticed the Irishman's eyes moving between her and the men. A spark of coherence in his expression gave her hope that his senses had returned.

"You really a doc?" he croaked.

"Yes."

He glared at her suspiciously.

"If I weren't a doctor and my oath of profession didn't require me to render aid to all who need it, I would gladly leave you to your own devices."

"An angel of mercy, eh?" He tried to rise, groaned, and settled back again to the walk. "Might as well do what the lady says, boys. I doubt she can hurt me any worse than you did."

With that dubious testimonial of faith, two men picked up the injured man—one lifting his shoulders and the other grabbing his ankles—and carried him the short distance to Olivia's surgery. The audience followed; they would have peered through the windows and watched Olivia patch up her patient if she hadn't sternly shooed them away.

Olivia directed the two bearers to lay her patient on the cot that served as an examination table. As they left she turned up the kerosene lamp and set it next to the cot, then filled a basin with soap and warm water.

"You're really a doc, huh?" The patient sounded skeptical. Olivia was familiar with the tone.

"Yes. Would you like to see my diplomas?"

"Uh!" He flinched as she set to work cleaning a cut over his eye and the bloody bruise on his cheek. "Go easy there! I'll take your word for it."

"If you persist in exiting rooms through windows instead of doors, Mr. Danaher, then you must get used to having glass plucked from your face."

"Ow!"

"There. That seems to be the last of it."

Olivia saw his eyes roam over a chipped metal cabinet that held her carefully labeled supplies and remedies—laudanum, ipecac, julep, calomel, digitalis, quinine, morphine, arnica, paregoric, carbolic acid, and many others. The sink beside the cabinet was also chipped.

"This is just a temporary surgery." She felt a sudden need to defend the shabbiness of the place. "I'm only visiting here from New York for a few months to care for a friend."

"Hmm."

"Mr. Talbot was kind enough to set up temporary facilities for me. Now, hold your head still, please."

He jerked when her fingers touched his chin. "I thought you said that was all."

"That was all the glass in your face. Don't be such a baby, Mr. Danaher. I'm just going to look at your eyes. From that bump on your head I'd guess you took a nasty blow."

"Several."

She looked carefully at the pupils of both eyes. He looked back at her in a rather disconcerting manner.

"Why were you fighting?"

He hesitated, then gave her a wry grin. "Nothing better to do at the time."

"You think bashing at each other is a responsible way for grown men to entertain themselves?"

"There are worse ways."

"Indeed?" She sniffed. "Turn your head a bit, please."

Olivia couldn't help but notice the strong line of his jaw and the small dent in his chin. If one ignored the fact that he was a scoundrel, Mr. Danaher could be considered a very attractive man. Unlike many of the miners, woodcutters, and mill workers she'd seen in town, her patient was clean-shaven—and clean, discounting the dust and blood of the brawl.

"I believe you have a bit of a concussion, Mr. Danaher. That would account for your confusion when you came around. Are you dizzy?"

"A little."

His eyes were surely the brightest shade of green she'd ever seen, and he was still looking at her in a most unnerving way.

"You may experience dizziness, nausea, and even vomiting for a day or so, but if you restrict your activity for a while you should recover quite nicely. Now, let's see what other damage has been done."

The emerald mocking of his eyes as she unbuttoned his shirt threatened her professional detachment, which was unaccountably feeling a bit fragile at the moment. As she peeled his shirt away from his chest, she gave him a cool look. "Don't let it bother you, Mr. Danaher. I am a physician."

His mouth slanted upward in a half-smile. "Doesn't bother me a bit. Ouch!"

Ignoring his yelped objection, she probed along his bruised ribs. "Apparently something here bothers you."

Another gasp met her investigation.

"You have a couple of cracked ribs."

"Yeow! Well, now you know they're cracked, maybe you can stop pounding on them."

"I'm scarcely touching you, Mr. Danaher. I'll wrap them for you, but these ribs are going to be very sore for a while. Perhaps that will teach you to avoid fighting from now on. I vow it's a crime. Most people would pay a fortune to have a body as fit and healthy as yours, and you abuse this God-given gift by drinking and brawling."

"Does the lecture come free with the doctoring?"

"I didn't expect to be paid for either. Don't worry, I'm quite accustomed to treating charity cases."

She wasn't accustomed to treating patients quite like Gabriel Danaher, however. Olivia was familiar with the details of male anatomy. She had dissected a male cadaver in her medical training and had disappointed the male students in the class by succumbing neither to hysteria nor to mortal embarrassment. In both Paris and New York she had treated male charity cases—drunks and indigents who could afford no other care—but most of her practice had been women and children. Young, healthy men consulted other men if they needed the services of a physician. Having a strong male body under her care was a new experience.

A new experience—and an unexpectedly unnerving one. As a young girl, Olivia had not giggled or sighed at the sight of a comely man as her companions at Miss Tatterhorn's Academy had done. And medical school had surely cured her of any fascination with the mysteries of masculinity. So the warmth that stole into her cheeks took Olivia by surprise as she observed Mr. Danaher's admittedly admirable physique. For all that he was "trash," as Amy had labeled him, the sheer animal perfection of him was rather startling to the senses.

Olivia cleared her throat and gathered her straying thoughts. "Just sit still while I get some bandages for your chest."

"I suppose this is going to hurt too."

She searched the chipped metal cabinet for an appropriate length of bandage. "I've treated children who complained less than you, Mr. Danaher."

"My father once told me that bearing discomfort in silence might be the manly thing to do, but it also encourages people to keep pounding on you."

Olivia gave him a chilly glance. "If you so dislike discomfort, perhaps you should avoid brawls like the one that just sent you flying out a saloon window."

He grinned, then winced at the movement of facial muscles. "Doesn't hurt while a fellow's still fighting."

There was a hint of teasing in his voice that almost made Olivia smile in spite of herself. No doubt the fellow thought he was charming.

"Be patient, Mr. Danaher. This will only take a moment." She unrolled the wide bandage and sat beside him, but the position was awkward. "Would you stand, please?"

He stood.

"Hold this end of the bandage."

She wound the length of gauzy cotton around his broad chest, ignoring his occasional yipe as she touched a tender area. "This will give you some protection while the ribs heal, but you should be very careful to not strain yourself until all the pain is gone."

When he swayed suddenly toward her and grasped her shoulders, Olivia's heart leapt in instinctive fright.

"Sorry," he muttered. "Got dizzy."

"Yes. Of course."

His breath was warm in her hair, the male scent of him hot in her nostrils. Several seconds passed before she could slow her breathing to normal. "The . . . the bandage is in place, Mr. Danaher. You may sit down now."

He didn't resist when she carefully pushed him away from her and steadied him as he lowered himself to the cot. The bronze of his face had tarnished to a greenish tinge. "Do you need a basin?"

"No."

"Just lie here, then. Do you have anyone I could fetch to help you home?"

His mouth crooked upward. "No."

"How far must you go?"

"A night's ride and a bit of the next day."

"I don't believe that's a good idea at all."

"I've ridden when I was in worse shape than this."

Olivia shook her head.

He slanted her an inquiring glance as his color returned. "No more lectures?"

"I rarely beat my head against a brick wall once it's proven to be unyielding. You're quite a stubborn man, Mr. Danaher. And not a very wise one, I might add."

He smiled slightly. "How old are you, Lady Doctoress?"

"I beg your pardon?"

"How old are you? I've been trying to figure it out. You sound as though you're sixty, but when you smile you look about fifteen."

Olivia tried to be indignant, but the last hour spent with this scoundrel had used up her supply of scoldings. "My age is really none of your concern."

He continued to look at her expectantly.

She huffed. "Very well. I am twenty-six."

"Going on sixty?"

She arched a brow. "And how old are you, Mr. Danaher? Thirty going on thirteen?"

"Thirty-four. And right now it feels like I'm going on seventy."

"You really should spend the night at a hotel instead of riding to wherever you live in the mountains."

"We're both stubborn." He sat up. The greenish tinge promptly returned.

"At least lie down until you can stand without turning colors," Olivia suggested.

Gingerly he sank back onto the cot and closed his eyes. "I guess I don't have to start right away."

Olivia covered her patient with a blanket, then carried the lamp to the little oak desk that occupied one corner of the clinic. She had no files to review or case notes to ponder. In the week since the clinic had opened she had seen only one patient—Rosie, a saloon dancer from the Lucky Lady.

So she sat and watched as Gabriel Danaher lay with eyes closed. Gradually his breathing became slow and even. His eyelids, which were fringed in dark lashes ridiculously thick for a man, twitched in the telltale flutterings of dreams. The stubborn Irishman was asleep; his body knew what it needed more than the man himself did. The corded muscles in his neck relaxed and his brows no longer held their puckered scowl. One of his long legs shifted and fell off the cot. Even the clunk of his boot against the plank floor didn't wake him.

After an hour of sitting at her desk, Olivia found herself struggling to not join the Irishman in his dreams. She had no work to distract her, and the man's sleeping presence had a mesmerizing quality. As if he were a hypnotic charm, he fixed her attention on himself—the brows that arched so devilishly over his eyes, the flat curve of his lips—which even in sleep seemed to retain a slightly mocking slant—the dark thatch of chest hair that escaped the bandage she'd wrapped around his ribs.

Looking at a man with such appreciation was most unlike her, and to regard a patient in such a fashion, even in passing, was very unprofessional. She certainly shouldn't be spending the night alone with him, yet a concussion patient couldn't be left untended to sleep. He needed to be awakened now and then to ensure complications hadn't developed.

Olivia was about to get up and do just that when a scratch sounded at the door.

Danaher was instantly awake. The benign clunk of his boot hitting the floor hadn't awakened him, but the mysterious scratching brought him bolt upright and clutching at his thigh for a pistol that wasn't there.

"Mr. Danaher, for goodness' sake lie down."

He shook his head, looking confused.

"It's just someone at the door."

The someone at the door was enough to make any man take notice. The woman cut a gaudy figure in a tightly laced corset and red silk skirt that reached only to her knees. Her hair color and lip rouge matched the skirt, and the full breasts that strained the corset laces were also accented with rouge.

For a few seconds the woman's gaze went to the man on the cot. She gave him a professionally appraising glance and then turned a cautious gaze on Olivia.

"Are you the lady doc?"

"Yes."

"Rosie told me to come. You gave her powders for her stomach a couple of days ago. She said you was a decent sort, even though you was a lady."

"How can I help you?"

The powder-caked face tightened. "Not me. My kid. She's awful sick." The woman reached outside the door and half dragged, half carried a thin, dirty child who appeared to be five or six years old. "None of the real docs will even look at her just 'cause her ma's a saloon dancer."

Olivia moved to take the child from the woman, but the little girl struck out and screamed. Her eyes were glazed with fear.

"I'll take her." The Irishman brushed Olivia aside and carried the struggling girl to the clinic's one cot.

"Hold her still, please," Olivia instructed him unnecessarily, for he had already subdued the little fists and kicking legs. His hands were gentle and competent—surprisingly gentle for a man who brawled because he had nothing better to do.

Olivia placed a hand on the child's forehead. The skin burned hot, and in spite of the coolness of the November night, the little girl's face glistened with sweat.

"How long has she been like this?"

"Only tonight." Tears trickled through the thick rouge on the mother's cheeks. "For a couple of days she's not eaten. Said her throat hurt. But tonight Amaryliss—she was watchin' her for me—Amaryliss comes to me and tells me poor little Pearl cain't hardly stand."

The saloon dancer watched anxiously as Olivia examined the girl, who fought continually against Danaher's restraining hands. Olivia was glad the man was willing to help. Small as the child was, the mother would not have been able to stop her struggling.

Only a brief examination was required to confirm Olivia's first instinct. Elkhorn might soon need every doctor it could get, and the town now couldn't afford to be choosy. The child had diphtheria.

Chapter 3

*I*n the dim lamplight, the hands of Olivia's gold pocket watch showed the hour to be nearing midnight. She snapped the watch shut and put it back in her skirt pocket. Did she have the energy to undress? She really should, Olivia decided wearily. Her navy-blue serge skirt and white linen shirtwaist felt sticky with sweat and smelled of antiseptic. She would sleep better in her nightdress—if she could find it.

She opened the closet that held her starched white surgery aprons. No nightdress. Neither was it in the drawers with the folded towels and sheets, nor in the bandage cabinet. Where had she flung the thing this morning when she dressed? No, not this morning. She hadn't gone to bed the night before. Yesterday morning, then. No wonder she was stumbling and nearly incoherent. Where was the cursed thing?

To the devil with her nightdress. She would sleep in her shift. Olivia pulled off her skirt, blouse, and corset, folded them neatly and precisely, and laid them on a chair. Then she gratefully sank down on the clinic cot, which had been her only bed since the beginning of the diphtheria onslaught. Amy sent down fresh clothing each day along with a basket of fresh bread and cheese. Olivia took her meals, when she had time, at the hotel and slept in the clinic. The discomfort was of small significance, for she spent very little time in bed. The few hours of sleep she managed to snatch might have been sounder on the feather mattress in the Talbot guest room, but she refused to expose Amy to the contagion.

Olivia blew out the lamp, pulled a blanket over herself, and tried to let her senses fade into the darkness. Her body was numb with exhaustion, but her mind still whirled with images. Joey Sanderson's face cracked in a smile. His red hair and freckles had blazed in the noonday sun when she'd seen him two weeks ago in front of Ford's Candy Store. But tonight, two hours ago, that red hair had been dark with sweat, his eyes dull and frightened, his freckles stark in a colorless face. Now he was dead. Joey Sanderson, Melissa Banks, Chin Su Li in the Chinese section of town, Aaron Campbell, and a half-dozen others whose names she didn't remember. A mother and her two sons had died within hours of each other. Another family lost three children in the same week. All of the dead paraded before her mind's eye. They had died an ugly death of choking, suffocation, or heart failure. Olivia had no tools to help them other than nursing their strength and praying that their natural defenses would conquer the disease. Despite the wonderful advances in medicine in the last decade, diphtheria was still an untamed monster. Seldom had she felt so helpless. Strong, basically healthy patients often survived diphtheria, but the people who came to her for help were seldom the strong and healthy type. Her patients were those who had no money to pay the fees of Elkhorn's other two physicians—poor, overworked mine and mill laborers and their children, who lived with both inadequate diets and an appalling lack of hygiene. They were fodder for the disease.

Olivia was grateful that being the Talbots' guest enabled her to treat these unfortunates without a fee. She wished only that she could work some magic to ward off the death that claimed so many of them. During her medical education and her two years of private practice in New York, Olivia had seen enough of death to become resigned to its tragedy, but she would never get used to watching a child die.

Still seeing Joey Sanderson's freckled, pale face, she sank into exhausted sleep.

Gabriel Danaher was a black shadow in the dark night. Slumped against the rough log wall of the livery building, he stared down Elkhorn's main street. A slight movement brought his face into the meager light of the thin crescent moon. The Irish cockiness that had so irritated Olivia Baron had been erased by harsh lines of fatigue. The eyes that watched Elkhorn slumber were narrowed with grim bitterness.

From stillness Gabe suddenly exploded into angry action. With a curse he slammed his fist into the logs of the wall. Pain shot up his arm and into his shoulder, a welcome distraction from frustration. Inside the livery, a horse whinnied.

"Damn! Goddamn hypocrites! Quacks! I'll see them both in hell!"

Bitterness rose like bile in his throat. He couldn't think what to do. After being awake for almost three days, his brain was grinding to a stop. There was nothing left to do but go back to the mountains and watch Katy and Ellen die.

Weighed down by more than exhaustion, Gabe stumbled into the livery and lit a lantern. His bay mare Longshot whickered a greeting.

"The bastards won't come," Gabe told Longshot as he lifted the blanket and saddle onto her back. "Too busy, too tired, and who the hell cares what happens to a pair of half-breed brats anyway?" He rested his face against the mare's body and inhaled her warm scent. "Offered old Cahill three hundred dollars, then offered to let him name his own price. The sonofabitch still wouldn't come. And the other quack—Traleigh—he wouldn't even answer me. Just shut the door in my face."

Longshot blew out a long breath as if in sympathy. Gabe shook his head. "Got to do something. Can't just go home. Come on, boyo. Think of something, dammit!"

As if in answer to his demand, an image came into his mind. A somber little face beneath a ridiculous hat. Hands that had bandaged his painful ribs.

"Want to see my diplomas?" she had asked.

He had humored her. How much training did it take to clean a few cuts and bandage cracked ribs? He needed a real doctor for his girls, not some odd, mousy spinster who dabbled at a man's job.

But the doctors wouldn't come with him, and probably neither would Olivia Baron. No woman would trek into the mountains a full day's ride with a man she already thought of as a brawler and a no-good.

"Want to see my diplomas?" Olivia Baron's words repeated insistently in Gabe's weary mind. She had diplomas, which meant she was a doctor of sorts, woman or not. Some fancy school of medicine had certified her worthy to practice medicine. Olivia Baron would be better than nothing.

Gabe could see no other way to give Katy and Ellen a chance. He gave Longshot a thump on the shoulder. "Stay here, girl. I've got one more visit to pay." He wouldn't let another doctor tell him no.

A few of Elkhorn's buildings had windows glowing with lamplight. Olivia Baron's clinic was not one of them. Gabe hadn't really expected her to be there. It was past midnight, after all. She would be at the Talbot house, sleeping. The thought of "Doctor" Baron in a comfortable feather bed while Elkhorn struggled through an epidemic made Gabe feel better about what he was planning to do. When the good doctor came to the clinic in the morning—assuming she came at all—she would find a patient waiting for her.

The door of the little office was locked, as he expected. A small window on the side was open, but it would be a tight squeeze to get his shoulders through. He would try only if he couldn't find another way in. He quietly moved around to the back, keeping an eye out for anyone else who might be on the street at this late hour. When he cautiously tried the back door, it opened. He raised a brow in surprise. Miss Baron ought to be more careful.

Gabe shut the door behind him and struck a match. Its dim glow showed the desk, cabinet, and sink just as he remembered. And the cot where he'd lain— Gabe froze. Someone was stretched out on that cot. A skirt and blouse folded neatly on a chair identified that someone as a woman. For a moment he didn't move. Then the match burned down to his fingers and he yelped.

The figure on the cot stirred, then was still once again. Gabe let out a slow breath. Apparently he wouldn't have to wait until morning to confront the doctoress.

"Doctor Baron."

She turned and burrowed deeper into the blanket.

"Doctor Baron." Gabe gently shook her shoulder. She woke with a start, jerked to a sitting position and looked around in distraught confusion.

"Take it easy, Doc. It's just me." He lit the lamp, which threw a ghostly pattern of light and shadow across the little clinic. Sitting on the cot and blinking, the doctoress seemed only marginally awake. The blanket had fallen to her waist, revealing a low-cut lacy camisole and the tops of her breasts. Who would have thought such a stiffly starched little lady would be downright feminine under all those layers of clothes?

Olivia's eyes slowly came into focus. "Oh my goodness!" She grabbed for the blanket and clutched it to her chin.

"You good and awake now, Doc? Remember me?"

Wide-eyed, she stared at him.

"Gabriel Danaher. You patched me up a while back. No-good brawling Irishman. Remember now?"

"Yes. Yes, of course I remember you." With visible effort she gathered her composure, brushing her hair away from her face. Unconfined, it was long and thick, not the dreary brown he remembered, but a rich, dark auburn shot through with pinpoints of fire from the lamplight. She was calmer now, though the blanket was still tightly clenched in her fists. He had to give her credit for a cool head.

"It's still night. What are you doing here, Mr. Danaher?"

"I need a doctor."

She gave him an appraising look. "Are you sick?"

"No. My girls are sick. Bad sick."

She sighed, and the weariness he heard in her voice was more than just tiredness. "Let me get dressed and I'll come with you."

He obligingly turned his back. The cot creaked. Clothing rustled.

"You can turn around now, Mr. Danaher. I have a buggy at the livery. Just let me get my medical bag."

"We don't have time to nurse a buggy up the mountain. You'll have to go on horseback." He turned around. She was starched and prim once again. Even her hair was scraped back into a neat little bun at the nape of her neck.

"Just where did you say you lived?" she asked uncertainly.

"Over a day's ride up Thunder Creek."

Her shoulders slumped slightly from their square set. "A full day's ride. That's impossible, Mr. Danaher."

A sharp stab of disappointment killed the small bit of hope he had allowed himself. For a moment or two she had seemed different than the other two. His temper began to slide.

"What is it with you people? Is there some clause in that doctor's oath you take that says you only treat people who are less than an hour away? Or maybe it's just that half-breeds aren't worth your trouble."

"Don't be ridiculous, Mr. Danaher. I . . ."

"Katy and Ellen are dying, and I can't find a single doctor in this town who gives a damn!"

Her voice sharpened. "A lot of people have died in this town, and more will die before this is over. There are three doctors here, and every one of us has been lucky to catch a few hours' sleep or a bite to eat over the last week. We don't have time to leave for Lord only knows how long to treat two patients when there are ten times that many who need us here. Bring your girls to town, Mr. Danaher, and I will gladly do everything I can for them. But I can't leave other patients unattended."

"They would never survive the trip. You *have* to come with me."

She sighed, a long, dispirited, weary sound. "I'm sorry, Mr. Danaher. I assume they have the same condition that has struck the town, especially since you were with me when that little girl came in. I can write down a treatment for you and give you some medications, but that's the best I can do. I have three other patients whom I absolutely cannot leave right now."

"There are two other doctors in town for those people to turn to. My girls have no one but me."

"Doctors Cahill and Traleigh have full patient loads already. They can't—"

He grabbed a metal basin that sat on the cabinet and threw it. It ricocheted off the wall and clanged to the floor. The violence felt good. The look of fearful surprise on the doctoress's face as she stared at the gouge in the plaster felt good. A flood of bitterness inside him strained against the seams of his restraint.

"I guess I'm going to have to persuade you." Gabe lifted his pistol from its holster and pointed it in her direction. She backed up frantically, as if she could escape a bullet by putting a few feet between herself and the gun. He followed until she was brought up short by a wall, then he jammed the barrel of the pistol against her, just under the breastbone. "Katy and Ellen are not going to die because no one cared enough to save them. You're coming with me."

"Mr. Danaher, this is insane." Her eyes grew large in a suddenly pale face.

"Insane or not, I'll do most anything to make sure they have a crack at getting well. Get your medical supplies, and if you want to throw a change of clothes in a bag, just don't take longer than five minutes. And don't make me do anything we'll both regret."

He backed off a few feet. The muzzle of the pistol didn't waver from its target. The little doctoress made a visible effort to collect herself. Gabe felt a twinge of admiration in spite of the anger making coils of his innards.

"I can't go with you. And I don't believe you would shoot me. Killing me won't help your ladies."

Gabe chuckled, and the sound was ugly even to his own ears. "No. But it might make me feel better. Now, go get what you need, or you'll likely find out I'm more villainous than you believe."

Her bolt for freedom was sudden and took Gabe by surprise. He'd underestimated her. She had guts, and she was fast, but not quite fast enough. He caught her before she reached the front door.

"Aaaaaaagh! Let me—!"

Only one scream escaped Olivia's mouth before Gabe clamped it shut with his hand, but it had been a loud one. He hauled her back against him and held her still with an arm clamped around her middle. For a slender little woman she was strong, and she struggled like a rabbit caught in a snare.

"Settle down, Doc. Don't make me knock you over your fool head. Use whatever sense God gave you and settle down."

Her struggles stopped, and gradually her breathing slowed to normal. Gabe felt a twinge of conscience. The slender waist under his hand and the soft curves of her breasts were uncomfortable reminders that she was a woman—a small woman at that—and incapable of putting up much of a fight. But weaker sex aside, the woman was a doctor. And she'd goddamned better help his girls whether or not she cared to.

There was no alarm from outside. No one in sleeping Elkhorn had heard Olivia's scream.

"Are you in a more sensible frame of mind now?"

At her hesitant nod, he released her. "Go get your medical bag." When she didn't move, he gestured her forward with his pistol. "Go get it."

She fetched a leather case from behind the desk. "This is criminal, Mr. Danaher."

"Take your coat. It's cold."

"I could have you prosecuted."

"Put on the coat. Gloves too. I don't want you to freeze to death before we get to the cabin."

With a disgusted sigh, she obeyed. He took a sheet from the cot and ripped it into strips to bind her hands in front of her.

"You don't have to do that. Your gentlemanly pleas have convinced me to come with you."

"You have a smart mouth, Doc. I just don't want you to get too smart for your own good." He picked up the medical bag and blew out the lamp. "Come on. We've got a long ride ahead of us."

The cold November air hit Olivia in the face as Gabe pulled her after him through the back door. High above the mountains, a thin sickle slice of the moon inadequately contested the night's darkness.

"Do you want the door locked?" Gabe asked.

The question seemed absurdly courteous under the circumstances. "Wouldn't that be rather like closing the barn door after the cow escapes, or in this case, is kidnapped?"

He locked the door.

"Do you enjoy thinking of yourself as a bully and a kidnapper?"

For a moment Olivia heard only silence filled with tension. Then he answered in a quiet, determined voice. "Like I said. I'll do anything I have to to give my girls a chance."

"I tell you once again that this is insane."

"And I'll tell you once again, Doc, that if I have to tie you to the saddle like a sack of flour, I'll do it. So behave yourself and save us both a load of trouble."

"I guarantee I'll be more trouble than I'm worth."

They exchanged glares for a moment, then Gabe grinned in a way that sent a prickle of alarm down Olivia's spine. He reached out toward her. She jumped back, but all he wanted from her was the scarf that peeped out of her coat pocket.

"You'll be less trouble with your mouth closed."

Before she could protest, he tied the scarf securely over her mouth. She sputtered helplessly into the gag.

"You can scream all you want now, Doc. No one's going to hear you."

They walked through the clumpy grass behind the buildings until they arrived at the livery stable. With every step away from the familiar clinic Olivia's panic grew. This Gabriel Danaher was not the brash, teasing man she'd sparred with in Shriner's Mercantile or the roguish Irishman she'd patched up in her clinic. This man was desperate, determined, and angry. He must love his Indian mistresses very much to stoop to such villainous means to bring them help. Surely the most dangerous man of all was one who thought his mission justified any means, no matter how illegal or brutal. The thought sent a chill down her spine that had nothing to do with the cold.

The door of the livery opened with a creak. Once inside, Gabe lit a lamp and shoved Olivia into an empty stall. He bolted the door. "Stay put. I don't suppose you have a horse stabled here."

She shook her head.

"We'll just have to borrow you one, then. Longshot can't carry us both up the mountain. Hope you can ride."

Again she indicated no.

"You'll just have to learn."

If she did as he said, he probably wouldn't hurt her. She would ride up the mountain, treat the women, and then ride back to town. Two of her three current patients were nearly recovered and would suffer little from her loss. The third had parents who would somehow find the means to pay Cahill or Traleigh. Poor Amy would be desperate with worry, but Sylvester wouldn't let her overtax herself. In a few days she would be back, and all would be set aright. In a few days . . .

Olivia tried to convince herself as she watched her kidnapper efficiently saddle and bridle a big roan gelding. This incident was an inconvenience and surely an irritation, but not a calamity. After she lodged charges with the local magistrate, she could forget about Gabriel Danaher for good.

All her calm good sense could not quite stem the tide of panic, however. What if these women died and Danaher blamed her? Or what if he wanted to ensure that she couldn't bring charges against him? How easy it would be to commit murder and rid oneself of a body in these wild mountains. Gabe Danaher was a scoundrel and a no-good, Sylvester had said. Just how no-good was he? With the lamplight casting ominous shadows on Gabe's bleak face, Olivia was ready to believe he might be thoroughly no-good in the worst sort of way.

He unlatched the stall door. "You really can't ride?"

She shook her head vehemently. Not only could she not ride; she was rather afraid of horses.

He grimaced, but there was no sympathy in his expression. "Too bad. I guess you're going to learn the hard way."

He took Olivia by the arm and led her outside along with the two horses.

"Grab the saddle horn, put your left foot in the stirrup, and swing your right leg over the horse's back."

She looked at him blankly.

"Come on, Doc. You're not that ignorant." He took her bound hands and wrapped them around the saddle horn, then reached down for her ankle.

Olivia kicked at him and sidled away, her face heating.

His eyes narrowed. "Do you remember what I said about tying you stomach-down over the saddle like a sack of flour?"

She nodded.

"Now get the hell on that horse!"

Salvaging what little dignity she could, Olivia managed to thread her foot into the dangling stirrup. The roan turned his head to give her an impatient look as she tried to pull herself into the saddle. This maneuver was much more difficult than it looked.

"Need help?" A broad hand landed on her posterior and pushed. Olivia catapulted into the saddle and hung there on her stomach. "Now swing your right leg over."

What she wanted to swing was a fist into Gabriel Danaher's face. His hand still rested indecently on her buttocks.

"Sit up, Doc. Or you're going to ride up the mountain that way." He gave her a light swat for inspiration.

She managed to get her right leg over the horse and her foot into the stirrup with very little grace. Her skirts bunched around her legs, revealing an unseemly length of calf and ankle. Danaher didn't seem to notice. He snapped a lead rope to the roan's bit and swung easily aboard his own horse.

"The reins are looped over your horse's neck, but you don't need to use them. Just sit there and behave."

As if she had any other choice! The roan gelding lurched forward to follow the lead horse. They plodded quietly through town. The mountains rose in front of them, a black, forbidding mass against the star-dotted sky. Once out of town there would be no one to help her, even if she did manage to escape.

Olivia thought desperately of throwing herself from the horse and running, but she knew Danaher would be on her in a trice and undoubtedly make good his threat of tying her over the saddle—if he didn't lose that Irish temper of his and shoot her. Sitting on a horse right side up was uncomfortable enough. She had no desire to spend the rest of the night with her posterior pointed toward the sky.

The road began to climb as they left the last of Elkhorn's buildings behind. At Gabe's urging, the horses lengthened their stride and broke into a trot. Olivia held on to the saddle horn as she jounced and bumped in the saddle. Her legs flapped awkwardly against the horse's sides, her teeth jarred in her head, and a very tender part of her anatomy felt as though it were being pounded to a pulp. Up ahead, Danaher looked as though he were part of his big bay mare. He didn't bounce in the saddle; his long legs didn't flap; his head didn't wobble in counterpoint to the horse's movement as Olivia's did. The supple grace of his harmony with the beast seemed to mock her awkwardness.

The road curved sharply to the right to run along the hillside above town. Elkhorn spread out below, dark except for a window or two winking lamplight into the night. The town looked like a rash of dark splotches on the faintly starlit valley, ugly and unnatural, but to Olivia it seemed the last outpost of civilization and safety. They turned, and the town disappeared behind the hillside. The road deteriorated to a rutted track that would tax the sturdiest of wagons. Olivia felt more helpless and alone than she had in her entire life.

Gabe twisted in his saddle. "You all right back there?"

Olivia muttered a denial into her gag. Danaher's horse stopped. Hers didn't. She trotted past her tormentor close enough to see the surprised lift of his brows. The lead rope tightened. With a sudden jerk, the roan swung around. Olivia's legs flapped as she struggled for balance. Her heels dug accidentally into the horse's sensitive flanks, and the roan shied violently to one side. Almost before she knew what had happened, Olivia

found herself on the ground. Her horse looked back at her with a satisfied gleam in its eye.

"Jesus Christ! You really are something!" Gabe dismounted and
strode over to where she sat among pine needles, rocks, and tangled
skirts.

She glared at him through narrowed eyes and thought of trying to kick
him as he pulled her to her feet. But she was too tired and sore to kick.

"Guess we can do without this now." He untied the scarf from her
mouth. "You can scream your head off, and the only ones to hear you
will be me and the chipmunks. Get back on the horse."

"That horse doesn't like me."

Gabe smiled unpleasantly. "I don't much blame him, to tell the truth.
But he doesn't have much more choice in the matter than you do. This
time try to keep your heels away from his flanks."

When Olivia didn't move, Gabe started toward her. Remembering his
hand on her rear the last time she'd climbed into the saddle, Olivia
managed to mount quickly, if not gracefully. Her horse gave a snort of
disgust.

"You and me both," she muttered.

They rode on, always climbing. Olivia could find no position in the
saddle that was either comfortable or secure. Her legs, buttocks, and
back all complained mightily, but after one request for a rest met with
curt refusal, she didn't ask again. Gabriel Danaher hadn't a speck of
mercy in him; and if she got back to Elkhorn alive, she'd find great
satisfaction in seeing him rot in jail for a very long time.

Finally, the stars overhead began to fade. The dark bulk of the mountains took on color and detail—gray rock glinting through evergreen
forests. Steep valleys with tumbling streams all but hidden by willow
bushes. When the first sunlight speared through the valleys, they
stopped.

"Ten minutes to do whatever you have to do." Gabe dismounted and
slung one of the gunnysacks from Shriner's Mercantile off the back of his
saddle. "There's some jerky in here if you can find it. I'll take the horses
down to water."

Olivia swung her leg over the saddle and closed her eyes from the pain
that knifed up her leg and back. She had thought she was numb, but she
wasn't numb enough. Practically falling from the horse, she landed on
the ground with feet that felt like stumps of lead. She stood swaying as
Gabe led her horse toward a little rill of water that tumbled down the
mountainside.

"Hop to it, Doc. We don't have all day."

"Aren't you going to untie my hands?"

"Nope."

Fury boiled up in her breast. She was exhausted, frozen, thirsty, hungry, and saddle-sore. Her bladder felt ready to rupture, and her legs were rubbery masses of pain—all because Gabriel Danaher thought his female companions had more right to medical care than the good people of Elkhorn. Now, to top it all, the ruffian wouldn't even loose her hands so that she could tend to herself.

"Still standing there?" Gabe asked as he led the horses back. "You've got about five minutes left."

Olivia asked through clenched teeth, "Would you please untie my hands, Mr. Danaher. I need to . . . to . . ." She felt her face heat.

"There's plenty of bushes over there, Doc. You can manage anything you need to do with your hands tied."

"Mr. Danaher! You're a . . . a . . ." At least a dozen descriptive names came to mind, none of them fit for the vocabulary of a lady. He turned his back to rummage through the gunnysack, and his lack of interest in her scolding made her even madder.

"You're a barbarian, Mr. Danaher."

He turned and regarded her with a stony expression. "You have about five or six minutes before you have to get back on that horse and ride another three hours."

With a sniff of disgust she stalked toward a thicket at the side of the trail. What she had intended to be an indignant march became somewhat ludicrous, however, when her legs declined to obey her will in any good order. She refused to look back to see if Danaher was watching her swaying and stumbling retreat into the bushes.

"Two minutes!" he called after her.

Damn the ignorant, rude, contemptible scoundrel!

Olivia managed to tend to her needs in spite of tied hands. As she rearranged her skirts, she looked back down the rough wagon track they had climbed. In the morning light, the rugged country didn't look quite as threatening as it had at night. Birds sang and twittered to greet the new day. A breeze stirred the aspen leaves that littered the forest floor, producing a swirl of warm gold.

The temptation to run was strong. Danaher and the horses were out of sight, and if she quietly slipped into the forest, perhaps he wouldn't find her. The ground was covered with dead leaves that would show very little evidence of her trail, and after he gave up and went on his way, she could simply follow the track to Elkhorn. With luck she would get there before nightfall.

She wanted freedom so badly she could taste it. For much of her life, Olivia had been in control of almost every situation she met. She had forged her way through a world fraught with obstacles and difficulties and done very well at it. Her helplessness in the hands of this coarse, rude man was as frustrating as it was frightening. She longed to take the situation back into her own hands, even if it meant walking alone down the mountain through the wild forest.

On the other hand, since she was this far up the mountain, did she owe Danaher's women what help she could provide? Obligated to her patients in Elkhorn, she firmly believed she'd been right in refusing Danaher; but now that the issue had been forced, could she put her own safety above the needs of the sick women up the trail?

On still another hand, Danaher was an immoral scoundrel of a ruffian, rough, unpredictable, explosive. The farther she could get from him, the better. She should take the chance to escape.

Yet his Indian floozies, as Amy had named them, were human beings, and they were suffering. The highest duty of a physician was to relieve human suffering, or so Olivia had always believed. Could she turn away from duty because she was frightened?

Olivia promptly forgot the dilemma at a sudden rustling behind her. She whirled to see a savage sight that made the blood drain from her face. Not ten feet away, eyeing her as a fox might eye a fat hen, stood an Indian in buckskin leggings, cowboy boots, and a threadbare wool shirt. Two ragged feathers decorated the coarse hair that straggled over his shoulders. Black eyes were as hard and grim as a snake's, and a feral grin pulled thin lips back from a savagely gleaming row of teeth.

The brute came toward her, and Olivia screamed.

Chapter 4

Olivia's scream pierced the morning quiet of the forest. Gabe dropped the piece of jerky he was cutting and ran toward the thicket, grabbing instinctively for his pistol. He brushed through the thick tangle of branches to meet a sight that made his heart drop. Facing Olivia was a Blackfoot warrior whose grim brown countenance confirmed Gabe's worst fears. His mission had failed after all.

The sound of Gabe's arrival made both Olivia and the Indian look up from a staring match. Olivia gave a strangled cry and ran toward Gabe. The Blackfoot stood like a statue.

Gabe caught Olivia as she pelted past him and held her in the curve of his arm. "Run! It's a . . . it's an . . ." She trembled like a frightened rabbit.

"I see what it is. Now hush."

He switched to Blackfoot, the language that had always been so melodious on Minnie's lips. But his words sounded like the rattle of dead bones. "They are gone, then. That is why you are here." Gone without his being there, without his even saying good-bye.

"They are not yet gone, Horse Stalker."

A stone lifted from Gabe's heart.

"But they are very bad. Much worse. Especially White Horse Woman. I was worried that you did not come with the doctor, that you took so

long. Squirrel Woman watches your daughters while I come to find you."
The Indian turned a questioning gaze on Olivia.

"This woman is the doctor," Gabe explained. "I took such a long time
because I couldn't find anyone else to come."

"A medicine woman?"

"So she claims."

The Blackfoot nodded acceptance. "It is good that you bring her. We
must ride fast now, or your daughters will join their mother in the village
of the dead. I hope this woman's medicine is strong."

"I will persuade her to make it strong," Gabe said grimly.

Olivia looked from one to the other of them as Gabe and the savage
conversed in a language that was gibberish to her. Gabe had put his
pistol back into its holster, which she took as a sign that at least they were
not to be immediately scalped and killed. The strange conversation
stopped, and both men regarded her with expressions that made her
nerves prickle with unease. She backed out of Gabe's hold and found
strangely enough that the Indian looked much more threatening to her
without Gabe's arm about her.

"You know this Indian?"

"He's a good friend. Meet Crooked Stick."

A friend of Danaher's. She had certainly made a ninnyhammer of
herself, screaming as if the world were coming to an end and cowering in
the shelter of Danaher's arm. "I . . . I'm pleased to meet you, Mr.
Crooked Stick."

The Indian nodded gravely, and Olivia felt hot blood rise into her face
at her recent display. Not that she could have known. He hadn't precisely
acted like a friend, after all; and even in this day and age when most
tribes were on reservations, all the stories and articles she had read about
Indians scarcely led one to regard them as allies.

"He says Katy and Ellen are much worse. We need to ride fast."

"Mr. Danaher, I don't want them to die any more than you do, but just
riding is task enough for me. I don't think riding fast is a possibility."

He took her arm and pulled her back toward the horses. "You'll ride
with me."

"You said your horse couldn't carry both of us up the mountain."

"Most of the climbing is done, and we'll ride your roan. He's bigger
than my mare."

The ride up the trail inspired Olivia to promise herself that if she
survived this journey she would never again climb atop a horse. Only
Gabe's arm wrapped around her rib cage prevented her from ending up
on the ground under the horses' hooves at least a dozen times. Her

repeated pleas to ride more carefully were ignored by Gabe and seemed to amuse the Indian.

If the physical duress of the ride was not enough, the forced intimacy of her position was even worse. Squeezed between the saddle pommel and Danaher's hips, Olivia was humiliatingly aware of her buttocks riding firmly against his groin. Her legs, indecently exposed from midcalf to the tops of her shoes, were practically on top of his, the muscles of his chest pressed insistently into her back, and more than once she felt his stubbled cheek brush her temple and his breath in her hair.

It wasn't the indelicacy of the situation that bothered her so much. After all, when lives were at stake, propriety was unimportant. What bothered her was her peculiar reaction to this manhandling. She had always been a very private person who required space between herself and those around her, but her body seemed to feel an illogical excitement from being forced into such intimate proximity with the Irishman. Obviously her body didn't have very discriminating taste.

Finally the hellish ride came to an end as they rode into a high mountain valley. On one side of the valley, a ridge of granite crags jutted toward the sky; on the other side, alpine meadows of winter-sered grass climbed steeply to a bare, rounded double mound that looked like a huge set of shoulders shrugging at the splendor around them. This high in the mountains, trees were stunted and warped into grotesque shapes by the wind.

Danaher's cabin was just below the timberline, set at one edge of a clearing surrounded by spruce and pine. The place consisted of a log cabin with a stone chimney set at one end, several sizable sheds, a corral, a henhouse, and a large square of dirt that held the autumn remnants of a vegetable garden. On a clothesline stretched between trees flapped two shirts, a pair of heavy cotton trousers, a skirt, and another pair of trousers that might fit a half-grown boy. The cabin and outbuildings looked like a well-tended homestead, not the hideaway where a miscreant scoundrel wallowed in sin with two mistresses.

An Indian woman stepped out of the house as they rode up. Her thick braids were silver shot through with flecks of jet, her skin brown and fragile-looking as sun-dried parchment. Crooked Stick returned her guttural greeting. Gabe swung to the ground and strode into the cabin without so much as acknowledging the old woman. Even considering his girls' critical condition, Olivia thought his behavior very rude.

Olivia felt the Indian woman's eyes on her as she precariously climbed off the tall roan.

"My mother, this woman is a medicine woman among the whites. She will help the little ones."

The woman looked dubious as Olivia lowered herself inelegantly to the ground. She made a curt-sounding comment in her own language. Crooked Stick laughed. "Squirrel Woman says she hopes you are a better doctor than horsewoman."

"You may tell her that I most certainly am. She is the mother of one of the girls?"

The old woman snorted, and a twinkle of humor in Crooked Stick's onyx eyes belied his impassive face. "She is their grandmother."

"She speaks English."

"Only when she wants to."

"I will do what I can for your grandchildren, madam."

The crone blocked Olivia's path as she started for the cabin. She spit several rapid-fire sentences in Olivia's direction and made no move to step aside. Olivia's legs felt like rubber after the long ride, and she had no agility to match the woman's repeated moves to impede her. Only at a rebuke from Crooked Stick did the Indian woman let Olivia pass.

"Make your medicine strong, Big Mouth Woman."

"Big Mouth Woman?"

Crooked Stick grinned. "Your mouth is always scolding. It must be big to hold so many words."

"Well, I—"

"Heed my warning. Katy and Ellen are Squirrel Woman's only surviving grandchildren. If they die she will tear out your hair as well as her own."

"If Squirrel Woman wanted to keep her precious granddaughters safe, she should have advised them to stay on the reservation rather than take up with a roving, immoral white man who would lead them into the white man's sinfulness and the white man's diseases."

"Many words, Big Mouth Woman. They make no sense."

Olivia sniffed indignantly and marched toward the cabin. She stopped and turned, prepared to offer a rebuttal to Crooked Stick's rebuke, but the two Indians had silently disappeared. The roan and Gabe's bay mare both looked into the brush with ears pricked, but there was no sign of either Crooked Stick or Squirrel Woman.

Olivia blinked, then exhaled a shaky breath. "What rude people."

The interior of Danaher's cabin was all gloom and smoke. Shutters kept out the morning sunlight, and smoldering wood in the fireplace burned with more smoke than flame. Near the fireplace were two pallets. Danaher stood between them, looking down at the figures who lay there.

The grief in his face was painful to see. No matter how unconventional and immoral his relationship might be with these women, he truly loved them. For a moment Olivia's heart softened toward him.

"You must see that the air is freshened in here, Mr. Danaher. And open the shutters, please. Fresh air will help the patients, not hurt them."

He lifted a bleak face full of despair.

Olivia looked down at the patients she had been dragged up a mountain to attend—and received a shock. Those pale little faces didn't belong to women. What kind of depraved monster was Gabriel Danaher?

"These are but children!"

"What the hell did you expect?"

She sputtered her indignation, unable to find the words to express her disgust of a man who would take advantage of females so very young. Danaher looked at her in dawning realization.

"You thought . . . my God! You pure-minded ladies certainly do muck up garbage in your imaginations. These girls are my daughters."

Olivia's face heated to instant fire. His daughters. Of course. No matter what Amy had told her, the girls looked much too young to be anything else. "I apologize, Mr. Danaher. I was led to believe . . . that is . . ."

"It doesn't matter." His mouth tightened to a grim line. "When I left they were awake and complaining. Now they look barely alive."

He was right. The girls were pale and quiet except for the harsh rattle of labored breathing, and they didn't stir at Danaher's gentle touch. If they weren't beyond help, as their father plainly thought, then they were indeed very close. But Olivia didn't believe in giving up. Life was a remarkable thing, and sometimes, particularly with the young, it won out against all odds.

"Let me examine them, Mr. Danaher. Go open the shutters and do something about that wretched fire. It's no wonder they're bad if this was Squirrel Woman's idea of treatment."

Danaher rattled about the cabin opening shutters and poking at the fire, but Olivia could feel his eyes on her as she bent over the girls. She was accustomed to suspicious scrutiny during examinations—all women doctors were used to such distrust. But Danaher's watchfulness sent a little prickle up her spine. The man had an air of desperation about him that was dangerous.

Olivia's examination confirmed what she had suspected—Danaher's daughters were suffering from severe cases of diphtheria. Elkhorn's epidemic had reached up into the mountains to claim two more young victims. Both girls had the characteristic fibrous, dirty-gray tonsilar membrane developed sufficiently that it interfered with both swallowing and breathing. One of the children showed swelling of the pharynx and larynx —she was definitely worse off than her sister. The stethoscope revealed hearts still beating strongly in the thin, laboring chests, however, so Olivia dared to hope that the disease had not progressed to irritation of that most vital organ.

She straightened suddenly and bumped against Danaher.

"Sorry." He took her by the shoulders to help her regain her balance.

Olivia hastily shrugged off his grip. "Mr. Danaher, I cannot work with you hovering over me like some specter of doom."

"Are they . . ."

"Your daughters are very sick. I'll be frank on that score. There is yet hope, I think, but I can't say right now what are the chances of their survival. Medical science has not yet isolated the cause of diphtheria, and current treatments are of little use. All I can do is help them regain their strength so they can fight off the disease."

Danaher's mouth flattened. "They're fighters." His voice was hoarse with emotion. "Both of them are fighters in their own way."

Olivia followed his unhappy gaze to the girls. They were twins, she realized. She'd been concentrating so on their illness that she hadn't noticed their identical features. Even struck down by sickness they were beautiful, with fine, high cheekbones set in oval faces. Their hair was raven's-wing black, thick and wavy. Now it was damp and lifeless, but in health, it no doubt set off their faces to perfection. "It's good that they're fighters, Mr. Danaher. We will help them fight."

For the rest of the day and most of the night, Olivia stayed by the twins' side. There were a number of popular treatments for diphtheria. Some physicians opened the blocked passageways and sucked out the obstructing mucus. Others preferred to hold the patient upside down while the throat was tickled with a feather soaked in goose grease in hopes the victim would vomit up the congestion (this was more practical with small children than adults, of course). Doctors Cahill and Traleigh in Elkhorn swore by sulfur boiled in limewater and dropped into the patient's nostrils with a quill.

Olivia was not convinced that any of these methods were anything but quackery. She had no doubt the disease was caused by some vicious microscopic organism—as others had been shown to be. Until that organism was isolated and an antitoxin found to combat its effects, the best treatment a physician could give was to support the patient's strength in fighting off the disease.

The twins were exhausted from their battle for breath, so the first thing

Olivia did was cut through the blocking membrane with a knife soaked in carbolic. This was a temporary solution, for the membrane would quickly grow back, but at least the children were able to breathe easier for a short time. And while they were temporarily relieved, she patiently dribbled a light broth into their mouths and helped them swallow by massaging their throats. The broth had been brewed by Squirrel Woman and smelled of an unpleasant combination of herbs. It was the only thing she had at the moment, however, and whatever it was, it seemed to be strengthening. In the late afternoon, when the twins had regained sufficient energy to object to her ministrations, Olivia counted it a triumph.

"Are they better?" The cabin door banged shut behind Danaher, who had been in and out all through the day, unable to stay and watch his daughters suffer yet just as unable to stay away.

"They're awake enough to try to spit out this concoction Squirrel Woman brewed. From the smell of it, I don't blame them."

Danaher sniffed. "Elm bark tea. Tastes awful, but the Indians hereabouts use it as a tonic."

"I saw what looked like a henhouse as we rode in. Do you have a chicken you could boil up into a broth? Now that they're able to swallow a bit, I'd like to get something more nourishing down them. And build up the fire without the smoke that Squirrel Woman was generating, please."

As the day progressed, the twins swallowed chicken broth with great difficulty, looking up at Olivia with confused eyes that were as green as their father's. They called for Danaher, and he spent long periods sitting with them. One he spoke to soothingly, brushing the damp hair from her brow in a gesture so gentle that Olivia had difficulty believing he was the ruffian she knew him to be. The other twin he teased and chided for her weakness in a way Olivia thought was intolerable, but the child seemed to respond with renewed determination to recover.

Finally, warm and clean, their stomachs full of broth, the twins settled into a sleep that was more natural than the near trance they'd been in when Olivia first arrived. Their breathing and swallowing was still painfully labored. The membrane had grown back quickly. Olivia didn't want to remove the obstruction again unless she had to, for the procedure had dangers of its own, including infection and excessive bleeding. She settled back into the cabin's one chair—a rocker—beside the pallets to watch and wait, the most frustrating part of any physician's role.

Danaher pulled a stool in front of the fireplace and sat beside her. "Will they live?"

"I don't know yet, Mr. Danaher. Their recovery depends mostly on them."

They sat in silence until Olivia could stand his quiet misery no longer. "Your daughters are identical twins, yet they seem very different in temperament. One lies on her pallet and does what she is told, the other fights everything."

A smile flickered across his face. "The quiet one is Ellen. She always tries to please, but inside herself, she always knows what she's doing and why she's doing it. If she doesn't want to do something, she'll find a way around it without making a scene. She generally ends up getting her way. Her sister is Katy." He shook his head and regarded Katy with a wry smile. "Even when her mother was alive she acted more like a boy than a girl. She's almost as good with a rifle as I am, and she'd rather be helping in the mine or taking care of the mules and horses than doing women's work inside the house. My fault for treating her like a son, I guess. Someday she'll have to learn she's a female, if she lives. . . ."

"Their mother must have been very lovely," Olivia interjected quickly to divert him from the gloomy thought. "The girls are beautiful."

"Their mother was the most beautiful girl on the whole Blackfoot reservation. They got her looks, except for the eyes. Those are mine."

"Their mother is Blackfoot, like Crooked Stick?"

"Yes. Many Horses Woman. I called her Minnie. We lived a year with her people, then she left the reservation with me. Squirrel Woman is her mother. Crooked Stick is her brother."

"Is Squirrel Woman still angry because you took her daughter? Is that why you didn't speak?"

Danaher chuckled. "Blackfoot custom forbids a man to speak to his wife's mother. It's a good custom. Prevents a lot of fighting."

"Oh." He was married to the Indian woman, then. At least he was that civilized. "Where is Many Horses Woman now? Should you perhaps send her a message that her daughters are ill?"

"It would be a message to the village of the dead. She died over two years ago."

"I'm sorry. It must be quite a task raising two girls on your own."

His brow furrowed. "It's not a task. Without them I would be . . . empty."

Katy stirred and opened her eyes. "Pa?"

"I'm here, Katy."

"I'm not going to die, Pa. I swear I won't."

"No, you're not going to die. Neither is Ellen."

She choked, and fluid spurted from her nose. Olivia quickly and efficiently wiped it away. "Let me look at your throat, Katy."

Katy glared. "Who are you?"

"She's a doctor, Katy. Do what she says."

Reluctantly, Katy obeyed.

"Do you think you could swallow some more broth?"

"Yeah."

"Pa?" came Ellen's voice. She had awakened also.

By the time the twins had managed to swallow most of the broth, they were fatigued enough to drop instantly back asleep. Olivia found her own resources almost exhausted as well. She couldn't remember the last time she'd slept, and though Danaher had earlier offered her a bowl of some kind of stew, she'd been too tired to eat. Yet the rest of the evening and the long night stretched ahead of her.

"You look done in, Doc. Why don't you sleep a bit while the girls are sleeping. There's a bed just beyond that curtain over there."

"Now is not the time to ease vigilance, Mr. Danaher. Your daughters are resting more easily, but they could turn to the worse at any time."

"I'll call you if that happens."

"Thank you just the same, but I've stayed awake for longer stretches."

"Well, then, since it looks to be a long night, I think I'll heat some coffee. Want some?"

"No, thank you. I don't suppose you have any tea."

He chuckled. "Just the elm bark tea that Squirrel Woman brewed up. It's a good tonic, I've heard. Might give you energy."

"I don't think so."

Gabe sat down at the rough-hewn pine table with his mug of coffee. The doc wouldn't be able to stay awake long, he guessed. He could see weariness etch her face and drag her shoulders into a slump. She might have stayed awake for longer stretches, but he doubted that those stretches included being kidnapped in the middle of the night and riding horseback up a mountain. For all that she was a prissy-looking little mouse, the woman had grit, no doubt about it. And to give her credit, once here, she did seem truly concerned about the twins. She might have looked at them and said there was no hope; or she might have given them a cursory treatment and demanded to be taken back down the mountain. But once she'd seen them, she'd launched into fighting the sickness as though she were fighting a war.

Gabe himself was nearly stumbling with fatigue. He had a notion to pull a stool next to Olivia's chair, where he could be closer to the twins, but he wasn't sure he could get up. Worry alone kept him awake. He couldn't rest until he knew for sure the twins would live—or until . . . The other possibility was unthinkable. If the twins died, the best part of his life would die with them. At least when Minnie had died, lust for revenge had spurred him to live—that, and the need to protect his daughters. If the twins died . . . How did one seek vengeance against a disease?

The night stretched on interminably. Time was measured by each labored breath, each restless toss or turn of Katy or Ellen. Twice they awoke—both at the same time, as if they were alike in their illness as they were in looks. Olivia spooned chicken broth down their throats, patiently cleaning up the mess that was produced as they tried to choke the warm liquid down. Gabe talked to them, sponged their faces, and told them all the things they would do together once they were recovered. And when they fell back asleep, both Gabe and Olivia sat and watched, waiting for the tide to turn one way or the other.

Shortly after midnight the moon sent its light slanting through the window and illuminated the twins in a pure white glow. Remnants of Irish superstition urged Gabe to believe it was a sign that all was well; the girls would recover. Nonsensical though he knew the notion was, for the first time since returning to the cabin he allowed himself the hope that Katy and Ellen would survive.

Apparently the pragmatic doctoress had no such fanciful illusions. She merely rose and closed the shutters against the moonlight. Then she condescended to ask for a cup of coffee, which she drank down with a grimace.

An hour later, with the twins sleeping peacefully, Gabe watched Olivia lose her battle with exhaustion. Somehow she managed to stay upright in the chair, and the only signs that she slept were the slump of her shoulders and the slight nodding of her head. Gabe smiled wryly. The lady doctor wasn't quite as tough as she thought she was. He carefully lifted her from the chair and carried her to his bed behind the curtain. She remained fast asleep when he laid her on the quilt and covered her with a blanket. In repose she looked younger and much less stern. Her hair had come loose from its severe bun and framed her face on the pillow in a soft, dark halo. Her eyelashes were dusky crescents against pale cheeks, and shadowed smudges of weariness beneath her eyes gave her a look of childish vulnerability. Gabe felt a rush of gratitude, for now he believed the girls would live. Reluctant though she'd been, Olivia Baron was their savior, and for that he owed her more than he could ever pay.

The night seemed to inch by, and each hour dragged on longer than the last. Gabe sat beside the twins, dozing and then waking with an alarmed start each time one of the girls turned or made a sound. Their time together paraded before his mind, and sometimes in the limbo between sleep and waking, he almost thought he was back with Minnie.

The day the twins were born came alive once again—how helpless he had felt, banished from their tipi while Squirrel Woman and the elderly midwife tended to his wife in her travail. Helpless, elated, excited, awestruck, impatient, fearful—so many emotions raging inside him that he'd almost been sick. The men had laughed at him. Some of the women as well. When the birth was over and he had beheld his two little girls—twins, just as Squirrel Woman had predicted—he'd been the proudest man on earth. Minnie had beamed as if the sun shone from inside her, even though pain still lined her face and her hands were bruised and in places raw from where she'd grasped a lodgepole to keep herself upright during the delivery.

How Minnie had loved their daughters. Gabe sometimes wondered if she would have left the reservation with him a year later if not for the twins. He had tried his best to make her not regret it, but she'd been no more comfortable with the white man's way of life than he had been with the Blackfoot. They made a life that they could both live, however. They loved each other; they loved Katy and Ellen. Gabe remembered romps in the snow in front of the little log cabin ranch house near Virginia City; Ellen's pride in learning from Minnie how to properly tan hides and how to build a tipi that was actually warmer in winter than their cabin; Katy cleaning her first squirrel, while Ellen's little nose screwed up in disgust. He remembered holding Ellen in the flickering light of the fireplace one winter night and explaining that the eerie chorus of howls floating down from the hills was the song of wolves, not ghosts; Minnie sitting in front of that same fireplace teaching the twins how to plait their hair into neat braids; him teaching the girls how to play chess and discovering that after a few weeks of practice, Katy could beat him.

Those had been the family days, the days when the four of them had had a future. Before Minnie had been killed, before Will O'Connell became Gabriel Danaher and grew hair down to his shoulders to become less recognizable, before he became a hunted man hiding in the mountains and digging for the riches that would let him hire enough men to confront Ace Candliss and his army of hired hands. His life had unraveled, and Katy and Ellen were the only threads left whole. His daughters and the hope of avenging Minnie were his only reasons for living.

Gabe glanced at the mantel above the fireplace, where two small buckskin cases, both in the form of lizards, sat propped against the stone chimney. The cases held dried portions of the twins' umbilical cords. Blackfoot tradition said that such an amulet ensured long life and health for the child. Boys' cords were preserved in cases shaped like snakes, girls' in cases shaped like lizards. Both were animals the Blackfeet be-lieved were never sick and lived very long lives.

The tradition had proved right. The twins hadn't been sick a single day in their young lives—until the diphtheria. In the face of this white man's disease, the amulets had failed. Gabe could only hope that Olivia Baron's medicine was stronger than Blackfoot magic.

Katy moaned, and the sound roused Gabe from his half-slumber. She tried to cough, but the cough congealed into a fluid choking. Then, un-easily, she relaxed again into sleep. Ellen didn't stir. Her breathing was deep and less labored than before.

Gabe got up and poured himself some of the strong coffee that was boiling down to syrup over the fire. Would the twins be fighting for their lives now if he'd been hanged two years ago and they lived in Widow Casey's comfortable home? They wouldn't be living in a one-room log cabin, sleeping in a drafty loft, keeping house with only chipmunks and an occasional bear for company.

It won't be forever, he promised them silently. One more year at this mine, and I'll have enough money to hire the men I need to go against Candliss. And when I have him, he'll tell the truth about what happened that day, and the law will take my revenge for me. For me, for you, for Crooked Stick and Squirrel Woman and all the people in the world who loved Many Horses Woman. Then I won't have to hide my face every time someone gives me a second glance, or look over my shoulder in fear that Candliss has hired some bounty hunter smart enough to trace me to these mountains. Then we can make a future again.

Katy tried to cough once again. She gurgled instead. Her eyes opened, and she half raised herself on her elbows. A great heaved breath resulted only in a choking sputter as fluid ran from her nose.

Gabe wiped the mess from her face. "Breathe, Katy. Breathe."

She labored to obey, fighting for precious air and getting very little. Tears ran from her eyes. Her color was more blue than pink, and her breathing was getting worse by the second.

Gabe hadn't time to move toward the bed to wake Olivia before the doctoress was there. Eyes puffy from sleep, hair in a cascade over her shoulders and back, she had neither the officious presence of a white doctor nor the awesome dignity of the Blackfoot medicine man. But she nevertheless took the situation in hand.

"How long has she been this way?" Olivia demanded.

"Just now. Well, no. The last hour or so she's been getting worse. Restless. Trying to cough."

"Get the lamp and hold it so I can see." She peered into Katy's throat. "Why didn't you wake me?"

"You said you'd done all you could."

Gabe knew from the frown that knit Olivia's brows that Katy wasn't good. He could have guessed that without the doctor's help.

"We've got to open up the air passage somehow. She's losing consciousness."

Gabe felt a claw of panic begin to tear at his gut.

The doctor straightened and regarded Katy thoughtfully. She chewed a moment on her lower lip, then her lips firmed into a line. "Get me some clean towels if you have any."

In the cupboard by the bed were towels that were mostly rags, but they were clean. He fetched them and hurried back to the cot, his stomach in his throat. Olivia had poured a strong-smelling solution into a basin and was immersing a scalpel and a length of tubing.

"Carbolic," she explained. "It prevents infection."

"What are you going to do? Can you do something?"

"I'm going to cut a little slit in her trachea and put this bit of tubing in so she can breathe."

He seemed to hear Katy's name in the pounding of his heart. "You're going to cut open her throat?"

Olivia looked almost apologetic. "Mr. Danaher, this is safer than trying to cut the membrane again, and it will solve the problem for a longer period of time. I've got to do something or we're going to lose her."

She was a quack, and she couldn't know what she was doing. After all, she was just a woman. He should stop her. But Katy . . .

"Hold her still, please, Mr. Danaher. She's unconscious now, but if she should wake and move, I could do considerable damage."

She didn't look at him, concentrating instead on placing a towel beneath Katy's neck and feeling the little girl's windpipe with her fingers. She expected him to go along with the madness, so confident in herself, in his obedience.

Feeling dizzy, he held Katy's head.

"This will take only a moment."

Lips pressed together in concentration, Olivia swiftly made a small incision. A soft whistle of air escaped Katy's windpipe.

"Would you mop up that bit of blood, please?"

There wasn't much of it. Just a dribble or two. But it was Katy's blood. Gabe's and Minnie's blood mixed together. Gabe felt dizzy again.

With efficient movements, Olivia inserted the small rubber tube through the slit in the windpipe. "Good thing this tube was in the bag. There. See, it's already stopped bleeding."

Katy's eyes fluttered open. Already her complexion had a healthier tinge. Olivia placed a finger on Katy's lips as they started to open.

"Don't talk, Katy. You were having trouble breathing, so I had to cut a little hole in your windpipe. Once you're well it will heal and you'll never even know it was there. But for now just lie quietly and try to breathe as normally as you can."

Gabe was glad to see that Katy was braver about the thing than he was. He sat down hard in the chair as Olivia bent to check Ellen. He didn't think he could stay awake any longer.

Gabe's eyes closed against his will, and momentarily he felt the light brush of cool fingers on his forehead. He looked up into a professionally composed expression that belied the tenderness of that touch.

"Why don't you make use of the bed, Mr. Danaher. I've had a few hours' sleep now. I'll call if I need your help."

Gabe obeyed and stumbled off toward the bed. He looked back just once to see Olivia outlined against the fire, calmly pouring herself a cup of coffee as if she performed such miracles as this every day. She grimaced as she sniffed the thick, hot liquid, settled into the chair, and smiled to herself as though she knew he watched her. The smile of an angel, Gabe decided, coming from the heart of a lion. How had he ever compared her in his mind to a small gray mouse?

Chapter 5

Sylvester, this is not my imagination. I'm sure something has happened to her. I didn't think much of it yesterday when the food I took her was untouched. After all, she's been running herself ragged with this illness in town. But she isn't at the clinic today either, and the bed doesn't look slept in. It looks as though she hasn't been there at all. She didn't even use the clean clothes I brought her, and you know Olivia. If she were fainting from exhaustion she still would change to clean clothes."

Sylvester regarded his wife with concerned eyes. In her condition, Amy shouldn't be fretting like she was. He realized Olivia felt an obligation toward those who were ill, but he was vexed that the woman was behaving in such an inconsiderate manner. Amy was a worrier; and in her delicate condition, peace of mind was paramount. After years of acquaintance with his wife, Olivia should know her disposition and take steps to ensure that Amy didn't fret about her.

"Sylvester, you're frowning. You think something has happened also."

"No, my dear, I don't, and I wish you would try to calm yourself. Most probably Olivia is staying with a patient who needs constant care. You yourself told me that she tends to lose track of time and circumstance when she's involved with someone else's problem."

"I don't believe that. If she were staying with a patient, she would let us know where she was. She wouldn't worry us like this. I've got the most awful feeling inside me that she's in trouble."

Amy's feeling was more likely a dyspepsia caused by her condition than a prescience about Olivia, but Sylvester supposed that he should make some inquiries, if only for the sake of his wife's composure. Not that he had the time to spare. Two belts had broken at the mill this morning, and the mill hands were grumbling again about their pay. Just last week they had lost two men to the lure of prospecting in the mountains, even though the first flush of discovery had long since passed in this area, and now three were absent because of illness. He needed to be at the mill to deal with these problems, and in truth if he weren't so concerned about Amy, he wouldn't have come home for the midday meal. Still, nothing was more important right now than his wife's happiness and the health of the child she carried. Olivia had to be somewhere nearby. How long could it take to find her?

"I'll look into the matter, my dear. But you must promise me to rest the entire afternoon. Have Mrs. Grisolm build up the fire in your bedroom so you'll be warm. I can't feel easy about that cramping you had yesterday, even though it went away after a time. When I find her, I intend to tell your friend Olivia that she should be here tending you, not running about town doctoring people who, if the truth be known, no well-bred lady should have anything to do with."

"You will find her, won't you?"

"Of course I will."

Sylvester didn't find Olivia, however. No one in town had seen her in several days, although Mr. Shriner thought she had been tending the Sanderson boy, who had died the day before yesterday, or was it the day after that? He wasn't quite sure. Of even more concern was Dr. Traleigh's indignant news that a Grub Wicker had brought his son to him for treatment because Olivia had not shown up at his shack as she'd promised. Traleigh told him that Dr. Cahill had also treated some of Olivia's patients because of the doctoress's neglect. As the doctor waxed eloquent about the unsuitability of females to be physicians, Sylvester listened with only half an ear. He now shared Amy's concern. For some reason, Olivia Baron had simply disappeared from Elkhorn.

Sylvester had no notion of how to solve the mystery. He was a mining executive, not a detective. Amy was going to be frantic until Olivia was found, and past what he'd already done, he had no idea how to proceed —beat the woods for the chit, he supposed, just in case the woman had taken a walk and gotten lost. It was possible that she had done something that stupid. After all, she was a greenhorn from New York.

If beating the woods didn't work, he would simply have to try his hand at becoming a detective.

*   *   *

After two days of watching, waiting, and hoping, Olivia allowed herself the satisfaction of victory. The diphtheria was in retreat, and both of Danaher's daughters were recovering. She removed the tube from Katy's throat and stitched the wound closed. The girl was stoic during the stitching process, then afterward begged a shot of whiskey from her father to ease the pain. Gabe started to fetch a glass, but at Olivia's shocked look he shook his head.

"You should be drinking that good chicken broth the doc made you, Katy girl. That'll make you feel better than a shot of whiskey."

"Pa!" Her voice was a hoarse rasp, and she grimaced from the soreness.

"Don't give me that look, Katy. Drink the broth and then lie back and rest like the doc told you."

Katy gave Olivia a poisonous look.

"Who made this broth?" Ellen asked from her cot.

"I did," Olivia admitted.

Ellen regarded her somewhat sympathetically. "It's awfully weak."

"That's because you're both still weak. It isn't good to tax the digestive system after a bout with illness."

Ellen sniffed disdainfully at the liquid in her bowl.

Both twins ate with a good appetite, however, and then promptly dropped off into peaceful slumber. In spite of their returning spirits, they had no strength to do much of anything other than eat and sleep.

Olivia also hadn't much energy after the ordeal. She slept in the bed behind the curtain, so tired that she scarcely noticed the lumpiness of the straw-ticked mattress. Nor did it bother her that the bedding smelled of Gabriel Danaher, a not-unpleasant male scent of leather and soap and sweat that she'd become well acquainted with when they'd ridden in such close company on the way to the cabin.

It must have been the man's scent that prompted Olivia to conjure him in her dreams. Once again she treated Danaher in her little clinic in Elkhorn. As her arms circled him to wrap a bandage around his chest, he pressed a pistol into her belly. She heard him pull back the hammer and saw his finger tighten on the trigger; all the while his green devil's eyes seemed to burn into her soul. She saved herself by waking up, but gazing into the darkness, she wasn't quite sure what she had saved herself from. The disturbing sensations the dream left in its wake prompted her to rise and pace the cabin—until she became awake enough to notice that Gabe sat in the darkness and regarded her with eyes that caught sparks from the fire. She made the excuse of checking on her patients and quickly returned to the privacy behind the curtain, feeling somehow that her dream had followed her into the waking world.

The next time she slept Olivia dreamed she rode with a kidnapper, the horse galloping beneath them, rocking them together with every stride, then woke to find herself intimately tucked into the curve of Danaher's body. At first reality was a mere extension of the dream, but when she stirred, a warm hand slid over her hip and came to rest on her thigh below the twisted nightdress. The contact of bare skin on bare skin brought Olivia fully awake.

She bolted from the bed, and the interloper woke with a start.

"Just what do you think you're doing?" Olivia demanded.

Danaher gave her a groggy frown.

"Mr. Danaher!"

"What?" He shook his head and blinked. "Oh. Sorry. I just wanted to lie down for a little while. Guess I dropped off."

A terrible possibility flashed through Olivia's mind. "Have you been sleeping here every night?"

"No. I've been in the loft."

"The loft?"

"Where the girls normally sleep."

Olivia had thought the ladder reaching up to the dark platform above simply led to a storage area.

"A couple of cots are up there. The girls like it, but my feet hang over the bed."

"Since I am considerably shorter than you are, perhaps I should sleep up there."

One arched brow lifted briefly at the coolness of her voice. "Don't get in a huff, Doc. I was catching a nap, that's all. I'm tired, just like you are. It didn't seem worth it to climb the ladder for forty winks."

"You were being inappropriately familiar."

His mouth slanted into a half-smile. "Was I? And here I thought I was dreaming."

Her face heated under his gaze, and his smile turned into a grin.

"Don't worry, Doc. When I intend to be inappropriately familiar with a woman, I don't go sneaking around to do it."

Her face grew hotter, and she suddenly despised Gabriel Danaher for being able to get such a reaction from her when a legion of medical students and instructors had tried and failed.

"I think I'll check on the girls," she said with a sniff.

It was merely an excuse to get away. The twins were sleeping soundly and peacefully, and Olivia knew it. She should have faced the man and given him a good dressing-down, but when Gabriel Danaher fixed her with those Irish green eyes of his, her command of language seemed to desert her along with her usual cool rationality.

From then on she slept in the loft and let Gabe have the bed.

For most of the girls' recovery, however, Olivia and Danaher managed a cautious truce. The diphtheria, though defeated, did not hasten to loose its grip. For a week the twins had scarcely enough strength to feed themselves, and the possible complications of the illness were serious enough that Olivia felt her patients needed constant attention. She and their father watched them together, most of the time managing a cordial, if somewhat strained, relationship. The Irishman made an effort to be kind to her, Olivia noted. When she showed her weariness, he insisted she sleep. He dug into a chest and pulled out a pile of fresh clothing for her to wear instead of her one skirt and blouse. His wife's clothing, he explained. He insisted she wear it, even though when she first appeared wearing one of Minnie's dresses, his mouth pulled into a tight line and his eyes darkened to green slate.

He continued to pamper her. When their unseasonably sunny weather gave way to gray clouds and a cold wind, he carried a pile of woolen blankets up to her cot in the loft—since she steadfastly refused to return to his bed and let him sleep on one of the girls' cots. If she didn't eat he scolded her. If she went outside without her coat, he brought it to her.

Danaher was merely showing his gratitude, Olivia knew, but she didn't press the point that she had done little besides help the children help themselves. As he had once told her, his girls were both fighters, and they'd mostly fought their own way back from death's door. But if her abductor believed himself in her debt, she would let him. She felt safer that way, for she had not yet decided whether to be afraid of the man or to be intrigued by him.

Most of what she knew about Danaher was not terribly encouraging. He threw things when he was in a temper; he wasn't above using a gun to get what he wanted; he had married an Indian woman and socialized with a fierce-looking Indian brave and an old crone who had threatened to rip her hair out. He had twin daughters whom he adored, one of whom drank whiskey and muttered in her sleep in language that was reminiscent of the New York docks. That much did Olivia know about Gabriel Danaher; and even though they spent long hours together, she managed to learn little more of consequence.

He taught her to play chess to pass the time while the twins slept. Olivia had always thought of chess as a game of the educated class, and yet this scarcely civilized prospector had a board and chess pieces that could have graced a table in some aristocratic mansion. He'd inherited it from an Englishman who'd come west with him a long time ago, Gabe told her.

"He was a swell if ever I've seen one," Gabe said one afternoon as they played—or rather he played and Olivia struggled to remember which pieces moved in which way. "He carried this fancy set in his saddlebags. Every night when we settled into camp, out the board would come and he had to have a game. He had a camera, too. Shot pictures of everything he saw." He moved to take her knight.

"Were you his guide?"

Gabe chuckled. "Hardly that. I was green as grass at the time. Never been farther west than the west side of New York City. He knew where he was going, though. Had all sorts of books on the Wild West, and wanted to see the country from the back of a horse, not the belly of a train. I ended up tagging along with him after I helped him out of a fix."

She captured one of his pawns. By his smile she gathered it was the move he had hoped she would make. "You lived in New York?"

"Came over on the boat with my ma when I was thirteen." He moved his bishop to threaten her queen. "She tried to stuff me with book learning, but I grew up with a strong back and a hard head. Got a job on the docks. Made pretty good money there. Enough to bury my ma in style when she died. Then this English fellow comes strollin' along like some idiot and gets jumped by the crew I'm working with."

She moved her knight to block his bishop. "Why did they attack him?"

Gabe shrugged. "He was English. They were Irish."

"You're Irish."

"True, but five on one doesn't seem sporting, so I took his side—just to even things out a bit. Didn't matter. We both got the stuffings beat out of us, and it wasn't healthy for me on the docks anymore, so I latched on to Avery and came west. He wasn't a sturdy sort, though. Died of pneumonia up near the Blackfoot reservation north of here. Too bad. He was a good man." He grinned and moved his queen. "I got the chess set. Checkmate."

Olivia sighed.

"You're more fun to play with than Katy." Danaher smiled wickedly. "She always beats me."

But Olivia could pry from Danaher nothing about his Blackfoot wife, or how he'd come to live at such an isolated spot in Montana's mountains with two beautiful daughters, or why he lived so separated from his fellow man that his closest neighbors—the people of Elkhorn—thought he lived in sin with two Indian mistresses. She thought about what Amy had said about his being a wanted man and didn't press too hard. She might learn something that she'd rather not know.

Olivia was sitting by the fire, reading one of the books that she had been surprised to find in the Danaher cabin, when Katy asked a thin-voiced question.

"You're not a real doctor, are you?"

"Yes, I am."

"Doctors are men."

Olivia put aside her book, went to Katy's bedside, and felt her forehead. No fever. And she was talking. Good signs.

"There are a lot of women who are physicians, Katy. For the past forty years women have been going to medical colleges and becoming doctors. The world is not quite so limited for women as it once was."

"I ain't never seen a woman doctor," the girl said, as though that fact made their reality improbable.

"Haven't *seen,* dear. Ain't isn't a word."

"It is if I use it and I know what it means."

Olivia pulled the blankets up to Katy's chin. "Are you warm enough?"

"Stop fussin' with me. I ain't no baby."

"No, you aren't. But you've been very sick. It wouldn't do for you to get a chill."

"I damn well don't get no chills. Where's my pa?"

"He's hunting."

"Damnation! And here I am stuck in bed with a nursemaid tuckin' me in."

The child's mouth should be washed out with soap, Olivia decided, and she was in great need of a firm lesson in manners. The more she recovered, the more hostile she became.

"That isn't very attractive language for a young lady, Katy."

Katy looked at her with contempt. "What's wrong with it?"

"As I said before, ain't is a word used only by the uneducated. Damn and damnation are foul language that mark even a man as an ill-mannered lout when he uses them."

"Don't pay Katy any mind," Ellen advised in a sleepy voice. "She *is* a lout, and she's proud of it."

"I ain't no lout. I can do for myself is all. You've got to be tough and smart to do for yourself."

"How do you feel, Ellen?" Olivia ignored the challenge in Katy's voice and laid her hand against Ellen's brow.

"Better."

"Feel as though you could eat something?"

Ellen made a face. "Broth?"

"If *I* was hunting with Pa, we'd have nice fat venison for supper," Katy boasted. "I'm a better shot than Pa, even."

"Oh, you are not!" Ellen declared.

"Am too! I shot that doe last month right behind the eye. Dropped stone dead without moving a foot."

"That's disgusting."

"You ate it all right."

"It's disgusting that you were out shooting it instead of home cooking it like a woman should be."

"Cooking is boring. I can bring in the meat. Why should I have to cook it too?" Katy slid a glance toward Olivia. "I bet she doesn't bother with cooking. She's a doctor."

"I'll bet she does."

"Bet you didn't know women could be doctors," Katy challenged.

"I did too. I read a story about Elizabeth Blackwell once. She's a doctor."

"Elizabeth Blackwell was the very first woman to graduate from a medical school in the United States," Olivia told them.

Katy looked uninterested in Olivia's contribution to the conversation. Ellen looked neutral.

"Are you a friend of Pa's?" Ellen suddenly asked.

"Well, not exactly. He knew I was a doctor, so he asked me to come up here and help you two get well."

Both twins looked relieved.

"I think I'm pretty near well," Katy announced. She threw the blankets back. "I think maybe I should get up and feed the mules. The sun's almost down."

Olivia pushed the girl back down and pulled the blankets up to her chin. Her struggles weren't effective in her still-weak condition, but Olivia wouldn't have wanted to wrestle with her when she was up to snuff.

"*I* think you can stay in bed another couple of days. And you can drink some broth."

Katy glared. "We don't need no woman to come up here and boss us around."

Ellen grimaced as she sipped her broth. "You *can't* cook, can you? I could surely tell you how to make a better broth. I'm surprised you remembered to take the feathers off the chicken."

The twins had progressed from pathetic little angels to ornery children. They were well on the road to recovery, Olivia decided, and it was time for her to return to Elkhorn.

The light of day was just fading into dusk when Gabe returned from his hunt. He stopped Longshot in the cover of the trees and watched the clearing and cabin—a habit born of two years of being a hunted man. He'd been loath to leave the girls with only Olivia to mind them, but they needed the meat, and the past few days he'd smelled a storm on the wind. Tomorrow or the next day they might be snowed in.

Gabe regarded the scene before him. Olivia leaned on the peeled aspen corral poles watching the mules, who gazed back at her with calm indifference. The twins must be well, or the doctor wouldn't be outside the cabin. No strangers or wildlife was about, or the mules would be agitated.

No smoke came from the cabin's chimney. The foolish twit must have let the fire die. It was a wonder some people could be so inept and still survive in this world. Good thing the doc wasn't as incompetent at medicine as she was in the simple arts of daily living. He supposed she'd always had everything done for her.

Still Gabe didn't move. He enjoyed watching Olivia watch the mules. She was always guarded when he was around, and more than once he'd wondered what she was like behind that shell of self-conscious dignity. What kind of woman sought to spend her life patching up strangers rather than nurturing a family of her own? What kind of woman knowingly plotted a course in life that brought so many raised brows and whispers? She wasn't so plain that she couldn't have caught herself a husband. In fact, when her hair came loose and she let herself smile, she wasn't hard on the eyes at all. The soft way her lips curved when she was amused could grow on a man. Her biting wit and stubborn self-possession might grow on a man as well, if it didn't inspire him to kill her first.

Olivia jumped and looked around as Gabe crashed through the trees into the clearing. "Venison for dinner," he announced.

"Oh. It's you."

"Were you expecting someone else?"

"Katy was spinning stories about an especially cranky bear who lives in these parts. She said he helps himself to one of your mules now and then. I think she was simply trying to scare me, though, for I'd just forced some broth down her throat and she would've rather had that hard beef jerky that's hanging in your vegetable cellar."

Gabe dismounted and untied the buck that was draped over a patient pack mule. He fastened a rope around the deer's hind feet, threw the rope over a tree limb, secured the end of the rope around another tree, and led the mule away. Thus suspended, the carcass swung gently back and forth, dripping blood onto the ground. "She was telling you true enough about the bear. We call him Bruno, and he's a mean cuss. Most of the creatures in these mountains are mean cusses, animal or human. You should not be wandering around outside the cabin without a gun."

Olivia stared at Gabe with knitted brows.

"You're hurt."

"What?"

"You're bleeding." She grabbed his arms and lifted them to display the blood on the shirt under his coat. "My Lord!"

"The deer's blood, Doc, not mine. I cleaned and bled it before I came back. The carcass is lighter that way, and you don't have to worry about the wildlife around the cabin coming after the innards."

He heard a little choking sound come from her throat and turned around with a grin on his face. "Come on, Doc. You can't tell me that a little blood bothers you."

Her mouth settled into a firm line. "I can assure you that I've seen enough blood that I don't faint at the sight."

"Well, I'll admit I was sloppy about it. If you'll heat some water, I'll take a bath."

"The fire went out." Her eyes focused momentarily on the ground, then rose to defiantly meet his. "I couldn't quite get a new one started."

"I guess I'll have to teach you about starting fires."

"I know how to start a fire," she claimed in an annoyed voice. "The wood is wet."

"You've just got to know how to make it burn. If you'll fill the kettle, I'll start the fire."

She looked at the buckets that hung by the rainwater cistern. "I'm not your valet, Mr. Danaher."

"You wouldn't want me to catch pneumonia because I couldn't get the chill out of my bones, would you? Just feel that cold wind and look at the gray sky. I just thought you might be grateful for me bringing in enough food to last us the next ten days." Gabe grinned at the disgusted look she directed first at the bloody deer and then him. The lady was fun to bait. One of these times she was going to crack through that cool exterior and send a fist flying at his face. Gabe allowed himself to contemplate the possibilities in the wrestling match that might follow.

"Do you hear what I'm saying, Mr. Danaher?"

"What?"

"I said I wouldn't be around to help you eat that poor bloody creature. It's time for me to be getting back to Elkhorn."

The pleasant mood that had started with the successful hunt and grown in the minutes watching Olivia suddenly evaporated. "Can we talk about that after I've cleaned up?"

"I'm not asking you, Mr. Danaher, I'm telling you. The girls—"

Suddenly tired, he turned his back and walked toward the cabin, leaving her sputtering. He didn't want to listen to her carping about leaving just yet. In a few days, maybe, when the girls were stronger. Maybe then.

"You can get your own blasted water!" he heard her spit at his back.

"Checkmate!"

Olivia sighed. She'd lost again. Not that she'd been concentrating that hard on the game. She was still seething from Danaher's rude refusal to discuss her leaving. His promise to discuss the subject after the twins were asleep and the delicious venison dinner he'd served hadn't quite smoothed her ruffled feathers.

"I'd think you'd be getting bored with winning by now," she told Danaher.

He grinned. "Winning isn't something that comes along often enough in life so that I'd get bored with it. Besides, in a few days, Katy will be whittling me down to size but good. I might as well take advantage of the easy pickings while I can."

"Thank you. I'm not sure I like to be described as easy pickings."

A muffled snort came from Katy's pallet. Gabe's brows knotted in a concerned frown. "Is she all right?"

"I'll look at her."

Olivia knelt beside the pallet and gazed down at the face that was doing its best to appear angelic, with thick-lashed eyes closed and mouth curved into a peaceful smile. The little hoyden had been feigning sleep while they played—Olivia had more than once detected a ferocious glint in her not quite closed eyes. Katy didn't like someone else playing chess with her father.

"So you think I deserve to be called 'easy pickings,' do you?" Olivia kept her voice low so that only Katy could hear the words. The little imp's mouth twitched upward.

"Is anything wrong?" Gabe started to rise.

"She's fast asleep," Olivia lied. "And so is Ellen." These two rascals certainly didn't need round-the-clock care from her or their father any longer. A few more days and they would be bouncing around the cabin like chipmunks. "They've really recovered quite nicely, you know. There's no reason for me to stay any longer."

Gabe frowned.

Olivia decided to try the polite approach. "I would appreciate it if you would take me back down the mountain tomorrow."

"Didn't you say there're complications that come out of diphtheria?"

"Sometimes there can be, but the girls are far enough along in their recovery that you needn't worry too much about that. Just keep them warm and quiet for another week or so."

He was silent, his brows drawn together in furrows of irritation. Olivia thought she knew what caused his hesitation. She'd encountered it many times before in loved ones who cared for and fretted over dangerously ill patients and then could not let go of the fear when the patients began to recover.

"They're going to be all right, Gabriel."

Her use of his first name brought his brooding gaze up to meet hers. What she saw in his eyes was not fear. She didn't know precisely what it was.

"You promised to discuss my going back."

"We're discussing it. I think the girls need your care for another couple of days. I can't be in here all the time to watch them. There's a load of wood to cut if we're going to stay warm, and I need to get back to work in the mine. That ore doesn't make me money by staying in the mountain."

Olivia expelled an exasperated sigh. "The girls don't need me anymore. I understand why you're concerned, but you should trust my evaluation. I wouldn't put them at risk by telling you something that isn't true."

"You've been up here almost two weeks. A couple of more days isn't going to hurt you."

"Mr. Danaher, there is at least one person in Elkhorn who needs me very badly, and a couple of more days might make a difference to her. I came to Montana to help Amy Talbot through her confinement. She's lost two babies before this, and I would not like to see her lose a third because I'm absent."

"There are two other doctors in Elkhorn to help Mrs. Talbot. Katy and Ellen have only you."

"Doctors Cahill and Traleigh are not as experienced in difficult childbirth as I am. When I worked in Paris and New York . . ." She trailed off, realizing from the hard emerald glint in his eye that he didn't understand. "I've done my best for Katy and Ellen, despite being kidnapped from my bed and dragged here like a sack of flour. I think you owe it to me to take me back."

Gabe got up, dragged his fingers through the disorderly black mane of his hair, and turned to lean against the split log mantel and stare into the fire. Brooding shadows flickered across his face. "I'll take you back in good time. But not tomorrow. There's a storm coming in. It'll be a couple of days."

Olivia recognized the finality in his voice. Not for a moment did she believe the excuse about a storm. The sky had been gray and a cold wind blowing for the last few days, but there was no sign of snow. At the end of a couple of days there would be another excuse, and then another. He wanted her here until Katy and Ellen were completely back to normal, and that might be several weeks.

"I'm going to hit the sack," Danaher announced.

He knelt beside the twins' pallets and looked down into their sleeping faces. Truly sleeping now, Olivia noted. They would be stronger tomorrow, and by the next day they would be on their feet. Why couldn't their stubborn father realize she was no longer needed? Typical pigheaded, intractable, unreasonable man!

"Good night." His eyes held hers briefly. Nowhere in his shuttered expression did she see a hint of understanding. He wouldn't relent until he was good and ready.

"Good night." The chill in her voice rivaled the nip of the wind that blustered around the cabin.

For a long while after Danaher had pulled the curtain around the bed, Olivia stood and looked out the window, feeling frustration rise in her chest in a tight, painful ache. Amy was a worrier. Once concerned about someone or something, she let the worry grow until it fretted every hour of her day. She was almost seven months along in her precarious pregnancy, and if anything happened now, the tragedy might rob her not only of the child but of life itself. A miscarriage this far along in pregnancy would be very dangerous.

Olivia could picture Amy fretting, not eating, losing sleep. She would feel responsible for Olivia's safety because she asked her to come to this wild part of the country. There was no way anyone could know she was safe—or relatively so—in a miner's cabin in the mountains.

As she watched out the window, the moon drifted from beneath the scudding clouds. The full, bright orb flooded the clearing with milky light, painting the corral, the henhouse, and the sheds in its brilliance. The big shed housed four horses, Gabe's bay mare, Katy's big Appaloosa, a little sorrel gelding that was Ellen's, and the roan Danaher had "borrowed" from the Elkhorn livery. Except for the roan, those horses had doubtless traveled down the mountain so many times they could find their way in the dark.

Not that it was dark. The clouds were becoming patchier, it seemed to Olivia, and the bright winter moon would light the track down the mountain almost as well as the sun.

Olivia made up her mind in an instant. Mr. Gabriel Danaher would discover, as had other men, that Olivia Baron set her own course in life and was not afraid to follow it.

Chapter 6

The metallic clink of the horse's shod hooves echoed through the night, somehow making the utter loneliness of the dark forest even emptier than it already was. Murdoch was the big Appaloosa's name, Gabriel had told Olivia, though why anyone would call a horse such a thing was beyond her. Murdoch wasn't any happier than Olivia, and Olivia wasn't happy at all clomping through the mountains down the track she hoped led to Elkhorn.

Perhaps taking off on her own hadn't been such a good idea after all. The night was bitterly cold, and the wind cut through her wool coat as though it were thin cotton. That same wind sang through the pines with a ghostly sound that made her shiver. Waving boughs made moon shadows leap and writhe along the path. Rocks and tree stumps seen only dimly in moonlight took on the form of beasts waiting in a sinister crouch until she had passed. But the eerie singing was only the wind, and the beasts were only inanimate wood and rock, or so Olivia tried to convince herself.

Murdoch was absolutely no help. Olivia had taken Katy's Appaloosa rather than the "borrowed" roan gelding she'd ridden up the mountain in hopes this horse would be a bit more tractable. It wasn't. When she had first put the saddle on its back the beast had given her a look of jaundiced disbelief. True, her three awkward heaves trying to lift the heavy saddle onto the horse's back might have made the creature skittish. And just when she finally managed to swing the thing up, a stirrup had hit her in the face and made her stumble back against the wall of the shed. That had made all four horses within nervous.

They had finally started on their way, though. Murdoch had balked at leaving his warm stall in the middle of a cold night. A good deal of thumping with her heels had been required to start him down the trail, and even now, when they'd been on the move for several hours, the horse took every possible opportunity to turn back. When she'd allowed him to stop and drink from a tiny stream that crossed the path, the stubborn creature had taken the halt as permission to start for home. Before Olivia had realized what was happening, Murdoch had swung around and headed up the trail, carrying her along as a helpless passenger. She sawed on the bit to no avail. Not until the brute stumbled on a root protruding into the trail did Olivia manage to jerk his head around and force him to reverse direction.

Now Olivia watched her mount every moment, and she could feel Murdoch watching her. With every stride his head swung around and his eye cast back in her direction. She was stiff, the insides of her thighs felt raw as they rubbed against the saddle leather, and her muscles were practically convulsing with shivers. A hot bath beckoned from the Talbot house at the end of the trail, a hot bath, safety, good food that wasn't sliced from the carcass of some poor wild animal within her sickened sight, steaming hot tea instead of bitter coffee, and a soft feather bed instead of a creaky, rope-sprung cot. How good Elkhorn would look when she rode in. Amy would welcome her with a great hug of relief. Sylvester would hem and haw and make his wife lie down in all the excitement, and Olivia would sleep for a week in that feather bed and not have to worry about Gabriel Danaher or his demon daughters.

Olivia sighed. Gabriel Danaher and his twin girls—the thought of them conjured up mixed feelings, especially of Danaher himself. He was certainly a man the likes of whom she'd never met. One moment a tease, the next a menace. An uneducated mining prospector who played chess and had a shelf full of books. A drunken brawler who loved his children to distraction, so much so that he let nothing stand in the way of helping them when they were in danger. Yet he isolated them in the mountains where they were a subject of lurid speculation, where they would never have companions their own age, never have an education past what their father's books could give them, never see the wealth of opportunity that was opening to women or find husbands who would love them.

Gabriel Danaher.

Olivia sighed and slumped in the saddle. Her aching muscles needed a rest. She reined Murdoch to a halt, stiffly lowered herself to the ground, and, keeping the reins firmly in her hand, stretched her back and legs to loosen the muscle kinks. A very faint glow to the east announced that dawn was breaking, but, surrounded by high mountains, the valley of Thunder Creek would have a wait to greet the sun. The dark forest seemed not quite so threatening, however. The night's spell was broken with just a hint of light behind the peaks. She would take a few moments to rest, Olivia told herself, then push on. Before the sun set behind the western mountains, she would be with Amy in Elkhorn.

Gabriel Danaher. The thought of him persisted. How could one not be moved by a man who was such a kaleidoscope of changing moods? Under it all she sensed something rock solid, something that would lead her to trust the man if she herself were sick or in trouble.

And of course there were those clear, emerald-green eyes, her conscience reminded her cynically. And the devilishly arched brows, the faint scar that gave a rakish cast to the chiseled features, the slightly quirked smile, and the barely perceptible Irish lilt to his words. She was being every bit as much of a goose as those silly adolescent girls in Miss Tatterhorn's Academy. At her age she should be past such nonsense. Even if she weren't, a man who got thrown out of saloons in drunken brawls, threatened her with a gun, kidnapped her, half killed her by dragging her up a mountain, and had a mysterious, slightly sinister past, was not a man that a sensible woman should allow herself to get moony about. What's more, his daughters, though their spirit and strength appealed to Olivia, were as uncivilized as little wolf cubs.

The wind suddenly whipped Olivia's bedraggled hair into her face. The dawn, she noted with some concern, had disappeared, and the faint morning light was almost drowned by scudding gray clouds that clogged the passes and blanketed the peaks.

Olivia pulled herself aboard Murdoch and pointed him down the trail just as the first flakes of snow kissed her face.

When Gabe awoke it was still pitch black. He lay perfectly still, searching for what woke him. The sounds that reached his ears were only ordinary sounds—the twins' gentle snoring upon their pallets, the crackle of the low-burning fire, the sigh of the wind through the pines. Somewhere far away a mountain lion screamed. That might have wakened him, but he doubted it. The eerie shriek was an ordinary enough night sound in the Montana mountains.

Something was not as it should be, however, and whatever was wrong had brought him from sleep. He rose, pulled on wool socks, and padded over to the pallets in front of the fire. In the dim red glow of the fire, the twins slept peacefully. He looked up the ladder to the dark loft where Olivia slept. He could see the foot of a cot, nothing more. He turned back toward his bed, then stopped. His eyes narrowed suspiciously. He turned and climbed the ladder, steeling himself for the fit of indignation that would greet him if he woke Olivia by trespassing on her solitary, virginal slumber. But when he reached the top of the ladder and bent over the cot, there was no explosion of maidenly indignation. There was no Olivia.

He cursed.

Gabe knew immediately what the little fool had done, but he confirmed it by taking an oil lamp and searching outside and inside. Olivia's coat and medical case were missing, and Minnie's two dresses that she had filled out so surprisingly well were laid neatly across the cot. Murdoch was gone from the shed along with a saddle, saddle blanket, and bridle. The saddlebags were all still in place, however. The little greenhorn hadn't thought to take food or extra blankets. Did she believe the ride to Elkhorn was an outing on a Central Park bridle path?

He cursed again—cursed Olivia for being a stubborn fool and cursed himself for letting her slip away without waking him. He stood in the door of the horse shed and looked up at the sky, where a bright winter moon ducked in and out of the clouds. The wind smelled like snow, and soon the clouds would coalesce into the first real storm of the season, unless he missed his guess. Even experienced woodsmen didn't want to be caught away from shelter during a good Montana snowstorm.

Gabe stalked into the cabin. The blockhead woman had made her own bed, he told himself, and she would have to lie in it. He couldn't leave the girls alone to go chasing after a twit who didn't know enough to come in from the rain—or the snow, as it were.

Careful not to wake Katy and Ellen, he swung the coffeepot on its hook over the fire and pulled a stool close enough to take advantage of the warmth. Damn the woman, anyway! Why couldn't she have waited another couple of days until the storm had passed? Why couldn't she have listened to him?

"Perhaps," a leprechaun's voice in his head answered, "she thought you were making excuses. You weren't very concerned about her desire to go back."

Another couple of days wouldn't have hurt her.

"Was it just a couple of days you wanted?"

I would have taken her back to Elkhorn. I'm not some monster who forces women against their will.

"Is that so?" the leprechaun observed. "You shoved a pistol into her belly and dragged her up the mountain against her will. But you're not some monster who forces women against their will."

That was different. The girls were sick. They would have died if I hadn't brought her. She saved them.

"That's right. Olivia saved them."

"Damn!" Gabe cursed aloud. He was in debt to Olivia Baron, and he couldn't sit here arguing with himself while she rode into trouble. If not for the coming storm, he'd simply let her ride down the mountain. She was right. The girls didn't really need her any longer. He shouldn't have been so reluctant to let her go.

The frightening thing was, Gabe finally admitted to himself, that he *was* reluctant to see the last of Olivia Baron—for reasons that had nothing to do with the twins. He liked her. For all her prim and fussy ways, for all her unwomanly independence and stubbornness, she grew on a man. She had strength, spirit, intelligence, and a deep kindness that she hid under a sharp tongue. She also had a damned feminine talent for filling out a dress. There was no way he could sit here and let that woman freeze to death in a snowstorm.

Gabe took the lantern outside and climbed with it to the top of a dead pine that stood at the edge of the clearing. Since the trouble in Virginia City, Crooked Stick—never very keen on staying on the reservation—had always been within reach of his sister's children. He defined his hunting grounds, legal or not, by proximity to Katy and Ellen. The lantern hanging on the pine should bring him within a couple of hours to stay with the twins. And then Gabe would ride out to have a word or two with Miss Olivia Baron about common sense.

Murdoch was not happy. Neither was Olivia, but it was Murdoch's unhappiness that was making the situation worse than it might have been. The horse wanted to go back to his little shed with its fresh straw and rich grain and other warm horse bodies to drive away the chill. Olivia was determined, however, to continue downward.

Olivia had never been one to curse—it wasn't ladylike, and her father had admonished her once: If she must become something as outlandish as a physician, at least she should guard her manners and remain a lady. She had heard more than her share of maledictions, however, and had never been more tempted to use them than right now. Sleet and snow pelted her face, which had just enough feeling left to smart from the sting. Her hair was sodden with snow, freezing water dripped down her back, and her hands in their fashionable leather gloves were blocks of ice. She couldn't feel her feet, what little sensation was left in her nose told her that it was running like a mountain stream, and on top of everything else, the flea-ridden, brainless idiot of a horse balked every other step and wouldn't walk faster than a slow shuffle that might get them to Elkhorn by the end of the year. Every few seconds the recalcitrant beast threw its head and rolled an eye in her direction, plainly accusing her of being a fool.

Well, she wasn't a fool. Or if she was a fool, she at least knew that snowstorms got worse with increasing elevation. Anyone could see that in the fall and spring snow blanketed the mountain peaks while the valleys and foothills were green. It stood to reason, therefore, that if they continued downward, they might emerge from the snow into rain, which wouldn't be much to her liking but at least would be better than this freezing, white corner of hell they were plodding through. If they were lucky they might get out of the storm altogether.

Olivia clutched her coat about her more tightly. The effort was useless; the cold wind cut clear through to muscle and bone. She thought about frostbite. She had treated the painful condition, and a few sad times even amputated toes and fingers of homeless unfortunates who'd had no shelter on winter nights. She'd never thought that she'd have to fear the condition herself. She would be a fine doctor and surgeon with two or three fingers missing.

Curse Gabriel Danaher for getting her into this. And curse herself for being a fool. Why hadn't she believed the damned Irishman when he'd told her there was a storm coming? No. She was so sure that the man was stalling, she had to ride out and see for herself, like a stubborn child who puts a finger on the stove to discover if it's hot. Damn Danaher. Damn herself. And double damn the imbecile nag she was riding.

She moved her lips to say the word. "Damn! Damn, damn, damn, damndamndamndamndamndamn!" Cursing made her feel better. It brought heat to her face and made her lips feel less numb. There was no one but Murdoch to witness her unladylike lapse, and if she went to hell for it, as her spinster aunt Eloise had once threatened, she would at least be warm.

By continuously thumping her heels against Murdoch's sides, she urged the reluctant horse down the trail. The snow fell at an alarming rate, whipped by the wind into white eddies that made seeing beyond Murdoch's nose almost impossible. The wagon track, faint even when bare rock and soil were visible, became a mere depression in the snowy landscape. Trees were no more than tall shadows that bent and swayed with the force of the wind.

Olivia wasn't quite sure when she stopped thinking of the storm as a troublesome and uncomfortable inconvenience and began thinking of it in terms of a dangerous disaster. Perhaps it was the first time she lost the trail and became tangled in a willow thicket. Or possibly not until the descent down a switchback when Murdoch slipped on a patch of ice and went to his knees, nearly pitching Olivia over the edge of a steep hillside. She began to realize that being caught outside in a Montana snowstorm was a good deal more dangerous than being caught outside of the shops on Broadway when snow began in New York.

By Olivia's estimate of the passing days, this day or the next was Thanksgiving. New York often had snow for the holiday. She remembered Thanksgiving dinners with her parents, aunt, uncle, and cousins, sitting by the big dining-room fireplace and watching white flakes swirl past the windows. She had thought those storms quite fierce, and perhaps they were, but they were gentle flurries compared to how Montana ushered in the holiday.

An hour passed; the trail disappeared. They made their way as best they could along the path of least resistance through the trees. Mother Nature seemed to take insult at a horse and woman challenging her power and threw everything she could in their way. Snowdrifts grew at a prodigious rate. The wind kicked the snow into blinding whirlwinds. Icy rocks seemed to leap out of the building snowbanks to make Murdoch stumble.

Much to Olivia's surprise, once the going got truly difficult, the big Appaloosa became a different horse. He plowed through the drifts with single-minded tenacity. Time and again he found the trail and followed it when Olivia could only see trees and snow. Either he had decided that forward was the only direction that Olivia would let him go, or he was one of those souls who needed a challenge before showing any energy at all.

Olivia was starting to admire the beast when he stumbled over an unseen obstacle and pitched her headfirst into the snow. Before she could feel the pain of impact, everything went black.

Amy Talbot lay on her feather bed, eyes fixed on the ornately designed pressed-tin ceiling. Her child moved within her, and she said a silent prayer of intense gratitude that she still carried it, that it was still alive. She had tried very hard to do what was right for the babe. As Olivia had instructed, she had eaten three good meals a day—vegetables and fruits and lean meat—even though she had no appetite. She had taken a short walk every day and had diligently tried to sleep at night. But how could she sleep when she still didn't know Olivia's fate?

Sylvester had tried to find her, God bless him. He had alerted the marshal and had even helped the search team comb the surrounding hills. Everyone thought she had gotten lost in the hills, Amy knew, though no one would say anything directly to her. They thought that Olivia was making calls on cabins up and down the little valley and she must have become lost. Not that the distance to any dwelling in the valley was that great, but Olivia was from Back East, after all. Montanans seemed to expect great stupidities of folks from Back East.

Amy didn't think that Olivia had gotten lost. She'd known Olivia since they had been girls together at Miss Tatterhorn's; and though her friend had pursued life with an intense determination that made her different from most young girls, she'd always had an abundance of good sense. She would not have lost her way, Amy thought. And if she had gotten lost in the dark, she'd have found Elkhorn again in the daylight. It wasn't as if the log cutters had left any trees in the area to conceal the town. Elkhorn was visible from anyplace upvalley or on the surrounding hills. Olivia would have found her way back.

Unless she'd been killed or injured. The mountains abounded with bear and mountain lions and wolves. She might have stumbled in the dark and broken an ankle. Unable to walk, she would have died of exposure, thirst, or starvation.

Amy closed her eyes. She didn't want to think about it. But she had to think about it. She was the one who had brought Olivia to Elkhorn for her own selfish purposes. If not for her, Olivia would be safe in New York. She had delayed accepting a plum appointment to the New England Hospital for Women and Children so she could come to Elkhorn and help Amy through her confinement.

She got up from the bed and went to the window. Snow was beginning to fall—the storm that off-and-on gray skies had threatened for the past two days. Now the clouds came right down over the mountains, hiding them from view. On the forested slopes and rocky peaks, snow had been falling since the break of day. All morning Amy had been watching the storm descend the slopes, wondering if Olivia was still alive somewhere out in the storm. Most likely not. Sylvester was usually right; and after a week had passed without finding her in the hills or discovering some clue to her whereabouts, he had all but given Olivia up for dead. Only Amy's prodding had forced him to continue asking questions. Probably Olivia was dead and they would never know what happened to her.

Tears squeezed out of Amy's eyes as she closed them against the pain.

Her arm rested across her swollen abdomen as if to cradle her unborn child. All her life she had wanted to be a mother. Since she had been a tiny girl she had mothered everything in sight—puppies, kittens, dolls, other children. At Miss Tatterhorn's she had mothered Olivia, trying to protect her from the gibes of the other girls who thought of her as an odd duck, and therefore fair game for their cruel teasing. Not that Olivia had cared. She had been too sure of her calling to care what others thought, but Amy's maternal instincts had flared.

Now, after one miscarriage and another stillbirth, perhaps she would have a child of her own. Olivia had said this pregnancy seemed to be normal. Olivia—how would Amy ever forgive herself for bringing her to Elkhorn to meet with some horrible fate? The child she had longed for so long—whenever she held it in her arms or looked upon its face, she would think of Olivia and wonder how she had died.

A soft knock on the door interrupted her melancholy reflections. "Amy, dear. Are you sleeping?"

"Come in, Sylvester."

He was smiling, his face ruddy with the cold and snow still melting on his lashes and side-whiskers. "I have news that may mean something about Olivia, my dear, but you must promise me not to get your hopes too high. I don't want you to have to endure a disappointment."

A small flicker of hope ignited in her heart. "What? Tell me, Sylvester."

"I was just talking to Gregg Smoot, the smith. You know he runs the livery as well."

"Yes?"

"He remembers something fairly strange on the last day anyone saw Olivia. Actually, it was that evening. Gabriel Danaher rode into town that evening and stabled his horse at the livery. In the early morning when Smoot got to the livery, Danaher's horse was gone, and so was a horse belonging to Smoot, a big gelding who was in the stall next to Danaher's mare. Now, horse thieving isn't that uncommon, but the strange thing is that payment was left for the gelding, and payment was also left for Danaher's stable fee—both in raw silver. I guess Danaher's got himself quite a silver mine up in the mountains."

Amy's eyes widened. "And you think Mr. Danaher took Olivia and needed a horse for her? Why would he do that?"

"Perhaps he had need of a doctor. He knew she was a physician because she treated him that time he got thrown out of the saloon."

"Then she might be alive?"

"If he took her, I don't imagine he'd hurt her—other than perhaps . . ."

Amy knew what Sylvester couldn't bring himself to say in front of her. Poor Olivia might be compromised in the worst sort of way. But even that was better than being dead, though ladies were supposed to prefer death to such disgrace.

"If this man took her, my love, I'm sure he has treated her with decorum. Olivia's appearance and demeanor are not the sort that would tempt a man to lasciviousness."

"Do you know were Mr. Danaher lives?"

"Well, no, not exactly. No one else seems to know the exact location of the mine, either. Danaher doesn't come into town often, and when he does, he usually keeps pretty much to himself. Around here, when a man doesn't volunteer information, folks don't ask too many questions."

"But you'll find him, won't you?" she asked anxiously.

"Oh yes. We'll find him." He looked out the window. The snow was falling harder now. "We won't be able to search until this storm is past and the snow melts off a bit, though. Meanwhile, I'm going to send to Helena for information on the man. Seems to me I saw a handbill there a while back with a sketch that looked a bit like him. Didn't pay much attention to it at the time. I guess I've gotten into the habit that everyone else around here has—live and let live. But if this fellow is wanted by the law for some reason, we may be able to get some help flushing him out."

"Oh dear! Poor Olivia. But in spite of Mr. Danaher being a scoundrel, I can't help but hope she's with him. Anything is better than her being dead, and us not knowing how or where it happened."

Sylvester gave her a worried frown. "Don't you fret now, Amy. If Olivia is with Gabriel Danaher, we'll get her back."

Amy placed her hand over her unborn child. Tomorrow was Thanksgiving Day, and she gave thanks that at least there existed this small morsel of hope.

"Olivia! Wake up, goddammit!" Gabe shook her, and when she didn't wake, he took off his glove and slapped her smartly across the cheek. He hadn't ridden all this way in a blizzard to allow the nincompoop to die and escape the lecture he intended to burn her ears with.

"Olivia! Open those goddamned blue eyes or so help me I'll hang you upside down from a tree to get the blood back into your lame brain." He shook her again.

Her eyes slit open, then closed again. She was as pale as the snow in which she lay, and a frozen crimson path from her hairline over her ear and down her neck glared in stark contrast.

"Wake up, you idiot woman! If you give up and die I'll kill you myself!"

Her eyes opened again. This time they stayed open and focused with difficulty on his face. "Gabriel." The sound came out of her throat as a pathetic whisper.

"It's about time you came around!" He brushed a dark, sodden lock of her hair away from her eyes, his gentleness a marked contrast to his voice. "I've been yelling at you long enough to wake the dead."

Her facial muscles twitched, as if she tried to smile but her cheeks were frozen in place.

He pulled the blanket more tightly around her and propped her against a tree that afforded some shelter from the snow. "I'm going to build us a fire and a shelter, because it for sure is going to get colder out here before it gets warmer. You keep your eyes open, you hear? If you go back to sleep, I'll make sure that you wished you hadn't."

She nodded her head slightly, and he got off his knees and started to collect twigs and deadfall that lay under the snow. Lucky it was so cold—too cold for the snow to get the wood wet. If he couldn't build a fire, they'd both end up frozen stiff as icicles. Every minute or so he checked to see that Olivia was still awake. The heavy wool blanket he'd wrapped around her and the heavy gloves he'd stuffed her hands into had brought a faint color of life back into her face.

Once the fire was blazing, Gabe cut a pine branch to sweep a small area free of snow. Then he collected more dead limbs, propped them against each other in a cone, and covered the cone with a canvas tarp and full, brushy pine limbs that he cut with a hatchet. The opening of the makeshift tipi faced the fire.

Olivia's eyes were sagging when he picked her up and carried her into the shelter. "Stay awake, Doc. You'll be warmer soon enough. I'd build a fire inside here, but with all this dead wood I used for lodgepoles, the place would likely burn down around our ears." He propped her against a roll of wool blankets and shook out another to wrap around them both.

"How . . . how did you find me?" she asked in a shaky voice.

"It wasn't hard. You followed the trail most of the way, and when you got off of it, you left enough tracks to follow. Most of them were filled in with snow, but under the trees, where the ground is a bit sheltered, there were enough left to tell me where you'd gone."

"Is Murdoch all right?"

"He hurt one leg pretty bad. Might be broken. I haven't had a chance to look at it yet, but I figure he's done for."

"Oh no! You wouldn't shoot him!"

This seemed to upset her more than their own precarious situation.

"Doc, a horse with a broken leg isn't any use to himself or anyone else. Shooting is a mercy. Believe me."

He recognized the determined set of her mouth and chin. It was the same look she'd gotten when she first looked at Katy and Ellen.

"At least let me look at him."

"You're in no condition to go out in that storm to doctor a horse. You really don't have a lick of sense, do you?"

She struggled out of the blanket he'd wrapped her in. "I have enough sense to know I'm responsible for that animal injuring himself. He was quite courageous, you know, struggling through every drift in our path."

"If he'd had any sense, he would have turned around and taken you back to the cabin before you even got him on the trail."

Olivia grimaced. "He did try." She headed out of the shelter.

"Goddammit, woman! I didn't ride out in this mess to have you freeze to death doctoring a stupid horse!" He took her arm to hold her back, but she merely shrugged him off. "Will you act like you have some brains in that head of yours?" he called out as he stomped after her.

Longshot and Murdoch stood tethered in the lee of the tipi, tails to the wind, heads down. Feedbags covered their noses.

"You think of everything, don't you?" Olivia said, looking at the feedbags.

"When you live up here, you learn not to go anywhere in the wintertime without making sure you have what you need. That's a lesson you could learn."

"I don't live up here, and I have no desire to learn anything about this benighted country." She ran her hand down the rear leg that Murdoch held off the ground.

"Don't tell me you're a horse doctor, too."

"No, but I know enough to see that this leg isn't broken. Only sprained."

"He still won't make it back up the mountain."

"We can devise a support for the leg if we have to, Mr. Danaher. I would think a little effort on our part would be preferable to killing a courageous animal."

"We'll talk about it—inside the tipi."

"I won't let you shoot Murdoch. It isn't necessary."

"I'll decide what's necessary and what's not."

"You at least should give him a chance. He's a very game creature. He shouldn't be disposed of as though he were some inanimate object that's lost its usefulness."

"You're going to get pneumonia unless you get inside. I'll be surprised if you don't get it as it is."

"Promise me you won't shoot him."

Olivia was a game creature as well, Gabe noted with more than a touch of irritation. "Okay. I won't shoot him if he can stumble up the mountain. I'm not going to drag him behind on a travois, though. That's ridiculous."

She smiled. Apparently the argument had heated her up enough to thaw her face. "That's good enough."

"Now, will you come back inside?"

The heat from the fire was beginning to penetrate the chill in the shelter. Gabe laid by enough wood to get them through the night and the next day as well, if necessary. Then he heated some coffee and pulled a slab of jerky from his saddlebags to fill their stomachs. Their little camp was almost cozy with them sitting in the doorway of the tipi, soaking up the heat from the fire and listening to the snowflakes sizzle as they fell on the hot coffeepot. After they had eaten, Gabe wrapped a blanket around both of them and settled back against the pine boughs he'd laid on the floor of the shelter. The objection he expected from Olivia didn't materialize. She was too exhausted to quibble about propriety as she willingly lay back against his chest and snuggled deeper into the cradle of his arms. Stubborn idiot or not, the woman felt good against him. She fit completely between the tops of his boots and the collar of his jacket, and his arms could almost wrap around her twice if they were that flexible. Her damp hair smelled like wind and snow, and the rest of her smelled like woman.

Gabe resisted the thoughts that crept into his mind. Olivia would scold him soundly and call them inappropriate. Gabe called them lust—and something more he didn't want to think about. He felt responsible for the woman, that was all. Just as she felt responsible for poor Murdoch.

Responsibility. That was all those strange feelings were. They certainly couldn't be anything else.

Chapter 7

*T*hey remained huddled together in the little tipi all through the night and the next morning as well, drinking hot coffee, eating jerky and dried corn, and sleeping sporadically when exhaustion overcame them despite the cold and the noise of the wind. It seemed to Olivia that the universe had shrunk. A world beyond the encircling trees was hard to imagine. All worries besides keeping warm and fed and sheltered from the elements became mere abstract concepts. Amy belonged to another world, New York, and her appointment to the hospital to an even more distant world. The only reality was the driving snow, the fire, the tipi, and Gabriel Danaher.

Olivia was surprised at how quickly a civilized person like herself could slip back to such a primitive state of mind. She shed modesty and decorum without a thought. If warmth was to be found in the arms of Gabriel Danaher, cocooned with him in layers of blankets, then she willingly surrendered to such an improper embrace. If she survived the storm, Olivia knew, she would think back on how thin the veneer of civilization had proved to be, and no doubt be frightened and dismayed by the revelation. But during those hours in the tipi, civilized priorities didn't matter. The only thing that mattered was warmth and survival.

Perhaps it was the need to survive that made Danaher's intimate presence not only acceptable but comfortable. More than comfortable, if Olivia admitted the truth. His arms about her were strong and reassuring. The solid wall of his chest was a welcome bulwark against the elements. His breath in her hair and on her cheek sent shivers down her spine that had nothing to do with the cold. When she looked up at his face, she saw none of the Irish cockiness, the teasing cynicism, or the obdurate stubbornness that he'd exhibited in the past. She had sometimes suspected that something deep and strong lay beneath the scoundrel on the surface, and within his blankets and his arms, she thought she saw it.

All through the night and next morning the wind drove sleet and snow against the tipi in a rattling symphony of cold. By midday the wind died, and the snow gentled and finally stopped altogether. The sun made brief appearances between scattering clouds and sparkled off a world of pristine white. Olivia emerged to find snow drifted almost to the top of the tipi on the windward side and the ground nearly swept clean in the lee. The horses stomped and whuffed a cold greeting, and the world suddenly clicked back into place, with Amy waiting in Elkhorn, a medical appointment waiting in New York, and a man who had forced her into circumstances that kept her from both of them once again controlling her life.

"Look at that sun." Danaher stomped his feet to get the blood flowing. "It'll melt a lot of the snow in a few hours. That's the way it is with these fall storms. They dump a couple of feet of snow on the ground, but by the next day or so all you have left is mud."

"This is beautiful!" Olivia had to admit. "How can the sky suddenly be so blue? And the trees have every branch and needle coated in white. It's almost blinding. I don't think I've ever seen anything look quite so . . . so clean and bright. It's picture-perfect."

"It's not going to be so picture-perfect once this stuff turns to mud, Doc, so we'd better get moving. I'll pull the canvas off the tipi and you pack up the rest of the gear—roll it in the blankets."

Glad of something to do, Olivia gathered the blankets they had wrapped themselves in, the coffeepot, and the jerky, packing them into neat, tubelike rolls that could easily be tied behind the saddle. Gabe made another roll of the big canvas tarp that had sheltered them. Then together they examined poor Murdoch's injured leg. A bloody scrape marred the leg below the stifle, and the fetlock was swollen to almost twice its normal size. While Gabe held the leg immobile, Olivia carefully cleaned the scrape of blood and debris and wrapped the fetlock in snowpacked strips of a blanket she convinced Danaher to sacrifice. She detected a gleam of amusement in his eyes as she treated the animal and was relieved that he was past the notion of shooting the poor beast.

Although, she remembered wryly, there were a few times coming down the trail that she could have shot the ornery Appaloosa herself.

In the bright afternoon sunlight, with the world once again resuming its normal proportions, Olivia felt a bit diffident as she worked on Murdoch, shoulder to shoulder with Danaher. She had never spent a night with a man wrapped around her and didn't know quite how to react. There was a new link between the two of them, and Olivia didn't know exactly what it was or how to define it. She was a woman of science, accustomed to analyzing and diagnosing until something was thoroughly understood and defined. A known quantity could be controlled, or at least dealt with. But this new and tentative bond that grew out of shared peril and forced intimacy eluded her analysis. She didn't know how to deal with it, and therefore she no longer knew quite how to react to Danaher.

"Well, now," he said as Olivia's ministrations to the horse were complete, "we'll see if old Murdoch can get up the trail."

Olivia brushed the dirt from her skirt—a useless exercise, since the garment was hopelessly soiled—then folded her hands together at her waist. She must say her piece right, without tweaking Danaher's Irish stubbornness. "Wouldn't it be easier for him to go down the trail than up?"

"Going down's harder on a horse, but either way he's not going to have an easy time of it on three legs."

"We must be closer to Elkhorn than to your cabin."

He regarded her keenly, and she could see a decision being contemplated in those green eyes.

"How far are we from the town?" she asked.

"About three hours on a good trail. Four with snow and mud, and with the two of us both on Longshot."

She wanted to repeat her arguments about the twins no longer needing her, about Amy's need for care, but he'd heard them all, and to carp would only push him into obstinacy.

"All right, Doc. You win. We'll go down."

Olivia smiled. A stone lifted from her heart.

"You know, you're not too bad-looking when you smile like that. You ought to smile more often."

"Why is it," she asked with an arched brow, "that a woman's worth is always judged on the basis of how she looks?"

"Because that's the easiest thing to comprehend about a woman." He grinned mockingly. "What's inside her head is impossible for a man to understand."

"It's about the same as what's in a man's head, Mr. Danaher."

"Then you ladies have my sympathy. There you go scowling again, Doc. You could scare old Bruno the bear with a face like that."

She opened her mouth for a sharp reply, then shut it. He was probably right, after all.

"In my profession, sometimes one forgets how to smile."

"You shouldn't let yourself forget something like that."

For a moment they looked at each other awkwardly, then Danaher broke the tension. "Ready to go?"

She sighed. "I hope to never sit horseback again when this is over."

He mounted and held out his hand. "Come on up, Doc."

After an ungraceful struggle, she managed to seat herself in the saddle in front of him. The cage of his arms and the solid wall of his chest against her back felt familiar and comfortable. This adventure had certainly eroded her ladylike sensibilities.

The snow was melting fast in the sun, and they found the trail easily. The going was slow as they picked their way through mud and deep drifts, but Longshot was surefooted, even carrying the weight of two people on her back, and trailing behind them on his lead rope, Murdoch did quite well on three legs. They didn't get far, however. The track angled gently down the side of a mountain and then curved around the mountain's shoulder to where it dropped back down toward Thunder Creek. Halfway down the valley they came into a wide meadow that gave them a good view of the trail ahead. Gabe reined in and grunted in disgust.

"Well, that's that."

"What?" Olivia asked.

"Look ahead. What do you see?"

Olivia looked. One mountain valley appeared much the same to her as another. "Trees, rocks, dirt, mountains. What do you want me to see?"

"The trail's been cut off. See that little lake down there?"

It did rather look as if the trail headed directly into the lake.

"A slide cut off Thunder Creek. Too much snow, too fast. See all the trees and boulders that came down with it—enough to block off the creek and back it up into a lake."

"You mean we can't get through?"

"That's what I mean, Doc."

Olivia's heart plummeted. "The snow's melting, though. You said so yourself."

"It'll take that pile a long time to melt—maybe not until next spring.

The creek will cut a path long before that and we'll be able to get through along the creekbed. The footing won't be good, but we'll be able to make it."

"But it might take weeks for the stream to cut through that snow and debris!"

"That's right."

"There must be some other way to get down to Elkhorn."

"Not that I'd take you over. You have trouble enough sitting a horse on a well-broken trail."

"What's that trail over there?" She pointed to a thin line that angled along one side of the valley above the tree line. "That looks like a good trail."

Danaher chuckled. "That's a game trail. Mountain goats, deer, and elk go along on it just fine, but a horse isn't quite as agile. I'm sorry, Doc—I really am. But you're going to have to spend a few more weeks enjoying my hospitality."

"A few more weeks . . ." Olivia felt like kicking something in her frustration. She didn't have weeks to spend up here on this godforsaken mountain. Amy was just over two months from delivering her baby. She had to get to Elkhorn!

"Could one negotiate that game trail around the slide on foot, leading a horse—if one were desperate, I mean?"

"Maybe—someone who was pretty close to being a mountain goat. Not you."

Olivia was accustomed to being told that something was beyond her abilities, and just as accustomed to proving it wasn't. She took a good look at the game trail and the ways it could be reached from their present location. She was still looking back when they turned around and headed up the mountain.

When they arrived at the cabin late the same night, Katy was dressed and sitting in the chair by the fire. Ellen was asleep in the loft.

"Crooked Stick left," Katy told them. "He saw you was only a couple miles down the trail, so he headed out. He's going up north for a while to join Lame Wolf's hunting band and wanted to get there before the weather turned bad again. Now that Big Mouth Woman"—she gave Olivia a malicious grin and repeated the odious name—"Big Mouth Woman, now that she's here to stay, Crooked Stick says you don't need him and Squirrel Woman's help."

"I'm certainly not here to stay!" Olivia said sharply.

"That's what I told Crooked Stick. I said you was a city woman, and you'd be outta here faster than a bear boltin' a beehive now that me and Ellen are on the mend." She slid a glance toward her father as if for agreement.

"I wouldn't have put it quite as colorfully," Olivia said, "but on the whole you're right."

"Well, Crooked Stick just took off. Said he'd check back before winter sets in real good."

Gabe took off his hat, tossed it onto the table, and swung the coffeepot over the fire. "Katy, I figure you should be in bed. I see Crooked Stick let you girls move back into the loft."

"We ain't sick no more."

"Aren't," Olivia automatically corrected. "You *aren't* sick."

Katy shot her a quick, hostile look. "We *ain't* so sick anymore that we need to sleep by the fire and need *her* telling us what to do and when to eat and when to take a leak."

"Katy! Show some respect to the doc and stop talking like a mule skinner. You know better."

"I ain't—" She backtracked at her father's glare. "I'm not bein' disrespectful, Pa; I'm just sayin' the truth. You don't need to hold her here no longer. Ellen and me don't need her. Honest."

"Your father knows that you don't need a doctor any longer," Olivia said emphatically, hoping to set that truth like concrete into Gabe's mind. "He was taking me back to Elkhorn, but a slide closed the trail down the mountain. I'll be gone just as soon as the trail is once again negotiable."

The mutinous set of Katy's jaw relaxed a bit. "I guess you really do want to get back to the city, huh?"

"I'd hardly call Elkhorn a city, or even a town. But yes, I do have to get back as soon as possible now that you and Ellen are recovering so well."

"I'm strong as a bear," Katy assured her.

"I'm very glad to see that you've made such an improvement."

"Ellen's good too."

Danaher interrupted in a stern voice. "You won't be strong as a bear for long if you don't get up to bed."

"Ellen's snoring kept me awake." She cocked a suspicious eye at Olivia. "I think I'll sleep down here."

Danaher took Katy by the shoulder and pushed her toward the loft. "Like you said, you're well enough to sleep in your own bed. And as far as snoring goes, you're about twice as loud as your sister. I should know. I've been listening to both of you sawing logs for the last decade or so."

"Oh, Pa!"

"Upstairs! Take the basin with you so you can wash your face and hands."

Katy marched truculently toward the ladder. Danaher handed her a basin and a kettle of water.

"Wash other places, too."

"Pa!"

"And put on a clean nightdress."

She rolled her eyes.

Danaher sat on the ladder and put a finger under her chin. "How about a good-night kiss, Katy my lass?"

Katy screwed up her face. For a moment father and daughter regarded each other, then she gave him a crooked smile. "Good night, Pa."

He received the peck on the cheek with appropriate solemnity. "Good night, White Horse Woman."

Katy grinned and kissed him again before climbing the ladder to her bed.

"White Horse Woman?" Olivia asked with a raised brow.

"Her Blackfoot name. She likes it much better than Katy. It was given to her by Minnie's great-uncle on her mother's side. Buffalo Robes was his name, and he was a big chief. Katy feels honored to have been named after the chief's favorite horse."

Olivia thought being named after a horse was somewhat strange, but she refrained from saying so.

"Did he name Ellen also?"

"Ellen is Lights Up the Sky."

"How did the chief come up with that?"

"There was a real show of falling stars the night the twins were born."

"Hmm. Interesting," she said around a yawn. "It's been a very long day. If you don't mind, I'll go to bed."

"Good idea. I'm tired too."

"Well, goodnight then. And . . . thank you, Mr. Danaher, for coming to fetch me in the blizzard. It was foolish of me to not listen to your prediction of the storm."

"You're welcome, Big Mouth Woman. It's nice to meet a woman who knows when she's wrong."

She grimaced at him and turned toward the ladder, then remembered that the loft had been reclaimed by its rightful owners. With only one other bed in the cabin, the situation was a bit awkward.

"I nearly forgot. I've been evicted from my bed."

She hoped he didn't interpret the forced intimacies of the last few days to be license for further improprieties.

"I'll fetch some blankets," she offered, "so you can make yourself a bedroll by the fire." Olivia had no intention of sleeping on the floor herself. After all, if not for Gabriel Danaher and his daughters, she would be sleeping in a feather bed in the Talbot house.

"I don't think we'll need extra blankets." Though Danaher's expression was carefully neutral, the devil's own light flashed in his eyes, so fast that Olivia almost missed seeing it—but she was becoming practiced at spotting the danger signs, and she was instantly suspicious.

"You'll be quite uncomfortable on the floor without them."

"I'm not sleeping on the floor."

"Really? You're going to make me sleep on the floor? Mr. Danaher, though you have many redeeming qualities, gallantry is certainly not one of them."

He smiled with that Irish cockiness that made her want to grind her teeth. "I think I'm very gallant, Doc. After all, I damn near froze myself stiff looking for you in the storm. And now I'm going to be gallant again by making sure you don't act on those stupid notions I saw going through your head when you looked at that game trail."

"Game trail?" She tried to sound innocent.

"You have many redeeming qualities," he mimicked. "But a talent at lying isn't one of them, Doc. I'm not having you sneak past me again and lead me on some wild-goose chase through the woods. You'd kill yourself trying to make it over that game trail, and then what good would you be to your friend Mrs. Talbot?"

"I'm not lying. I had no intention of sneaking out tonight to try that ridiculous trail." That, at least, was the truth. She would have waited for the daylight and sneaked away when Danaher was in his mine or off killing some poor deer. She'd had her fill of nighttime horseback rides. Besides, tonight she was very tired.

"Somehow, Doc, I just don't trust you. You're a woman whose stubbornness puts those mules out there to shame."

"*I'm* stubborn as a mule? I'm sure I haven't come near *your* accomplishments on that score. You should sprout long hairy ears any day." She flounced over to a wooden box in one corner where the linen and extra blankets were stored. "But I for one am too tired to continue this futile conversation." She yanked out the blankets and carried them to the hearth. "I can tell you've no intentions of letting me have the bed, so I shall sleep here."

" 'Fraid not."

"What?"

From some corner of the cabin he had produced a rope, and he dangled it almost tauntingly. "You'll not only sleep in the bed, but tied to it."

"You're joking."

"Nope. I'll get you to Elkhorn when it's safe, and not until then. I don't fancy you taking off again. Now, do you want to get in your nightdress, or are you going to sleep in your clothes?"

Olivia backed up a step. "This is ridiculous. I've no intention of letting you tie me to the bed, particularly if you're going to be in it."

"Well, now, I wasn't asking your permission, Doc. And I figure I've slept on the ground too many times already for your sake. A man my age gets used to the luxury of a bed."

Olivia backed another step as he advanced, rope in hand. Her helplessness against this man struck her with renewed vigor, leaving her shaking with angry frustration.

"You don't have a civilized bone in your body, you unprincipled scoundrel. This is outrageous. I give you my word that I won't leave this cabin tonight."

He shook his head. "Not good enough, Doc. There's water in the bucket there if you want to wash."

She flung the blankets at him and dodged his grasp, even though she knew the situation was hopeless. He just wasn't going to listen to reason, and she didn't have the strength to stand against him. But surrendering to such humiliation without a fight was against every instinct.

"Come on, Doc. We're both tired. You don't need to worry about me taking liberties. I've resisted you so far. I figure I can go on resisting you until the trail's open again."

She had backed herself into a corner, literally. There was no place to run. He grasped her wrist in an iron grip and knotted the rope firmly around it.

The urge to strike out at him was almost irresistible, but the look in his eyes stopped her. Gabriel Danaher had a thoroughly ungentlemanly nature and an unpredictable temper. He just might hit back.

She glared at him and gathered what composure she could. "At least let me wash."

Some minutes later, Olivia was stonily silent as Danaher snuffed the oil lamp and settled onto the bed beside her. The bed was not a big one and the straw-ticked mattress was not firm. Danaher's greater weight produced a definite downward slope in his direction. Unable to brace herself with her hands, which were tied to the iron bedstead, Olivia couldn't prevent herself from sliding against him. She struggled with her legs to push herself away.

"Stop squirming or we'll neither one get any sleep."

Olivia froze. Danaher's heat burned through the thin cotton of the nightdress, which had once belonged to his Minnie. He'd come to bed in his long underwear, she realized, for neither belt buckle nor the rough folds of denim trousers came between them. What did rise between them to prod her buttocks was warm and hard. Olivia had a physician's knowledge of its identity and purpose, but she'd never before been so close to getting a more practical knowledge of the thing.

She inhaled in a sharp gasp when Danaher's arm circled her waist and settled her more firmly against him.

"Go to sleep, Doc. We both need the rest."

She stayed very still for what seemed an eternity—until Danaher's breath ruffled her hair in the shallow, constant rhythm of sleep. She was not going to be completely compromised after all, Olivia concluded. If her relief held the smallest twinge of disappointment, Olivia excused it as a deviation of exhaustion. She was a sensible, civilized, educated woman of twenty-six, after all. Any sordid interest she might have in Gabriel Danaher was simply the product of the barbaric circumstances of her situation, or perhaps the lingering spell of their hours wrapped together in a blizzard. It would most certainly disappear once she was back in her own world.

The picture of Katy planting a good-night kiss on her father's cheek suddenly came into her mind, and her annoyance with Danaher relented a bit. She'd give the man credit for some good qualities, but on the whole he was a thoroughgoing philistine who belonged back in the Dark Ages. Not at all the type of fellow she might feel attracted to.

As sleep overtook her, consciousness narrowed down to the weight of Danaher's arm around her waist and the hard warmth of his chest pressed against her back—and then, finally, to exhausted oblivion.

Olivia woke to the discomfort of cold feet. Sheets and blankets both were twisted around Danaher's legs, leaving her feet and calves bare— very bare, for her nightdress had rucked up around her thighs. Reluctant to completely leave the comfort of sleep even though a bright bar of sunlight fell across the bed from a gap in the curtains, Olivia buried her legs under a flap of blanket and allowed herself to drift back toward sleep. It was then she became aware of rustlings in the cabin.

"She's gone," came a loud whisper.

"Good!" declared a louder voice. "Just so she didn't take poor Murdoch again!"

"Sssssh! Don't wake Pa. He's still asleep."

"The sun's been up for an hour!"

"He was real tired. He'll probably sleep till noon."

"At least then it'll be too late to go after that stupid woman."

"Do you really think she's stupid enough to try to get over a mudslide?"

"She's from Back East" was the answer, as though that was sufficient to establish just how stupid Olivia was.

"She could be in the privy, or the henhouse."

A quiet shuffle of feet padded to the window. "Don't see her out there."

"Maybe we should wake Pa and tell him." Now the whisper held a note of worry. "She could get killed."

"She's not *that* stupid. The first time she falls and skins a knee she'll come running back. You want some coffee?" The pothook that hung over the fire squeaked.

"Pa doesn't like us to drink coffee. Says it'll stunt our growth and stain our teeth."

"Pa's asleep. Besides, I need something hot in my stomach before I go out and look at Murdoch's leg."

"Pa said we weren't to go outside."

"You're as bad as that woman. Do this. Don't do that. If I have to stay cooped up in the cabin much longer I *am* gonna croak."

"Well, you can't just have coffee for breakfast. I'll fix some biscuits and gravy."

Danaher snorted in his sleep, bringing momentary silence on the other side of the curtain.

"Now you've gone and woke Pa."

"That's all right. He'll want to eat breakfast too. And I bet he won't let you go traipsing around outside, either."

As the voices came closer, Olivia suddenly realized that she and Gabriel Danaher, innocent though the night had been, were in a most compromising position—not a sight to be witnessed by the eyes of innocent children. Her gown was still twisted around her thighs, and Danaher had shifted one underwear-clad leg to rest possessively over hers. She struggled to free her hands.

"Pa, it's morning!"

The curtain suddenly slid back, revealing a room full of sunlight and two little surprised faces. Danaher woke with a start. In one fluid, instinctive motion his hand reached for the pistol that hung from the bedstead.

"Pa!" squealed two voices in unison. The twins didn't look at the pistol in their father's hand; their round eyes fastened on the woman tied to his bed.

Olivia wished she could dissolve into the air and disappear.

"How many times have I told you girls not to startle me when I'm asleep." He shoved the pistol back into its holster and looked down at Olivia as if just remembering she was there. Casually he flipped the blanket over her bare legs.

"Pa!" Katy admonished. "What're you doing?"

"Trying to get a good night's sleep without this one"—he stabbed a finger at Olivia—"sneaking off into the woods and without you two bouncing around like a pair of busy little mice instead of resting like you should be. You're barefoot! Where are the moccasins Squirrel Woman made for you?"

"Somewhere."

"Go find them. You too, Ellen."

Both girls looked from their father to Olivia. Finally, Katy pressed her lips into a firm line and set her jaw. "You . . . you didn't marry her, did you, Pa?"

For a moment Danaher seemed nonplussed. Then he laughed. "No, Katy. I didn't marry the doctor."

"You told me ladies only slept with men they married."

"We didn't sleep together like married people sleep together. There's only one bed, and I didn't want to sleep on the floor." He chuckled. "Besides, I figured I better tie her to something or she'd be out the door again. Would you want her tied to a chair all night?"

Katy smiled maliciously, but didn't say anything.

"Go find your moccasins while I fix some breakfast. You too, Ellen."

"I'm going to get dressed and look at Murdoch."

"You're going to put on a warm robe and then go back to bed after you've eaten."

"Pa!"

"Do as I say."

Katy stomped away, leaving a slightly smiling Ellen in her wake.

"I'll fix breakfast, Pa."

"No, Ellen. I want you and Katy both to rest for another couple of days."

"But Pa! The house is a mess. You said you needed to get back to work in the mine. Someone has to wash the clothes and cook and . . ."

"I'm sure Dr. Baron is very capable of running a house with two children."

Ellen gave Olivia a resentful frown before following after her sister. Olivia wanted to pull the blankets up over her head and forget that she'd ever awakened. The day was not going to be a good one.

Chapter 8

*T*he next three days convinced Olivia that pursuing medicine, with all the prejudices and obstacles thrown in her path, was a much easier road for a woman than keeping house and raising children. On-and-off snow alternating with sun turned the valley of Thunder Creek into a quagmire of ice and mud, ending Olivia's hope of getting down the mountain trail. Assured that even Olivia wasn't fool enough to try the journey to Elkhorn in the current conditions, Gabe spent his days in the mine, leaving her to the mercy of two fractious girls who didn't want to be confined to their beds and a cabin full of chores to be done.

When he first disappeared down the mine tunnel, Olivia wondered how Danaher could bring himself to crawl down that dark, tight, damp gullet of the earth; closed-in places had always made her uneasy, and the mere thought of being in the narrow mine drift gave her chills. Not many hours passed, however, before hiding in the belly of the earth seemed a sensible alternative to being trapped with Katy and Ellen in the cabin.

Ellen was certain that the household was going to come down around their ears without her to care for it. Only the threat of calling Danaher from the mine kept her in bed, where she vented her frustration in criticizing every move Olivia made. There was much to criticize, Olivia admitted. She'd been raised in a wealthy New York home that had servants to attend to such mundane chores as fire tending, wood chopping, laundry, cooking, and mending. During her medical education, she'd lived in genteel rooming houses where those services were included in the monthly rent, and then she'd moved back in with her family in New York while she started up her practice. She never had need of skills in ax wielding, fire starting, and biscuit making, and her sewing education at Miss Tatterhorn's had been limited to the decorative, not the useful.

Around noon Ellen complained of the cold. Indeed, the fire had burned very low. Olivia had forgotten to watch it while she wrestled with the intricacies of peeling and cutting vegetables for a soup. When she added wood, what fire was left turned to smoke, most of which billowed out into the room.

Coughing, Ellen came down the ladder. "First you freeze us. Now we're going to choke to death. Don't you know anything useful?"

Olivia refused to let a twelve-year-old get the best of her. "I know a number of useful things, Ellen. Unfortunately, tending a fireplace is not one of them. The wood must be wet."

"It's not wet. You don't put a big chunk like that on a little bitty fire. You need to add smaller pieces first, then the log." Her nose twitched. "That's more than just wood smoke. Did you burn the coffee?"

"Well . . ."

"Yes." The girl opened the lid of the enameled graniteware coffeepot and grimaced. "We'll have to soak this in baking soda."

"I'll take care of the fire, and I'll soak the pot in baking soda. You go back to bed."

"But what about Pa's dinner?" Ellen glanced dubiously at the potatoes, carrots, and turnips in the soup pot. "Pa usually comes out of the mine a little before dark, and he'll need more than vegetable soup."

"I'll put some venison in it and make some biscuits. Now, Ellen. Back to bed."

"If you say so." She surveyed the smoky cabin, the piles of vegetable peelings on the table, and the crusted coffeepot. A gleam appeared in her eye, and suddenly her smile was strangely content. "Call me if you need help with something, though."

Halfway up the ladder, Ellen paused and looked down. "I'm sorry I was unmannerly, Miss Baron. You know, you shouldn't feel bad about being so ignorant about such things. My ma told me once that a girl has to start from real young to learn all the things she needs to take care of a man's home. I guess you've been real busy learning to be a doctor and didn't have any time to learn to be a woman. But a doctor's a good thing to be."

Olivia bit her lip to keep from laughing as Ellen climbed the rest of the way up the ladder. The girl was transparent as crystal. She'd just realized that Olivia wasn't competition; the bungles in the house only made Ellen look good in her father's eyes and would make him appreciate what a fine hand she was at keeping him comfortable on this godforsaken mountain.

Katy was a bit tougher to handle. It wasn't uncommon for patients to regard inactivity during recovery as a greater curse than the original illness, but Katy carried restlessness to an extreme. She bounced out of bed so often on one excuse or another that Olivia thought she would wear out the rope springs of the cot.

First Katy offered to chop firewood. Olivia thanked her politely and ordered her back to bed.

"Your father can cut more wood this evening," she told Katy.

"Oh, he'll be too tired."

"Then I'll cut it."

Katy laughed. "You? You'd cut off your foot with the ax."

"Thank you for your concern, dear. I'll try to be careful. Now, back to bed."

Her second excuse was to check on Murdoch's leg.

"I redressed it this morning," Olivia told her. At Katy's dubious frown, she smiled, for once feeling she was on her own ground. "I am a doctor, Katy."

"You're a people doctor. Murdoch's a horse."

"I did notice that."

"Yeah, well, docs around here sometimes fix up animals. I guess they know what they're doing. But you're from Back East."

"Murdoch's leg will be fine, Katy. But you won't if you don't stay quiet for the next few days. Back to bed."

And so it went for the entire day. As the long hours passed, the twins became bored with baiting Olivia and started on each other. Ellen complained that Katy was hogging the warmest blankets. Katy griped that Ellen kept her awake with her snoring. Ellen retaliated by throwing a book at Katy, and Katy countered by refusing to give it back, then reading aloud and sniggering at such tender passages that struck her as particularly ridiculous. The battle went on until Olivia, who had always prided herself on her patience with the ill and cranky, was tempted to tie the little monsters to their cots and stuff gags in their mouths.

Shortly after the sun dropped below the mountain, Danaher crawled from the mine, crusted with dirt and sweat. He washed in a bucket outside the cabin before coming in.

"We always pour buckets of water over ourselves like that," Katy announced from the loft as she watched her father out the window. "Even when it's freezing cold. I'm always dirty as he is, 'cause I either help in the mine or tend the horses or load ore all day long."

"Those sound like difficult, dirty jobs for a young lady."

Katy snorted."I ain't no young—"

"I'm not," Ellen corrected. "Ain't isn't a word."

"I *ain't* no young lady." Katy smirked at Ellen. "I can outwork, outshoot, outload, and outride any boy I've ever met. And I can outspit 'em, too."

"Who'd want to," Ellen muttered.

Olivia sighed wearily. "You two can come down for supper now. Put on your moccasins and robes."

"Did the fire die again?" Katy asked contemptuously.

"No, but it's nippy just the same. I want you to stay warm."

If Ellen had any doubts about her superiority to Olivia, those doubts must have faded upon tasting the evening meal. Olivia had intended to serve venison stew, but she added too much water and the concoction became soup, which in itself would have been satisfactory if she hadn't added too much salt as well as too much water.

Danaher choked on the first spoonful, but he manfully swallowed it down. To kill the taste of the soup he reached for a biscuit, but his hand stopped halfway to the plate. The biscuits were a lovely golden brown on top and charcoal black on the bottom.

"Careful, Pa," Ellen warned. "I think she forgot the baking powder."

"Baking powder?" Olivia grimaced. "Oh gracious."

Danaher picked up a biscuit and tapped it against the table, where it left a slight dent in the wood.

"I couldn't find a recipe," Olivia explained. "I thought just flour, water, and salt . . ."

Ellen's sympathetic smile was more of a smirk.

Katy sipped at her soup. "Ewwww! This tastes like horse piss."

"Katy!" Danaher chided. "Watch your language."

"Well, it does."

Danaher's mouth twitched in a smile. "Maybe it does. But you should try to be polite."

Olivia felt about as tall as a thimble. Rachel Olivia Baron was a woman who was good at everything she tried, or so her father had once boasted. She wasn't accustomed to being inept at anything, and she certainly didn't want to become accustomed to it. Bungling something—even something as unimportant as stew and a batch of biscuits—was a great jolt to one's pride. So was being laughed at by a pair of disagreeable little girls and their equally irritating father. She'd be damned, though, if she would let the lot of them get the best of her.

"I think Katy is recovered enough to do the cooking tomorrow," Olivia announced with a magnanimous smile.

Both green-eyed, cream-colored, perfect oval faces turned to look at her in surprise.

"*I* don't cook," Katy declared.

"Is that so?"

"I do stuff that's more important."

"Perhaps my talents lie elsewhere as well."

Ellen lifted a lip at her sister. "You'll think cooking is important when your stomach starts growling. If Katy's well enough recovered, then so am I. I'll do the cooking tomorrow."

"And I'll work with Pa." Katy grinned.

"No you won't," Olivia said. "It's starting to snow, and even if the sun comes out tomorrow, everything will be cold and wet. You can stay inside where it's warm. Perhaps Ellen can give cooking lessons to us both."

Ellen beamed, and Katy growled an unintelligible comment under her breath.

"I'm glad I'm gonna be out there tomorrow." Danaher stabbed a finger in the direction of the mine and grinned.

Over the next several days Olivia allowed the twins more time out of bed and was sorely tempted to take their place on one of the cots. Danaher did not insist on tying her to the bed after their first night back in the cabin, but neither did he volunteer to leave the bed to her. Indignantly she wrapped herself in a blanket by the fireplace and declared that he could have the bed to himself. Her attack of modesty, however, lasted only long enough for the cold of the floor to seep through the blanket into her weary bones. Danaher's soft snores convinced her that it was safe to tiptoe back to the bed. She rolled her blanket and placed it between them under the quilt as a chaste barrier, but when she woke in the predawn darkness, the blanket had been unrolled and spread over the both of them. Danaher's breath ruffled her hair, and one of his large, callused hands rested casually on her hip.

Gingerly Olivia extracted herself from beneath Danaher's hand without waking him. She added a log to the fire, swung the coffeepot over the coals, and sat wrapped in a blanket in the rocking chair, awaiting the dawn while the rest of the house slumbered.

On the floor or in the chair she couldn't sleep other than in short, uncomfortable snatches that seemed to leave her more tired than no sleep at all. But Danaher's bed held dangers more grave than uneasy sleep. Her hip was still warm where his hand had lingered, and Olivia didn't like the attraction of that warmth, an attraction that had much more to it than merely not being cold.

All in all, sleepless nights in the chair seemed to be the safer choice. Olivia sighed. The wait for the Thunder Creek trail to open was going to be a long one.

During supper of the third day—a "cowboy hash" prepared by Ellen—Danaher announced that he was leaving for a few days to bring in more game.

"Need to bring in a couple more deer or elk before they all head for lower country. Most of 'em are probably gone already, as cold as it's been the last week."

Katy was jubilant. "I'll go with you, Pa!"

"No you won't. Not fresh out of a sickbed, you won't."

"Pa! I'm better."

"I know you are, Katy my lass. Otherwise I couldn't trust you to keep Dr. Baron from heading down the trail if these snowy days we've been having suddenly turn warm. We wouldn't want the doctor to get herself into a situation she couldn't handle." Danaher grinned at Olivia.

"It's been snowing off and on for the past three days," Olivia pointed out. "Why is it any more safe for you to go hunting than me to head down the trail?"

"Because I know how to take care of myself, and you don't."

"Why don't you just take care of both of us and take me with you? We could go down the trail to check the slide and you can shoot your deer on the way back."

"It hasn't even been a week yet. The creek won't have gotten through that slide yet. Maybe if we get a warm spell and this snow melts off, then it might make some progress."

"It wouldn't hurt to check."

"It would be a waste of time. Besides, I spotted a couple of deer moving in the trees across the valley today. They're probably still there."

Olivia sighed in frustration.

"I'll check the slide when I get back, Doc. In the meanwhile, stay here and take care of my girls."

"I thought they were supposed to take care of me." Olivia lifted a brow. "Like prison guards."

"You keep them on the road to getting well, and they'll keep you from killing yourself."

Or drive her to suicide, Olivia thought privately.

*   *   *

Katy sat on her cot, legs crossed beneath her Indian style, chin cupped in the palm of one hand, staring out the loft window. The morning was still a fragile blue, and the sun was merely a promise still hidden behind the mountains, but she could sense the day was going to be a fine one—and she was stuck in this stupid cabin, or at best in the stupid clearing, waiting on a tenderfoot woman who didn't know up from down or crosswise from straight. Her father would leave her behind all because of some fussy, schoolmarmish crow of a female who couldn't be trusted to have the sense of a gopher.

She could hear her father moving around the cabin, and the woman as well. Their voices were low—probably trying to not wake her and Ellen. No worry about Ellen. She'd sleep sound as a rock if a two-ton boulder crashed down the mountain and ripped through the cabin. But Katy's senses were a good deal better. Her father should know she'd be awake—he was the one who'd told her that sleeping light was a good way to stay alive in this world. She halfway hoped he would climb the ladder and tell her good-bye. He could apologize for leaving her here at the same time. She deserved an apology, and she sure as hell wasn't going to make the first move and go downstairs to say good-bye to him, the traitor.

Outside, the first gray light of morning brightened to gold. The cabin door creaked open, then shut. A few minutes later, hoofbeats thudded against the soft pine-needle and grass carpet of the clearing. Katy hurried to the window for a last view of her father, but he was already gone. The woman stood staring into the trees, hands on hips and backbone stiff as a stick. Katy clamped her lips together and huffed out a disgusted snort. She almost wished she could get sick again, just so her father would return and have cause to regret leaving her behind. Almost, but not quite. Being sick wasn't a bit fun; and if she were sick, she'd have to follow the lady doctor's orders that much longer.

She crawled back under her blankets and tried to cheer herself by imagining how it might be when her father returned. The hunt hadn't gone well without Katy along, but by then his regrets would be too late. He'd leave the measly amount of game he had bagged with Ellen to clean and smoke while he and Katy took the doctor back to Elkhorn. Her father would want Katy along to scout a way through the slide while he hung back to take care of the greenhorn woman.

At first look, the slide would seem as if it were still impassable, but Katy would find them a way through. Her father would send the woman on her way down the trail, and then Katy and he would have a nice, companionable ride back to the cabin—and it would be just the three of them again: Pa and Ellen and Katy. They didn't need anyone else to be

with them, especially some ugly, bossy, tenderfoot woman from Back
East.

Well, maybe she wasn't that ugly, but she was bossy. She'd been gentle
and caring while Katy and Ellen were sick, but Katy knew they could
have pulled through without her. It took more than diphtheria to kill
O'Connells, even when they were pretending to be Danahers.

That woman had better not get any ideas about staying. She'd slept in
Pa's bed; Katy had seen with her own eyes. What went on between men
and women in beds wasn't clear to Katy, but she was certain that only
married couples slept together—unless the woman was a whore. Olivia
Baron wasn't a whore, so did that mean she had plans to marry Pa? Her
father had laughed at the notion, and the woman had turned green when
Katy had mentioned marriage. She might have had second thoughts by
now, though. After all, any female in her right mind would fall in love
with a man like her pa.

Katy tried to imagine what life would be like if such a horror should
happen. It was too awful to think about. Since her mother had died,
three had become the perfect number. Pa didn't need anyone else demanding a part of his love. He didn't need anyone else to take care of
him or share his adventures or sit with him in front of a fire, listening to
him tell the stories about the Little People that his mother had once told
him.

The sooner Thunder Creek carved a route through that slide, the better off they all would be, Katy decided. Meanwhile, for the doctor's sake
as well as theirs, the O'Connell girls should make it clear that they
weren't shopping for a stepmother. It wouldn't be kind to let the woman
get her hopes up, after all.

"Ellen!" Katy whispered sharply and reached out to nudge the other
cot. "Wake up, slugabed."

"No," came a muffled reply from under Ellen's blankets. "It's barely
morning."

"Pa's gone."

"Stupid. Of course he's gone. He told us he's going hunting."

"He didn't come up to say good-bye."

Ellen's tousled head emerged from the pile of blankets. She glared at
Katy. "He didn't want to wake us up. You should be as considerate."

"You want to sleep all day? We've got things to do."

"Like what?"

"Like watch out for that woman."

"Dr. Baron, you mean."

Katy lowered her voice. "We got to get rid of her."

"Pa said she was supposed to stay here till he got back."

"Yeah. I know. But I'm talking down the road. I think she's aiming to get her claws into Pa."

"Don't be silly. She's going back to Elkhorn and then back to New York. She's talked about nothing but going back since she got here."

"Yeah, but she's old, and she ain't got a husband. Women get desperate if they ain't married by eighteen, and that's a fact. I've seen that woman look at Pa like a hungry dog looking at a bone."

"That's stupid. You don't know what you're talking about."

"Oh, don't I? They sleep in the same bed, you know."

"That's just 'cause there's only one bed downstairs. Besides, last night she slept in the chair. I went to the rail and looked."

Katy sighed. "Don't matter. They did it once. Men and women sleeping together any time means there's something going on between them."

"Oh yeah? What, Miss Know-it-all?"

"I don't know exactly! But it's not good."

"You're just looking for mischief, like you always do."

"Do you want to take a chance on her horning in on our lives? I say we make sure she doesn't want to stay longer than she has to."

Ellen looked dubious. "She was nice to us when we were sick."

"Pa dragged her up here. She didn't even want to come. She didn't care if we died. It's true!" she insisted as Ellen frowned. "I heard her and Pa fight about it when we were still sick."

"She really didn't want to come?"

Katy lowered her voice to a conspiratorial whisper. "Pa pulled a gun on her!"

"Goodness!"

"She's not a very nice lady."

"Well, she certainly doesn't know a single thing past doctoring, that's for sure."

"All we need to do is make sure she *really* wants to leave when that trail opens up."

Ellen looked thoughtful, then smiled. Katy smiled also. Ellen was quiet and boring most of the time, but when necessary, she could get even more creative than Katy in raising hell. Olivia Baron was going to be sorry that she hadn't let Pa shoot her rather than meet the O'Connell twins.

The fact that she actually missed Gabriel Danaher revealed to Olivia just how much her judgment had slipped since being dragged from relatively civilized Elkhorn to this hermit's cabin in the mountains. Remembering Elkhorn as civilized compared to her current situation was bad enough, but missing Danaher—well, that showed what extreme circumstances could do to a woman's mind.

The promise of a fine day had faded into a gray, sulky sky when Olivia went out to check Murdoch's healing leg. The cold wind brought a promise of more snow on the way. It stung her cheeks and numbed her nose as she walked to the shed. The gusts tore the wood smoke from the chimney top and scattered it in ragged puffs among the trees.

Olivia gratefully took shelter in the shed and let the warm scent of horse thaw her nose. She wondered if Danaher would return because of the lowering weather. Probably not. Anyone who lived in these mountains in wintertime had to be all but immune to cold.

The big Appaloosa regarded her suspiciously as she pushed into the little box where he was stabled.

"Don't worry, my friend. I've learned my lesson. Next time I steal a horse, I won't take you."

Murdoch grunted as if in satisfaction.

"Now, let's take a look at that leg."

Katy had been to the shed earlier in the morning and reported that Murdoch's leg was swelling again. Olivia ran her hand down the fetlock. It wasn't particularly sensitive or warm, and the swelling looked better to her instead of worse, but she'd have to do something, or Katy would insist on sitting in the shed herself to make sure her horse was all right.

"We'll just put some hot wrappings on that for a while, all right, Murdoch? I'll fetch the kettle from the house."

The horse gusted out a warm, grainy breath and gave her a tolerant look.

"Just wait here a moment." Olivia decided she rather liked animals as patients; they didn't talk back, and one could tie them in one place without feeling guilty about it. She reached into the bin where she'd thrown the rags she was using to wrap the fetlock, and something bit down on her fingers with a sharp snap. She yelped and jumped back, making Murdoch sidle away in alarm. The culprit still hung ferociously onto her fingers.

"A mousetrap?"

"Do you need help, Dr. Baron?" Katy leaned against the door of the shed, her eyes wide with innocence, but the dimple in her cheek bore evidence of an impish smile beneath the innocent surface.

Olivia's eyes narrowed. "How did a mousetrap get in the bin with the rags?"

"I put it there." Katy sauntered into the shed. "Otherwise the mice would've made a nest of those rags. Sorry I didn't think to tell you. Here—" She opened the wire jaws of the trap. "Ooooh. That looks like it hurts."

"It does."

"Well, it could have been worse," Katy philosophized. "You could have reached in there and grabbed a dead mouse. That's something that really makes Ellen screech—the stiff little bodies and the tiny lips pulled back from the teeth."

Olivia shook her hand to ease the pain in her fingers. No real harm was done, she supposed, and to lose her temper would only be playing into the little scamp's hands. At times she'd regretted that she'd never married and had children. Now she began to think that she'd been lucky.

It was evening before Olivia realized that all-out war had been declared. Ellen had prepared supper, so Olivia volunteered herself and Katy to wash the dishes. Turning her back to clear the table was a mistake, for when she first dunked her hands in the soapy water, she found a water snake enjoying a swim through the suds. When the thing slithered between her fingers, she jumped halfway across the cabin while the twins stifled giggles. She tried to picture what her mother would have done in the way of discipline had she ever behaved in such a monstrous manner. But she hadn't ever been such a hooligan, of course. In fact, she'd never even been spanked, a fate which these two richly deserved.

The best Olivia could think of was to send the little demons off to their cots—scarcely a punishment, for night had fallen and it was nearly time for bed, anyway. They marched up the ladder with eyes twinkling in mock-serious faces. Olivia discovered the reason for their cheerfulness when she turned back the covers on her own bed and found grit from the mine liberally sprinkled on the linen.

The time had come, Olivia decided after she had shaken out the sheets and remade the bed, to fight back. In medical school she had learned that the best defense against such spiteful attention was to turn the pranks back upon the perpetrators. Therefore the anatomy class who had banded together and given her cadaver an appearance below the waist of being lustfully alive found that agar, a gelling-culture media, had been poured into the laboratory coffeepot. She sat innocently sipping her tea and charting the arteries of the leg while her fellow students groaned at the gelatinous black mass that poured into their cups. And then there was the poor fellow who had glued a detailed sketch of the male reproductive organs to her teacup. Shortly thereafter he found the same sketch on the student bulletin board with appropriate notations as to deficient development of certain attributes and naming the unfortunate syndrome after himself.

Those devilish twins didn't know what they'd gotten themselves into when they started a war with Rachel Olivia Baron.

Ellen woke to the smell of bacon and coffee. The first light of morning bloomed a pale gray at the loft's one window, and the lantern glow from below confirmed that the doctor had risen early. The warmth of her bed beckoned her to stay a bit longer, but duty called. No doubt that woman would burn the bacon and scald the coffee unless Ellen supervised.

Not until she moved to throw the bedcovers back did Ellen realize that they were wrapped around her so tightly and tucked under the mattress so firmly that she couldn't escape. Katy's work, no doubt. She had enjoyed their little jokes on the doctor so much that she decided to play one on Ellen. Sometimes having a sister just wasn't worth it.

"Katy!"

A muffled mutter came from the other cot.

"Katy, this isn't funny! Get up and let me loose."

Something between a snort and a snore was Katy's answer.

"Right now, Katy! I mean it!" Ellen lifted her head far enough to look at her twin in the other cot and a horrible suspicion hit her. Katy looked every bit as immobile as Ellen.

"Wh . . . what? Hey! Somebody made the damned bed with me in it! Ellen!"

"It wasn't me, stupid. I can't move either."

"Then it had to be . . ." They spoke the words together just as the ladder creaked and that woman's head appeared above the loft floor. She was ominously cheerful. Flour smudged her cheek and a black streak of soot decorated her forehead like warpaint. Ellen hoped she hadn't tried to make biscuits again.

"Good morning, you two. How did you sleep?"

Katy jumped on the warpath before Ellen had a chance to speak. "What's the idea of tying us down like this?"

The doctor was all innocent charm. "You looked so tired last night that I was worried about your overdoing it so soon after your illness. I know how difficult it is to remain quiet when you're beginning to feel your energy return, so I thought I'd ensure that you remain in bed today."

Ellen had to give the woman credit. She was almost as devious as Katy.

"We wouldn't want you to be sick again when your father returns."

Katy growled like a cornered bobcat.

Ellen tried to reach the doctor with reason. "We're going to have to get up to make a trip to the privy."

The doctor turned a slightly amused regard Ellen's way. "It's much too cold for you to be traipsing to the outdoor privy, dear. I know the bedpan isn't the most pleasant alternative, but it's better than losing your health, isn't it?"

Ellen groaned.

"Perhaps if you're very quiet all day, you might get up for supper. I think you'll be sufficiently rested by then."

"You mean we don't get breakfast?" Katy cried.

"Of course you do. I'll be up to feed you as soon as the bacon is done."

"You expect us to just lie here all day?"

"Oh no. That would be excessively dull. Later on I'll come up and read to you from one of your father's books. I noticed a history of the American War of Independence in the bookcase. Perhaps you'd like to hear a few chapters of that."

Katy glared down the ladder as the doctor disappeared. "She's going to torture us, the old harpy. Dammit! She can't keep us here all day."

"Yes she can," Ellen snapped. "Nice going, Katy. Next time you pull a dog's tail, find out if the dog bites."

"Go stuff a sock in your mouth."

Ellen sighed morosely. It was going to be a very long day.

Chapter 9

*S*upper that night was a small victory for Olivia, or perhaps a major victory; after three tries she managed to mix up a good batch of biscuits and to cook them in the cast-iron Dutch oven without burning them. The corned-beef hash was acceptable as well, and she'd found a dusty can of peaches for dessert. The cabin was cozy from the fire she had finally learned to keep from burning out, and a day's worth of not too neatly chopped firewood was stacked in the shelter of the cabin's eaves.

She was an intelligent woman, after all. Learning to do such routine chores was certainly not beyond her capabilities. In fact, she felt a flow of accomplishment that was no less satisfying than when she had successfully set her first broken bone. She also felt a burning ache in her arms and shoulders from a day spent in unaccustomed physical labor, but somehow the ache only added to the warmth of self-satisfaction.

The twins, released from the prison of their beds just before supper, were subdued and sulky, as Olivia expected. Ellen got even more sullen when she noticed that the food was at least marginally palatable. Realizing one is replaceable in the scheme of one's own personal universe is a blow to the self-esteem, particularly to the young.

"The hash isn't up to your standards, Ellen. But I am learning."

"It's not bad," Ellen conceded reluctantly.

"Why should you learn to cook?" Katy asked petulantly. "In a few days you'll be back in town being waited on."

"I sincerely hope so. But I never turn up my nose at learning. You never can tell when you'll need some craft or talent you discover."

Katy sniffed scornfully.

"Are we even?" Olivia inquired with a smile.

Katy and Ellen both looked down at their plates. "What do you mean?" Katy demanded.

"You know what I mean. Did you enjoy your day of rest? Did you perhaps learn something during all those hours of quiet contemplation?"

"We did it for your own good," Katy said.

"Just as I thought you should rest for your own good. I can see the value in staying quiet when you've so recently been ill, but I can't quite fathom the benefit of having one's fingers smashed in a mousetrap and finding a snake in the dishwater."

Ellen looked up from beneath the curtain of long, black lashes. "We didn't want you to think that . . . well, Katy says spinsters get desperate as they get on in years. We didn't want you hatching any ideas about our pa. Katy said you sleeping in the same bed was a real bad sign. So we figured we'd make sure you didn't want to stay. Nothing personal, ma'am."

Olivia's face heated. In a way the girls were right; she'd allowed herself to get much too familiar with Gabriel Danaher, and the isolated and primitive nature of the situation had inspired feelings and responses that were entirely unsuitable. It was rather daunting that two supposedly innocent children could read her so well and a lesson to herself in how far she had slipped.

"Girls, you don't need to worry about my getting any romantic notions where your father is concerned. Believe me, the moment the trail to Elkhorn is passable, I will be on my way."

Katy appeared to relax, then frowned. "I suppose our pa isn't good enough for a city lady like you."

"Your father is a fine man."

"He's very handsome," Ellen added.

"Yes, he is."

"He's smart," Katy offered. "And he's a dead shot with a rifle and pistol both. He can outwit just about anybody who comes along—with a little help from me."

"I can imagine."

"He's going to be rich someday from everything he's taking out of the mine," Ellen told her. "And we're going to have a horse ranch in California where it doesn't get so cold, with pastures that go right down to the sea."

"But he'll never get married again," Katy hastened to add, apparently remembering her original purpose. "Of if he does, I feel sorry for the gal he marries. He's got a temper like a badger and he can be twice as mean."

Olivia saw Ellen's confusion and then the sudden enlightenment as a smile twitched her mouth. "Yes," the quieter twin agreed. "Sometimes Katy and I have to hide beneath the bed when Pa's in a temper, or he'd beat us for sure. I'd hate to see what he'd do to a wife."

"You poor dears," Olivia murmured, hiding a smile. She didn't have to imagine Gabriel Danaher in a temper; she'd seen that spectacle. She couldn't imagine him directing it at his girls, however. The notion of Katy and Ellen hiding from a rampaging Danaher was a bit out of character for all concerned.

"And he's a mean drunk," Katy added.

"Indeed?"

"Drinks all the time."

"That's a shame." Olivia watched the play of emotions on the twins' faces. They were anxious to convince her their father wasn't a good catch and at the same time offended that she might think herself too good for the man they obviously worshiped. Life was certainly confusing when one was twelve years old. Actually, life could be quite confusing at twenty-six as well.

"Suppose we simply agree that no more pranks are needed to convince me to go, and I'll promise not to—"

"Wait!" Katy held a finger to her lips for silence. "Listen. What's that?"

For a moment all Olivia could hear was the usual night silence, then the sound came—the merest hint of a rustle in front of the cabin. Her heart rose into her throat and hammered in alarm. Thoughts of old Bruno the rogue bear leapt into her mind.

"Keep talking like we didn't hear," Katy instructed. Her face had suddenly taken on an expression that was years older than her tender age. Olivia and Ellen stuttered into a halting, meaningless conversation as Katy took a shotgun from its place over the fireplace mantel and checked the loading.

"Will a shotgun stop a bear?" Olivia asked.

"Not likely. But it ain't a bear."

"How do you know?"

"Bears ain't sneaky. Old Bruno, for instance. He generally comes crashing right up to the mule pen to let you know he's paying a call."

"Then what—"

A sudden, loud knock on the cabin door answered Olivia's question. Her immediate relief that the visitor wasn't a bear faded before misgivings of who would be traveling this isolated valley at night.

Ellen started for the door.

"No," Olivia told her. "I'll do it."

"Wait." Katy opened a bin beside the fireplace and took out a revolver. This cabin, Olivia noted with some wonder, was an arsenal.

"Take this." Katy handed her the pistol. "And look tough. I'm right behind you with a shotgun."

The door rattled with another loud knock. Olivia opened it. The man on the other side might as well have been a bear; he was built like one. When he saw her, his beefy face split in a grin.

"Well, hello, missus. Didn't expect to find no one like you out here. Your man in?"

Olivia wished very much that her man—or rather, the man of the house—was in. "Well, uh, no, not right now." Out of the corner of her eye she saw Katy move into sight of their visitor. "But he'll be back anytime."

"Well, I'll bet he will. If I had a woman as looked like you, ma'am, I surely wouldn't leave her by her lonesome in a spot like this."

"He's close, really. Very close. He would . . . uh . . . probably hear me if I called him."

"Well, that's fine. Is this your little girl?" His gaze shifted to Katy, who returned his stare with one of her own. "You know how to use that shotgun, missy? I'd hate to see it go off by accident."

"If it went off," Katy assured him grimly, "it wouldn't be by accident."

"Well, now, I can see where you'd want to be careful, but me and my partner are just honest prospectors. We was headed down to Elkhorn, but there's a big slide across the valley where it narrows up. We'd go around the mountain and down Dead Man's Gulch, but that's a mighty hard trail, and my partner's got a bum leg. Got kicked by a horse about a week back."

"Of course you must come in," Olivia said, overriding Katy's warning frown. To refuse the men shelter would be unthinkable with one of them hurt and the moist, heavy feel of the air promising snow before morning.

"Thank'ee, ma'am. I'm Jeb. Jebediah Crowe. And that skinny fella over there's Slim McNab. Just let me help ol' Slim off his horse. If that's coffee brewing, it surely would feel good in our cold stomachs."

More than coffee went into the two prospectors' stomachs. When Olivia offered them the leftover corned-beef hash and biscuits, they attacked it with relish and declared her the best cook in the whole of Montana.

"They must not have eaten in a while," Ellen whispered to Katy just loudly enough for Olivia to hear.

After the men had eaten, Olivia looked at Slim's leg. The injury had started out as a simple fracture, but the leg had been unattended for a week. The tissues around the bone were badly swollen, and the bone ends had moved far out of place. Setting it was a chore that made Olivia wish for once that she had a man's brute strength.

Slim doused himself with a full bottle of whiskey that Jeb brought in from their saddlebags. Jeb polished off another bottle for good measure. The big man seemed scarcely affected by the prodigious amount of liquor that disappeared down his gullet, and he had no trouble restraining a screeching Slim as Olivia set the bone.

"You're better'n most sawbones," Jeb commented when the job was done. Slim snoozed before the fire in a drunken stupor, his leg neatly splinted and compresses applied to the inflamed flesh. "But I guess a woman needs to be a jack-of-all-trades out here, just like a man. I swear, though, ma'am, a young, pretty thing like you don't look old enough to have birthed those two fine girls of yours."

Olivia was about to clear up the man's misconception that she was the girls' mother when Katy interrupted. "She's our stepma. And our pa's the jealous type, and mean into the bargain. I wouldn't want to be here when he comes back, if I were you."

"Well, now, missy. Slim and me don't mean no harm, and we cain't go nowheres with Slim laid up and the only decent trail to Elkhorn closed."

"Of course you can't go anywhere," Olivia said, submitting to Katy's lie. Perhaps it was safer, after all, to have these men think she was the wife of a dangerously jealous husband. "You're welcome to take shelter here for as long as you need to."

Jeb smiled, revealing an incomplete set of tobacco-stained teeth. "That's mighty nice o'you, ma'am. I can see you have your hands full with these here girls. That one's got a mouth on her, hasn't she."

"Yes, she does." Olivia raised a brow at Katy, who sighed dramatically.

"Oh, Ma!"

When all was settled for the night, the two men took the twins' cots in the loft and Katy and Ellen moved into the downstairs bed with Olivia. Ellen complained of the crowding, but Katy seemed satisfied with the arrangement.

"At least they can't sneak down that ladder without us hearing them," Katy said. "And if they're planning to make trouble, they'll get more than what they bargained for." She picked up her pillow to reveal the .44-caliber revolver that she had earlier forced into Olivia's hand.

"Katy! You're not sleeping with a gun under your pillow," Olivia whispered. "You'll blow our heads off."

"No I won't." Once again the girl's face took on that unchildlike mien, a hard maturity that made Olivia feel as though Katy, not herself, were the adult here. "This isn't the first time I've slept with a gun under my pillow, and I figure it won't be the last."

For once Ellen didn't chide her sister for her hoydenish attitude. Olivia followed her example and stayed silent, hoping that Katy was taking too dim a view of their guests.

"I don't really believe they mean any harm," Olivia ventured as they scrunched together in search of a comfortable position.

"I guess a female from Back East wouldn't know," Katy said condescendingly. "But there's generally two types of fellows that roam this far up in the mountains. There's those runnin' from the law, and there's those that have just plain been thrown outta every town they come to 'cause they're skunks. Otherwise they'd be goin' where the mining's easier and the weather's warmer."

Olivia wondered which one of those crude categories Gabriel Danaher fell into.

"I wish Pa would come home," Ellen said in a small voice.

Olivia also wished that Gabriel Danaher would come home. She'd much rather deal with the skunk she knew than the strange skunks in the loft.

The next morning, Jebediah and Slim attacked Ellen's biscuits and gravy like wolves. A triple batch of biscuits had disappeared down the gullets of the two prospectors before Olivia and the girls sat down at the table, and half the next batch vanished as well. There was scarcely enough left for the three of them, but as Ellen prepared to make a fifth batch, Olivia told her not to bother. She had very little appetite after lying awake all night listening for sounds from the loft. The two girls could divide her share and she would be very comfortable with just coffee.

Slim burped an apology as he pushed back his stool and patted his stomach. "Don't mean to eat you outta house and home, ma'am, but it's been a long time since I had a decent meal."

Olivia was surprised the two men could eat at all considering the volume of whiskey they had consumed the night before. "How does your leg feel this morning, Mr. McNab?"

"Just call me Slim, ma'am. The leg hurts a bit, but a couple'a shots o' whiskey will fix me right up. I'm mighty grateful to ya for your trouble."

"Yes'm," Jeb echoed. "We sure do appreciate your kindness. We was talkin' last night that we'd be ungrateful sonsofbitches if we left a pretty gal like you here alone with these two little girls and tried to make it down Dead Man's Gulch, even though the weather looks to be clearin' and Slim's got his leg fixed nice and proper. So we decided to stay and take care of you ladies until your husband comes back." He gave Olivia a grin that told her he didn't really believe she had a husband close by. No doubt he'd be all too willing to take on Danaher's woman and Danaher's mine if Danaher himself didn't show up to claim them. Or perhaps they were villainous enough to make sure he didn't show up.

"That's very kind of you, but really not necessary."

"Well, now, sweet thing, we think it is. You don't know what kind of scum can be roamin' around these mountains."

She was beginning to learn, Olivia reflected sourly.

"Missy," Slim said, eyeing Ellen's uneaten serving of biscuits and gravy, "if you're not gonna finish that grub, I'd be glad to do the honors."

Jeb's gaze at Olivia was very similar to Slim's covetous stare at Ellen's food. A chill ran down Olivia's spine, and she was suddenly very glad that Katy was so proficient with a shotgun.

Danaher couldn't have picked a better time to return. Olivia didn't hear him ride in, but Katy's eyes brightened and she smiled. "Pa's back." She gave the miners a smirk that told them now they were in trouble.

Olivia followed Katy out the door, their two uneasy-looking guests on her heels. The clearing was empty. Her heart fell. "There's no one here."

"You don't expect him to just walk in when he can see two strange horses in the corral with the mules, do you? He isn't that stupid. He's out there with a gun, waiting to find out what's going on."

Gabriel Danaher behaved very much like a man who was running from someone or something, but right now Olivia didn't care. She would have given a year of her life to see him stride out of the forest right then, with his mocking Irish smile and his barbaric shoulder-length hair blowing in the breeze.

"Pa!" Katy called out. "Ma's got breakfast ready for ya. Ya better come in before these billy goat prospectors eat it all."

"Kid's got a mouth on her," Slim noted. "Someone oughta turn her over a knee and teach her some respect."

"You wanna try it, mister?" Katy challenged.

"Well, I just might, little missy. I think you're pullin' ol' Slim's leg when you say your pa's out here. In fact, I'm beginning to wonder if you have a pa at all."

"Are you accusing us all of lying?" Olivia demanded.

"Well, ma'am, if I was a woman out here alone with two pretty little girls, for whatever reason, I figger I wouldn't want just any fella that drifts by to know I didn't have a husband to protect me. No sir."

"I can assure you that the girls have a father, and he's not a man whose anger should be taken lightly."

Jeb had been listening with his mouth lifted in a skeptical smile. Now he joined in. "That's just fine, ma'am. 'Cause if you didn't have a claim staked on you—well, females is scarce in this country around here, and you'd have all sorts of fellas up here gawkin' and makin' pests of themselves and maybe even gettin' greedy and jumpin' claim on that mine over there. Why, Slim and me been lookin' for a good deposit since the start of summer and come up empty-handed. I figger neither one of us would mind settlin' down with a good-lookin' woman and a load of silver just waitin' for someone to dig it out."

"This load of silver's waiting only for me, lads." Gabe was suddenly there, as though he'd materialized out of thin air instead of walked out of the forest. He cradled a rifle in one arm. "The mine's claimed, and so is the woman."

The prospectors took Gabe's measure and apparently didn't like what they saw. Jeb's mouth turned downward in a sullen droop.

"Didn't mean no harm to your wife and girlies, mister."

" 'Course you didn't." He cast a glance at Olivia, who could have sworn his eyes were actually twinkling. "My *wife* probably told you what a jealous cuss I am. Two sensible gents like you know enough to stay away from another man's woman, and even a dimwit knows that a man's likely to cut off the pecker of anyone touching his daughter. Fathers aren't really reasonable where their daughters are concerned."

Slim turned pale, and Olivia didn't think it was because his leg pained him. She suppressed a smile. It was very, very good to have Danaher back.

Jeb didn't look quite as intimidated as his partner. "We wasn't about to touch the little girls, mister. Or the woman neither. We just stopped here 'cause the trail down Thunder Creek is closed, and Slim had a leg that was broke."

"Trail's still closed. I was just down the way."

"We was headed into Elkhorn for supplies—ain't got much left but a bit of bacon and a sack of beans. 'Preciate your wife offering us a place till the trail opens."

Olivia was beginning to regret her largesse. Danaher plainly trusted the two men no more than Katy did, and an eyebrow cocked in her direction let her know he wasn't pleased. But surely there wouldn't be any trouble now that he was here.

"My wife just can't turn away people in need. Katy, Longshot and Ears are in the trees over there. Go fetch them in. Ears is packing an elk and he doesn't like it much, so be careful." He eyed Jeb and Slim, who cautiously eyed him back. "If I'd known we had company, I would've shot two."

Jeb squinted closely at Danaher. "Ain't I seen you somewheres?"

"I don't think so."

"I know your face." He chuckled, sounding rather like a bear grunting. "Y'ain't got it plastered on no wanted posters, have ya?"

Danaher's face was impassive. "Not as far as I know."

"Well, I seen ya somewheres."

"I don't think so. If I'd seen you, I'd know you. A man your size is hard to forget."

Jeb swelled with pride. "That's true, ain't it?"

The day did not improve as it got older. If Danaher didn't trust their guests, he did seem to enjoy the corner Olivia had backed herself into by taking shelter behind their "marriage." Olivia didn't appreciate the provoking sense of humor that prompted her "husband" to take advantage of the situation. At noontime when Olivia brought his dinner out to where he was butchering the elk, he held his arms wide and smilingly demanded a wifely kiss.

"Come on, my lass. You'll have to do the kissing. If I weren't a mess of blood and bone, I'd grab you and show how much I missed my pretty wife."

Not having any connubial experience, Olivia wasn't sure if a real wife might have told her husband to forget his silly demands and get back to work. Probably not. A wife was supposed to be respectful and obedient to her husband, even if the husband was acting like a jackass.

Jeb looked up from where he was chopping firewood, and nearby, Slim paused in his whittling. Katy stopped stacking the wood and stared, frowning.

"Well, sweetheart." Danaher's eyes crinkled in a fan of laugh lines. "Aren't you going to show me how much you missed me?"

Gingerly Olivia leaned forward and pecked him on the cheek. His three-day growth of beard was rough on her lips, and he smelled of pine, wood smoke, and the fresh Montana wind. Her heart jumped as he breathed suddenly into her ear. "I can see you don't know what a wifely kiss is, Doc."

She pulled back abruptly. "Eat your dinner and get back to work, *husband.*"

He smiled a leprechaun's smile. "Yes, ma'am."

Supper that night was elk steaks and sweet potatoes from Ellen's vegetable cellar. Ellen declared it was her welcome-home dinner for her father, her tone making it clear that the sugar-glazed potatoes, flame-charred steaks, fried bread, and wild blackberry pie was her doing entirely.

"Little Ellen's the best cook in Montana," Danaher boasted. "Takes after her mother."

"My *real* mother," Ellen clarified.

Olivia saw Ellen's triumphant gaze slide her way. Both twins had been treating her like a piece of overripe garbage since she had given their father his little innocent peck on the cheek. The truce they had forged to present a united front to Jebediah and Slim was apparently only a temporary one. Now that their father was back, the lines of war had been drawn once again.

The evening was a short one, a blessing for which Olivia was grateful. The cabin was filled with negative tension, all directed toward her. Jeb and Slim cast furtive looks her way, and their eyes held an unpleasant promise that she didn't want to think about. She'd seen hungry men look at food that way. Montana certainly must be short on women if a plain spinster such as herself was regarded as a choice cutlet worth slavering over.

The twins' regard wasn't much more pleasant. They were marginally polite only because their father demanded it. Olivia supposed their hostility had peaked so sharply because she now posed as Danaher's wife, and Danaher seemed to take great delight in small gestures of husbandly affection such as an arm around her waist or holding her hand—only because he knew it embarrassed her. He did seem very fond of embarrassing her. Knowing their father's twisted sense of drollery, the twins should have understood, especially since it was Katy who had first shackled her with this fantasy wifehood.

But then, Olivia reflected, at twelve years of age, emotions are unlikely to be reined in by reason. Sometimes at the ripe age of twenty-six emotions were just as unruly.

Nevertheless, Olivia was grateful to the cold, snowy evening that sent them all early to the warmth of their blankets. Jeb and Slim climbed the ladder to the loft, comforted by a bottle of Danaher's Irish whiskey. Katy and Ellen settled into pallets by the fireplace, both casting scorching looks at Olivia as Danaher snuffed the last of the lamps and headed toward the curtained bed.

"Coming to bed, Olivia?" In the darkness his voice was laced with a mockery that was meant for her ears only. Dread knotted her stomach. She'd almost forgotten that as Danaher's "wife," she would be expected by the two men upstairs to share her husband's bed. If she didn't they would no doubt consider her fair game to be hauled into theirs. She'd shared Danaher's bed before, tied to the bedstead like a trussed hen, and the whole night Danaher's long body had curled around hers. The whole night she'd lain awake wondering at her response to the most improper situation. The whole night she'd had to fight, not him—for if he had decided to take more ardent advantage of her, she couldn't have fought him—but herself. Her own primitive femininity had proved a more dangerous adversary than Olivia could have ever guessed.

And now she had to sleep with Danaher again and act as though it were a normal thing for her to do. She could almost feel voracious eyes peering down from the darkness of the loft. Life is subject to change without notice, her father had once warned her. How right he had been. If someone had told her a month ago that she would stray so far from the paths of propriety, she would have laughed and called the doomsayer a jester.

"Olivia, you're going to catch cold if you stand there long enough."

Olivia suddenly hated the rustic cabin that had only a meager fireplace for heat, the mountains that had made it impossible for her to get home, and Danaher, that irritating, irreverent, disrespectful transplanted Irish troublemaker.

A white ghostly apparition suddenly flew out of the darkness toward her. Olivia ducked.

"Your nightdress," Danaher said softly. "You can go behind the curtain to change, if you like. I'm going to put more wood on the fire."

Olivia sighed and picked up the nightdress. It may have been a short evening, but it was going to be a very long night.

By the time Gabe climbed into the bed behind the curtain, Olivia was securely cocooned in Minnie's old nightdress with the buttons done up to her chin. He couldn't see the buttons in the dark behind the curtain, but he knew there wasn't a one of them unfastened, because he knew Olivia. Not only was the nightdress locked up tight, but the covers were pulled around her like a suit of armor.

The sheets on the bed were as cold as the night air, and on this night, the air was very cold. He was glad he had another body in bed to pump out warmth. Glad for more than just the warmth, if he were honest about it. He enjoyed teasing Olivia because she was so easy to ruffle, but there was a grain of truth in his blarney. Perhaps that grain of truth was why she riled so easily. He didn't think of Olivia as plain anymore. He'd been blind to ever think she was drab. Her smile might not be sweetly feminine, but it had a distinctive lift to it that made him want to smile in return whenever he saw it. Her eyes had snap and energy, and her hair had highlights of red and gold that made him think of a glossy chestnut mare he'd once owned. That female had been fractious as well. She'd tossed him off three times before he got the hang of gentling her. If he put his mind to it, he wondered, could he gentle this one as well?

Not that he wanted to. Saint Patrick and his sainted mother knew he didn't have time or use for a woman right now. He had a job to do, and there were bounty hunters and lawmen aplenty who would cut him down before he could do it—if they were lucky enough to find him in this remote spot or if he were dumb enough to place himself in their path. For Minnie's memory he had a vow of vengeance to fulfill, and for his own sake a charge of murder to disprove. Soon he'd have enough money to ensure the girls' future no matter what happened to him. Then he could ride down from these mountains and confront Ace Candliss. With Gabe's pistol stuck up his nose, Ace would likely see the advantage of telling the truth about what he and his brother had done on that cursed day two years ago. Then, if the law refused to take care of the man, Gabe would do the job.

But first he had to scratch enough money from this mine to give the girls the good life they deserved—and to make sure they were never prey to men like the Candliss brothers. Money could do that. Stumbling across this rich silver deposit had been a piece of true Irish luck.

Irish luck—he would need more than his share of it to live through a confrontation with Candliss and his pet lawmen. But if he did survive, maybe then he could think about a woman. But that woman certainly wouldn't be a spinster from Back East whose idea of cologne was disinfectant, who didn't mind sewing up a man's gut but blanched at the sight of a freshly killed deer, whose idea of fresh-baked biscuits was charcoaled bricks.

But, damn, the woman was warm lying next to him, and even as she lay in his bed stiff as a stick he could hear the beat of her heart. It was a warm heart, for all that she tried to be a clinical scientist. It was a heart that softened for children and horses and grubby devils like the men upstairs who were down on their luck.

He tugged and tucked the covers until they were wrapped in the same cocoon—for warmth, he told himself, though he knew that he lied. He wanted to be next to her, with her warm skin and gentle curves. She didn't smell like carbolic tonight; she smelled of wood smoke and warm flannel and woman—a heady perfume.

She tried to escape toward the edge of the bed when he moved closer, but the tightly wrapped bedclothes held her fast.

"It's all right," he whispered in her ear. Why had he not noticed before that her ears were so small and dainty—like the rest of her? "We're married, remember?"

"Yes." Her voice held a finely honed edge, even in a whisper. "And it would be a pity if your wife were startled out of a nightmare and just happened to land a few telling blows to anatomically sensitive areas before she came to her senses."

He could hardly suppress a chuckle. "Ever the sweet tongue you have, lass."

"Shouldn't you be listening for what our dubious guests are doing rather than harassing me? They might take it into their minds to bother the twins."

"Nothing is going to move in this cabin tonight without me knowing it. Besides, if either of those jackasses picked on Katy or Ellen, he'd likely get more than he bargained for."

"They're just children."

"Doc, it's not Katy and Ellen those two want. It's you."

"They might get more than they bargained for if they bothered me, as well."

"Right they would. They'd get me all over them."

She stiffened when he pulled the covers more tightly around her shoulders, but relaxed when he did nothing more. His body wanted to do a good deal more, for he was definitely rising to the occasion. He wished the occasion were what his body thought it was.

The two drifters in the loft weren't the only ones who looked at Olivia Baron and saw one hell of a tempting woman.

Chapter 10

*B*y the time dawn paled the sky, Gabe felt as though his veins were running with lead. In spite of his reassurances to Olivia, he hadn't dared to sleep while Jeb and Slim were in the cabin. He had lain awake the whole night listening to Olivia's even breathing and feeling the warmth of her body next to his. He deserved to be sainted for keeping his hand from nestling in the smooth indentation of her waist or caressing the soft swell of her breast. He had noted with amusement that her shoulders were squared even in her sleep, and with something other than amusement he had inhaled the fragrance of her skin and the fan of silky hair that covered the pillow.

Perhaps if he had stayed awake only to keep guard, he wouldn't be so tired, but resisting temptation was hard work. He wasn't a saint, after all. Far from it. And mortal man could only resist so much.

Olivia's eyes blinked open, then closed. With a childlike murmur she turned her face into the pillow and sighed. Gabe grinned and landed a light slap on the softly rounded behind that had been tempting him all night.

"Mmmmrph?"

"Wake up, my love."

"Arrrrgh!"

"Don't you know that it's the wife's job to rise on such a cold morning to put more wood on the fire and start the coffee brewing."

She opened one eye and regarded him balefully. "I'm not a wife."

"You'd best convince those two upstairs that you are."

"You're a cruel man, Mr. Danaher. I'm beginning to think it's a good thing you live so far from civilization."

"There's wood piled by the fireplace."

"Katy's closer. She's tough."

"She's still sleeping."

"Then convince our guests that you're an unusually considerate husband by doing the chore yourself."

"They'd never believe it, Doc. They're better judges of character than that."

"Posh!"

In the end it was Olivia who built up the fire and made the coffee, not because she was so anxious to play her role, Gabe suspected, but because she rolled over to go back to sleep and felt what had been growing between them—a reaction Gabe was helpless to restrain. That part of his anatomy simply had a mind of its own. The sight of her bending over the fire to fill the coffeepot didn't help to curtail his discomfort. He needed to go to Elkhorn and relieve himself on some willing whore. He'd been without a woman too long; that was why he was standing to attention every time Olivia Baron smiled or frowned or, God help him, bent over the fire as she was doing right then. The pressure of frustration made him long to take something or someone apart with his bare hands.

Before the morning was out, he nearly got his wish.

Olivia made a passable batch of griddle cakes and bacon for breakfast, and Jeb and Slim watched her every move as she hovered between the griddle and the table. The meal was quiet but intense with the drifters silently lusting and the twins sulking. Ellen was obviously annoyed to be upstaged as the cook—even though the bacon was slightly singed and the griddle cakes were somewhat soggy in the middle, sins that Ellen would never commit. Katy had her nose out of joint for who knew what reason. Gabe was beginning to think that twelve-year-old girls were beyond anyone's understanding. Jeb and Slim were easy enough to understand. They were suffering from the same disease that Gabe was. But Gabe didn't trust them to behave quite as much as he trusted himself.

After the meal, Jeb gave a mighty belch that broke the tension. "I been thinkin'."

Probably an unaccustomed feat, Gabe reflected.

"Slim and I was talkin' about your woman last night. Out here, ya know, females are as scarce as owls' tits, and it only stands to reason that what females there are oughta go to those what can keep 'em."

"An interesting notion," Gabe admitted.

"Well, now, I coulda run off with the woman when we first came, but bein' the sorta fella that likes to play straight up, I figgered I should give you a chance to keep her."

"Seems fair."

Gabe saw Olivia pause in a trip from the griddle to the table. Her cheeks were a rosy red, and he guessed it wasn't from the fire. The twins were both stony-faced.

"So," Jeb continued. "Fair's fair. I figger we can wrestle for her. If Slim didn't have that bum leg, I'd wrestle him, then you could take on the winner. But Slim ain't in no shape to do right by a woman, so for now it's just you and me. Maybe later I'll have to fight ol' Slim for her."

"That sure you're going to win?"

Jeb just grinned.

"Finish your hotcakes, then, and we'll get to it."

Jeb slapped the table. "You're a good man, Danaher. It's a shame I'm gonna have to break you in two."

"Yeah," Gabe agreed. "That would be a shame."

Olivia pulled Gabe aside as they all rose from the table.

"Say your good-byes now, missus," Jeb advised. "There might not be much left to say good-bye to after I'm done. But don't worry. I'll make you fergit him soon enough."

Gabe allowed Olivia to pull him into a corner as Jeb and Slim went out the door. "Go up into the loft," he ordered the twins. "Katy, take the shotgun. If anything happens, you know what to do. I'm holding you responsible for Ellen and Olivia's safety."

"Yes, Pa." She grimaced. "Can't we watch?"

"Go."

Olivia shook his arm to get his attention. "Are you insane? That man is a gorilla! He'll tear you into pieces so small I won't be able to stitch you back together!"

Gabe gave her an innocent smile. "Don't you think you're worth fighting over?"

"I'm not an object prize to be awarded to the strongest! And even if I were, that man must weigh half again what you do. Why didn't you just tell him I wasn't up for bid?"

"I doubt he'd have listened."

"Then send him on his way!"

"You were the one who invited them to stay in the first place."

"Oh for heaven's sake, Danaher, stop being contrary! Just tell the man I'm not a negotiable item and don't fight."

Danaher was flattered that she was so concerned. Could it be that a New York City sophisticate could be the least interested in an Irish barbarian? More likely she feared to have herself and the twins left unprotected if he got his brains bashed out on a rock.

"Don't worry, Doc. I'll win. He may be a gorilla, but I'm not a runt myself, and unless I miss my guess, I've got speed on him."

Fists on her hips, she looked angry and worried at the same time. "What if you miss your guess and lose?"

"Then Katy will make sure those drifters leave politely, right after they've dug a hole to put me in."

"You're impossible!"

"It comes with being Irish, or so I've always been told."

"Well, if you get broken in two, my fee to put you back together is going to cost you more than you make at this little mine."

"Is it, now?"

"It is!"

He laughed. "You're a cantankerous female. How about a kiss to send me into battle?"

"Be serious! This is no time for your antics."

"I am serious. I'd wait until after my victory, but since you're so convinced that I'm soon to be a red smear on the ground, I think I'll get a taste of the prize before I fight."

Her mouth opened in surprise as he came down upon it. She didn't fight. Perhaps because she was so shocked, or because she was just as curious as he about how this kiss would be.

It was delicious, lips soft and giving, mouth sweet, yielding. Heat engorged his body as he pulled her closer, fitting her to him like a piece of a puzzle sliding into place beside its mate. Her breasts and belly burned holes in his self-control, and his hands slipped to her buttocks to press her closer to the center of his desire.

Suddenly she twisted in his grasp. The spell was broken.

"Mr. Danaher!"

It took a moment for him to get his heart and breathing under control, and for all her protestation, he noticed that her pulse raced, fluttering like a butterfly under his hand. "That was definitely worth fighting for, Doc."

Her color rose even higher. "You're fighting for no such thing! You shouldn't be fighting at all, you nincompoop!"

"Time to fight the gorilla. Fetch that can of bacon grease and come along outside."

"Damn you, Danaher!"

Fuming, Olivia had no choice but to do as she was bade, fear, anger, and humiliation washing over her in successive tides. Danaher was every bit as bad as Jebediah. They both belonged back in the Stone Age—simpleminded, lecherous cavemen. They should be dragging their knuckles and swinging clubs. Not that she was much better, conscience reminded Olivia. She hadn't fought Danaher's kiss nearly as hard as she ought.

She snatched the can of bacon grease off the shelf. Curse Danaher anyway! He was going to get himself maimed or killed, and Olivia was going to be forced to watch. Worse, she had no doubt that bloodthirsty little Katy would blast Jeb to smithereens with the shotgun, an invaluable experience for a growing young lady of tender years, and then Olivia and the twins would be left the task of picking up Danaher's pieces and putting them back together again, if possible. Like Humpty Dumpty.

Fear for Danaher suddenly overwhelmed all other emotion. It was unbearable that he might get hurt or even killed defending her, for that was exactly what he was doing. Never before in her life had she needed defending. It was a terrible burden to have to depend on someone else's strength rather than your own.

Jeb and Danaher shucked their shirts and boots and greased their bare chests and arms with the bacon grease—protection from both the cold and an opponent's grip. They faced each other in a sunny area of the clearing where the snow had melted and the ground was covered with dead grass and pine needles. Crouching, they grinned, both of them like idiot schoolboys, Olivia thought. Then they circled, eyes narrowed, tension evident in the bunch of shoulders and the clenching and unclenching of fists. The circling seemed to Olivia to go on forever. It ended abruptly when Jebediah sprang.

Danaher easily stepped aside and left the bigger man with empty arms. Jeb turned and charged again, like a bull, his head lowered. Danaher smiled and stepped aside again.

"Goddammit! Stand still and fight!"

"In my own good time, my boyo."

"I'd hate to say you was chicken, Danaher."

"I'd hate to say you look damned ugly half-naked."

Jeb growled and launched himself forward once again. This time Danaher didn't avoid the rush. He stuck out a leg and tripped his attacker, then pounced on the downed man. They crashed to the ground with a bone-jarring thud. Each grappling for a good grip on the other, within seconds they were coated in enough pine needles to make them look like porcupines rolling in the dirt.

Until now, Slim had looked on impassively. Now he shouted encouragement. "Go git 'im. Git your thumbs into his windpipe."

To whom he shouted was uncertain. Probably, Olivia thought, the little man would be satisfied whoever won, just so enough blood was spilled.

The porcupines stopped their rolling. Jeb struggled to free himself from the vicious lock Danaher held on his throat. He flopped like a fish, his face growing redder and redder. Danaher strained as well. Every muscle and sinew stood out in bold relief. He made a brutal, beautiful picture—a panther compared to Jeb's bear.

Olivia clenched her fists at her sides. Danaher was going to win after all. Thank the Lord! He was going to survive so she could kill him for acting like an idiot.

Then Jeb reached both beefy arms over his head and clasped his hands around the back of Danaher's neck. He forced Danaher's head down to crash against his own thick skull—once, twice, three times. Danaher lost his hold. Jeb turned around and was on him in a flash. He pinned him to the ground with his great bulk, sausagelike fingers squeezing his throat.

Olivia's hand flew to her throat in sympathy for Danaher's ordeal. Frantic, she considered running for Katy and the shotgun to put an end to this travesty of a contest, then noticed to her dismay that Slim wore a pistol.

Danaher had been so sure of victory, the cocky fool. Had speed on Jeb, did he? The arrogant, overconfident jackass! What could she do? What in hot, burning Hades could she do?

Danaher stopped trying to pry Jeb's hands from his throat and punched his fingers up toward his assailant's eyes. Jeb screeched and let go, rolling back onto the ground clutching his face.

"Oh my God!" Olivia put her face into her hands. Sometime in the past days she had begun to think of Danaher as an essentially gentle man, but the Danaher of this moment, greased like a heathen warrior, nose running blood, eyes glittering in a battered face, was someone she didn't know. He fought like an animal. Both men did. Untamed, brutal, savage animals.

What had she expected? Olivia asked herself cynically. The Marquis of Queensbury rules? This was wild Montana, not New York, and this contest was not for a winner's purse or a championship or honor; it was for her.

She lifted her face and opened her eyes. Danaher was atop his opponent, using Jeb's ears as handles and banging the man's head against the ground. A man without Jeb's thick skull would have passed out. Jeb only grunted. He heaved up like a human earthquake. Danaher rolled off but managed to get his arm wrapped around Jeb's neck and his knee lodged in the small of his back. For a moment both men were very still.

"I can break your back, boyo."

Jeb grunted agreement.

"Give in?"

"Hell yes," Jeb croaked.

Danaher immediately released him. Olivia feared Jeb would take advantage to turn and fight again, but he didn't.

"You're a better man than I figgered, Danaher."

"And you're a better man than I figured. You almost had me a couple of times."

"Damn right I did. You got lucky." He tugged on his ears and grimaced admiringly. "And you got a mean streak a mile long."

The two of them strolled into the cabin as though they'd not been near killing each other minutes earlier. Olivia stared after them in amazement. Slim came up to her and tipped his hat.

"Too bad I got this here bum leg, ma'am. Your man's a tough one, but I'd fight him. You're a fine-looking female, a passable cook, and you've got a talent at patchin' a man together."

Slim tipped his hat again and followed the other two men into the cabin. Olivia heard the twins clamber down from the loft, their voices an excited counterpoint to the men's laughter. She blew out a whuff of disgust. Montana wasn't simply a wild and far-off land; it was a different world altogether.

According to their own rough style of honor, Jeb and Slim were much better behaved after Gabe won the wrestling match. Their glances in Olivia's direction became wistful instead of lustful. The tension eased. The two prospectors helped out with chores, and Gabe went back to the mine.

Ellen couldn't understand what all the fuss had been about. The reason for the morning's fight eluded her. She couldn't imagine why Jebediah wanted Olivia in the first place. What would any man want with her? She was ignorant in most matters of keeping house, and her cooking skills were crude at best. To Olivia, baking a batch of acceptable biscuits and frying griddle cakes that were done all the way through was a major accomplishment. She couldn't steal an egg from under a hen without getting pecked, she couldn't clean a squirrel or skin a rabbit. What good was she to a man?

Being a doctor was a fine thing, Ellen supposed, but it really wasn't the sort of thing that a man sought in a woman.

In a way Ellen felt sorry for Olivia. As the day warmed to an unseasonable temperature and rivulets started to run from beneath the snowpack, she noted that the woman repeatedly looked down the valley of Thunder Creek toward the unseen place where the stream tumbled into Elkhorn Creek and from there ran the miles down to Elkhorn town. Her expression was both worried and hopeful. Probably she longed for her friends and servants and fancy carriages and people exclaiming about her because she was a doctor. She hated the peaceful little clearing and the cabin that Ellen loved. She probably hated all of them as well. The foolish woman was so wrapped up in wanting to get back to her fancy life that she couldn't even see what a fine man Ellen's father was. If she ever learned he was wanted by the law, she would probably jump to turn him in.

Not that Ellen wanted Olivia to become attached to her father. Heavens no. Ellen and Katy and their pa were doing just fine with only the three of them. Still, a snooty lady like Olivia Baron looking down her nose at them was irritating. All the men in the cabin treating Olivia as if she were something special—something to fight over. That was even more irritating.

Ellen paused in her sweeping and looked out the window. The *thuk, thuk* of Jeb's ax was as regular as the beat of a heart, and Katy was busy stacking the firewood that flew off the chopping block. Nearby, Slim sat on a tree stump and whittled a piece of wood, his splinted leg stretched out in front of him. Katy's shotgun was propped conspicuously by the stacked firewood. Katy didn't trust the two prospectors, in spite of Pa's demonstrating to Jeb that he could beat the daylights out of him. Or maybe Katy just liked to show everyone how tough she was. That was more likely.

Pa was still in the mine, even though the sun was almost ready to drop behind Thunder Ridge. Dealing with the trouble Olivia had caused had lost him valuable time in the tunnel. Yet Pa still looked at Olivia with that warm light in his eye. Katy had made a mistake in making up the story that Olivia was Pa's wife. Their father enjoyed his part in the story much too much.

Ellen put away the broom and knelt by the fireplace to shovel out the ashes. She heard Olivia sigh from where she bent over a recipe at the table. The woman had a sigh that could fill a whole room at times—especially when she was trying to cook. She had volunteered to make supper tonight, since Ellen was busy cleaning the cabin and doing laundry. Ellen didn't credit her with thoughtfulness, though. No doubt the snooty woman wanted to show everyone that she'd become a passable cook. Ellen suspected that some of the food prepared by herself over the last couple of days had been credited to Olivia, and of course the old witch hadn't bothered to make sure that credit was given where it was deserved.

With a grimace of disgust, Ellen thrust the shovel into the pile of ashes below the grate. The energy of her attack sent white swirling into the air to settle everywhere but on the shovel. The fire had burned hot the night before, leaving a pile of fine white ash among the dirty gray—ash almost as fine and white as powder.

Ellen suddenly knew how she could reveal Olivia Baron for what she was.

Olivia's amazement at the sudden change in masculine attitudes had softened over the day from astonishment to bemusement. As they sat down to the supper she had prepared, Jeb and Slim were on their best behavior. Along with Gabe, they had sluiced themselves in the icy wash water in back of the cabin. Faces clean and hair slicked back, they sat at the table with hearty appetites lighting their faces. If a bit of wariness lingered in Gabe's eyes, the two prospectors apparently didn't note it, for they were bluff and hearty as if the three of them were longtime friends.

Katy, of course, didn't bother to hide her suspicious aversion to the two. If her father weren't at the table, no doubt she'd have her shotgun propped against her stool. Ellen was out of sorts for reasons Olivia couldn't begin to fathom. The girl had been sulky all day.

Gabe was the person Olivia's eyes and mind kept returning to, however. He'd spent all day in the mine, which saved her the trouble of not speaking to him. She was still angry about the fight—the brutality, childishness, and uselessness of it. Not to mention the sheer audacity of fighting for the possession of *her*, as if she were a heifer on the auction block.

She was angrier still about the kiss. Her mind had come back to it time and again all day, reliving every humiliating moment of it. Humiliating, disgraceful, and . . . intriguing, inspiring a wild mix of emotions. She had been a party to that kiss in spite of herself; in some contrary way, she'd enjoyed it. She was an idiot, and Danaher was an even greater idiot, kissing her then marching out to slay the dragon like some legendary knight. He could have been seriously injured, maimed, even killed. He could have told Jeb that Olivia was fair game and let her defend herself. But he hadn't. For all his outrageous conduct, hidden deeply—very deeply—within Gabriel Danaher was a spark of chivalry. Danaher would probably be the last to admit it was there, but it *was* there. And its existence made it impossible for Olivia to get too angry with him for his horde of offenses.

"What do we have here?" Gabe took the plate Olivia handed him and inhaled. "Rabbit stew?"

"Katy got a couple of rabbits this afternoon."

"Hit 'em dead on the noggin with a slingshot," Katy elaborated. "One stone for each rabbit."

"Good shootin'," Slim said. "Never used a slingshot, myself. Mebbe you could show me."

The struggle between pride and her dislike for Slim played across Katy's face. "Mebbe."

"Good stew." Gabe raised one brow. "You make it, Olivia?"

"Yes, I did. Don't sound so surprised."

"Yer a right good cook, ma'am," Jeb commented. "It's fine to marry up with a good-lookin' woman, but if she cain't cook . . ." He ended with a rude snort.

"My feelings exactly." Gabe's smile seemed innocent, but Olivia could detect the hint of devilry there. "A woman's place is in the kitchen! Always has been. Always will be."

Olivia arched a brow that promised revenge for that remark.

"A woman's got a good place in bed," Slim reminded him with a lewd chuckle.

"Watch yer manners, Slim." Jeb frowned indignantly. "There's young'uns here."

"They ain't so young that they don't know what's what. Hell, my ma married up when she was thirteen."

"Your ma warn't married at all, if'n my guess is right."

"You got no call to say that."

"Just my guess." Jeb reached for a biscuit. "These look good. Yaller and brown on top like I like 'em."

"They do look good." Gabe took two. "There's nothing like a good biscuit. When I was courting Olivia, I told her: Ollie, lass, I don't care if you can't read or write or only bathe once a month, but you gotta make good biscuits. She was so taken with me that she went right out and learned."

Jeb wrinkled his brow. "Once a month seems like a lotta bathin'."

Gabe bit into his first biscuit and chewed with enthusiasm. His expression froze. The bronze of his face paled to fishbelly white.

Olivia saw Ellen smile slightly, and a pang of dread chased away her half-amused anger at Gabe's raillery.

Gabe chewed. His mouth pulled up in a valiant half-smile. "Good," he choked.

Jeb took half a biscuit in one mighty bite. His eyes widened, his nostrils flared, and his mouth puckered. Morsels of the bread dropped from his mouth to his plate. "What the hell? Jesus! What's in these?"

Olivia felt her face grow red. There was nothing out of the ordinary in the biscuits; she had followed the recipe to the letter, and the last two batches she had made had turned out quite well. Ellen's smile made her terribly suspicious, though. The little imp was trying to look innocent, but she couldn't quite hide that puckish satisfaction. Olivia took a bite of her own biscuit and almost spit it out. It tasted like soot and gritted like sand on her teeth.

"Good," Gabe repeated, smiling weakly. "That's my Ollie."

"Pah!" Jeb threw the rest of his biscuit in the fire. "If these show how much the woman was taken with you, Danaher, I'd'a looked somewhere else for a wife! Christ! She's tryin' to poison us!"

Olivia didn't know quite what to do. Gabe was still trying valiantly to swallow his biscuit, Jeb was trying to get the taste from his mouth by digging around his teeth with his napkin, and Slim was laughing so hard that tears rolled down his cheeks. Ellen and Katy both sat innocently on their stools, reptilian smiles on their little faces. Both of them looked satisfied as a snake who'd just swallowed a fat mouse.

Olivia sighed. How fortunate that she had become a physician. Obviously she wasn't cut out to be a wife and mother.

Ellen was smug. It wasn't every day that she bested Katy in cleverness, but her twin had been frankly admiring at the way she'd managed to substitute white ash from the fireplace for baking powder in the pantry, and thus in Olivia's biscuits. She'd also laced the salt with the stuff, so the dough got a double dose. Yes indeed. Ellen got great pleasure from watching scorn heaped on the snooty Dr. Baron and from seeing her turn red as her faults were displayed for all to see—or, rather, taste.

Now Ellen was paying for her pleasure, however, sleeplessly staring into the night and wondering what form Olivia's revenge would take. Stupidity was not one of the doctor's faults; the woman would know who had sabotaged her attempt at cooking, though she might not know exactly how cleverly it was done. No doubt she would tell Pa, and Pa would turn her over his knee for a couple of good swacks, or worse, sit her down and tell her how all nine children in his family had respected their elders whether or not the elders had deserved it. Knowing her pa, that tale was probably a load of horsefeathers, because her pa didn't respect anything that he hadn't decided deserved his respect.

Still, the lecture would be better than the swacks. Not that a spanking hurt so much, but she was getting a bit old to be turned over her pa's knee. Such a thing was humiliating for a young lady who, after all, was mistress of her household. Besides, Katy was usually the one who misbehaved and had to bear the consequences while Ellen looked on in righteous innocence. Ellen was fairly sure she wouldn't like being on the receiving end of her father's displeasure.

All in all, the imaginings of the night were not restful, and when morning came, Ellen was certain her grim fate came with it.

The morning began with no sign of retribution, however. Jebediah and Slim left before the sun rose, and Pa teased the doctor about her bad cooking chasing the two away. Olivia snapped back something about being able to sleep in the chair again, though Ellen didn't know if she were inviting Pa to take up nightly residence in the chair or if she were claiming the chair for herself. Ellen didn't like the light in her father's eye when he looked at that woman, and the doctor showed as much color as a rouged-up saloon dancer when she glared back. Her pa ought to know better than to get worked up over a Back East city lady, a spinster doctor at that. What more could Ellen do to convince him the woman wasn't worth a second glance?

Still, today Ellen had problems of her own to worry about. Although Olivia hadn't accused her yet, she surely would. Ellen wondered if she could play innocent and lie. Maybe Katy would get swacked instead. Katy was used to it, after all. But then her twin would get credit for the trick, and Katy probably knew less about baking biscuits than Olivia did.

Breakfast was a peaceful meal—and tasty, because Ellen made it. No mention was made of last night's baking catastrophe. Ellen began to think that Olivia was deliberately prolonging the torture by making her wait and wonder. She had thought the woman was more straightforward than that. But maybe not. Ellen had played dirty the night before. Perhaps playing just as dirty was part of Olivia's plan to get even.

By noon Ellen could stand it no more. Her father had gone into the mine after breakfast, and Katy was in the mule corral repairing the gate, so Olivia and she were alone in the cabin. Olivia had been scrubbing the table where they ate with a scrub brush and lye soap, muttering something about her hands never being the same; but now she was gazing out the window as she so often did, to where the valley of Thunder Creek narrowed into a V. A little frown etched a vertical line between her brows, and her eyes had softened with a faraway look. Ellen decided the time was right. They would have it out about last night right here and now.

"Uh . . . Olivia?"

The woman turned, one delicate brow slightly arched.

"Don't . . . don't you get tired of people calling you Dr. Baron all the time? It sounds like they're talking to a man." Ellen wanted to kick herself. That wasn't at all what she meant to say.

"No, actually. Ever since I was your age I wanted to be a doctor, and I had to work very hard to become one. So when people call me doctor, the title sounds good to my ears."

"Oh." Now was her chance. The woman had an expectant look on her face. The time was right. "Why would you rather be a doctor than get married?"

"Because helping sick people makes me feel good. Besides, being a doctor doesn't mean I can't get married. Many women physicians marry and have children."

That wasn't good news at all!

"Ellen, are you perhaps trying to work your way into explaining last night's biscuits?"

Ellen's heart pounded. She knew! Of course she knew. After all, the woman wasn't stupid. "Did you tell Pa?"

"No. Not yet, at least. I thought it might be something that you and I could talk out. What was it you put in them?"

"Ash from the fireplace."

"I thought it might be something like that."

"I put it in the salt and the baking powder. It was really white, so you couldn't have seen it."

"Do you know you could have made all of us sick?"

Ellen hadn't thought of that.

"And you made me look like an absolute fool, but I suppose that was your purpose."

"Uh . . . yes, ma'am."

Unbelievably, Olivia's tightly pressed lips relaxed into a slight smile. "Your father didn't come off too well, either, after bragging about his wife's biscuits."

"No, ma'am." That was also something Ellen hadn't thought of. Her pa had looked pretty silly, and he might not see the humor in that. Could be she was going to get more swacks than she'd thought. "Are you going to tell Pa?"

Olivia gave Ellen a long, pensive look, and the longer she was looked at, the more uncomfortable Ellen became. Maybe the ashes in the biscuits hadn't been such a clever idea after all.

"Throw another log on the fire, Ellen, so we can sit here and keep warm while we talk about this."

Feeling uncharacteristically meek, Ellen did as she was bid and sat herself on a stool in front of the fireplace. Olivia sat in the rocker. "I haven't decided if your father needs to know about this. Maybe it's something we should settle just between the two of us."

What did she want from her? Ellen wondered suspiciously.

"Ellen, why don't you tell me why you've been sulking like a two-year-old and why Katy has been throwing daggers at me with her eyes? I know you girls didn't like the thought of me trying to capture your father's attention—you made that plain enough—and I thought we cleared up that misunderstanding and were quite nicely even for the little tricks you played on me."

Ellen remembered only too well just how Olivia had gotten even. It was a good thing Katy had been tied to the cot; she'd been so full of steam that she might have exploded right through the roof. Ellen hadn't been too happy herself.

"Then when Jeb and Slim showed up, I thought maybe the three of us had reached a truce. Was I wrong?"

The woman wasn't scolding or yelling the way Ellen had envisioned. Her unruffled composure made Ellen feel more than a little guilty.

"Do you want to tell me what this is all about?"

Ellen hung her head. "I didn't see what all the fuss was about," she mumbled. "They were fighting over you! Pa was fighting over you."

"And . . ." Olivia encouraged.

"And it just seemed that everybody thought you were something special, you know. And you aren't . . . well, I mean, maybe you are, but you're not something special to a *man*. At least not if they knew what you were really like—that you were a doctor, and not somebody's wife who can keep a house and cook . . . and things."

Olivia looked as if she was trying not to smile. Ellen couldn't think of anything she'd said that might be amusing.

"So I tried to show them that you really aren't worth all that fuss."

Olivia bit her lip. "I see. You were jealous, so you tried to make me look bad."

"I wasn't jealous! Why would I be jealous?"

"You and Katy are still afraid I'm not going back to Elkhorn, aren't you?"

Ellen didn't know exactly how Katy felt. She only knew how she felt.

Every time her father's attention wandered from her or Katy to Olivia, Ellen's heart hurt, and that seemed to happen more and more often. He had never teased their mother; he teased Olivia. He had smiled a lot with their mother; but he laughed with Olivia, or at her. To Ellen it didn't make any difference. Her father had become different since Olivia had come.

"I saw you kissing Pa."

"When he was butchering the elk? Your father was just teasing to make me mad, Ellen. Knowing him as well as you do, you must know that he enjoys provoking people."

"He's only that way with you," Ellen said. "Besides, I saw you kiss him another time, before the fight. That wasn't teasing."

The woman's face turned a rosy red. "Your father was joking, Ellen. And I . . . well, maybe when you're older, you'll understand. But just because I let him kiss me doesn't mean I'm not going back to Elkhorn."

"You promise to leave?"

Olivia sighed. "Don't you think your father should be able to marry again if he found someone he was happy with?"

That wasn't the statement Ellen had expected. Olivia should be saying something along the lines of she couldn't wait to get back to Elkhorn and then far away to New York. "What?"

"Don't you think your father should find happiness in another marriage?"

"We're happy just the way we are." Ellen couldn't tell her the way it really was, couldn't tell her about the flight from Virginia City or that it was the three of them against the world. There wasn't room for a fourth. "You don't understand."

"When you find a man to love someday and want to marry him and take care of him, how would you feel if your father were jealous and tried to drive him away?"

Ellen had never thought of that. She assumed she would marry someday after Pa showed the lawmen how wrong they were and got even with Mr. Candliss for hurting their ma. "I guess I wouldn't like it."

Olivia raised one brow.

"Does that mean you and Pa are getting married?"

"No, dear. Your father will be fortunate if I don't take Katy's shotgun to him before that trail opens."

"You don't like Pa?" Ellen didn't know whether to be glad or angry.

"Your father's a good man. You're lucky to have such a loving, loyal, protective father."

"But you don't like him." Ellen wanted to be very sure.

"I'm not going to marry him."

Ellen would have rather heard that Olivia didn't like her pa at all—hated him, in fact, in spite of his kissing her. But Olivia didn't sound really certain how she felt. One would think that a woman with enough nerve to become a doctor would be sure of everything.

"Are you going to tell my pa what I did?" Ellen wanted to make sure of the original question.

"Are there going to be any more tricks?"

"Not from me. And—I guess I'm sorry for last night. You're not really as snooty as I thought you were."

"Then I guess I won't tell your father. Maybe you can help me do some sewing this afternoon. I've never been very good at stitching anything besides incisions, and if I'm to continue to wear this dress without tripping myself, I need to take up the hem."

"Sure. I can show you a real fast hem stitch. And maybe we could lengthen some of my skirts and Katy's trousers . . ."

She rambled on, thinking that when the woman smiled she really didn't look half as ugly as Katy said she was. In fact, she was even pretty, and not snooty at all.

Chapter 11

A week passed in relative peace. In winning Ellen's regard, Olivia had earned herself a taskmaster the equal of any professor of medicine at Cornell. The girl was determined to make up for her earlier pranks by teaching Olivia the art of frontier housewifery, without which she seemed to feel no woman was complete. They mended, sewed, baked bread, smoked, pickled, and jerked the meat of the elk Danaher had brought in, cleaned, stretched, and tanned the skin. They cleaned floors, boiled clothes, and turned under the garden plot for planting in the spring. In return, Olivia entertained Ellen with stories from her school years, taught her the medicinal value of some of the plants—now dry and brown—that grew in the alpine meadows just above the cabin, and showed her how to splint the broken leg of an injured marmot that they found one day while hanging out the wash.

Katy watched their exertions with a curled lip and took great pains to stay out of their way. Danaher teased Olivia about finally seeing the light and preparing to get herself a husband when she returned to civilization. She ignored him as she tried to ignore almost everything about him since the fight—and the Kiss. She had begun thinking of that kiss with a capital K, which was both nonsensical and disturbing, and she found the fewer encounters she had with Danaher, the less thoughts of the Kiss intruded on her mind. During the day, she didn't have to worry about avoiding him, for from dawn until sunset he worked in the mine. After supper

Olivia found tasks to keep herself busy and away from the trio of father and twins, who spent the evening hours playing chess or checkers, reading, telling wild Irish tales to each other, or working on the lessons that Danaher insisted the girls study. When the time came to retire, Olivia would wrap herself in blankets in the rocking chair and curl herself so she faced away from the bed where Danaher lay. When he offered to give her the bed and take the chair himself, she answered with a curt "No, thank you."

"Doc, you're stubborn enough to be an Irishwoman," he had replied.

"I wouldn't dream of depriving you of your bed." In truth, she had no wish to spend the night in comfort if it meant being enfolded in the masculine scent that clung to his bed and being warmed by the heat his body had left in the straw-ticked mattress. Even in the cold, uncomfortable chair she had difficulty fending off schoolgirlish thoughts that were born of the dark and the sound of him breathing nearby.

Days passed with intermittent snow, sleet, and wind, and then, a week before Christmas, the cold gave way to a late Indian summer. Olivia was gratified to watch Murdoch mend without a limp. Ellen's splinted marmot seemed content with the big wooden crate and old rags they had given him as a nest, and cooking and sewing became more of a routine than a challenge. The heap of ore waiting to be hauled down the precarious wagon track to the mill in Elkhorn grew every day until Danaher announced that he would have to dynamite the tunnel to loosen more of the ore vein. The twins and Olivia ceased their midday activities to watch, and Katy laughed when Olivia nearly jumped out of her skin as the charge fired and the ground jolted beneath their feet.

"You're going back in that tunnel right now?" Olivia gasped as Danaher headed toward the mouth where dust was still billowing after the earth's heaving cough.

"Don't worry, Doc. I'll come out again." He grinned at her over his shoulder, his face dark with the grime of the morning's work. "And if I don't, Katy will get you down the trail once it's open. Won't you, Katy my lass?"

Katy smirked at Olivia's misgiving. "With pleasure."

"Don't worry, Olivia," Ellen comforted. "Pa knows what he's doing. The tunnel's very solid, even after a blast. If the rock weren't so solid he wouldn't have to use the dynamite."

Olivia hated the fact that she worried so about Danaher in the tunnel. Any decent human being would be concerned for another's safety, but her anxiety for him went beyond that. She needed to get back to civilization for more than just Amy's sake. Her heart needed a good dose of reality.

The next day at noon, Katy asked Olivia to take Danaher his dinner in the tunnel. She wasn't feeling well, Katy claimed with a woeful look, and Ellen was busy hanging out the laundry.

"You can't get lost," Katy claimed innocently. "There's only one short tunnel, no branches, and Pa's at the end of it. There's no pits or anything. It's perfectly safe."

Olivia's idea of perfectly safe was not a black hole reaching into the belly of the earth, and she was tempted to tell Katy that Danaher could skip his dinner if Katy herself didn't feel well enough to take it to him. Katy didn't fool Olivia for one moment with her pathetic slouch and pitiful eyes. The little wretch wasn't a bit sick; she simply enjoyed putting Olivia in an awkward position. Either Olivia could admit her irrational fear or she could go into the tunnel and be scared out of her wits. The gleam of triumph hidden in Katy's eyes goaded Olivia into foolish bravado.

"Of course I'll take it in, Katy. You do look poorly. I expect you'll have to spend the rest of the day in bed to make sure you're not coming down with something serious."

Katy's eyes narrowed a bit, but she marched obediently up to the loft, apparently feeling boredom was a price worth paying to see Olivia shivering in her shoes. But Olivia was determined not to shiver in her shoes, at least not where Katy could see her.

The mine tunnel was a five-minute walk from the house, and Olivia spent all five minutes trying to bolster her courage. It was only a tunnel. Rock, dirt, dust. That was all. She had a lantern to dispel the dark, and Katy had assured her there was no way she could get lost. It was a short tunnel. Only three hundred feet or thereabouts, Danaher had once told her. Olivia couldn't picture how far three hundred feet actually stretched. She hoped passionately that it was very, very short.

It wasn't. Three hundred feet seemed an eternity, and less than a minute after entering the dark maw of the mine, Olivia's racing heart and clammy palms screamed to her that she'd been swallowed by the earth and would never again see daylight. The lantern pushed back the darkness in a feeble sphere of illumination. All else was stygian. Forward and back, up and down became meaningless. More than anything, Olivia wanted to abandon the bucket with Danaher's dinner and cling to the rock wall for support. But if she yielded to fear she would remain in this place clutching that wall until Danaher found her. What a ridiculous and humiliating spectacle that would be!

She continued forward, breathing deeply to keep her panic at bay and telling herself that reason was stronger than fear. It was only a dusty old tunnel, after all.

By the time she saw Danaher's light and heard his off-key humming along with the clang of his pick, Olivia felt as though she'd descended most of the way to Hell itself.

"Well, look who's here! Have Katy and Ellen finally driven you into the earth to seek shelter?"

Olivia couldn't remember when she was more grateful to hear a human voice. Even Danaher's. Especially Danaher's. She set down the lantern and the bucket. "I . . . I brought your dinner."

"You're panting like you just climbed a mountain. What'd you do? Run all the way back here?"

"Of course not. I . . . well, I . . ."

"Come over here and sit on this rock." He took her arm and sat her down, then squatted beside her, regarding her closely in the light of the lantern. "Scared spitless, aren't you, Doc? I can hear your heart beating from here."

Olivia couldn't deny it. Her pulse pounded against his fingers on her arm. Even she could smell the fear that emanated from her every pore. Danaher would certainly get a good chuckle out of what a ninny she was.

"Why the hell did you come in here?"

"Katy . . . Katy . . ."

"Oh yes, I figured Katy worked into this somehow, especially when she saw you turn ten shades of white when I blasted yesterday." He lifted a brow. "I thought you were smart enough to not let Katy get the better of you."

Olivia sighed. Her pulse was beginning to slow to a more normal rate just from hearing Danaher's voice. "I've done smarter things than let her goad me into this."

Nodding, Danaher smiled a peculiar smile, neither condescending nor derogatory. "I had a friend once—a big moose of an Irishman on the docks of New York. He was scared to death of small spaces. Got the shakes every time he had to go down into the hold of a ship. Finally wouldn't go at all, so he lost his job. One of the bravest men I've ever known, though. Once saw him pull a friend out of a burning saloon when no one else would go in after him."

Olivia swallowed. She wondered if the hold of a ship was as bad as the belly of the earth. The darkness was beginning to close in around her again.

"I think I'll eat dinner out in the light today. I need to haul this cartload of ore out anyway."

The cart was not nearly as full as the others she'd seen him haul out of the tunnel. He was making a special trip to help her out, and at that moment she was supremely grateful.

"You take this lantern, I'll take the other, and we'll put the bucket on the ore cart."

He hitched himself to the cart with a leather harness that crossed over his chest and shoulders. Katy had teased that the harness made him look like a mule. Olivia didn't agree. To her he looked like a savior. She didn't object when he took her hand in a firm clasp and pulled her beside him as he started forward. The ore cart rattled and clanked behind them as they progressed. In their wavering little circle of light, they seemed to go nowhere. The blackness was infinite, and Danaher's hand was the only thing that kept her from falling into the abyss.

They walked for an indeterminate eternity before Olivia's reeling senses forced her to stumble to a stop. At the moment it didn't matter that she was acting the fool; all that mattered was the walls of earth that pressed in upon her and the black vortex of terror that whirled in her mind.

"Olivia."

She could scarcely hear Danaher's voice over the sound of her own racing heart.

"Olivia—Lord, woman! You're cold as ice. It's all right, Olivia. Hold on to me."

She did, clutching at the leather braces of his harness. His arms went around her and drew her close. One hand tangled in her hair and pressed her head into the hollow of his shoulder.

"Close your eyes."

"I c-c-can't."

"Yes you can." Gently he settled her head against his broad chest. She closed her eyes as he had directed. The sharp edges of terror were dulled somewhat by the engulfing warmth of his solid body.

"Think of something relaxing and wonderful."

She groaned in despair.

"A meadow in summer. Flowers poking through the grass. A breeze pushing white, billowy clouds through a blue sky."

One by one Olivia's muscles relaxed as she concentrated on the picture he painted. His hand rubbed up and down her spine in a relaxing caress. Just so he might comfort one of his girls when they were frightened.

"There's a stream running between grassy banks, and in places high up on the meadow, the winter snow hasn't melted and lies in crusty white ridges covered with a red fuzz. The girls call it watermelon snow, because when you crush it in your hand it smells like watermelon."

His deep voice vibrated somewhere in the recesses of her mind, driving back the fear into a place where she, like a lion tamer with whip and chair, could keep it under control. She opened her eyes, emerging from a sunlit meadow full of wildflowers and watermelon snow to the wavering light of the lanterns in the dark belly of the earth. Her vision was full of the blue flannel of Danaher's shirt and the leather braces that crisscrossed his chest. He was solid muscle and warm strength. The cage of his arms was a haven she didn't want to leave, but leave she must if they were to emerge from this hellish place.

Gently she pulled away. "I . . . I'm quite all right now. Thank you."

The eyes that surveyed her were so dark green they were almost black. No raillery, teasing, contempt, or condemnation waited there to jump out at her. Only concern. "You okay?"

"Yes." She was much better, but felt an inexplicable desire to melt back into those strong arms. Seldom in her life had she been held and comforted; she always was the one doing the comforting, it seemed. Amazing how effective the treatment was. Amazing that Danaher of all people would do it.

"We're not far from daylight."

"Then let's go."

They were much farther from daylight than was comfortable for Olivia, but she managed to whip back her phobia long enough to emerge from the hillside. Never had sunlight and wind and the murmuring of the pines been so welcome. She felt like falling to her knees and singing a hymn of praise to the open air. But she had damaged her dignity enough for one day.

"I'm sorry I acted so foolishly in there." Self-consciously she retrieved her hand from Danaher's grip, as he had shown no sign of loosing it himself.

"There's not a person alive who's not reduced to blubbering by something."

Somehow she couldn't picture Danaher in such a state, then remembered his desperation when Katy and Ellen had been near death. She was touched both by his kindness in the tunnel and now his indirect admission of his own vulnerability. Not many men of her acquaintance had such compassion and honesty. She certainly hadn't expected such qualities in Gabriel Danaher.

"I suppose you're right, but I didn't think that I could be brought to that condition." She gave him a sheepish smile. "Pride."

His eyes twinkled. "And stubbornness?"

"Maybe a touch."

He shook his head as he shrugged off the harness, like a horse released from its traces. "Care to share some dinner?" He took the dinner bucket from the ore cart and sat down on a sunny rock.

Olivia had just sat down beside him when all thoughts of dinner were drowned in Katy and Ellen's high-pitched shrieks.

The screams were not shrieks of terror, as Olivia discovered when she reached the cabin, out of breath and running, a good hundred yards behind Danaher. The girls' squeals had welcomed their uncle, who had returned from Lame Wolf's hunting band for a visit. Crooked Stick certainly did have a wanderlust, Olivia reflected as she tried to catch her breath.

"I thought I told you to stay at the mine."

"You did," Olivia shot back at Danaher. "But that was ridiculous. If something had been wrong, you might have needed help."

"And you might have come pelting into Lord knows what. Don't you ever do what you're told?"

"Well, you needn't get huffy about it. It's only your friend Crooked Stick, after all."

Crooked Stick looked from Danaher to Olivia and back to Danaher. He grinned a most un-Indianlike grin. "I come to bring you game, Horse Stalker. Now Big Mouth Woman live here, you have three women to feed and no time to hunt."

"I've had time to hunt, but thanks anyway."

Crooked Stick darted a glance Olivia's way. "Glad to see you still alive, my brother. Women more dangerous than grizzlies, and you have three."

Danaher snorted. "Why can't you be impassive and dour like Indians are supposed to be?"

"Squirrel Woman sends greetings. Said to tell Big Mouth Woman to take good care of her grandchildren or she will skin alive."

Olivia joined in. "You can tell Squirrel Woman that Mr. Danaher is taking fine care of her grandchildren without my help, since I will very shortly be on my way."

Now Crooked Stick turned into the classic impassive Indian Danaher accused him of not being. He regarded Olivia with an unreadable expression. "Squirrel Woman had a dream. She knows."

"She knows what?" Danaher asked.

"She knows." Crooked Stick lifted one black brow, and Olivia got the feeling he enjoyed playing the mysterious prophet.

"Well, if she knows so much"—Olivia propped her hands on her hips and eyed Crooked Stick with an arch look—"I do wish she'd sent word of when that bothersome trail to Elkhorn will be open."

Crooked Stick shook his head. "Big Mouth Woman set foot on wrong path."

"I'll set my feet on any path that will take me from here to Elkhorn."

"No use arguing with her, Crooked Stick. You'll lose." Danaher nodded his head toward the pony that patiently waited with the deer. "Let's take care of the meat. Doc, why don't you and the girls go make up a plate of dinner for Crooked Stick."

When Olivia and the twins had disappeared into the cabin, he turned to Crooked Stick. "You showed up at a good time, my brother."

Crooked Stick grinned. "Need help with new woman?"

"There is no help for that woman." Gabe grimaced as the words rang false in his mind. "Well, I guess that's not quite true. She's a good woman. She's a damned good woman, but she fits in here about like a square peg fits into a round hole. She needs to get back to her own place."

"Trail not open."

"Have you seen for yourself?"

"No. But I know."

"Like hell you do. It's been warm for a week. The stream might have cut through that slide. I want to take her down the mountain with me and check on it."

Gabe secured a rope to the deer's hind legs.

"Big Mouth Woman big trouble for Horse Stalker," Crooked Stick said with a canny look. "Make man part stand up like big bare pine hit by lightning." He chuckled. "Woman not so ready to put out fire, eh?"

"Dammit, Crooked Stick, you've got a mind like a New York sewer."

"Don't know what New York sewer is. Know women, though. Squirrel Woman right. This she-wolf got you sniffing up her tail."

"Jesus! Give you a bone and you'll gnaw it to nothing before you're done."

"You try to get rid of her before she's got you on your back whining like a pup."

Gabe tossed the rope over the branch and pulled as Crooked Stick led the pony away. "You've got it wrong, my friend. Come back here and help me pull this deer up."

Crooked Stick took a grip on the rope and heaved. "Horse Stalker not so good at lying like other white men. Got woman trouble."

Gabe snorted. "If you can stay with the girls for a day or so, I'll get rid of my woman trouble. Ordinarily, I could leave them here on their own. Katy can take care of most anything that might come along. But there were a couple of drifters here a few days ago. I wouldn't want them to double back this way and make trouble."

"I stay, but it won't work."

"The trail might be open."

"Don't matter, my brother. Women like burrs. Don't shake off so easy."

"Horseshit. You don't know a thing about women, you big-talking fake. You've never had a wife."

"Don't have to step off a cliff to know the ground hard when you hit."

With the deer well out of reach of small predators, Gabe tied the rope off and wiped his hands on his trousers. "You ready for some dinner?"

"Big Mouth Woman good cook?"

"Not really. But Ellen is, as you well know."

"Better make her learn. No good have a woman who can't cook."

Gabe shook his head and retreated toward the cabin, leaving Crooked Stick grinning in his wake.

Like so many plump, complacent pigeons they perched on the drawing-room settee, love seat, and wingback chairs. At least that was the image that popped into Amy Talbot's mind as she served tea, coffee, and sweet Christmas cookies to five respectable ladies of Elkhorn. To be truthful, they were not all plump, or complacent. Cornelia Stanwick looked like a winter-bare twig on which someone had hung a dress, and Margaret Norton, with her drooping cheeks, pursed lips, and snapping eyes, actually resembled a dragon more than a harmless little pigeon.

Penelope Shriner took a sip of her tea and regarded Amy critically. "You don't look well at all, Amy dear. You really should try Dr. Acker's English Elixir that Henry got into the store last week. It's much more soothing than Dr. Goullard's Celebrated Infallible Fit Powders that I was using. Truly wonderful, I tell you."

Margaret Norton harrumphed. "Of course she's not feeling well, Penelope. She's more than seven months gone with child, poor dear. I always say the good Lord knew what he was doing when he gave the task of childbearing to women. If men had to endure the consequences of their little pleasures, the race would come to a quick end."

"These fancy tonics are mostly useless, in my opinion," Bess Walpole chimed in. "I've always sworn by my grandma's remedies. She had a cure for everything under the sun, you know, and her concoctions worked better than any store-bought tonic I've ever known. Better than a visit to the doctor as well. When we were children, she gave us a tonic made from soaking rusty nails in vinegar for a blood purifier. And she cured my little Henry of the whooping cough with her special owl broth. I wish she'd been here when the diphtheria swept through town. Back in '52, when we lived in Iowa, she cured our neighbor's baby of diphtheria by treating him with mashed snails and worms in water."

Margaret wrinkled her nose. "The cure sounds worse than the disease, my dear. And I'm fairly certain your sainted grandmother didn't have a cure for Amy's condition."

"Oh, I feel quite fit, I assure you." Such a lie. Amy examined the fine bone china of her teacup but didn't take a sip. The tea tasted sour somehow. Everything she ate or drank tasted off, her back ached miserably, her hands and ankles were bloated, and to top it all off, her head pounded.

"You're very brave, dear," Cornelia said. "But we all know how wretched one gets when one is this far along. And you must be dreadfully apprehensive, seeing that your other attempts at childbearing ended so tragically. And having your friend disappear like she did must certainly have upset you."

"Yes, it did." Amy swept them with a rather uncharitable glance. Not one of them had treated Olivia with more than the barest courtesy, and that grudgingly given. "It still does."

Sylvester had sent an inquiry about Danaher to Helena, and the answer had come back only a week ago. No one by the name Danaher was wanted by the law. And as to the description Sylvester had sent, there were at least a dozen known felons at large who were in their late twenties to early thirties, tall, with shoulder-length black hair. Amy thought with some exasperation of the unimaginative description Sylvester had sent with his inquiry. Amy had only seen the man once or twice, and then from under a curtain of eyelashes that hid her unseemly curiosity, but she could have painted a much more vivid picture of him. His hair wasn't just black; it was burnished black with a sheen that defied the Montana dust. His eyes were the green that made one think of a deep, still pool along the shaded banks of a river. His mouth was as gracefully shaped as a woman's, but its harsh line and the cynical curl at the corners created a tension that made one want to keep a safe distance. His face, though it was a handsome face all in all, made her think of a predator. If he was wanted by the law, she pitied the men who might come hunting him, and she pitied even more anyone he might be hunting.

That Olivia might have fallen prey to such a man made Amy's heart twist in anguish, even though Olivia's being with him would be infinitely better than Olivia's lying dead in some remote gulch or valley where no one would ever find her.

"You know, Amy dear, although it's hard, you really should not let your friend's misfortune upset you so," Penelope Shriner advised. "You have the health of your unborn child to consider, and it will not benefit from your fretting."

"I'm not fretting, Penelope. But she was . . . is . . . my very dearest friend, and she came to Montana to help me."

"But it isn't your fault that she fell into trouble," Margaret Norton said with an arch wave of her hand. "Women who step outside the proper feminine sphere put themselves at risk. They barge into situations where women shouldn't be. They forfeit the consideration afforded the weaker sex because they don't act like women."

"Oh fiddle! Olivia Baron is the kindest, sweetest lady one could ever hope to meet."

"If she were a lady, Amy, she wouldn't have been traipsing around alone at night without a male escort."

"She was a doctor visiting her patients!"

"A lady has no call doing such work."

"Even if that were true, would that justify her getting hurt or killed?"

"Of course not, dear," Penelope conceded in a soothing tone. "Margaret just wanted to point out that you shouldn't feel responsible for what happened. And worrying only upsets your equilibrium and saps the strength you'll need to bear your little one."

"That's right," Bess Walpole agreed. "After all, she might have run off on her own with that man you think she's with. A woman that unconventional, one just can't predict what she would do, can one?"

"Well, I don't believe that Danaher fellow has her at all," Cornelia Stanwick said. "If the man wanted a bit of sport, there are plenty of soiled women in this town who would have accommodated him."

The women murmured in a woeful chorus of agreement.

"I think Sylvester is wasting his time and all of our husbands' time trying to go up the mountain after that man."

"He's simply leaving no stone unturned," Amy said. "He knows how I feel about Olivia."

Amy did wish that Sylvester hadn't been quite so open in his investigation of Danaher, however. Olivia's reputation would certainly suffer from

152   EMILY CARMICHAEL

having her abduction trumpeted about town. But men didn't think about such delicate things as feelings and reputations. Sylvester had inquired all over town for someone who knew where Gabriel Danaher's cabin was, and he made no secret about why he wanted to go there. For a while it had seemed that no one knew how to find Danaher, but every man in town was willing to join a citizens' posse to confront the man. Such activities were like a game to men. They enjoyed broiling about preparing for their little sortie, filled with self-importance and indignation, having a fine time regardless of whom they were hunting or whom they were rescuing.

Finally a man who worked at the mill said he knew where Danaher's mine was—he thought. Ten men from the town, including the husbands of all the ladies at Amy's tea party, had dashed boldly up the mountain only to find that snow and a mudslide blocked their way.

Amy had allowed her hopes to rise when the posse departed, and again when they returned with news that the trail was closed. Perhaps that was why Danaher hadn't brought Olivia back. Perhaps he had no evil intentions toward her at all, but had simply needed a doctor, and the slide had trapped her in the mountains with Danaher and his Indian mistresses. Perhaps Olivia had even gone with him willingly and could find no way to get word back to Elkhorn because the trail was closed. Perhaps. Perhaps. Best to hope while she might, because if Olivia was not with Gabriel Danaher, then surely she was dead and Amy would never know her fate.

"Well!" Bess Walpole's chins wobbled indignantly. "If that man did take her, he surely should be punished. Montana will never become civilized as long as such wild behavior is tolerated."

"He won't be punished," Cornelia said, "unless our men do it on their own. Here we are the newest state in the Union, and still no law and order to speak of. Just as I was saying the other day . . ."

The ladies chattered on, about the changes statehood might bring, about the Elkhorn Trading Company's new shipment of yard goods, about the Christmas dance to be held at the Mason's Fraternity Hall. Their voices and laughter clattered painfully in Amy's head. She wished she could make an excuse to end the little party. Sylvester had encouraged her to have the ladies over. She was depressed, he had said. Feminine company would cheer her up.

She wasn't depressed, Amy thought. She was anxious, but anxious wasn't the same thing as depressed. And having the ladies over hadn't cheered her up one bit. Their attitude toward Olivia's disappearance made her furious, and it was all she could do to retain her good manners and not tell them exactly what she thought of their small-mindedness and self-righteousness.

If Olivia were here, she would laugh at Amy's protective instincts and be philosophical about this flock of puffed-up hens. Could Olivia still laugh? Amy wondered. If Danaher had truly kidnapped her and done unspeakable things to her, could she be philosophical about the disaster and go on with the rest of her life?

Amy almost dreaded the inevitable time when the mountain trail would be open once again. She wanted to continue to hope, and yet she wanted to know.

Most of all she wanted Olivia back, safe and sound. She wanted her baby to be born alive and with all its parts in the proper place. She wanted to be through with being as bloated as an overripe pumpkin. She wanted this nightmare winter to turn into spring.

Yes she was anxious, and sad, and afraid.

She put a hand on her burgeoning belly and felt a healthy kick against her hand. Olivia, she silently cried. Be alive and well, and come back to me.

Seventy miles south, near Virginia City, another also brooded over someone's disappearing without a trace. His contemplation, however, was more vindictive than wistful. Ace Candliss tapped his fingers on the polished oak surface of his desk and looked through the window of his office to the wide valley that was some of the best grazing land west of the Mississippi. *His* valley. His land. With sweat, brains, and determination he'd made it into one of the biggest ranches in Montana. He and his father before him—and his brother Buck. He was rich, powerful, and a damned important man. No inconsequential, no-account Irishman should be able to challenge a Candliss and get away with it.

Ace turned away from the view and focused on the man who sat across the desk from him. Cal Rodgers had been in his employ for six years. He'd known his father, and his brother. Only a passable cowhand, with a gun Rodgers was a master. He also had the hunting instincts of a bloodhound—and the same unflagging loyalty to whoever paid his wages. With sagging, unshaven cheeks and eyes bloodshot from sun, wind, and a fondness for rotgut whiskey, Rodgers even looked a bit like a hound.

"I've got a job for you, Cal."

"Somethin' more interestin' than pullin' cows outta snowdrifts, I hope."

Ace smiled. "I think the rest of the crew can manage that without you. I heard from a friend in Helena." He lifted a letter from his desk and handed it to Rodgers. "Some fellow in Elkhorn has been making inquiries about someone who fits Will O'Connell's description. Wants to know if he's wanted for anything."

"Lots of men fit O'Connell's description."

"This one supposedly speaks a bit like an Irishman. There might be more than one mick in Montana with black hair and green eyes. Then again"—he grinned like a cat who'd spotted the first fat robin of spring—"there might be only one."

Rodgers grunted skeptically.

"If this isn't O'Connell, your ride won't be a complete waste of time. I want you to look at some horses in Jefferson City and stop in Boulder to look at the Hereford bull I'm thinking about buying."

"But mostly you want me to bring back O'Connell's head on a stick."

Ace raised one brow into a sardonic arch. "What a lawless idea. Montana's a state now, Cal. We can't just take the law into our own hands like that."

"Hmph! Right."

"Besides. I want to see the man swing on the end of a rope. I want to see the look on his face when they fasten that noose around his neck."

"So you want him alive. That's harder."

"I don't pay you high wages because you're good at roping and branding."

Rodgers shrugged. "Whatever you want, Mr. Candliss. If this is O'Connell, I'll bring back a big enough piece of him to hang."

"Good man."

"You want me to get started now?"

"I'll let you know when. I'm setting up an appointment for you to talk to U. S. Marshal Shreve Wilkinson in Helena. He should be able to tell you how to find this fellow who was asking questions."

"Why don't Wilkinson go after O'Connell himself? He's the law."

"Says he's too busy to go riding off on a wild-goose chase. Guess he figures I'm not."

"Or you want O'Connell more than the law does."

"I do," Ace agreed with sudden intensity. "And if I have to do Wilkinson's job for him, then I will."

After Rodgers had left, Candliss penned his letter to Wilkinson. Then he sat looking out the window at his valley. He was suddenly more aware than usual of the pain in his crippled leg, an ache coupled with the hurt gnawing his heart ever since Will O'Connell had killed Buck. The sore leg he would have the rest of his life, but the other hurt might diminish somewhat if he could only see O'Connell on the end of a rope.

Ace smiled. The hunt was on. The scent was found. Now was the time to loose the hounds.

Chapter 12

*T*he ride down the trail was a mostly silent one, with Olivia bundled warmly against the cold breeze and perched atop the "borrowed" roan gelding, which Katy had named Curly. Patiently following in Longshot's footsteps, the roan didn't give Olivia the trouble it had when she'd first ridden up this trail. Perhaps it knew that the warm stable at the Elkhorn livery was ahead. Lacking orneriness from her mount, Olivia had nothing to do but relax in the saddle and watch Longshot's broad rump rise and fall with every stride. More interesting was Danaher's back and behind, which seemed magically glued to his horse. How he stuck with his saddle in such a natural, powerful rhythm was beyond Olivia's imagination. She slid around most uncomfortably, and every movement of her horse seemed to send her in a different direction. She was never going to be a horsewoman.

But then, she didn't need riding skills—or any of the other skills that were necessary for survival in this godforsaken place. She was going to spend her life in New York, where she could take a cab, carriage, or omnibus wherever she wanted to go. She didn't need to know anything about horses, or how much lard to put in biscuit dough, or how to stack firewood so it wouldn't tumble down around her when she fetched wood for the fire. Nor did she need to know how to make soap or dip candles, how to snatch an egg from under a hen without getting pecked, or how hot a griddle should be to fry hotcakes. In a way she would miss all those things that Ellen had been so eager to teach her and Katy had been so doubtful that she could ever learn.

Olivia allowed her gaze to linger for a moment on Danaher. She would miss him also, though it hurt her pride to admit it, even to herself. She had come to realize over the past few weeks that her valued self-reliance contained an element of snobbery. She'd thought herself immune to masculine charm, much too intelligent and practical to be drawn to a set of broad shoulders, a pair of muscular arms, a smile that hinted of the devil and promised paradise at the same time. But in spite of herself, she was drawn to this impossible man.

Never before had her emotions warred with each other the way they battled over Gabriel Danaher. After what he had done to her, she ought to despise him. She didn't. He was exasperating, irritating, crude, brutal, and violent when it suited his purposes. But he was also understanding, gentle, loving to his daughters, and patient. And he had an infectious laugh that made her want to smile, even when he was laughing at her.

Gabriel Danaher really was extraordinary. If she had met him when she was eighteen, would he have carried away her heart?

Of course not! Olivia answered her own question. For one thing, he wouldn't have wanted to. Her talents lay in intellect and dedication, not in feminine charm. For another thing, at eighteen, she had been well set on the path to a future she was determined to have. Not that she had ever disliked men; they were simply superfluous to her goals. They still were. *He* was. To moon over an enigmatic outcast like Gabriel Danaher was addlepated foolishness, and if she hadn't been living under such trying circumstances, her mind certainly never would have wandered along that path.

Nor would she have allowed herself to be charmed by those trouble-making imps that were Danaher's daughters. Both were little devils in their own right. Katy was the more obvious hellion of the two, but Ellen had her own little demon inside her. Any woman who took on the raising of those two would be driven to the madhouse. Olivia had doubts that Danaher himself could survive them.

This ride down the trail was much more pleasant than Olivia's last journey this way. The sun burned in a deep-blue sky. Pines and spruce etched themselves against the brightness like sharp spears, their multiple shades of green set off by the dying gold of aspen leaves that littered the forest floor and drifts of white snow that clung to spots where sun and wind couldn't reach. All in all it was a beautiful day, even considering the sharp bite of the wind. She would miss these mountains with their scent of pine, the crystal-clear air, the cloud shadows scudding across wide-open meadows and rocky peaks. Their sweeping power left one with a feeling of awe, almost like being in the presence of God Himself.

However, it was good to be going home, Olivia reflected. If the trail was open, she would be with Amy and Sylvester for Christmas, safe once again where she was needed, where she knew what was up and what was down, where her life was an orderly journey along a road that led to a carefully thought-out goal. Lord, how she hoped Amy and her unborn babe were still well, and the patients she had so unwillingly deserted had found good treatment elsewhere.

Suddenly Olivia wished Danaher would say something to her. He hadn't so much as turned to look at her since they started down the mountain. Brash and provoking as he was, this silence wasn't at all like him. The set of his broad shoulders was almost brooding, as if he, too, were lost in reflection. No doubt he was angry at the time and trouble to take her back.

They rode on, and she left him to his silence. Already she missed him, and she hated that she did.

By the time they came into view of the slide, the sun was resting on the western peaks. Olivia's backside hurt, her shoulders ached, and her face smarted from the cold wind. She was too tired to be brave about the disappointment when Danaher announced: "Well, I didn't really think the creek would cut through this soon, but I guess it was worth a try."

A tear slid down Olivia's cheek—as much from anger and frustration as despondency. Anger that Amy would have more days of waiting and worrying. Anger that she was still mired in a confusing world where she didn't belong. Anger that she wasn't as disappointed as she should be—not for herself at least. Anxious about Amy, yes. Frustrated that she wouldn't, after all, be getting back to her own familiar life. But something inside her was glad that today wasn't the last time she would see Gabriel Danaher.

She hastily wiped the tear away before Danaher could see it. "How much longer, do you think?"

"Hard to say. If it stays warm like this, not much longer." He turned his horse so he was facing her—the first time he'd really looked at her since the trip had begun. "Doc," he said, sounding a bit uneasy. "My mother once told me that the Irish invented stubbornness, Irish males in particular, and I guess I fall into the mold. It's hard for a stubborn man to apologize, but I guess I owe you one. I'm sorry you're stuck up here on this mountain. I know it's not easy for a lady like you, and the girls and I haven't exactly made it any easier. All things considered, you've been a fair sport about it."

Olivia was nonplussed by the sudden apology.

"But to be honest, I'd do the same again, if Katy or Ellen was sick."

Olivia smiled. "Well, Mr. Danaher, to be honest, if Katy or Ellen were sick, I guess I wouldn't blame you. If I had children, I suppose I'd do the same thing if the situation called for it." She looked wistfully down the trail. "No real harm would have been done if it hadn't been for that blasted slide."

"Don't look so discouraged, Doc. New York will wait for you, won't it?"

New York would wait. Olivia just hoped that Amy and her baby could wait awhile as well.

As they headed back up the trail, the sun slipped behind the mountains and the air grew noticeably colder. The sky was surrendering to wind-whipped low clouds and the air smelled of snow. Danaher led them into a thick copse of pine and spruce to make camp. The thicket was littered with dead wood they could use to fuel a fire, and the trees provided a barrier against the rising evening wind.

"You build a fire," Danaher instructed. "I'll put up a shelter and get us something to eat."

"Just don't expect me to clean that poor something you find for supper."

"I'd think you'd be used to blood and guts, Doc."

"Medicine is not blood and guts, Mr. Danaher."

"Can't do much doctoring in these parts without getting into a mess of both," he warned.

Danaher was gone on his hunt for supper longer than Olivia expected. She had a fire built—a new skill that gave her a ridiculous feeling of pride—and coffee heating by the time he came back with two dead rabbits.

"All that time for a couple of rabbits?" Olivia teased. "Katy could have brought back twice that many in half the time."

"Found some tracks I wanted to follow for a bit. Old Bruno's been around here."

"Old Bruno the bear?"

"That's right. THE bear. Anyone prospecting these mountains runs into him sooner or later." Dahaner quickly and efficiently prepared his kill for the spit while he elaborated. "Bruno's old, with a gimp leg and a bad temper. He'll eat cattle, mules, horses . . . people. Last summer he broke into old Joe Petrowski's cabin two valleys over. Got Joe while he was sleeping, I guess. Not much left of the old man when I found him."

Olivia's stomach roiled. She suddenly lost her appetite.

"I didn't know bears were man-eaters."

"Most aren't, but Bruno's old and crippled. He goes after the easy prey, if he can, and I figure for a bear that size, people are pretty easy pickings if he catches someone without a rifle, and unless you hit just the right spot, even a rifle won't stop a grizzly. The skull's too thick."

"Oh dear."

Danaher spitted the rabbits over the fire. "Nice fire, Doc. You're getting to be quite a frontierwoman."

"Will the fire keep the bear away?"

"Don't worry. Bruno's headed up the valley—probably looking for a place to hole up for the winter. That's why I followed the tracks for a ways, to make sure he wasn't going to circle back. We'll have to keep a sharp eye out tomorrow to make sure we don't run into him. That'll slow us up some."

"The slower, the better," Olivia declared with a sigh.

Gabe grinned. "Backside sore?"

"Everything's sore. Besides, I'm in no particular hurry to get back to the cabin and Ellen's lessons about stitchery, laundry, and fireplace cuisine."

Danaher chuckled. "She has been keeping you busy, hasn't she? You may have made a mistake in winning her over. How did you do that, by the way?"

"A secret between us women, Mr. Danaher."

"Whatever it was, too bad it didn't work on Katy."

"Katy is an entirely different case. I think she considered my departure as her Christmas gift." Olivia smiled wryly. "You've raised that girl to be a quite unique little person."

"More like she raised herself and just dragged me along in her wake."

"My father once had very similar words to say about me."

"I'll bet he did." He poked at the rabbits, which sizzled and gave off a delicious aroma. "I think our supper's done."

When Danaher handed Olivia the stick that impaled her supper, she tried to devise a graceful way to get the meat into her stomach, which was beginning to rumble. "Just . . . uh . . . how does one eat a rabbit on a stick?"

She watched as Danaher twisted off a leg and bit into the meat.

"Like this," he said between bites. Juice coated his chin and dribbled onto his shirt.

"I'm afraid I slept through my lessons in barbarian etiquette at school." Olivia grimaced and tried to twist free a likely piece of rabbit anatomy. She twisted and twisted. Hot grease ran down her hand and arm, but the haunch didn't come free. "Would it be too much to ask for a knife?"

"Not at all." He slid a long-bladed knife from a sheath at his hip and flipped it casually in the air so that it stuck in the ground a foot from the log on which she sat.

"And a fork?" she asked hopefully.

He feigned ignorance. "A what?"

"You *are* a barbarian."

"Barbarian, Irishman—same thing, according to some folks."

After the rabbits were consumed and the horses watered and hobbled, Olivia washed as well as she could with a potful of snow melted and warmed over the fire. Then she attacked the wind-whipped snarls of her hair with her comb. No matter how tightly she wound the bun at her neck, the Montana wind always tore enough loose to make it a tangled mess. Tonight, after being in the wind all day, she felt as though her head were full of rats' nests.

"Let me do that." Danaher brushed her hands away from her hair and took the comb.

"Mr. Danaher!"

"You don't live with two daughters without learning how to untangle hair, Doc. A brush would be better."

"When you snatched me from the clinic, you didn't give me much time to pack a complete toilet."

"Then a comb it is. This is a mess." He ran a hand through her loosened hair, making shivers travel up her spine.

For a while they sat in silence, Danaher working carefully through the snarls and Olivia staring into the fire as though mesmerized. The feel of his hands working with her hair was sensually hypnotic, and along with the flickering of the fire put her into a trance of pure physical awareness. At the edge of her consciousness, Olivia heard his voice talking of the twins—how Ellen used to howl when he combed her hair, how Katy had once cut her beautiful long tresses into a shaggy, ear-length bob. But his hands were the center of her universe—the gentle pressure on her scalp, the occasional brush of his fingers against her neck. Strength seemed to seep out of her; a warm liquid flood of sensuous lassitude took its place.

How many different sides did Danaher have? Brutal brawler, gun-wielding kidnapper, arrogant upstart, loving father, carnal tempter, rescuer, taunter, barbarian, desperado? And now he was playing lady's maid, or was it seducer? Olivia had never suspected that a woman could be enticed through hair combing, but she knew if Danaher progressed to more carnal caresses, she would be sorely tempted to let him have his

way. The feel of his fingers working at her hair, the comb gliding over her
scalp, his hand steadying her head and sliding down over her cheek all
produced a raw, twisting ache inside her that was both frightening and
thrilling.

"Done," he declared some time later. "Are you still awake? You
haven't made a peep in the last ten minutes."

Olivia had to control her body's urge to simply lean back against his
broad chest and surrender herself to relaxation—or whatever else came
along. "I'm still awake."

"You'd better turn in. Tomorrow's going to start early."

Rising from the log was a great effort, but Olivia managed it. "Thank
you for untangling my hair."

"My pleasure."

She heard the truth of that in the huskiness of his voice. Deliberately,
she didn't turn to look at him. That bronzed face with its teasing smile
and devilishly arched black brows might be the undoing of her. Self-
consciously, she braided her hair and washed her face in the warm water.

"Good night, Mr. Danaher."

She could feel his eyes upon her as she took refuge in the shelter.
Finally he replied. "Good night, Olivia."

Olivia burrowed into the darkness of her bedroll, listening to Danaher
splash in the wash water. His boots dropped onto the ground with twin
thuds, and the pine needles under his blankets rustled as he settled into
the shelter. He tugged at the bedroll and wrapped the blankets around
them both so they could share the heat of their bodies. The world
abruptly became warmer. Olivia didn't protest. Civilized propriety
seemed superficial and meaningless in this wilderness. The first flakes of
a snowstorm flew past the shelter opening and hissed in the low-burning
fire, making the shelter seem cozy in comparison to the outside.

"Warm enough?" Danaher asked. He had curled himself around her,
his arm about her waist, his chin resting on the crown of her head.

Olivia felt ridiculously comfortable and not a bit ashamed. "I'm fine.
Are we in for another blizzard?"

"I don't think so."

She closed her eyes and let herself drift with the sensation of his body
pressed against hers, his heat invading her pores, his scent enveloping
her. He seemed to exude an aura of masculinity and confidence, and she
was swallowed by it. Deep in the core of her femininity, she wanted
more. She wanted to be a part of him, body and soul. Impossible. Ridiculous. It could never happen. It should never happen. And still that unreasoning part of her wanted it.

Somewhere in the mountains, a pack of wolves sang a mournful serenade to the snow-laden sky. The sound struck a chord of loneliness deep in Olivia's heart. As if sensing her feelings, Gabe shifted so that he looked down at her. "Don't be afraid of the wolves. They're not going to bother us."

"It's such a forlorn sound."

"So it is. Like the whole world is lonely."

His face was very close to hers, and Olivia didn't have a chance to fend off his kiss when it came. Nor did she really want to. His mouth moved gently over hers—more comforting than demanding. He tasted of wood smoke, roast rabbit, and passion, yet she wasn't afraid. The warm tension that built inside her as he deepened the kiss seemed right and natural— as much a part of these untamed mountains as the wolves' wild song.

He drew back finally. His eyes seemed to drink in the features of her face. "Good night, Olivia."

"Good night," she answered in a quiet voice.

He settled back into their blankets, curling himself around her. One hand brushed her cheek in a soft caress. Never before had Olivia felt so full and yet so empty.

Gabe woke long before dawn. Moonlight flooded into the three-sided lean-to, and all around their campsite the trees cast long, spearlike shadows in the milky light. New-fallen snow glowed in the brilliance of a luminous winter moon. The little storm was over.

A bigger storm was building inside Gabe, however, and it wasn't nearly over. It had begun as curiosity, matured into fascination, and now . . . Now, he didn't know what his feelings for Olivia Baron were. Lying in their little shelter, wrapped together in blankets that trapped and mingled their body heat, feeling her firm little behind innocently snuggled against his groin, some feelings were very definable. Lust. Need. Animal desire. But underlying those common passions was something else. He liked the woman, dammit! She was damned exasperating at times, but always interesting. Contrary to the core, she nevertheless didn't have a mean or petty fiber in her entire body.

And getting back to bodies, she had shifted in her sleep so that her breast lay almost directly beneath his hand and one of her legs pressed against his inner thigh. The woman was going to kill him with frustration before the sun rose. His hand itched to close over that temptingly full mound. His sex, hard with raw need, ached to plunge into the female heart of her and slake its appetite.

Gabe took a deep, steadying breath, but the scent of her inflamed his senses even more. How had he let himself come to this state? Even if he were able to seduce the woman, he had no right. She wasn't someone to be trifled with. Feelings ran deep in her, and through her prickly exterior he sensed a fragile heart. He had nothing to offer other than a very uncertain future, and she had everything she wanted in her own right. Olivia Baron had worked hard to get where she was, and a hard-nosed Irishman with vengeance on his mind and the law on his tail wasn't likely to be in her plans. No more than two hellion girls who were growing up fast and wild as two mountain lion cubs.

If he had an ounce of sense, he'd go back to thinking of Olivia Baron as an eccentric, pain-in-the-ass spinster who had questionable taste in hats and strange ideas of a woman's place in the world, Gabe advised himself.

But then, he was an Irishman, and as his mother had told him more than once, Irishmen didn't have the sense God gave a woolyworm.

She stirred. Her breathing quickened with approaching wakefulness. Gently Gabe removed the hand that rested so comfortably on her breast. If he were half a gentleman, he would have withdrawn that hand the moment she'd slid herself so snugly into the cup of his palm. He wasn't a gentleman, though. Not even half, and he'd never claimed to be.

She burrowed deeper into the blankets and the comfort of their mutual warmth, rubbing against his already inflamed groin as she did so. For a moment Gabe thought he would lose control, turn her onto her back, and teach her the practical uses of all that anatomy she had studied in medical college. But he didn't. Instead, he ended his torture by shaking her awake.

"Wake up, Doc. Time to hit the trail."

"Mmmph!"

"Shake a leg, woman. You'll sleep the whole day away."

She opened one eye, then closed it. "It's still dark," she mumbled.

"The sun will be up before you know it."

"Hmmph! Feels cold out."

"Get up, lazybones. Heat the coffee. While you do that, I'll saddle the horses."

He unwrapped himself and pulled on his boots. At the departure of his heat, Olivia shivered and opened her eyes with a resigned sigh. Stiffly, she sat up and blinked at the pale-gray sky where dawn was just beginning to drive the stars into retreat. "If I ever again sleep in a feather bed, I vow I'll think I'm sleeping in paradise."

He handed her a wool coat as she threw off the blankets.

"Oh!" she exclaimed as she emerged from the shelter, "just look at the new snow! It's beautiful."

Looking at Olivia instead of the snowy splendor of the moonlit mountains, Gabe said, "Yeah. It's a sight, all right."

They were in the saddle shortly after the sun rose. In spite of his eagerness to roust Olivia from the shelter at such an early hour, Danaher set a pace that she had no trouble maintaining. He seemed to be enjoying himself. Strangely enough, Olivia discovered that in spite of a sore posterior and aching muscles, she was enjoying herself as well. The ride was like a journey into a place apart from the real world. Traveling through these craggy ridges and sweeping valleys, she didn't feel like Doctor Rachel Olivia Baron, spinster, eccentric only daughter of a wealthy New York banker, a member of New York's socially elite on one hand and dedicated minister to the sick on the other. No indeed, here in these mountains, she felt very different, with different priorities, different needs. A part of her she'd scarcely known was blossoming out here, and that part of her grew almost sad at the thought of returning to the sterile and lonely world of her real existence.

As they rode in comfortable silence, Olivia marveled at how at ease Danaher seemed—in the middle of nowhere, without a soul other than herself for miles and miles. "You grew up in New York?" she asked him.

"From the time I was thirteen. Before that it was Ireland."

"And you came west with an Englishman?"

"True."

"How did you learn to get by in a wilderness like this—lighting fires in a snowstorm, building shelter, hunting, tracking greenhorns through blizzards?"

His smile surprised her, because always before when she had ventured onto territory too personal he had answered with an expression of stony reserve. Perhaps he also felt the peculiar closeness that this wild land seemed to engender.

"Some things you just learn because you need them to live. Other things you're lucky enough to have a teacher. After Avery died, I lived with the Blackfeet up in northern Montana for a year and a half or thereabouts. Married the twins' mother. Many Horses Woman."

For a short while he seemed lost in memory. Then he continued.

"Those people know a lot about living with the land, not apart from it. They're masters of many useful trades—tracking, hunting, survival. One old brave called Tall Man was the best shot with a rifle that I've ever seen. Before he took me in hand, I couldn't hit the side of a barn."

"Did you start mining after you left the Blackfeet?"

"No. Minnie and I settled on a ranch near Virginia City. The land was cheap, and the Blackfeet had taught me a thing or two about horses." He smiled ruefully. "The cattle I had to learn about. Made some mistakes the first couple of years, but finally got the hang of it. We did all right, selling horses and cattle mostly to the Army."

"Then how did you end up at that lonely mine?"

A raised black brow told her she'd gone beyond the limit. "What about you, Doc? How did you end up treating people's bellyaches and setting broken bones?"

"There's a lot more to being a physician than that, Mr. Danaher."

He grinned. "Most of the sawbones I've known are as likely to kill you as cure you, but I'll admit that when the girls were sick I was willing to give just about anything I had to find a doctor. Can't say I expected to find a woman, though."

"Woman physicians aren't that uncommon. It's been forty years since the first woman was awarded a medical degree in this country—Elizabeth Blackwell, at Geneva College in New York. Since then hundreds of women have studied medicine. There are prominent women doctors even in the West."

"Why you?"

"I beg your pardon?"

"You're a good woman. Seems like somewhere along the line a man would've snatched you up."

"I didn't study medicine because I couldn't find a husband. I became a doctor because that was all I ever wanted to do from the time I was twelve. That was when a doctor named Mary Putnam helped my mother through a very difficult miscarriage. She saved her life. I'd never met anyone so competent, or confident, or so full of feeling for people who were frightened and hurting. I determined right then that a doctor was what I had to be."

"Your family didn't think you were crazy?"

Olivia grimaced at the memory of her father's amusement when she'd first talked about her ambition. "At first they did. But their experience with Dr. Putnam—Dr. Jacobi, now that she's married—made their attitudes more reasonable. My father is a saint, really. When he finally accepted that medicine is what I wanted, he supported me wholeheartedly. When I graduated from Cornell, he threw an enormous party for me. I vow he invited the whole state of New York. Then he provided funds for me to study in Paris at the École de Medicine for my clinical work. Unfortunately, many American hospitals still don't admit women for graduate clinical experience."

"Never a thought of getting married and having children?"

Olivia considered a moment, then answered honestly. "Every woman has some thoughts of marriage and babies, I think, no matter what her ambitions. There are many woman physicians who are wives and mothers as well."

Danaher was silent.

"And what are your ambitions, Mr. Danaher? Are you going to get rich from your mine and take the world by storm?"

For a moment Olivia imagined that the bright day had become shadowed by the sudden darkness that flooded his eyes.

"I'm already rich from that mine," he finally said. "Just not quite rich enough. When I get rich enough, you can be sure that I'll take what I want by storm."

The look on his face sent an unexpected shiver through Olivia. She wondered if she wasn't better off not knowing some things about Gabriel Danaher.

They rode on in companionable silence. Now and then Gabriel would halt to examine the ground or the brush beside the trail. When she looked a question at him, he explained.

"Bruno's been by here. He's following the trail upvalley. Wouldn't want to blunder into him unprepared."

"Oh," Olivia said uneasily.

"Don't worry. Looks like he came through here earlier this morning. He's long gone by now."

In spite of his assurances, Danaher continued to be very watchful, Olivia noted. She began to imagine grizzly bears behind every tree and lurking in each shadow.

Midmorning, Danaher reined in his horse and cocked his head as if listening.

"Stay here." Pistol in hand, he turned off the trail toward an outcropping of weathered gray rock. After a cautious look at something in the rocks, he holstered the pistol. Olivia took that as a signal she could join him. She kneed her horse forward.

"What is it?"

Danaher pulled a pine branch back from the outcrop and revealed the opening of a cave. Sunlight penetrated just far enough to reveal several small shaggy forms lying in awkward, bloody heaps.

"Looks like Bruno discovered a litter of wolf cubs and had himself a snack."

"Oh, the poor things!"

Fuzzy gray puppy coats were streaked with blood. Legs and heads were bent at impossible angles. Except for one. Coat dark with blood and a leg hanging uselessly, the surviving pup faced them with teeth bared and eyes blazing.

"Look at him!" Olivia exclaimed. "So small and so brave!"

"He's got guts for a baby," Danaher agreed.

"How old do you think he is?"

"Couple of months. No more." He unholstered his pistol.

Olivia grabbed his arm. "What are you doing?"

"I'm going to do him a favor. He's in pain. He can't survive."

"Maybe the mother will come back."

"If she did, she'd probably kill him herself or just let him starve. Nature isn't a kind mother, Doc. She doesn't have room for the injured or crippled."

"No, Danaher. Don't. Please."

"Damnation, Doc! First the horse. Now a wolf?"

"Murdoch healed up just fine."

"This is a wolf! Not a horse who'll stand still and let you treat him."

"It's a baby."

"A baby wolf! Those may be milk teeth he's flashing, but they'll do just as good a job at tearing you up as the full-sized ones."

"You could muzzle him."

He lowered the rifle. "Jesus Christ!"

"Blasphemy, Danaher? Shame on you."

"A plea for help. Doc, you're light in the head. Suppose you did manage to patch him up. What are you going to do with a wolf?"

"Once he's healed, we'll turn him loose."

"He'd never survive on his own. He's too young, and he doesn't have a mother to teach him how to hunt."

She hesitated, not looking quite so sure of herself now. "Keep him?" she ventured.

"You're going to keep a wolf in New York City?"

"I meant you. He's young enough to tame."

"Maybe. Maybe not. A wolf isn't a dog."

She cast the pup a distressed look. He had stopped snarling and regarded them with wary, frightened eyes.

"You can't just shoot him."

The look on Olivia's face was as pathetic as the one on the pup's. Danaher shook his head and kneaded his brow. "Awww, God help me."

She was a know-nothing greenhorn and a sentimental fool into the bargain, but she pulled at his heart with her determination to heal any living thing that was in pain. Pulled at his heart and befuddled his brain. It appeared he'd just acquired a wolf.

Perhaps it was Danaher's gentleness with the frightened, injured wolf cub that knocked the last leg from under the grudge Olivia held against him for kidnapping her. Or perhaps she had actually forgiven him days ago when he fought that huge ox of a drifter to defend her, or the night he had cajoled Katy into giving him a good-night kiss. No matter. At some point she had stopped thinking of Danaher as a scoundrel and started thinking of him as a man who made her smile when she was near him, and sometimes laugh. Throughout her life she'd had much satisfaction and personal fulfillment, but little laughter. Laughing with Danaher felt good.

The rest of the day they rode at a leisurely pace. Their furry patient, who rode in a sling hung from Longshot's saddle, needed frequent attention to his injuries, and the country through which they rode seemed to hold them to its own tempo—the slow circling of an eagle overhead, the meandering of the wind through the trees, the lazy tumbling of a creek down a stairstep of ice-coated beaver dams. Olivia found herself smiling every few moments—though just exactly why she couldn't fathom. Danaher, also, smiled a lot, she noted. When he smiled, he did it with his whole face. The smile started in his eyes and traveled to his mouth. She remembered the warm, strange joy of being kissed by that mouth and felt her face heat. Someday, she told herself sternly, she was going to recollect this interval in her life and conclude that she'd suffered temporary insanity.

She tried to concentrate on her sore posterior and aching back. They were things she could deal with.

Katy had convinced herself that her father and the doctor had made it down the trail to Elkhorn. She hadn't misbehaved enough in her young life to deserve that woman's coming back—at least, she didn't think she had. So her heart dropped in disappointment on the day before Christmas when the two of them rode up to the cabin; she had expected only one. Stupid Ellen bounced up and down as though she was glad that the woman had come back.

"The trail's still closed?" Katy glared at Olivia as the doctor walked into the cabin with her bedroll and medical bag. It wasn't the woman's fault that the trail was still blocked, she knew. But Katy had been looking forward to getting back to the familiar threesome, and having someone to blame made her feel marginally better.

While Crooked Stick and her father greeted each other, a great rush of anger welled up in Katy. This interloper, this greenhorn, know-nothing, useless female from Back East was worse than a thistle burr on a saddle blanket, and just as impossible to get rid of. Her father was so befuddled by the woman that he wasn't even aware of what a useless bother she was. Worse, Olivia had a peculiar expression on her face when she looked at her father—almost friendly, as if something had happened between them during the time they'd been gone.

The woman smiled that weasel smile of hers and addressed Katy as if she couldn't tell Katy would just as soon spit at her as talk to her. "We brought something with us that you should like, Katy. Your father told me you've always wanted a dog."

Her father laughed. "This isn't exactly a dog."

"He's become quite tame."

"He's a pup. Wait until his leg heals and he grows a bit."

"A pup?" Katy asked.

"A wolf cub," her father said. "Bruno was ambling up the valley today and killed all the litter except this one. I was going to do away with it, but Olivia was busy wrapping him in bandages before I could cock the pistol."

"That's not true. You were holding him still while I was wrapping the bandages."

"More like holding his teeth away from your flesh."

"He hasn't tried to bite since."

Her father grinned. "Just don't turn your back on him."

"We will have to give you new name," Crooked Stick declared to Olivia. "Woman Who Walks with Wolf."

"Big Mouth Woman suits her better," Gabe said.

Katy's mind was divided between curiosity about the wolf cub and anger that they were bantering about something her father had shared with that woman when he should have shared it with her. Curiosity won out.

"Where is it?"

"In a sling on your father's saddle," Olivia said. "We'll have to fix it a bed by the fireplace."

"You think you're going to bring that wolf into my cabin and treat it like one of your patients?" Her father's voice was amused rather than annoyed, Katy noted, and the cheeky look Olivia gave him from under her lashes was amused rather than resentful. He chuckled. "I guess you do."

Her father wouldn't have been so tolerant if *she* had wanted to bring a wolf home. That was a sure thing!

Katy's temper was mollified somewhat by the cub, which she promptly named Hunter, since Olivia hadn't been enterprising enough to give him a name. Her father and Crooked Stick built the pup a box with sides too high for him to escape, and Olivia and Ellen lined the bottom with soft leaves and pine needles. Katy couldn't pretend disdain as she would have liked, for the little gray face with its pointed nose and furry ears appealed to her more than her resentment did.

Before he left, Crooked Stick sat beside Hunter's box and watched Katy feed him meat scraps. In just a few minutes she had taught the pup to accept such offerings without taking the fingers that held the meat, and the clever little thing was taking each piece quite carefully.

"Smart animal," Crooked Stick commented, watching him. "His life is not what it was, yet he accepts."

When Katy looked up, Crooked Stick no longer looked at the wolf; he looked at her.

"Your life is not what it was," he said gravely. "You should be as smart as wolf, White Horse Woman."

"What do you mean?"

"You know what I mean."

"My life isn't going to change. Not until Pa and Ellen and me leave here and go after Ace Candliss."

"If wolf had refused to change, he would be dead."

Katy stuck out her lower lip.

"Squirrel Woman say to me once that her granddaughter is stubborn as a bull buffalo."

Katy grinned suddenly, picturing Squirrel Woman's face screwed up in concentration, reading her portents and interpreting her dreams.

"Tell my grandmother that not very many people mess with a bull buffalo."

"There are no more buffalo," Crooked Stick reminded her.

With that ominous statement, he left her alone with the wolf.

Crooked Stick left that afternoon to return north, in spite of the twins' begging him to stay for Christmas. This time he was bound for the winter camp of Buffalo Hump, whose sister's daughter was Rain Falling Fast.

"Horse Stalker reminds me that man should have a woman," he announced.

"*I* remind you?" Her father had all but choked.

"Rain Falling Fast good woman. Not too young, not too old. Not so smart like Big Mouth Woman. Doesn't talk back."

"I didn't remind you of anything!" her father insisted.

Crooked Stick just grinned and went on his way. With his departure Katy felt deserted. Crooked Stick understood her. He didn't always agree with her, but at least he understood. Her father had understood her once, but since that woman had come, he didn't have time to think about Katy and what she was feeling. And Ellen had gone over to the enemy. She thought the doctor was a "real lady," as she had told Katy the last time Katy complained to her of the intruder's shortcomings. Her own sister had been pulled into the woman's web.

She spent the afternoon repairing the henhouse roof. Pounding nails relieved some of her vexation, but not much. When suppertime rolled around, a knot of anger still made her chest ache and her spirits sag. The knot pulled tighter when her father told them he'd spent the afternoon teaching Olivia to shoot. They had spent the afternoon at target practice and hadn't invited her along. Katy was surprised that woman knew which end of a rifle was which, and when her pa said that Olivia had a natural talent, Katy couldn't help the sound that came out of her mouth.

"What was that, Katy?" her pa asked in an ominous tone.

"Nothing."

"Maybe you could go target shooting with Olivia tomorrow and give her some tips."

"I've got work to do."

"Tomorrow's Christmas Day," Gabe reminded her with a grin. "I think you could take the time off to have some fun."

"What's fun about keeping some greenhorn female from shootin' herself? What's she want to learn shootin' for, anyway?"

"You're being rude, Katy."

"Well, hell! She's got the lot of you buffaloed into entertaining her and acting like she's something special, but not me!"

"What's gotten into you, my lass?"

"No!" Katy almost shouted at her father, all the frustration in her heart rising into her throat. "What's gotten into you?"

"I think you should go to bed and think about your manners for a while."

"Good! This table's too crowded anyway!"

Escape to the loft was a relief, though part of her felt bad for the look on her father's face. She heard the murmurings below, and guessed that they were talking about her. Let them talk! She didn't care. She got into her flannel nightdress and huddled under her blankets in the dark, wishing with all her might that things were as they'd been before she and Ellen had gotten sick—even better, before her mother had died. Katy remembered how Many Horses would tell the Christmas story each year on Christmas Eve. She took the foreign story the reservation missionaries had told her, changed the scene to Montana, and cast the characters as Blackfeet. When the story was finished, her mother would tell the Blackfoot legend of how Napi, the old man, had created the whole earth from a ball of mud, and how he had then roamed the new earth, piling up rocks to make mountains, gouging out river valleys, making all the animals and birds, designing the people of the world and commanding how they should live.

The sound of footsteps on the ladder interrupted Katy's memories of Christmases past. Someone sat down on the edge of her bed.

"Katy?"

A hand landed lightly on her shoulder—Olivia. After days spent in her care, Katy recognized her gentle touch. "Go away."

"We didn't mean to leave you out this afternoon, Katy. We thought you were busy with the henhouse."

"Leave me alone. I don't care what you did this afternoon."

"You shouldn't listen to Crooked Stick's teasing about your father and me, Katy. There's certainly nothing to it. Even if there were, even if your father remarried some day, it wouldn't mean he loved you any less."

"Git! I don't want to talk to you."

She heard a sigh. The weight lifted from the cot, and steps descended the ladder.

Next morning dawned gray and cold to match Katy's mood. Her pa went into the mine early with a promise to be out in time for Christmas dinner and gifts. Olivia and Ellen were tending to the wolf pup, who had chewed his bandages off during the night, and they were wrapped up in talking about how to keep the cub away from Ellen's injured marmot, who occupied a box across the room. Katy tromped alone into the woods to set a string of rabbit snares. She fancied a rabbit fur hat to keep her ears warm this winter, and she certainly didn't fancy hanging around the cabin with Ellen and that woman.

Two hours later she returned to the cabin and was greeted by Ellen coming from the mine at a dead run, her face beet red and her chest heaving to catch a breath.

"Katy! The mine!"

"What?"

She gasped. "The mine! It's caved. Pa . . ." she wheezed. "Pa's inside."

Chapter 13

*T*he dust that still hung in the air near the tunnel mouth almost obscured the twins as they pelted up the trail toward Olivia, Katy in the lead with Ellen trailing not far behind. Clutched in one of Katy's hands was a trio of hares, in the other a tangle of snares. The girl threw them all in a heap and shot straight for the mine entrance.

"No you don't!" Olivia interposed her body between the child and the tunnel. Katy pushed her aside. Olivia lunged after her and thrust her back against the hillside. "You're not going in there. Rocks are still falling. I can hear them."

"My pa's in there!"

"Rushing in and killing yourself isn't going to help him!"

Ellen, tears streaking the dust on her face, stumbled up to them and grasped Katy's hand. "He could still be alive. It just now happened."

"Did you see it?" Katy asked grimly.

"We were bringing Pa's dinner up the path when it happened. The ground shook and dust exploded out of the tunnel, just like when Pa dynamites the rock. Oh, Katy! What are we going to do?"

"The both of you just settle down!" Olivia's mind clicked away, grasping for a plan. As it almost always did during emergencies, an unemotional clarity slipped into her thinking and left it free of fear or hysteria. In medical college and in her graduate studies in Paris, she had gained a reputation for being cool in tense medical situations. This crisis was no different; a life was at stake. Now was the time for clear, quick thinking. Later she could collapse in a heap and cry.

The ground rumbled and more dust roiled from the mouth of the tunnel. Ellen shrieked. "It's not finished! Oh God! Oh please don't let this be happening!"

Katy struggled to get free of Olivia's grasp. Olivia gave her a firm shake.

"Don't be stupid, Katy. I need you here to help."

"Pa!"

"We'll get him. Now think. Your father has some way to contact Crooked Stick. What is it?"

"A lantern in the big pine. But Crooked Stick's gone up to visit Buffalo Hump's winter camp. He's too far to see the signal."

"Are there any other miners around here who could help?"

"No. No one."

What a fix. She couldn't even send down to Elkhorn for help. She had never wanted to see Jebediah and Slim again when they left, but now she'd give ten years of her life to see them riding up the path.

"Katy, go to the cabin and get every shovel, pick, crowbar, and spade that's down there. And the wheelbarrow. Ellen, you get a clean sheet we can rip into bandages and my medical bag. And lanterns. Hurry, now."

The girls were calmer once they had something to do, but Olivia was beginning to feel the claws of despair rip at her composure. The thought of Danaher trapped in that dark, suffocating tunnel threatened to send a streak of unreasoning panic through her. He might be gasping for air, or lying crushed and broken, in pain, buried alive to await a slow, agonizing death. Would they be able to dig through the debris that covered him, or would it be immovable, forcing them to wait and grieve, knowing that he could be slowly dying while they floundered helplessly?

Katy returned with a wheelbarrow and two shovels, a pick, a crowbar, and two sets of sturdy work gloves. A moment later Ellen puffed up the path carrying Olivia's medical bag, two lanterns, and a sheet.

Olivia donned a pair of gloves. "Ellen, you stay here and tear that sheet into bandages."

"I want to dig."

"We can't all three dig. It sounds like things are more stable in there now, but if the tunnel collapses again, there would be no one to go for help."

Where Ellen would go for help Olivia didn't know. But at least she could try.

"Light one of the lanterns and put it in the pine tree. Maybe we'll be lucky and someone will see it. Katy and I will take the other."

In the tunnel, the air was thick with dust. Olivia felt as though she were swimming in the stuff. The mine was blocked halfway down the tunnel by rocks and dirt.

"Pa!" Katy shouted at the wall.

"Gabriel! Can you hear us?"

No answer. Katy looked at the cave-in with wide, hopeless eyes. Olivia didn't think she'd ever seen the tough little girl look so fragile.

"We dig." Olivia tried to sound optimistic. "Set the lantern down and let's move the wheelbarrow over here. Be careful with that pick. I don't want to have to wheel you out of the mine."

"The wheelbarrow's to wheel Pa out of the mine, isn't it? You think he's dead."

"I don't know what condition he's in, Katy, but you and I can't carry him out of here if he can't walk."

They dug, and called, and dug some more. The blockage was not as tightly packed as Olivia had feared. Their shovel and pick made good progress through the debris. But if the rockfall extended to the end of the tunnel, there was no hope.

Olivia had no sense of how much time passed. Before long her shoulders burned with pain. Through the gloves her hands were raw. Her throat rasped from breathing dust and endless shouting that got no answers. Beside her, Katy grunted with exertion as she pried rocks and boulders from the pile, and Olivia heard similar uncivilized sounds coming from herself.

It didn't matter. None of it mattered. The only thing of importance was that they find Danaher. The thought of leaving him here, buried in the earth, those green eyes staring forever into the darkness of this hellish place twisted her heart with pain—a pain she was sure would be with her the rest of her life. Olivia found herself praying as she worked, though she had always believed that God rewarded efforts rather than prayers. When effort wasn't enough, when the task was impossible, then a miracle was her only hope.

Olivia was so intent on her work that she scarcely noticed when Katy stopped grunting with exertion and started crying, doubled over in an exhausted, miserable heap.

"I can't!" the girl wept. "We . . . we can't get through."

"Rest, Katy."

The child whimpered an unintelligible reply and rocked with her head in her hands.

Olivia kept working to the tune of Katy's quiet sobs. She finally loosened a particularly large rock, and as it tumbled down the pile, a shower of dirt and pebbles came with it. When the dust cleared enough for her to see, she held up the lantern and discovered open space on the other side.

"Gabriel! Can you hear me?"

She had shouted the same words a hundred times during the last hours. This time an answer sounded above the echo of her words.

"Olivia?"

"Gabriel!"

"Pa!" Katy screamed.

"Gabriel, where are you?"

"In a damned cave-in, that's where I am!"

The flood of relief that washed through Olivia made her so weak she couldn't lift her shovel. Hot tears spilled down her face. She had her miracle. If Danaher was cursing his ill luck in that tone of voice, he couldn't be too badly hurt.

Katy grabbed the shovel that rested in Olivia's limp hands and attacked the rockpile like a little demon. She quickly enlarged the hole enough to scramble through. Olivia grabbed the lantern and followed. Danaher lay propped against one rock wall. Dirt and small pebbles buried one leg.

"Pa! Are you all right?"

Danaher grimaced. The lantern light glimmered on a dark crimson trail from his hairline down the side of his face and into his collar.

"I think I'm all right. I made it this far after the first cave-in. Started digging, then a second cave-in sent some rocks down on me. Just woke up."

"Let me see," Olivia demanded, the cool physician once again. "Katy, hold the lantern up here."

A gash just above his right temple sent the stream of blood down his face, but the cut was shallow. "Can you move everything? Is anything broken?"

"I can't move my leg."

"Which one?"

"The one you're sitting on."

"What? I'm not . . . Oh, yes I am." She hastily moved. "Sorry. I thought that was a pile of dirt."

"Now I can move it." He grinned, and the dirt on his face cracked into a spiderweb of lines.

She almost cried at his attempt at humor. "Be serious! Is there anything else? Ribs? Fingers?"

"I can't move my ribs."

"Oh blast you, Danaher!"

She did a quick once-over to make sure his neck and spine and ribs were uninjured.

"Pa, we thought you were dead for sure!"

"You know it takes more than a little cave-in to kill an Irishman, Katy. I sure am grateful you came in here to get me, though." He glanced up at Olivia. "Something must have scared you a bunch to get you back into this tunnel, Doc. Didn't think my hide meant that much to you."

Her fingers stopped in their examination of his ribs. What he said was true. She hadn't once given thought to her earlier fear of the tunnel. Until now. "I wish you hadn't mentioned that, Mr. Danaher."

Surprisingly, his hand moved to cover hers where it rested on his chest. "Who's going to need more help out of this tunnel, lass? You or me?"

"Don't tease her, Pa! If it weren't for the doc, I woulda been caught in that second cave-in, and Ellen would still be screaming her head off like a useless ninny."

Danaher smiled. "Is that so?"

Katy sent a shamefaced glance Olivia's way. "And she kept right on digging after I gave up and started crying."

"Interesting. I guess we both owe the doc our lives, then, don't we?"

"Yeah. I guess."

"And don't think I won't collect on the debt from both of you, but I think we should get out of here now. Can you walk, Mr. Danaher?" Olivia tried to keep the trembling from her voice, but the walls were closing in and she felt as though she couldn't breathe.

"I can walk." Shakily, Danaher got to his feet. He put his arm around her, ostensibly for support, but Olivia felt strength flowing from him to her. How ironic that she was the rescuer and yet he was the one giving her help.

"Remember the meadow," he said as Katy crawled through the hole in the blockage. "And the wildflowers, and the creek."

Olivia took a deep breath and thought of the meadows they'd ridden through coming back to the cabin. The stream splashing down layered terraces of beaver ponds, the eagle that had circled far above their heads one afternoon. All those lovely things, and the fact that Danaher was alive. Danaher was alive. The steel band of his arm held her tight; his warm, living breath tickled her hair. The walls of her fear slowly receded.

* * *

A hastily thrown together Christmas dinner was a happy but subdued affair that evening. The twins were exhausted. Ellen's voice was raspy from shouting into the tunnel. Katy slumped over her plate and picked at her food, and Olivia was so tired she could scarcely keep her eyes open. The liveliest person at the table was the one who by rights ought to be dead, as Olivia had declared the moment they emerged from the mine. Spending one's days in such a place was tantamount to delivering an engraved invitation to the Grim Reaper.

"Surely you're not going back in there," she had cried when Danaher remarked that the cave-in had revealed a new silver vein.

"And what else would I be doing?"

"Working at something that doesn't involve getting buried under tons of rock!"

"Ah, well, I tried my hand at ranching for many years, but that was a good deal more dangerous than mining."

His grim tone held no hint of a joke, but Olivia couldn't imagine he was serious.

"I can't think that getting your foot stomped by a cow is as deadly as having a mine come down around your ears."

Danaher merely shook his head and smiled. He seemed to be taking his brush with death very lightly, and yet his mood was distracted. When they arrived back at the cabin, he brushed off Olivia's attempts to examine his injuries until the girls were washed and fed. While the twins slumped wearily over their plates and Olivia picked at her food, Danaher ate a hearty dinner and scoffed at Olivia's fears about the mine. The cave-in was a freak occurrence, he insisted. Besides, if a man wanted to make money by poking at the earth, he had to take his licks when the earth decided to poke back.

The man definitely needed a good talking-to, Olivia decided.

Gifts were exchanged after dinner—bright ribbons and peppermint candy for Katy and Ellen, a rabbit-fur hat for Danaher (hunted down by Katy and stitched together by Ellen), and a beautifully delicate natural filigree of native silver from the mine for Olivia.

Strangely, it was one of the best Christmases of Olivia's memory. The girls' warmth toward her meant more than any ordinary gift could have. When she had clawed her way through the barrier of rocks that had trapped Gabe, Olivia also had broken through the wall of Katy's hostility, it seemed, for Katy's eyes had sent her silent messages of gratitude all evening.

The night was a beautiful ending to a disastrous day. They all had much to give thanks for. Olivia looked at Gabe sitting on a stool by the fire, his face ruddy from the flames, and once again felt the awful fear of thinking he was gone forever.

The twins willingly trundled off to bed once the dishes were washed. Determined not to be put off any longer, Olivia got her medical bag and marched over to the fireplace, where Danaher sat and stared into the fire with a furrowed brow.

"You're going to let me have a look at you."

"Am I?"

"Yes."

"Always the doctor."

"What else would I be?"

"That's for you to say, I suppose."

"Take off your shirt, please."

"Yes, ma'am."

Considering what could have been, Danaher had suffered very little hurt. Minor scrapes and bruises, knuckles raw from digging, a gash and lump on his head, and two bruised ribs. He endured patiently while she snipped the hair around the head gash and stitched it shut—not his normal behavior at all. Olivia wondered if the blow to his head could have caused more damage than was apparent.

"None of your usual complaining, Mr. Danaher? I thought you didn't believe in suffering pain quietly."

"I guess tonight I'm just grateful to be alive."

"That's a very sensible attitude. I wouldn't have thought you capable of it."

"I might be capable of quite a few things you wouldn't think."

She cleaned the last of the blood away from the stitched cut and surveyed her handiwork in the lantern light. "It seems I'm forever patching you up, Mr. Danaher. If you don't stop letting your fellow man and Mother Nature beat up on you, you're not going to live to be an old man."

"I'll try to remember that."

"You've a couple of bruised ribs. You should be familiar with the procedure for that. Do you want me to bandage them?"

"Yes."

A bit surprised, she ripped the sheet Ellen had brought for bandages into wide strips, had him hold one end, and wound. "This would be very much easier if you stood up."

He stood.

"I don't think the ribs are broken this time. Is this too tight? Does it hurt?"

"No. The reason I wanted the bandage was to get you to put your arms around me."

She laughed.

"I'm not joking."

Something in his tone sent a stab of panic and a frisson of something more exotic shooting through her. She felt like dropping the bandage and backing out of his reach, even though she was only halfway finished.

"You're always joking."

"No. I'm dead serious." His arms had been stretched out to the side to allow her to wrap, but now his hands came down upon her shoulders.

"What are you . . ."

Her frantic question was silenced as his mouth slanted across hers. She struggled only briefly as his arms enveloped her and pulled her close. His scent, his warmth, the rasp of his stubble across her skin, the insistent hunger of his mouth on hers—it all released a flood of desire in her too powerful to resist.

She pulled back, trying to regain her equilibrium. His lips traced a fiery path up her throat to her ear. "Mr. Danaher . . ."

"In the mine you called me Gabriel." The warm whisper in her ear sent a tidal wave of sensation vibrating through her body. "Call me Gabriel."

"Gabriel . . ."

He was unbuttoning the bodice of her gown. She tried to tell him to stop this foolishness, but her lips wouldn't obey. His hand slipped inside her bodice, under her shift, and cupped her bare breast. The calluses on his hand rasped against the tender skin, not hurtfully, but with a sensation that thickened the sweet, honeyed lethargy that was rising inside her. Her breathing slowed to a languorous relaxation; her head dropped back, too heavy for her to hold erect. He pressed a kiss to the base of her throat.

"The twins . . ."

"Are sleeping like little logs."

In one last effort at good sense, Olivia tried to back away from his caresses. A single short step and her back came up against the wall. She had no retreat from hands busy with the rest of the buttons that fastened her gown from hem to collar.

"Gabriel," she whispered. "We shouldn't do this."

"Yes we should."

"I'm not . . . I'm not . . ." She had been going to use the classic objection that she wasn't that kind of woman. But she was that kind of woman, it seemed. Her whole body seemed swollen with need, and between her thighs was an ache and throbbing that testified to exactly what it was that she needed. She was ready to surrender both virtue and virginity for the touch that would assuage that sweet, agonizing ache.

"I know you're not that kind of woman," he said, as if reading her mind. "You're not a woman that a man can take and then walk away from. You're a woman who spins webs that are invisible until a man runs into them. Then the web clings and holds fast and won't let go no matter how he tries to shake it off."

Her gown slipped to the floor and his hands ran lightly over her shift, exploring curves, hills, and valleys with an intimacy that brought a hot flush of desire to Olivia's skin. Then he took the sides of the thin garment and stretched it tightly over her breasts until the swollen mounds and erect nipples were clearly outlined. "Lord and Saint Patrick but you're beautiful, Olivia Baron. How did I miss that when I first saw you?"

His hands traveled down her sides, stretching the thin material to outline her waist, belly, hips, and thighs.

"You're goddamned gorgeous."

He reached for the laces of her shift, the last bulwark between her and utter vulnerability. Suddenly frightened, she intercepted his hands and held them away.

Unperturbed, he smiled at her. In the lantern light his green eyes seemed to glitter with sparks of gold. "You care about me, Doc. And you want this."

She opened her mouth to deny it, but nothing came out. Nearly losing him today had made her realize how much she did care about him.

"You're a woman who grows on a man, and you've grown on me until every thought that goes through my mind has you hitched to its tail, and you're dancing through all my dreams."

His hand escaped hers and closed over one breast. The warmth of it burned all the way down to her toes.

"I found out a couple of things in that mine today." His thumb traveled lazy circles around her nipple, and his eyes seemed to look straight into her soul. "I found out you love me."

She started to disavow any such foolishness, but he gently shook his head to silence her.

"I also stared long and hard at death, and I discovered that life is precious, life is short, and only a fool doesn't reach out to take what he wants and what he needs. And I want and need you so much that I'm just plain going to go up in flames if I don't get you."

Both hands joined in the caressing now, pressing her against the wall and lifting and cupping her breasts. His body crowded her, loomed over her, and when he ducked his head and began to suck at one nipple through the thin cotton of her shift, Olivia thought her knees were going to go out from under her.

"I can understand if you want to go slow," he murmured against her skin. "We can go as slow as you like; we've got the whole, long night."

He lifted her against him, and the hard column of his male arousal pressed into her belly. As his hands slid down to her buttocks, she instinctively opened her thighs to allow him to soothe the ache between them. His fingers brushed across the place where sweet longing had almost become pain. Every bit of strength seemed to leave her body as he delicately teased and tantalized. A gush of hot, creamy moisture met his explorations.

"You're ready right now, aren't you, lass? Your blood's turning to steam, and you want me moving inside you."

Her arms around Gabe's neck, she clung to him to keep from melting into a molten pool on the floor. She had never guessed that feelings like this existed, that the heart could race, the pulse pound, the body flush with such exquisite, burning fire. Danaher's every touch, every word made the fire burn hotter. She was helpless against his assault and the contrivances of her own body.

He carried her to the bed, closed the curtains, and proceeded to make short work of her shift. Naked and unembarrassed she lay between his straddled legs, under the searing blaze of his eyes. She felt weak as a kitten and strong as a lioness, helpless, flushed with power, frightened and exultant at the same time. She could see the muscles of his jaw tighten as he looked at his prize, see the twitch of his sensuously curved mouth and the labored rise and fall of his chest, and she wanted him more than she'd wanted anything in her life.

With slow movements—as though one slip of control would precipitate a cataclysm—he stripped off his shirt and wool undershirt. He fumbled with his belt and trousers, peeling them down to release his sex in an impressive display of masculinity. Trousers and long underwear discarded, he knelt on the bed like a naked Apollo, broad shoulders, lean hips, sinew-corded thighs, and unabashed desire. She could have cried at the beauty of him.

"You are beautiful," she whispered.

He laughed. "Then we're well matched, you and I."

She reached out and tentatively touched the hard shaft that rose from his groin. He caught her hand and folded her fingers around him, his hips arching forward to send him sliding against her hand.

"Lord!" he groaned softly.

Fascinated with the game, Olivia tried a caress on her own. His head fell back and the cords in his neck stood out with the effort of control. With a low growl he pulled away and calmed his breathing.

"Curious little cat." He took her hands in his and pressed them to the pillow on either side of her head, caging her. "If I let you have your way, this game will end very soon and very abruptly." He lowered his head to trace a line up her throat with his tongue, ending at her mouth. "You're so appetizing I could eat you," he whispered against her lips. "Open your mouth."

She obeyed, and shivered at the delicious sensation of his tongue plunging between her lips and possessing her mouth. He left her wanting more, moving to tantalize her breasts, her navel, the insides of her thighs. She heaved up against him with animal sounds escaping her throat.

He laughed softly, and she could feel the warmth of that laugh fan the most private secrets of her body. A single kiss he pressed between her thighs, then slid up her body to take her mouth once again.

"Dr. Baron, for all you know about the body, you didn't know about this, did you?"

His finger slid into the most intimate recess of her body, and she arched with the acute pleasure of his invasion.

"But you know now, don't you, lass? You're warm and welcoming inside."

He spread her thighs wide, and she didn't resist. The prod of his sex made her gasp with bliss.

"I'll go easy, lass, I promise, though God knows right now I want to pound into you until we're both raw and bruised."

He eased inside, spreading her, stretching, tearing, and finally possessing. The pain was only part of the ecstasy, the wonderful feeling of completion, of wholeness.

"Wrap your legs around my waist, love. That's good."

She gasped as he seated himself even more deeply inside her.

"You're like silk inside, Olivia. Hot, wet silk, and I'm going to go mad if I have to control myself much longer."

She moved against him with an instinct she didn't know she possessed. He groaned softly, withdrew, and thrust again.

She grasped him tighter. "More. Oh please, more."

Again and again, faster and still deeper he plunged. She clung to him and reveled in his driving possession, every fiber of her body attuned to him, moving with him, contracting around him, until with a moan and one final powerful thrust he wrenched her with him into an eruption of rapture, the muscles of his buttocks convulsing in the rhythmic desperation of release. Her whole body seemed to contract around their joined flesh, then surge upward in flight. Spasms of bliss sent her higher and higher, until the stars themselves were left far behind and warm darkness enfolded her in welcoming arms.

Olivia woke to a cold nose pressed against hers and a blast of warm, ripe breath. She opened her eyes to meet yellow eyes. Hunter's head separated the bed curtains. His tongue lolled in a wolfish grin.

"What are you doing out of your box, you imp?" she whispered.

Hunter blinked, an innocent look on his puppy face.

"I think we'd better put you back, big boy, before you decide to make Ellen's marmot a midnight snack." Olivia swung her legs over the bed, and an immediate raw tenderness between her thighs reminded her in no uncertain terms of the night's activities. She glanced at Danaher, who was still fast asleep.

"Come on," she whispered to the pup, grabbing a blanket from the foot of the bed to wrap around her nakedness.

Hunter seemed content to stay in his box when she put him back. Olivia debated how to modify the little kennel to confine him, then realized the absurdity of standing in her bare feet on a freezing floor in the middle of the night wondering how to build a better wolf kennel. Her mind was taking any path it could that didn't lead toward her recent cavortings with Gabriel Danaher. Yet she had to think about it. She'd never been one to avoid facing reality.

She added a log to the fire and watched it blaze to life, then pulled her chair close to the fireplace and sat. She thought of the rocker as her chair because she'd spent so many nights sleeping in it, and should have spent this night in it as well. But what was done could not be undone, not by all the regret in the world; and Olivia wasn't sure she regretted anything. As she stared into the fire, she recalled only too clearly the paradise Danaher had taken her to. Seduction had always seemed like an ugly word to her, but the actuality of what had happened to her—to them both—had been far from ugly. Sex was not the awkward, embarrassing, and messy process described in her medical texts. Nor was it the quick, furtive groping in the dark that she'd pictured. In reality it was moving beyond words, more powerful than she would have ever guessed, especially with someone beloved.

Beloved. The word stuck in her mind and wouldn't budge. She hadn't realized that she loved Gabriel Danaher until he told her she did. Perhaps he had more insight into her soul than she did, because he was right. She had gone into that tunnel after him without a thought for her

fear of that dark, confined throat of hell, and not until she was sure
Danaher was safe did her own fear return. And how little persuasion had
she needed to fall willingly into his bed. She had behaved with shameless
abandon, allowing him to do unbelievably intimate things to her body
and enjoying every moment of it. Worse, she had brazenly caressed him
in a very private, personal manner.

Olivia sighed and rested her head in her hands. How could she have
fallen in love with such a man? A man she knew nothing about, really. A
man who could never fit into her life, and whose own existence was so far
removed from her own aspirations as to be on another world. Perhaps it
was a passing insanity, and yet right now this passion seemed firmly
rooted. It had germinated and grown while she wasn't looking, and now
seemed to rule her foolish heart.

A hand fell on her shoulder, and she started with a little squeak.

"It's only me," Danaher said softly from behind her. "I didn't mean to
scare you." He massaged her shoulders, then combed his fingers through
her hair, which hung down her back in a tangled cascade. "Are you
sitting here plotting revenge against the scoundrel who seduced you?"

She smiled and leaned back against him. "Well, I'm thinking of the
scoundrel, it's true. But scarcely in terms of revenge."

"I won't say I'm sorry, lass. I'm enough of a scoundrel to want you
again right now."

"Have you ever been in love, Gabriel?"

"Yes."

"Your Blackfoot wife?"

"Yes. When I lost Minnie, I thought my life was over. If not for the
girls, I would have gladly died."

"Do you love me?" The question was a brazen one, but Olivia didn't
believe in playing guessing games. She didn't know anything about love.
She was beginning to think that she didn't know a lot about life in general. But she did know that men and women lusted much more often
than they loved, and it was important to her that the night's embrace had
come from something more than animal desire.

He hesitated for a moment that seemed very long, then answered in a
quiet voice. "Yes, Olivia. I love you. For whatever it means to you, I do
love you."

She sighed as his fingers massaged her temples. "I don't know what it
means. Do you?"

"No," he replied with a chuckle. "But you'll want to find out, won't
you? Knowing you, you won't be satisfied until you've analyzed and
probed it to death." His hands dropped to her shoulders and kneaded

her muscles, then lower to brush her breasts. A frisson of desire shivered through her body, making her gasp in pleasure. "Why don't we forget what it means and just accept this bit of time that's been given to us?"

"That sounds rather hedonistic."

"What it is is practical."

Olivia was sure she didn't agree with such a philosophy, but his hands were massaging magic into her body, and thought was giving way to desire.

"Come back to bed, Doc. You're going to freeze out here, and I'm burning up with good old-fashioned lust."

She didn't object as he picked her up from the chair and carried her to the bed. The mattress was soft and still warm from his body heat, and her cold skin quickly heated as he covered her with himself. Instinctively her legs parted to welcome him, and she felt him smile against her mouth as he kissed her.

"I do love you, Doc. I love you so much it goddamned hurts."

The rest he told her with his body.

Chapter 14

Morning invaded their little curtained sanctuary in bright spears of sunlight and the aroma of sizzling bacon. Reluctantly Olivia surrendered the pleasant lethargy of sleep, only to meet wide green eyes observing her through the parting of the curtains.

"Good morning," Ellen said solemnly. "I'm making griddle cakes."

Olivia opened her mouth but couldn't think of an appropriate response. What did one say when caught red-handed in such a situation—especially by a child? Her lover's child.

Lover! Oh merciful Lord! What had she done? She glanced to Gabriel's side of the bed for support and found herself alone.

"Pa's been in the mine since before sunrise. He said we should let you sleep and call him for breakfast. Are you ready to get up? There's warm water for washing in the kettle over the fire."

"Oh my! It's late. You should have awakened me."

"Pa said you needed to sleep."

Ellen didn't seem at all upset to find Olivia in Gabriel's bed. In fact, she looked like a cat with a bowl of cream, humming to herself softly as she beat the batter and set the griddle on the fire to heat.

"I'll go up to the mine and yell for Pa and Katy," she said when Olivia had washed, dressed, and brushed her hair.

While Ellen was gone, Olivia went to make up the bed. She drew a sharp breath when she saw the dark crimson stains that splotched the sheets—virgin's blood, and she had been the virgin who bled. As voices sounded outside the cabin, she pulled up the blankets and quilt over the telltale spots, then smoothed and tucked until the bed looked as though no one had ever slept in it, much less tumbled around on the mattress in unrestrained passion. She had just tucked in the last corner when the twins and their father burst into the cabin.

Olivia turned quickly, feeling illogically as though she'd been discovered in some misdeed. Gabriel stood just inside the door, looking at her as though he might eat her for breakfast rather than Ellen's griddle cakes.

"You're both filthy!" Ellen pushed her sister and father back out the door. "Wash before you eat."

Katy slipped past her sister and darted to the table for a piece of freshly cooked bacon.

"Quit that, Katy! Your hands are covered with dirt!"

"It ain't gonna kill nobody."

"Go wash!"

"I'll wash at the sink," she conceded, grabbing the kettle of hot water from its hook over the fire.

Ellen leveled a stern look at her father, who raised his own dirty hands in surrender and backed out the door. "Yes'm! Yes'm! I'll wash."

He glanced at Olivia, and the glitter in his eyes drew her forward as a magnet draws iron. "I'll bring you a clean shirt," she murmured, her eyes not leaving the door even after he'd disappeared.

"Olivia!"

Ellen's voice broke the trance. Olivia started as though she'd been asleep.

"Pa's shirts are in there." Ellen pointed toward a wooden trunk.

Gabe had broken the ice on the wash trough and was sluicing frigid water over his bare torso when Olivia arrived behind the cabin with his clean clothes. His dripping hair glistened in the morning sun. Rivulets of water traced the contours of his chest and ran enticingly down his flat, muscle-ridged belly into his trousers. With a monumental effort, Olivia kept her eyes from following.

She had no idea what to say to him. What did a woman say to a man who had performed such incredibly intimate acts upon her body as Gabriel Danaher had last night? How did a woman slip back into the role of sane, civilized lady when she had acted like a brazen tart only short hours before?

Gabriel dried himself with a rag, took the long-sleeved woolen undershirt she dumbly offered, and pulled it quickly over his head. Unembar-

rassed, he unbuttoned his trousers and stuffed the shirt inside. Olivia
flushed as her eyes were drawn inevitably to the open fly. Suddenly
breathing became difficult, and something warm and liquid curled in her
belly like soft, flowing honey.

"Good morning." His voice broke the spell. Her cheeks burned. She
was sure her face was red as fire as she dragged her gaze up to meet his.
He looked at her from under lazily half-lowered lids, and his eyes were
warm with shared intimacy.

"Good morning," she answered softly. "You took off your bandage."

"I didn't really need it."

Grinning, he took the wool flannel shirt and her hand along with it,
pulling her toward him and into his arms. With one finger he tilted her
face upward. "How are you this morning?"

"I . . . I'm quite well."

"Are you?"

"Yes. Of course."

"Sore?"

Olivia felt her face grow even hotter. "Yes."

"So am I."

"Really? I didn't know men got . . . that is . . ."

"Yes. We do." He grinned wickedly. "I don't suppose you have some
magical salve in that medical bag of yours—something you could rub
onto the affected organ to soothe the ache."

Her eyes widened. "You're shameless!"

"And so are you. Beautifully shameless, and I love it." He kissed her—
no chaste good-morning peck but a hungry onslaught that pried her lips
apart and possessed her mouth in a way that made her ache to have him
between her legs and loving her once again. His open trousers left no
doubt that he was ready to comply with her body's demand.

"Tonight," he whispered against her ear, sending sweet shivers down
her spine. "I've never been so eager for the end of the day."

A giggle brought them both back to their senses. They looked up to
see two sets of black braids disappear around the corner.

Olivia shook her head. "I don't understand your daughters."

"Kids aren't made to be understood, are they?"

"For the longest time they regarded me as some evil Jezebel who was
out to seduce your affections, and now that I have, they're giggling with
delight and treating me like part of the family."

"Don't strain yourself trying to understand my girls," Gabe advised.
"God made them, and only He knows how their little minds work." He

gave her backside an affectionate pinch. "And what's this about you seducing me? Give credit where credit's due."

She raised a brow. "I had no part in it?"

"You definitely had a part in it. But you were the seduced, my lass, and I was the seducer. If you want to practice your skill at seduction, I'd be glad to let you have your turn tonight."

Arm in arm they walked around to the cabin door, lured by the aroma of bacon and griddle cakes. This wasn't real or right, but that didn't matter. Olivia wanted to sing like a lark on a fresh spring morning.

The interlude that followed was more peaceful than any time that Olivia remembered in her entire life. New Year's Day came and went unnoticed. Gabriel spent long days in the mine, breaking up and removing the ore from the new vein that had almost cost him his life. Katy often helped him; and when she wasn't in the mine, she was outdoors in the cold chopping and stacking firewood, repairing fences in the mule corral, tending horses, or chinking between the logs of the cabin to stop the cold winter drafts.

In spite of her constant worry about Amy, Olivia enjoyed her days. A good deal of satisfaction was to be had running a household and being able to do almost everything for oneself. She found a new combination of seasonings for elk stew that even Ellen complimented, and her yeast bread and biscuits were almost as good as Ellen's. Katy, also, took a hand in her education, and most days they spent at least a short time target-practicing with Gabriel's rifle. Katy laughed at her efforts at first, but the girl was a good instructor. Being much the same size as Olivia, she was able to share techniques for holding the rifle steady and improving aim.

The days were peaceful and pleasant, but it was the nights Olivia lived for. Wrapped in Gabriel Danaher's arms, she reveled in the strength that surrounded and flowed into her, basked in the fire of his eyes, and burned in the delicious heat of passion. She felt protected, cherished, secure, and desired. Something inside her knew what they did wasn't right; the world they created wasn't real, but a stronger part of her didn't care. Enfolded in darkness, warmed by the fires of love, she and Gabriel created a world that held only the two of them, a world in which they decided what was real and what was right.

Olivia was not the only one thrust into a new world in those few weeks. One snowy morning Katy came inside, leaving half a pile of firewood uncut. She wandered around the cabin, fiddling with the fire that already burned perfectly well in the fireplace, giving Hunter a few minutes of rough and tumble on the floor, and feeding scraps to Ellen's marmot, whose box had been placed well out of the wolf cub's reach.

"When're you gonna turn it loose?" Katy asked Ellen, who was busy making a hat out of the rabbit skins that Katy had brought back the day of the mine cave-in.

"In a couple of days. Olivia says his leg's pretty much healed."

"Oh."

Katy drifted to something else, every once in a while throwing quick glances Olivia's way. Finally, her mouth tightened into a firm line, her brows puckered in a determined frown, and she spoke.

"Olivia . . . uh . . ."

"Yes, Katy?"

"What're you doin'?"

"I'm mending one of your father's shirts."

"Oh." She picked up the poker and stabbed at the fire a time or two, then squared her shoulders. "I was wondering . . . well . . ."

"What is it, Katy?"

Katy glanced at Ellen and turned red. "Don't you have something to do somewhere else—like outside?"

Ellen gave her a puckish grin. "It's cold outside."

Amazingly, tears glistened in Katy's eyes and threatened to overflow.

"Ellen," Olivia said, "I haven't checked the hens this morning. Would you do it?"

"It's too cold for them to lay."

"I think you should check them anyway."

With a martyred sigh and a glare at Katy, Ellen set the rabbit skins aside, pulled on her coat, and left.

"Now, Katy. Tell me what's wrong."

"I'm sick somethin' dreadful."

Olivia laid her hand against the girl's brow. "You don't have a fever. How are you not feeling well?"

"I got a pain in my belly, and . . . and . . ." Tears overflowed, washing clean trails down dirt-smudged cheeks.

"And what? Are you throwing up?"

"No. I'm bleedin' something awful." Her voice lowered to a horrified whisper. "I'm bleedin' from my . . . from my bottom parts."

Olivia managed to stifle a smile. Obviously, this normal feminine event was unexpected and terrifying to Katy, who seldom admitted fear of anything. "Katy, you're not sick."

"What d'ya mean? I'm probably dyin'. My innards are twistin' in knots, and I'm bleedin' like a gut-shot deer."

"Your mother never told you about women's monthly flow?"

"What?"

"Sit down, my dear. I'll explain, and while we're talking, we'll rip these rags in a size you can use to keep the blood from staining your clothes."

A half hour and a hundred questions later, Katy was finally satisfied that she wasn't dying, though she was none too happy at the prospect of such inconvenient messiness and discomfort every month for years to come.

"This is something that women simply have to put up with, Katy. It's a price we pay for being female."

Katy made a rude sound. "When you pay a price, you're supposed to get something in return. What's the good in being female?"

"There are quite a few advantages to being a woman, dear, although sometimes one does have to look hard to find them."

"Name one."

Olivia smiled, thinking of lying in Gabriel's arms, thinking of the joy she'd seen on the faces of women who had just borne the painful travail of birthing a babe. She thought of Amy, so happy that she might at last have a child. She thought of her schoolmates at Miss Tatterhorn's, sharing girlish confidences and happily chattering over fashions. But Katy wouldn't understand these things. Appreciation of one's femininity came with time and maturity. Olivia herself was just learning what it was to be a woman.

"You'll have to take my word on this one, Katy. In any case, being female isn't something you have a choice about. You simply have to make the best of what you're given."

Katy grimaced.

"And as for the discomfort that comes with bleeding, I've always found that pampering yourself and staying in bed only makes the pain last longer. On the other hand, you wouldn't be wise to go riding about on horseback or overtiring yourself with strenuous activities."

"What? I should stay in and help around the house?" She made the possibility sound like the cruelest torture.

"Why don't we both spend the rest of the day making you a dress to celebrate the occasion?"

"Don't seem like nothing to celebrate!"

"You're growing up, Katy. If you're to discover the advantages of being a woman, you'll have to try your feminine wings. It doesn't mean you have to give up any of your other activities. Your trousers will still be there when you want them."

"A dress, huh?"

Olivia smiled to see a spark of interest in Katy's eyes.

Ellen and Olivia and Katy spent the rest of the day cutting and sewing a dress patterned after one Olivia remembered from her girlhood—sadly out of fashion now, she was sure, but the alpine meadows below Thunder Ridge were hardly Paris or New York. Ellen and Olivia sewed, while Katy supervised the styling. She balked at flounces and a bow in back, and only allowed a small amount of lace around the cuffs and the neckline. The long sleeves, she insisted, had to be roomy enough for her to swing her arms.

In the end they fashioned a very plain little dress, but when Katy donned it, the effect was stunning. Her glistening black hair, vivid green eyes, and satiny olive skin needed no enhancement. The dress fit perfectly around her slender little waist and modestly clung to just-budding breasts. Her clunky boots sounded a rather jarring note in the ensemble, but she had no other shoes.

"You are stunning," Olivia told her. It was the first time she had ever seen Katy freshly washed, nails clean, hair brushed and glistening in the rays of the afternoon sun that slanted through the cabin windows.

"I look stupid," Katy insisted.

"You look just like me," Ellen offered with an impish smile.

"Like I said. I look stupid."

"This will be quite a surprise for your father."

"I can't let him see me like this!"

"Oh no, young lady! We didn't go to all this work to have you turn tail and run."

"I never turn tail and run! But I look . . ."

"Like a beautiful young woman. Ellen and I have cooked a marvelous supper for your debut, and as soon as your father gets out of the mine, we're going to have a grand celebration."

Katy grunted.

"You climb up to the loft and hide until Pa gets here," Ellen directed.

"Are you sure my trousers are still there?"

"They're folded on your cot," Olivia assured her, "for whenever you want them."

"Well, all right. I'll show myself to Pa, then I'm gettin' back to normal." Katy gathered her skirt awkwardly in one hand and climbed the ladder to the loft, stumbling and cursing the dress most of the way up.

"Ladies don't cuss," Ellen called merrily after her.

Olivia put her arm around Ellen's shoulders. "One thing at a time, my girl. One thing at a time."

*   *   *

Daylight was long gone by the time Gabe emerged from the mine and walked down the path toward the cabin. The mine had been warm compared to the night air, and the sweat of his exertions froze on his clothing before he was halfway to the cabin. Dirt caked every inch of exposed skin, and even with a half-frozen nose he could smell his own stink. Maybe he would chase the twins and Olivia up to the loft, pull out the tin tub, and take himself a hot bath with the water he knew would be heating over the fire. On second thought, maybe he would chase just the twins up to the loft and let Olivia give him that nice bath. A number of entertaining possibilities sprang from that line of thought. Having a woman to end the day with was nice. In fact, it was more than nice—it was downright addicting.

Olivia and Ellen met him at the door with wide smiles that at once put him on guard. Something was brewing besides supper.

"You're late, Pa!"

"Yeah, but I got five loads hauled out today."

"My goodness but you're filthy, Gabriel!"

"I been grubbing in the dirt like a mole. What do you expect?"

"I expect you'll want a bath and clean clothes before supper. Ellen, fetch your father a clean set of clothes."

"Doc, you read my mind."

Olivia smiled, and suddenly Gabe wanted to skip the bath—as much as he'd been looking forward to it—skip supper, and go directly to bed.

"And if you read my mind right now," he continued in a whisper for her ears alone, "you'll be turning red as a berry any minute."

"Behave yourself," Olivia warned. "Your daughters have a surprise for you this evening."

"And what would that be?"

"You'll find out in good time."

"Not even a hint?"

"I'm not snitching. Sometimes we ladies have to stick together."

Ellen came running back with clothes and tub and placed both in front of the fire. "Now, hurry up, Pa. Supper's almost ready."

As Ellen scrambled up to the loft, Gabe started to peel off his grimy clothes. "I don't suppose you'd like to help," he said hopefully.

Olivia threw him a tolerant smile as she poured water from the kettle into the tub, then she too headed toward the ladder. "I think you're old enough to bathe yourself. Just don't take too long or I'll send Ellen down to drag you out."

"Where's Katy?"

"In the loft with Ellen."

"What are you three plotting up there?"

"You'll see."

So his daughters had a surprise for him, Gabe thought as he stripped off the last of his clothes and sat down in the steaming water. What would it be this time? Katy was usually the one to spring surprises—as in the time she had cut her hair into a ragged bob that ended at her ears, or the day she brought home a porcupine and wanted to make a pet of it. (How she had gotten the spiny animal in the box was something he had never quite figured out.) Of course, her crowning achievement of surprises had been the day she rescued him from hanging and jumped off a waterfall to avoid being left safely behind, dragging her reluctant sister along with her.

Ellen had her share of talent at surprises as well. Gabe had long suspected it had been the quieter twin who had actually cut Katy's hair. And then there had been the day when Ellen had gotten so fed up with Katy's boasting about riding a certain half-broken horse that she had sneaked out from under her mother's watchful eye and ridden the beast herself. The result had been a broken arm and a hard knock to the head, but she had declared getting Katy to shut up about that horse was worth the price.

Yes indeed, when his twin daughters had a surprise for him, Gabe's instinct was to run and hide. He had every reason to be apprehensive.

When the bathwater became chilly enough to make further procrastination uncomfortable, Gabe reluctantly got out of the tub and dressed. Calling that he was decent, he dragged the tub to the rear window to dump it. A cascade of footsteps descended the ladder behind him.

"Don't turn around!" Ellen chortled.

Gabe sighed and listened to the quiet fuss of female flustering behind him.

"Okay!" Ellen chimed. "Now you can turn around."

He turned. For a moment he thought he was seeing double. But no, Ellen had never had that glint in her eye. She was more subtle about her mischief. That was Katy's glint in the stunning young lady who stood between Olivia and Ellen.

"Katy?"

All three females looked at him expectantly, Katy most intently of all. The dress she wore clung fetchingly to nascent curves. Her face was scrubbed and rosy. Her hair, tied back with one of the ribbons he always brought the girls from town and which Katy never wore, was so glitteringly clean it shone in the lamplight. Her hands were clasped demurely at her waist; even the nails were trimmed and clean.

"Katy! You look so . . . so different!"

She instantly wailed. "I *told* you I looked stupid. Stupid, stupid, stupid!"

"You don't look stupid!" he vehemently denied. "Katy, you look beautiful! And grown up. You remind me of your mother the first time I saw her."

Not to be mollified, Katy pouted. "I look like Ellen!"

"What's wrong with that?" Ellen demanded.

"Yuk!"

"Now wait a minute!" Gabe thought fast to avert a war. "You two are twins. Of course you look alike—on the outside. But only someone who didn't know you would say you really look like Ellen, Katy, or that Ellen looks like you."

"You mean *I* don't look like Ma?" Ellen wailed.

"You both look like yourselves."

"You just said we look alike!" Katy reminded him indignantly.

Gabe looked toward Olivia in mute appeal.

"Girls," she intervened, "what your father means is: your mother gave you both beautiful faces and lovely dark hair and clear skin, and your features are very much alike." She threw Katy a twinkling look. "Especially when you're both dressed like girls. But you've each put your own stamp on the features your mother gave you."

"You don't think I look like Ellen?"

"No more than she would look like you if she put on trousers and a shirt."

Katy glowered at her father. "And you don't think I look stupid?"

"Definitely not. You're turning into the woman I always knew you could be."

"Oh."

"Boots and all."

Katy glanced down at her feet and grinned. Ellen giggled.

Nurtured by the warmth of Gabe's approval, Katy's femininity seemed to unfold like a blooming flower throughout supper. She ate in moderate forkfuls instead of stuffing her mouth faster than she could swallow, as was her usual manner at the table. She passed food politely instead of grabbing, and twice she corrected her own grammar. After supper, instead of immediately running upstairs to change into her trousers, as she'd threatened to do, she sat quietly with her father in front of the fire and whipped him in chess.

"I'm glad to see these duds don't slow a body's thinkin'." She twinkled at her defeated opponent, and the mischievous dimple was very evident in her cheek.

"I was hoping maybe they would," Gabe said with a grin.

"I could beat you dressed in baby didies."

"Don't get cocky, my lass. Three nights ago I beat you twice in a row."

"I let you win."

"Did not."

Katy smirked, then grimaced and looked at Olivia, who suggested: "Perhaps it's time for you girls to get up to bed."

Olivia gave Katy a hot-water bottle to take with her upstairs, and Gabe suddenly understood why Katy had chosen today of all days to dress the part of a female.

When both girls were upstairs and the lantern in the loft was doused, he smiled at Olivia, who poured hot water over a pot that earlier had been set to soak. "So my Katy has become a woman, has she? I wondered why she looked so pale off and on tonight."

Olivia raised a finger to her lips. "Don't tell her you know. She swore me to secrecy. I assured her that having been married, you knew all about these woman things, but she just rolled her eyes."

Gabe rose from his stool, put his arms around her from the back, and whispered into her ear. "I know all about these woman things, do I?" Her ear was a delicacy too tempting to resist. He bit it softy and felt her shiver in his arms.

"You know much more about woman things than you should, my good man."

"You seemed pleased enough with my knowledge last night. Leave the damned pot. The fire's burning low. We ought to be in bed."

"Whose fire is burning low?" she asked with a chuckle. "Not yours, I think."

"You're right about that. I flame up every time I look at you."

"Is that why Katy beat you so handily?"

"Katy is capable of beating me at chess without you to distract me."

"But you thought tonight would be an especially good time for her to win."

He smiled. "Don't change the subject, woman, or I'll carry you to the bed and remind you good and well what the original subject was."

Her eyes laughed up at him. "What was that?"

"My lust for you." Putting words to action, he picked her up in his arms and started for the bed.

"Gabriel!"

"Don't shriek, Doc. We don't want an audience."

"I haven't changed into a nightgown yet."

"You're not going to need one, and I'll see to your undressing."

She laughed softly when he dumped her onto the straw-ticked mattress and whipped the curtains shut. They rolled together; he ended on top, kissing her. She smelled of wood smoke and woman, and her mouth tasted of coffee and desire, a warm, wet cavern that was impossible not to get lost in.

Gabe released her only long enough to free her of her clothing. The buttons and hooks were stubborn, his fingers awkward with impatience. Finally her bare flesh warmed his hands—full breasts flattened against her ribs as she lay beneath him, tiny waist, flaring hips, slender legs that tapered to delicate feet. He combed his fingers through the triangle of soft curls that adorned her woman's parts. She sighed, lifted and opened her legs to give him better access to her.

"You're a shameless hussy, Olivia Baron." He pressed his mouth against her ear and felt her shiver at the warmth of his breath. "And it's a good thing for me that you are."

Her mouth willingly opened as he captured it. His body was hungry for her, and his soul was famished for her ardent response. She arched against the hand that stroked between her thighs in teasing caresses, and he savored his power to rouse her. Gently he circled the tiny erect bud that was the center of her passion, then dipped his fingers into the tight, moist well of her sex. In and out he delved. Inside, deeper, faster, until she gasped and contracted around his fingers.

He kissed her again, swallowing her cry of pleasure and starting the process again by rubbing his shirt tantalizingly across her breasts.

"You are wicked!" she whispered in mock dismay. "You don't even have your clothes off."

"If I had my clothes off and I could feel you against my bare skin, our games would be over before they began. I like the anticipation."

Her eyes lit with mischief. "You like to drive poor innocent women past control, but you don't like to go there yourself." Her fingers opened the buttons on his shirt and then started on his union suit. A hot spear of desire lanced from her every touch straight to his groin. The confining pressure of his trousers was raw and painful as he swelled even larger with need.

"Be careful, woman, or you'll get what you're asking for."

"Really?" she asked with an innocent smile. She had his shirt off and the top of his union suit around his waist. His belt was the next to go. Her hand paused at his fly.

"This is a very curious swelling you have here, sir. Your trousers appear to be in danger of giving way."

Her hand caressed the strained denim between his legs in sweet torture. He caught his breath and let her play, enjoying the throbbing anticipation. His thighs trembled with the torment; sweat beaded on his bare chest and brow while her long, supple fingers molded the swollen column of his desire and played like a puppy with a new bone.

Finally he could take no more. He brushed her hands away and made short work of the rest of his clothing. "Now see what you've done!" He wedged himself between her thighs and pinned her firmly to the mattress.

"I did a very good job, I would say!"

"Damn right you did."

He could wait no longer. Her legs wrapped around his hips as he took her. She was as ready as he, hot, silken, moist, and welcoming. Three hard strokes brought him to a powerful climax, and she gasped into the hollow of his throat as she followed him into ecstasy. For a moment he felt engorged with power, his body a focus of potency and vigor. The dark earth and bright stars above it whirled to his command, all to pleasure the woman who still clung to him, her face buried against his shoulder and her ragged breath warming his skin.

Slowly the fury of explosion died, leaving the glowing embers that never died when Olivia was near him. He eased his weight off her, carrying her pliant body with him as he buried both of them beneath the blankets. She looked up. Her eyes were bright, swimming with tears.

"Olivia! Did I hurt you?"

"No." She smiled and sobbed at the same time in that inexplicable, illogical way of women. "You bring me such joy, Gabriel."

The surge of protectiveness that flooded through him was as strong as the swell of renewed desire. His hand slid down the smooth curve of her back and cupped her buttock as he stiffened once again with need. But when he brushed the tousled veil of hair from Olivia's face, he could see that she had fallen asleep. A slight smile curved her lips; one of her hands rested against his chest, fingers twined in the mat of curly black hair.

He sighed and kissed the top of her head.

In this dark, curtained-off little chamber of passion, the world seemed far away. Vengeance had once been a sinister, burning need that was the focus of every day; now its glow seemed dim beside the fire that Olivia Baron had lit within him. Her fire was passion and need, but also warmth, laughter, joy. Her body stirred him to desire, but her eyes, her voice, her laughter warmed his soul. The grim quest that had consumed his life couldn't compare to that. For the first time since Minnie's death he was tempted to take up life again, not just for the twins' sake, but for himself as well. How far would he have to flee to leave Montana, murder, and vengeance far behind him?

Yet, even if by some miracle Olivia would come with him, what could he offer her? He was rough, uncultured, and unmannered—and the riches that came from this little mine couldn't make a silk purse out of an Irish sow's ear. What would his gentle lady say if she knew he had a hangman's noose waiting for him in Virginia City? She'd been afraid of him once. Would she be afraid again? Horrified? Disgusted?

Gabe pulled the blankets closer about them both and looked down at the dark blur of her hair. Her face was still nestled in the hollow of his throat. Her legs wrapped intimately around his, bringing their bodies almost as close as when they made love. He sighed, deciding that love was far more brutal than simple revenge.

Chapter 15

*F*or a moment Olivia didn't know what had awakened her. Then the ache squeezed her loins and back, and she grimaced. A sudden warmth between her legs bore witness that her cramps were not mere pains of sympathy with Katy's plight.

Reluctantly she climbed from the warm bed and hurried barefoot across the cold plank floor to the bin where she'd stored Katy's rags. As she fashioned a pad and then donned a warm nightgown and socks, the cold only made the cramps more severe. In spite of her philosophical advice to Katy, Olivia agreed that a woman's monthly curse was a high price to pay for the privilege of being female, especially if one were not destined to have children.

The thought of children brought Olivia up short as she added wood to the embers glowing in the fireplace. She could have very easily not had this particular monthly curse. How long had it been since her last? Over a month, surely. She had lost track of time in this isolated little world in the mountains, and she had given the consequences of her behavior scarcely a thought.

Foolish, foolish woman! So many times she had treated unfortunate girls in the charity clinics who had also not given pregnancy a thought when they succumbed to their own desires, and she had pitied them for their foolishness as much as for their sad situations. Most of them at least had the excuse of youth and ignorance. What excuse did Olivia have?

She was a mature, educated woman, a physician, no less! Yet she could have so easily ended up with a child in her belly and no husband to claim it. For once her menstrual cramps were a welcome discomfort. This time she would not pay the price for her imprudent conduct.

The wood she had added to the fire had ignited, and flames danced merrily on the grate. Olivia added a larger log and swung the kettle into position to heat. Then she pulled over the rocker and huddled in it for warmth. Gabriel Danaher warmed her much better, both body and soul, but reality sat upon her heart like a lead weight. She couldn't return to Gabriel's bed, or to his arms. This foolishness between them had to end.

A cold nose nudged her hand, and she looked down to see Hunter grinning wolfishly up at her from beside the chair. He jumped in and out of his box at will now, no longer quite the baby he'd been when she and Gabriel had first brought him to the cabin. Since Ellen's marmot had been released to its wild home, Hunter had the run of the cabin.

"You've adjusted very well to your new life, haven't you, love? What a smart fellow you are."

She had adjusted also—too well, and she hadn't been smart at all in doing so.

From her place by the fire, Olivia could look out the large back window of the cabin to see the night gradually give way to the dawn. As she and Hunter sat by the fire together, the black outside turned to gray, gray slowly brightened, until finally the highest part of Thunder Ridge caught the first of the sun's rays. She knew from experience that if she sat there long enough she would see the sunlight slowly creep down the ridge, and when the sun rose high enough, a bright flood would pour between the eastern peaks and wash through the valley with the clean light of a new day.

That was what Olivia needed—a clean, bright new day.

A warm hand fell on her shoulder from behind. "You're up very early," Gabriel said.

Olivia put her hand over his, wishing the world were something other than what it was. "It's going to be a beautiful day."

"Looks like it."

It was January, and Olivia had been gone from Elkhorn eight weeks. Amy's babe was due in February.

"Gabriel, I think we should take advantage of the good weather to ride down and check on the slide."

He was silent for a moment, but she felt his hand tighten on her shoulder.

"I doubt it's open yet," he said finally.

"I'd like to check, just the same."

Gabriel nudged Hunter aside and squatted beside her chair. "Still so anxious to leave, Doc?"

He was beautiful with the morning light behind him, his black hair tousled and lying every which way over broad bare shoulders, his eyes still dark with sleep. He had pulled on his trousers, but his chest was naked except for its mat of curling black hair. Gabriel Danaher was a magnificent animal; he was also a splendid man, and Olivia loved him dearly. No, she did not want to leave. But she must.

"It's not that I'm eager to leave . . ."

He folded both her hands in his. "You're freezing. Come back to bed."

"I can't. Gabriel . . . I . . ."

"Have your woman's time. I know. There were spots of blood on the sheets, and since I know well that you're no longer a bleeding virgin . . ." He grinned devilishly.

Olivia's face grew warm.

"Doc, I was married for more than ten years. Like you said, I know about these woman things. Now come back to bed and warm me up before I catch pneumonia and you have a patient to treat."

"Gabriel, what we're doing isn't right. You know it as well as I. When I woke up with my monthly flow upon me, I realized there could have been grave consequences to our behaving as though we're man and wife. It's immoral, irresponsible, and a terrible example to set for your daughters."

"Katy and Ellen love you just as much as I do, Olivia."

"Love." Olivia sighed. "Do you love me, Gabriel? Truly love me? Or is love a word you use in place of desire."

He smiled wryly, almost regretfully. "Love. Desire. One things leads to another. I do love you, Doc. You've got me hooked like a hungry trout, and I'm not even fighting it."

Olivia hugged her knees to her chest in the little rocking chair. He loved her. All the times she'd heard him say it, and this time it sank into her heart and nestled in a warm glow. That made it so much harder to be good, and it had been hard enough before.

He threaded his fingers through hers. They were long, blunt, and rough from hard use and merciless applications of the scrub brush. The juxtaposition of her white, tapered fingers upon his darker skin seemed to fascinate him for a moment. Then he exhaled a sigh that sounded rather like it came from a man about to jump off a cliff.

"Olivia, marry me."

She could only stare at him in surprise.

"I'm not exactly a high-class woman's idea of the suitable husband, but you'd never be without love and you'd never go hungry. That much I could promise you. I've made enough money from this mine to buy us a place far away from here, wherever we want to go."

He stood up and frowned into the fire, an odd expression, Olivia thought, for a man proposing marriage.

"Gabriel, I didn't bring up the subject of my leaving as a goad to obtain a proposal."

"I didn't figure you did. You just made me realize that keeping you means more to me than . . . Well, there were some things I thought I had to settle before thinking about a future. But now I want you to be my future. A man and a woman who love each other ought to be together."

Olivia was dumbfounded. He stood there, legs apart, arms crossed over a broad, bare chest, looking like a barbarian contemplating mayhem rather than a man proposing marriage to the woman he loved. His scowl was fierce, with black brows drawn down ominously over slitted eyes, awaiting her answer as though he would hog-tie and chain her if she dared to say no.

But Olivia knew he wouldn't do any such thing. In spite of a certain talent for violence, Gabriel Danaher was a gentle man. He would defend himself and his with ruthless savagery if needed, but he didn't glory in his ferocity, as some men did. He was kind, loving, intelligent, and had feelings that ran deep into his heart. This much she knew about him, and not much more.

Olivia wanted to run her fingers over those fierce black brows and soothe his face into a smile. She wanted to see the light in his eyes and the dent in his cheek when he grinned. She wanted to say yes she would marry him and love him for the rest of her life.

Marry Gabriel Danaher. Marry a man she knew almost nothing about, a man with secrets in his past and in his future as well. How had he come to live this secluded life in the mountains? He had never said, dodging her questions as if they were bullets. And what were these things he had wanted to settle in his future? More secrets, and he didn't seem inclined to elaborate.

Marry Gabriel Danaher. A violent man. A tender, loving man. Only God knew what or who he actually was. Yet she would trust him with her life, her body, her soul. She loved him. Life didn't have to be a lonely, flat plain of sterile dedication to others' problems and others' ills. She could say yes and have a life for herself, with a man she adored, two lovely girls to watch grow, and perhaps children of her own. She could say yes and see Gabriel smile.

Gabriel Danaher wasn't of her world, though. Olivia couldn't picture

him in New York, not on the docks where he'd once earned his liveli-
hood, and certainly not living among the rather snobbish liberal intellec-
tuals who were her friends. He didn't belong in her world any more than
she belonged in his. Even if his wretched mine made him a wealthy man,
Gabe would always be rough-and-tumble, lacking formal education and
civilized manners, without a shred of gentility about him. Her father
would take one look at him and scold her for even being seen with such a
man, much less marrying him.

But then, right now her father would look at Olivia and not recognize
her, she was certain. Who was the woman who had been living in this log
cabin, cooking in an open fireplace, sleeping on a straw-ticked mattress,
and bathing in the same tin tub they used to wash clothes? Certainly not
Olivia Baron of the prominent New York banking Barons, not this hoyden who sat shivering in a threadbare flannel nightdress considering the
pros and cons of a marriage proposal from a virtual stranger whom she'd
been making love to every night without a qualm. Making love to, and
loving . . .

Perhaps she didn't know who Olivia Baron was any more.

Gabe's eyes had never left her. They pulled at her, demanding an
answer.

"Gabriel . . ." She looked up into his face, into those deep-green
waiting eyes, and she couldn't say no. But if she said yes, she'd be giving
up ambitions that had sustained her since childhood, yielding everything
she was and all that she'd worked for so hard over the past years. "I don't
know what to say."

He squatted down beside the chair, the frown suddenly gone. "Say yes,
Olivia. Love isn't something that should be taken lightly. It doesn't come
along that often."

"I do love you, Gabriel." She lowered her head and hugged her knees
more tightly. Her mind was at a stalemate. "I need time to think."

"Then stay here and think. I won't rush you, Doc. I don't want to lose
you."

"I can't stay here. If I stay, I'll end up in your bed again. You'll smile at
me or touch me"—she shivered again, this time not from the cold—"and
there I'll be."

He smiled, and something in her roused at the possessiveness in that
smile.

"Don't look like that!"

"Like what?"

"Like a cock strolling through a henhouse. There's much more to
marriage than just lust—or even love!"

"You think I don't know that?"

"Gabriel, I don't want us to jump into something that will make us both unhappy. We need to spend time apart to think about what we really want."

His mouth tightened.

"Besides, Amy needs me. I have to go back to Elkhorn. If you still want to talk about marriage, I'll come back after Amy's baby is delivered in February."

"February? Goddammit, Olivia, there are other doctors who can take care of Amy. I need you. Katy and Ellen need you. We could be married and long gone from here by February. I want to start a new life. You made me realize that I *have* to start a new life."

"Gabriel, I made a promise to Amy."

"You made a promise to me also."

"What promise was that?"

"It was in your eyes when you said you loved me, and every time we made love. Your heart was in your eyes, and every bit of it was mine. Don't take it away."

She couldn't deny it. Every bit of her heart was his, but she had always believed a person should be ruled by the head rather than the heart.

"Gabriel, I have to go back."

He didn't argue further, but withdrew into that cold stranger who had forcibly taken her from Elkhorn—a man with ice in his eyes and anger in every move.

When the twins came down from the loft, he announced that they were riding down the trail to check the slide—all of them.

Katy rounded on Olivia. "You're still goin' back to Elkhorn?"

"I have to go back, Katy."

"Why?"

"A very dear friend is depending on me to deliver her baby."

"Ellen and me thought maybe you'd be staying now. We figgered you liked us."

Olivia took Katy's hand. "I not only like you, Katy, I love you. I love you girls and I love your father. But sometimes obligations have to take precedence over love."

"Then you're coming back?" Ellen asked.

"We'll see." From the look on Gabriel's face and the silence that surrounded him, Olivia had doubts that he would want her to come back.

The ride down the trail was strained. At first the girls filled the valley with their noise. Katy periodically cursed Murdoch; apparently Olivia was not the only rider the ornery Appaloosa gave trouble to. Ellen chided Katy for cursing, and from there the two of them found myriad subjects to argue and discuss. Soon, however, the tension between Gabriel and Olivia cast a pall over even the twins' spirits, and the lively disputes sputtered into silence. Young Hunter seemed to be the only member of the party enjoying himself. He trotted beside Olivia and Curly, ears pricked, eyes bright, pausing to pounce on anything that dared to move in the brittle grass.

Olivia's cramps abated as the morning grew older, but her mood didn't lift. Gabriel rode at the head of their party in brooding silence. No doubt he had taken her insistence on leaving as rejection, of both his proposal and his affection. Olivia hadn't meant it to be a refusal, but she told herself it was for the best. She and Gabriel were as mismatched as any couple could be. She truly did love him, but she could never be the wife that he needed; he loved her, Olivia believed, yet he didn't understand what she was—a physician as much as a woman. Things that were of paramount importance in her life had little meaning for him.

Love and lust notwithstanding, they would never be able to make a life together. The final realization made her immeasurably sad.

As if to taunt her, the mountains were especially beautiful that day. Dazzling white snow blanketed the peaks and lay in deep drifts on the north side of the valley, almost blindingly bright against the deep azure of the Montana sky. Spruce, fir, and pine wore their winter finery. Icicles sparkled from every needle, and snow lay along the boughs like white ermine on a fine lady's shoulders. The air smelled of cold and pine and watermelon snow.

She would sorely miss these mountains, with their vast silences, sweeping heights, and peaceful valleys. She would miss the singing of the wind through the pine and spruce; she would miss the dazzle of snowfield and glacier; she would miss the quiet clearing around Gabriel's cabin with its fragrant carpet of pine needles. She would miss the twins with their arguing, their pouts, their smiles and laughter.

Most of all she would miss Gabriel Danaher.

The slide looked a bit different from the way it had the last time Olivia had seen it. The lake that had backed up behind the barrier was now just a frozen pond; most of the dammed water had escaped through a notch between the avalanche debris and the opposite valley wall. To Olivia the way looked passable through the notch that Thunder Creek had carved for itself. One would be required to ride upvalley around the pond, contour carefully along the steeply sloping valley wall on the other side, and then pick a way through the frozen mud and boulders in the notch. She couldn't see the other side of the slide, but she imagined a bit of slipping and sliding would take one safely down the other side.

"It's still not passable," Gabriel declared in a voice that rang with finality.

"I think it is," Olivia protested.

"You hardly have the experience to judge."

"You'll forgive me if I mistrust your objectivity in saying it's not."

He scowled at her. "We'll take a closer look. Katy and Ellen, you stay here."

"Oh, Pa!" Katy said. "Why?"

"Because Olivia and I are going to have some words with each other, and we don't want two pairs of curious ears listening in."

"Oh." She shrugged. "Okay."

On closer examination, the passage seemed to Olivia to be precarious but very possible, if one were careful.

"It's too dangerous," Gabriel insisted.

"If we were to wait until it's perfectly safe, we'd be waiting until summer. Or perhaps you'd prefer to wait until someone builds a paved road through the valley."

"You're getting real uppity, Doc."

"Gabriel! This is not a casual matter to me. I *must* get back to Elkhorn. Amy Talbot is depending on me, and she's undoubtedly worried sick over my disappearance. I can't leave her any longer than absolutely necessary."

"Are you running to Amy, Olivia? Or are you running away from me?"

Both, Olivia admitted to herself. Her good intentions wouldn't weather a determined effort by Gabriel to seduce her. She would end up once again in his arms, his bed. Next time she tried to come back to reason and escape to her own world, the feat would be more difficult, perhaps even impossible. She would convince herself that love would somehow make everything all right, and enter into a marriage that would probably be a disaster for them both.

"I have to go, Gabriel."

"We'd never make it. The mud's too soft."

"Posh! It's frozen."

He said nothing, only scowled.

"If you don't want to take me, I'll proceed alone."

His mouth tightened into an ominous line. "I could force you to come back with me, and I have half a mind to do just that. You're risking yourself for your own damned stubbornness, and nothing else."

"What would you do, Gabriel? Tie me over the saddle like a sack of flour, and then tie me to the bed again once we get to the cabin?"

Angry red crept up his neck and stained his face. "Damn it all, Olivia! You're stubborn enough to give mules lessons." He signaled the twins to ride over. "I'm taking Olivia to town. You girls ride back to the cabin and stay there. Take Hunter with you. And behave!"

"Pa!" Katy and Ellen both wailed. "Why'd you let us come if we can't go all the way to town?"

"Because I didn't think the goddamned trail would be open, that's why!" He glared at the twins, the little wolf, the mountains, the debris slide, and the sky.

The fiercest glare, though, he reserved for Olivia.

The man's stink filled Sylvester's tiny office at the back of the mill—stale sweat, tobacco, and whiskey. Sylvester managed to contain his grimace; the fellow looked very much like the sort who might take offense at such a thing. He also looked like a fellow whom a wise man did not want to offend—not if he wanted to keep his skin intact.

Still, he wished he didn't have to breathe.

"What was it you wanted to see me about, Mr. . . . uh . . ."

"Name's Rodgers. Cal Rodgers. I work for Ace Candliss down in Virginia City."

"Ace Candliss. Don't believe I know the man."

"Well, ever'body down Virginia City way knows him. In Helena too. He's gonna be a big man now Montana's a state. Thinkin' about runnin' fer senator. Big man."

"Well, what can I do for you and Mr. Candliss?"

"The boss heard tell in Helena that you been askin' questions about some fella who's holed up in these mountains around here." Rodgers dug into his vest and produced a letter Sylvester had written to the U.S. marshal in Helena. "Says the fella has black hair, green eyes, and he's Irish."

"Yes. The man's name is Gabriel Danaher."

"Well, the boss is lookin' for a man like that. Name's not Danaher. It's O'Connell. Will O'Connell. He's got two half-breed kids with him, or at least he did. He mighta ditched 'em by now." From his other vest pocket Rodgers took a tattered handbill and passed it over the desk to Sylvester, who gingerly opened the grimy piece of paper.

The sketch on the handbill might have been Danaher; it was hard to tell. Below the sketch was an offer of three hundred dollars, dead or alive. The crime: murder. Sylvester thought of Olivia and felt his heart drop.

"O'Connell killed the boss's brother. Killed a woman too, though that's no account, since she warn't no more'n a lousy Injun."

"Danaher might be this O'Connell fellow. He doesn't have children with him, as far as I know, though it's rumored he lives with a couple of Indian women. I inquired about him because we suspect he had something to do with the disappearance of a friend of my wife."

"You know where I can find him?"

"Yes. He has a mine up by Thunder Ridge. We tried to get to him earlier, but the trail's been blocked by an avalanche. As soon at it's clear, I plan to take some men and ride up there again."

"You think it might be clear now?"

"I doubt it. The weather's been cold. Besides, the man who knows how to find the cabin took his wife to the doctor over in Butte. He won't be back for a week or so."

"Guess I could wait that long. I've got some business down in Jefferson City and Boulder that'll take me a week or so."

"If the man is truly wanted for murder, perhaps we should ask the law to take care of this."

"Mr. Candliss likes to take care of things the efficient way, ya know? An' the law in this place ain't exactly efficient. Don't worry, Talbot. Everyone will get their shot at Will O'Connell once Candliss has him— includin' the law."

Amy held up the little blue nightie she was embroidering. The babe was a boy—she was convinced of it—therefore she was making the entire layette in blue. She also had a long list of names: George, after her father; Keaton, after Sylvester's father; Scott, after her grandfather; Edward, after Sylvester's grandfather; Joshua, just because she liked the name. Of course, Sylvester favored Sylvester Jr., but Amy didn't think Sylvester Jr. was a name to hang on a boy who would probably grow up in wild Montana.

She laid the nightie on her stomach, which protruded to make a handy table. Lord knew she couldn't get close enough to any other table to do close work. She had difficulty believing she was only eight months gone with child. If the babe grew for a full month more, surely she would split at the seams. Olivia would laugh at the notion and tell her that women were designed to accommodate such things.

Olivia . . . The thought of Olivia brought a twinge of fear mixed with hope. She had to believe that she was safe with Gabriel Danaher somewhere on that mountain—stranded but safe. She had to believe, she needed to believe. Otherwise how could she get through every day?

Hoofbeats and a horse's whinny outside the house stole Amy's attention from her sewing. She didn't get up to see what the commotion was— she was much too ponderous to be jumping up at every noise. She only hoped that Sylvester hadn't brought the mill manager home for dinner again. The man was uncouth and ill-mannered in the extreme. He grunted like a pig when he ate, brayed like a donkey at Sylvester's lame jokes, and sprayed food from his mouth when he laughed.

"Madam!" Meg Grisolm the housekeeper bustled breathlessly into the parlor. "Madam, you'll never believe! Miss Olivia's come back, fit as a fiddle, and she's brought that rapscallion no-good Irishman with her!"

Amy's heart jumped, then seemed to take off flying. "Mrs. Grisolm! You wouldn't jest with me."

"No, madam! I wouldn't do such a thing! You sit right down," the housekeeper ordered when Amy started to rise. "Miss Olivia will be in soon enough for you to see for yourself." She raised a contemptuous brow. "What shall I do with the Irishman, madam?"

"Oh my! Is Olivia free to leave him, do you suppose? Perhaps he's brought her back to demand a ransom or some such thing!"

"Now, why didn't I think of that?"

Amy looked up to see Gabriel Danaher's lean, dark form in her parlor doorway. Olivia was beside him.

"Olivia!" Amy struggled to her feet. The two figures before her blurred suddenly as tears came to her eyes. "Olivia. Olivia . . . !" So much else needed to be said, but Amy could think of none of it through the joy of seeing Olivia alive and well.

"Amy! Oh my dear, I've been so worried about you!" Olivia came forward and grasped Amy's hands. "Let me look at you. Oh, you look fine!"

"Aren't I just big as a barn?" She caught her breath and blushed, remembering suddenly that a man was in the room. He smiled at her, and her heart jumped. The man was a scoundrel, but he was certainly an arresting one.

The villain gave Olivia a look Amy couldn't begin to interpret. "You think your friend would buy you back—seeing that your being here is so crucial?"

Olivia looked at him with daggers in her eyes.

He shrugged and smiled. "It was Mrs. Talbot's idea."

"Don't pay Gabriel any mind, Amy. His bark is much fiercer than his bite."

Amy did her best to follow Olivia's advice and ignore the man. "My dear, where have you been? All were convinced that you were dead, and I imagined the most horrible things! Oh, Olivia, you can't conceive how worried I've been, and Sylvester, also."

"Sit down, Amy, before you get too excited. It grieved me to worry you, but there was no help for it. Mr. Danaher applied to me one night to treat his daughters, who were very ill with the diphtheria. It was very late at night, and I assumed I would be back the next day, or the next, at the very latest—so I didn't leave word. But a storm came along to prevent my return, and then an avalanche closed the trail. As soon as we were able to get through, Mr. Danaher brought me back."

Amy noted the glance Olivia exchanged with the man. In their eyes was a story that went far beyond sick children and snowstorms, and Amy vowed to worm the full tale from Olivia later, when the brooding and quite dangerous-looking Gabriel Danaher was gone.

"What goes here?" Sylvester strode in like a knight looking for a dragon to slay. His eyes fastened on Danaher, and his wind-reddened face turned a shade paler. "You!"

"Talbot," Gabe returned mildly.

"What is this? Is Olivia—oh, there she is. If you've hurt her, you scoundrel, I'll see you rotting in jail until you're dust."

"Does she look like she's been hurt?"

"You have a nerve, fellow, showing your face here after abducting a decent woman and, and . . ." He looked as though he wanted to say something else, but he glanced at Amy and pressed his mouth firmly shut.

"I suppose I could have let her ride down the mountain alone."

"You'll not be so cocky when you get your just deserts, and I assure you that you will."

"Sylvester!" Olivia chided. "Please calm yourself. I don't know what you think Mr. Danaher has done, but he certainly deserves no censure on my account. I went with him to treat his children for the diphtheria and got stranded on the mountain by an avalanche. He didn't abduct me."

Danaher arched a brow in a way that made him look the very devil, Amy thought, and Sylvester turned a disbelieving scowl on Olivia. "You mean you went with this blackguard voluntarily?"

"I see no reason to insult Mr. Danaher, Sylvester. He's treated me with nothing but courtesy. And of course I went with him voluntarily. His children were sick, and I am a physician."

"Children? You have children?" Sylvester's eyes narrowed.

"He has two daughters who were very ill."

"Interesting."

"Interesting is hardly the word," said Olivia. "They almost died."

A strained silence seemed to stretch the air into impossible scarceness, until Amy almost couldn't breathe. "Olivia," she said into the silence, "you must be exhausted. You look like death warmed over, dear. You must go to your room to wash and change into some decent clothing. Dinner is almost ready. And, of course, Mr. Danaher is welcome to stay and refresh himself."

"No, thank you, Mrs. Talbot. You're very kind, but I have to be on my way."

Olivia glared at Sylvester as he opened his mouth to speak. Looking somewhat abashed, he clamped his lips shut and satisfied himself with merely giving Danaher an angry look.

"I'll see Mr. Danaher out," Olivia said. She took the man by the arm, looking small and almost fragile beside his well-muscled frame. Amy thought Olivia's hand on his arm looked far more comfortable than it should have.

Olivia had never mastered the art of dissembling, and her story had a false ring. Amy could scarcely wait to get her friend alone so she could hear the real tale.

"I'm sorry, Gabriel. I've never seen Sylvester display such foul manners." Olivia couldn't imagine what had come over her friend's husband. Even Amy had at first looked at Gabriel as though he were some mangy dog who had wandered in from the street.

"Don't let it bother you, Doc. People like Sylvester Talbot think they're still in their high-toned society Back East. If you don't play by their rules, they figure you for trash."

With a flash of guilt, Olivia wondered if that was the way she thought. The people in the New York and Paris clinics that she had treated, poor people, hardworking laborers, denizens of the street—she had been eager enough to treat their ills, but had she looked at them with the same disdain that Sylvester and Amy showed Gabriel?

She tried to banish the uncomfortable thought with a smile. "What terrible rules have you broken?"

"Marrying an Indian woman was one of them. Maybe someday I'll list the rest of them for you."

There would be no someday. Olivia saw the realization in his eyes and felt it in her heart. Tears suddenly flooded her eyes.

"Gabriel . . ."

He took hold of her chin and turned her face toward him. Silently he watched as the cold wind whipped the tears into wet sheets on her cheeks. "You really don't know what you want, do you, Doc?" he finally said.

"I used to know," she whispered through a throat tight with pain.

"Yeah. I used to know exactly what I wanted, too, but I changed my mind when I learned to love you. Maybe we've both grown up a bit, eh?"

"Gabriel . . ."

"It's okay, Doc. Maybe you're right. Maybe the whole thing's impossible."

He pressed his lips to hers in a brief, dry kiss that held no passion, only regret. As Gabriel mounted his horse and rode away, leading Curly behind him, Olivia bit her lip until she tasted her own blood.

Chapter 16

Sylvester Talbot, I don't care what you think of Gabriel Danaher. You will not set the marshal on him like a hound on some poor fox. At least not until I find out from Olivia what really happened up in those mountains."

"My dear, you're upsetting yourself. Danaher is not worth your concern, and Olivia would no doubt agree that the scoundrel should be locked up. I'm sure she defended the man simply because she was intimidated by him."

"If she's intimidated by Mr. Danaher, why is she out front alone with him when she could be safe inside with us?"

"If she has an ounce of sense, she's warning him to stay away from her in the future."

"She said she went with him willingly."

"A fabrication if I've ever heard one. The man may have needed a doctor indeed, but no decent woman would go off with that sort of man of her own free will. He's an outcast and a misfit, and a criminal besides."

Sylvester didn't want to tell his wife about his conversation with Rodgers; it would only upset her to know that her friend had been in the hands of a killer these past weeks, and that wouldn't do at all. Danaher had to be the same man that Rodgers and his employer sought. When Sylvester had heard that the Indian women living in the mountains with the man were his daughters, not his mistresses, Sylvester had become certain of the matter. A name was easily changed when it became inconvenient.

"Well, I don't believe Mr. Danaher is any worse than ninety percent of the men who drift out here. People distrust him because he's a such a solitary fellow. He brought Olivia back unharmed. And if my intuition is correct, there's something between them. If Olivia cares for him, then he can't be the scoundrel everyone seems to think he is."

"Amy, the fellow is a squaw man. He lived with an Indian woman and had children by her." And probably murdered her, but that wasn't for Amy's delicate ears.

"The women he lives with now—"

"Are his half-breed children."

"You didn't tell me this before."

"I only just found out, from someone who knew him in Virginia City."

"Having an Indian wife isn't so bad."

"Not a crime, certainly. But is a squaw man the sort of company you think Olivia should keep? A man with half-breed mongrel children, for heaven's sake!"

"Children are children, Sylvester."

"You haven't lived in the West long enough to know how people regard such things. And neither has Olivia. The man is an undesirable scoundrel. I think he should spend at least a few nights in jail for what he did to Olivia." A few nights, or however long it took Rodgers to return to Elkhorn.

"Sylvester, I'm surprised at you. Your attitude is most uncharitable and un-Christian. Didn't you tell me once that in the West almost every man has a past that doesn't bear looking into? As long as Gabriel Danaher didn't hurt Olivia, then we have no quarrel with him."

"Really, Amy, this is not a woman's concern. Let me decide what happens to Mr. Danaher."

"It certainly is my concern, because Olivia is involved. And I'll not have you upsetting her by voicing these attitudes within her hearing. Once she's rested and recovered, I'll learn from her just exactly what sort of man Mr. Danaher is."

"Amy, Olivia should spend her time trying to forget her ordeal with Mr. Danaher, not remembering it."

"I suspect it might not have been such an ordeal. Intuition, dear. It tells a woman much more than any words could say."

Sylvester shook his head. "And we're giving women the right to vote. Lord help us!"

"Now, mind what you say," Amy instructed when she heard the front door open and shut, signaling Olivia's return. "Poor Olivia is bound to be upset."

"She looks fine to me," Sylvester said under his breath as Olivia walked into the room.

"That," Amy returned softly, "is because you're not a woman."

Gabe rode to the livery to stable Longshot and settle with the smith for Curly, the horse he'd taken on that night in November—it felt like an age ago—for Olivia to ride. Gregg Smoot gave him an odd look as he rode up and dismounted. Gabe wasn't surprised. He'd swiped the big gelding, after all, even though he'd left money in payment.

Smoot didn't seem upset about the horse, however. "Oh hell," he said. "You left good money for him, and he's cantankerous as a mule when he wants to be. Keep him, for what it's worth."

"Thanks," Gabe replied.

"You ain't been down the mountain in a while, Danaher."

"Trail's been closed."

"Yeah. I know. Bunch of us rode up trying to find you. Sylvester Talbot's been raisin' hell, thinkin' you made off with that skinny little crow of a lady doc that came to tend his wife."

"I had her," Gabe said in an even tone. "Needed a doctor, and she was the only one who'd come. She's back where she belongs now."

Smoot chuckled. "Got stranded by the slide, eh? By doggies, Danaher, but you got bad luck. If you're gonna get stuck in the mountains with some female, at least make it one who's got some heat in 'er." Smoot winked. "Ya know—to keep ya warm when the wind howls and the snow blows."

"I'll keep that in mind next time. Make sure the horses get some grain, will you? They had a long ride."

"Sure thing," Smoot said, taking the reins. "When'll ya need 'em?"

"Three or four hours. That oughta give 'em time to rest."

"Jest don't make off with no more of the town's ladies," the smith called after him with a laugh. "Or if ya do, pick a lady who's gonna be worth your while."

Gabe stopped at the first saloon he saw. Ordinarily he wasn't a drinking man, but Olivia Baron gave him a need for strong liquor. The stronger, the better. Damned woman was the stubbornest, most addleheaded female he'd ever met. He could see her refusing him because he was an ignorant Irish lout, not loving him because he didn't have gentlemanly ways or pretty manners, but the woman insisted she loved him, dammit! She loved him, but wouldn't marry him. She loved him but had to get back to her goddamned friend to play doctor.

He ordered a bottle of whiskey. The barmaid gave him an inviting smile, but it didn't move him. She was pretty enough. Buxom, well-padded, and womanly. But right now he was fed up to his gullet with females.

"Just whiskey," he told her.

"Whatever you say, handsome."

He watched her walk away with her broad hips swaying provocatively between the close-packed tables. A card player smacked her buttocks and laughed. "Hey, Dulcie! Whaddya have for me tonight, sweets?"

Dulcie gave him a playful nudge with her hip. "Depends on what you have fer me, handsome." She tossed the man a smile over her shoulder as she sauntered on to the bar.

Gabe compared Olivia to the buxom saloon girl. Olivia was a spare reed compared to the barmaid's broad curves, slender enough that he could grasp a buttock in one hand—as he had more than once to pull her closer when he was inside her, to move her in the rhythm of his loving. But she had enough curves to satisfy any man, and a fire inside her that made her more of a woman than any other he could recall.

Queer that men saw her as starched and drab. He had when he'd first met her. She didn't show her real self to the world—the soft heart beneath the high-buttoned bodice, the compassion behind the stern looks, the laughter that could suddenly bubble from her serious little face. All high-class modesty and stiff propriety, she could melt into warm honey at the right touch from the right man. Yet she didn't think he was the right man, damn her.

Well, she could take her fancy diplomas and let them keep her warm in New York City. What did he want with a woman who had such high-toned notions, such crazy ambitions? What did he want with a woman at all? He had other things to think about—things that Olivia had made seem unimportant.

"Hey! Is that you, Danaher? You dirty dog of a woman-hogging skunk, you?"

The insults were shouted without rancor. Gabe looked up to see none other than Jebediah Crowe giving him a beefy grin from one of the poker tables. He cursed under his breath.

"Got loose of the ol' apron strings for a spree, didya?" Jeb slurred. "Come an' join us, man! Another sucker's money is always welcome, eh, gents?"

The other two men at the table eyed Gabe without interest and nodded assent.

"I'm drinking, Jeb. Not playing."

"A man can do both. Come on, ya skunk. I figger ya owe me a chance to get even."

Gabe carried his chair to the table and joined the game, partly to avoid a scene with Jeb, and partly because thinking about the cards might leave less room in his mind for Olivia. Jeb, already obviously drunk, toasted him with a mug of tanglefoot—a concoction of mountain sage, cayenne pepper, and tobacco boiled in water and flavored with a large volume of alcohol. "Join me, you low-down son of a badger."

Gabe held up his whiskey bottle. "Got my own, thanks."

"This here Irishman fights meaner'n a cornered weasel," Jeb warned his fellow players with a chortle. "Don't get on his bad side, gents."

The "gents" didn't stay at the table long enough to have need of Jeb's warning; they left two hands after Gabe sat down—either because Gabe won both pots or because Jeb's breath stank like the concoction he was drinking.

"Where's the little woman?" Jeb asked as Gabe dealt seven-card draw. "Left her up in the mountains all by her lonesome again with those two hell-raisin' girls?"

"Nope."

"She come to town with ya?"

"Yep."

"Well, hell! She oughta join us!"

"Don't think she'd want to. You want cards?"

Jeb discarded. "Gimme three. That's a high-class wife you got there, Irishman."

"She's not my wife." Gabe figured if the man stayed in town long enough, he'd see Olivia around. Coming clean with the truth might save her an embarrassing encounter. "And she's too high-class for either of us, my friend. I bet twenty."

"Whaddya mean she's not your wife?"

"My kid told you that to keep you behaving like you oughta. She's a doctor who got stranded up there by the slide. Bet."

"Jesus Christ! A lady doctor? Little gal with tits like that?"

"Bet."

Jeb scowled at his cards. "Raise twenty. That kid o' yourn needs to be taught a lesson. Lyin' can get a female into a heap o' trouble."

"She doesn't need a lesson by the likes of you, friend. What have you got?"

"Two pair. I don't take kindly to being lied to, Danaher."

"Full house." Gabe raked in the pot with his hands.

"If'n I'd known you hadn't put your brand on that heifer, I'da taken her without bothering with a fair fight."

"Take my advice, Crowe. Stay away from women like her. They've got more twists and turns to them than a man can follow, even when he's sober."

Jeb's beefy face puckered in a frown. "Lady doc, eh? She warn't half as fetchin' as these gals down here," he said, his gaze wandering appreciatively to the barmaids and saloon dancers. "But I don't like bein' lied to."

Gabe dealt one card down and one up. "Five-card stud. Deuces and jacks wild. Bet."

Still sullen, Jeb peeked at his facedown card. "I'll go for ten."

"Call." Gabe dealt another faceup to both of them.

"Maybe if I see her around town I'll just let that little lady sawbones know what she missed. It ain't right that she lied."

"Keep away from her, friend."

"If she ain't your wife, then you got no call to be sayin' who can be with her and who cain't."

"Just stay away from her. And bet."

Jeb looked down at his cards. "Twenty."

"Raise ten."

"You're bluffin'."

"Bet or fold."

"I call. You're bluffin' about the woman. She didn't like what you got between your legs, maybe she'll cotton more to mine." He grinned woozily.

"Last card. Bet."

"Hell. Fifty and I get the woman."

Gabe looked calmly at his facedown card. "Seventy. The woman's got no part in it."

"I'll see seventy and raise twenty."

"You got that much money?"

"Hell yes! Those two gents that were here before couldn't play poker worth a hoot. I took 'em so hard their heads was spinnin' round and round."

"I call. What've you got?"

"Three of a kind." He flipped the facedown card over to match the pair he had showing, then took a big, satisfied draught of his tanglefoot.

Gabe turned over the ten of clubs that completed his straight flush. "You lose."

Jeb sputtered and slammed his mug down on the table. He looked at the cards, then eyed Gabe in a manner reminiscent of Bruno. "You're a skunk, Danaher."

"You should learn not to play poker when you're drunk." He gathered up his winnings. "I think I've taken enough of your money for one night."

Jeb glared.

"And about Miss Olivia—remember that last time you took it in your mind to bother her, you got off with a few scrapes and bruises. Next time I might not be so charitable."

As Jeb watched Gabe go, a red haze colored his vision—partly from the cayenne in the tanglefoot and partly from anger. It was one thing to beat a man into the ground in a wrestling match. That was just good sport. But it took a low-down, scum-sucking, sonofabitch to make a fool of a man over a woman, and it appeared that Danaher was as low-down and scum-sucking as they came. Not only that, but he'd horned in on Jeb's poker game, chased off the two gents who'd been losing to Jeb, and then taken every last dollar Jeb had won in three nights of cheating.

Sonofabitch! He'd have to think awhile to come up with a way to get even. His brain was a little fuzzy right now, but he'd think of something. Something bad. Something smart. That skunk wasn't half as smart and tough as ol' Jebediah Crowe.

"Show him," Jeb muttered as he gathered the cards, then scattered them in an angry explosion of pasteboard. As his head sank woozily toward the table, a hand jerked, knocking over the mug of tanglefoot. His face splatted into the bitter brew that flooded the table, and he smiled as he inhaled the fumes. "Show her, too. Bitch. Show them both."

Jeb was still smiling as he passed out.

Longshot wasn't keen on being saddled after just a few hours' rest. She swung her nose around and flicked her lips back as Gabe tightened the cinch.

"Bite me and you'll be missing a few teeth, my lass. I'm in no mood to put up with any more female shenanigans. Understand?"

Longshot whickered an objection.

The light from a single lantern cast only dim light in the livery barn. Gregg Smoot had grained both horses and cleaned the packed dirt and gravel from their feet, and his boy had curried them until their coats gleamed. They were rested enough. There was no reason why Gabe shouldn't head up the trail toward Thunder Ridge.

Katy and Ellen were alone at the cabin. He had to get back. In the mine, ore waited to be blasted out. And somewhere men waited to be hired to ride against Ace Candliss and his outfit. Montana might be a state now, but it was still a wide-open and wild land where the powerful made their own laws. Ace Candliss had had the law on his side when he'd tried to hang Gabe with no trial and no proof but his own word; maybe the law would listen to Gabe's side of the story if he had Candliss by the short hairs screaming out what he and his brother had done that day.

The familiar litany failed to rouse its usual heat in Gabe's blood. Revenge, it seemed, had become more of a chore than a passion. Olivia Baron had stolen his passion and reserved it all for herself.

It would be nice to see her just once more. Once more.

He had to get back, Gabe reminded himself. Katy and Ellen were alone at the cabin.

The twins were better at taking care of themselves than most men were. They could be alone for a few days.

There was work to be done at the mine, he argued.

But one day more or less wouldn't matter.

He was a fool, Gabe scolded himself. Wounds didn't heal if they were opened again and again.

Bullshit. He ought to tell Olivia to watch out for Jeb, anyway. And his horses were bone tired. He was bone tired. What would staying just one more day hurt?

Gabe unsaddled Longshot, led her back to a stall, and settled down to sleep in a pile of clean straw.

"I knew there was something between you and that man, Olivia. You can't fool me."

Olivia gave the lines an impatient flick, and the horse drawing their buggy tossed its head and picked up its trot. "All I said was that I hoped the weather didn't close in on him on the way up the mountain."

"It was the way that you said it."

"Nonsense."

"And the gloomy face you've pulled all morning."

"That's absurd."

"I think he's devilish handsome."

"*You* were the one who first told me he's a scoundrel."

"I was merely repeating rumors—a churlish habit of mine. And now that you tell me the two females living with him are his daughters—well, any man who cares for his children the way you say he does can't be a total villain."

Olivia stopped the buggy in front of the Grand Hotel. "Mr. Danaher isn't a villain at all, Amy. He's good, kind, and intelligent. The worst I can say about him is that he's stubborn and high-handed, but most men share those faults. Over all, he's a fine man."

She climbed down and tied the horse to the hitching rail, then helped Amy lower her bulk from the buggy.

"So Mr. Danaher is a fine man. Go on."

"I'm acquainted with many fine men that I'm not enamored of, Amy."

"I saw the way you looked at him," Amy protested.

"What way?"

Amy attempted an imitation. Her eyes went limpid and her mouth curved in a dreamy smile.

"You look like a cow with indigestion in every one of your stomachs."

"Oh piffle!" Amy objected indignantly. "I know what I saw. Your eyes went all misty."

"Probably from a speck of dust. I'm not sure you should have come to town with me, Amy. You look pale."

"I thought I looked like a cow."

"I was teasing, dear. But you do look pale."

"I'm fine. Really. This baby is going to be splendidly healthy, and so am I. You see? I've adopted that positive attitude you're always nagging me about."

"You're sure you feel well?"

"Quit worrying, Olivia. A few minutes' rest and a cup of tea in the hotel dining room will set me right."

They sat down at a table under the window and looked out at the gray day. The mountains were hidden by clouds, and fat flakes of snow drifted lazily from the sky. Olivia wondered if Gabe had made it back to the cabin before the snow started in the mountains. She doubted it. Could be he would have to wait out the storm in a brush and canvas lean-to—this time without her. Her heart twinged painfully.

"Where are you?" Amy asked.

"Pardon?"

"Where are you, Olivia? Somewhere far away, from the look on your face. Thinking about Gabriel Danaher?"

"Of course not."

"Olivia, I'm your best friend. You can tell me."

Olivia looked down at her cup of tea for a moment, then sighed. "I am going to miss him."

Amy smiled. "You *are* in love with him!"

"Once you get to know him, he's a hard man not to love."

"Oh, Olivia! I always knew you hid a romantic heart under all that single-minded ambition."

Olivia twisted her mouth into a wry grimace. "I could have chosen much more wisely."

"Does he love you?"

"So he says."

"Did he propose? Are you going to marry him?"

"Of course not, Amy. We're completely unsuited."

"But you're in love."

"Love is but a temporary madness, or so I've always believed."

"You don't really think that, Olivia!"

Olivia gazed out at the gloomy day. "I'd like to."

"Oh, Olivia! I can see you're in sore need of a lecture. I can't credit that you would simply let the man walk out of your life because he's not some high-nob gentleman from New York."

"That's not it."

"And if he has no money, there's any number of ways a smart man can make money here in the West. It's still a frontier, seething with opportunity."

"I suspect he's already dug up his fortune."

"Well, what then? Is it medicine? Lord knows the West could use more competent doctors. So many of them who come out here are fugitives from family and responsibility, or they're lungers looking for a cure. But you're different. Why, once people realized what a fine physician you are, you'd be in demand."

"I don't think I'm really cut out to be a westerner, Amy."

"Nonsense! If *I* can live a thousand miles from nowhere for the love of a man, certainly you can too. You were always ever so much more competent than I at everything we did."

"That's not quite true. You were better at art, sewing, French . . ."

"Useless disciplines—except sewing, perhaps. I did excel in stitchery, didn't I?" Amy blinked. "Oh my!"

"What? What is it?"

"Just a back twinge. Nothing. It's gone now. I suppose one must expect these minor discomforts when this far gone with child."

Olivia smiled at the pride in Amy's voice. "I think we should go home where I can examine you."

"Nonsense."

"Amy, why did I come to Montana to help you if you won't listen to me?"

"Very well. If you insist. But you must fetch that package of lace from Shriner's first. I ordered it special, and if I don't pick it up, Margaret Norton will see it and talk Henry out of it. Would you mind?"

"Only if you promise to sit here and rest."

"Yes, Olivia, of course. But I'm fine, I assure you. It was a twinge. Nothing, really. I'll just sit here and have another cup of tea."

"Then I'll be back directly."

Olivia walked through the freezing wind toward Shriner's Mercantile. The weather was getting worse fast. She thought of Gabe, remembering the hours they had spent cocooned together listening to the wind, their shelter almost buried in snow. She remembered other things as well; how could she not? The warm coziness of the curtained bed where she lay in Gabriel's arms; the splendid anticipation she had felt when he had arched above her, an imposing black shadow in the darkness of their private little world; the lovely sensation of wholeness when he filled her and moved inside her, taking her to completion. The twins' laughter echoed in her mind, their arguments and complaints as well. Katy's impish smile. The quiet warmth in Ellen's face. Even little Hunter was there to haunt her memories, with his puppy grin and bright eyes.

You see, she said to Gabriel in her mind, *a wolf can be tamed.*

Perhaps Gabriel could be tamed as well. But that thought was absurd. Gabriel wasn't wild; he wasn't a wolf who needed taming. He was simply . . . unsuitable. Or was he? Had she made a grave mistake? Was Amy right in thinking her a fool?

Shriner's Mercantile was mercifully warm from the potbellied stove in the center of the store. Olivia shut the door behind her to block the freezing gusts that followed her in.

"Miss Baron," Shriner greeted her. "So good to see you back. Sylvester spread the news this morning that you were safe. We were all very worried, you know."

"Thank you, Mr. Shriner. I'm grateful that you all took so much trouble on my account, but I was never in any danger. Mr. Danaher treated me with great courtesy the whole time we were stranded."

"That's good to hear. And how is Mrs. Talbot?"

"She's well. She sent me to pick up her Flanders lace."

"It's in the back. I'll be just a few minutes finding it. Can you wait?"

"Certainly."

Mr. Shriner was gone for more than a few minutes. Mrs. Walpole came into the store and gave Olivia a reserved greeting, curiosity keen on her face. Olivia drifted to the back of the store to avoid her. The door opened and shut again. Olivia concentrated on the display in front of her, unwilling to endure more curious stares.

The display was hats—the same hats she had been looking at the first time she had seen Gabriel Danaher. She picked up the straw concoction that had attracted her attention that day. It looked silly to her now. She put it on and looked in the mirror, pictured wearing it in a Montana snowstorm, or to keep the sun off her face, and chuckled to herself.

"It doesn't look any better now than it did last time I saw you in it." Gabriel's voice made her nearly jump out of her skin. She could almost believe she'd been hurtled back in time to the first moment she'd seen him. "Gabriel! I . . . I thought you'd be up the mountain by now."

"I had a couple of things to take care of as long as I was in town."

"Oh." Self-consciously, she took the hat from her head, then smiled. "I think last time you said the hat would look better on some prospector's mule."

"Something like that. I'm afraid tact isn't part of my charm."

"No? Well, I've been told that I lack that particular virtue myself."

He stood there staring at her. Olivia fiddled with the hat, her eyes fastened on the buttons of his coat in order to avoid meeting his gaze. She felt his regard like a veritable force pressing against her. Her mind whirled, part of it clamoring for her to say something to keep him from leaving, to say she was sorry for being such a foolish ninny. But the other part told her that what she felt was an illusion born of isolation and danger. Here they were back in civilization, and they had nothing to say to each other more meaningful than empty courtesies. The notion of making a life with him was ridiculous.

"How is Mrs. Talbot?"

"She's well."

The silence stretched.

"Are you staying in town long?" she finally asked.

He sighed, and it sounded a bit sad, Olivia thought. "No. I don't think so. When the snow lets up, I'll be off."

"I suppose you don't want to leave the girls alone too long."

"No."

She met his gaze, then hastily looked away. She couldn't meet those deep-green eyes and tell him good-bye yet again, coward that she was. "You'll come by the house and say good-bye?"

Silence.

"Please say you will."

"Then I will."

"There's Mr. Shriner with Amy's order. I must go."

She felt his eyes follow her as she picked up the package of lace and went out the door. The freezing wind seemed to cut to her very soul. Fool that she was, why couldn't she just let him go?

*　*　*

True to his word, Gabriel stopped at the Talbot house before he headed up the trail to the cabin. Mrs. Slater showed him into the parlor, where Olivia waited alone. Amy had retired to her room for a nap, complaining of a backache, and Sylvester had pointedly gone to his second-floor office when he'd seen Danaher ride up.

"Olivia." Gabe took off his hat and stood in the middle of the room looking somewhat out of place. In the Montana wilds, wrestling a mountainous miner, or outlasting a winter blizzard with nothing but brush and canvas for shelter—there he was the master. But in Amy's parlor, with the ornately carved Victorian furniture, the gilt-framed artwork that crowded the walls, the marble statuary that crouched in every corner, he seemed as misplaced as a wild weed in someone's tame ornamental garden. Suddenly Olivia found herself longing for the high sweeping valleys and pristine peaks to which Gabriel was returning. The feeling pricked her anger. She shouldn't miss the wilderness, but be grateful to be delivered from it.

"Are you leaving?" she asked.

"Yes."

Though his hat was in his hands, he looked not at all apologetic. In fact, his stance was almost arrogant. Surrounding him, the gewgaws of parlor decor appeared ostentatious and tawdry.

"It's still snowing. There must be four inches on the ground."

"It's not snowing hard enough to matter."

Her anger climbed another notch. He shouldn't be standing there so coolly; he could at least feign regret at leaving her.

"I . . . I wanted you to come by because I have some things upstairs for the twins—some ribbons, a looking glass, and some other things."

"They don't need things, Olivia."

Was that a note of accusation in his voice? An implication that what they needed was her? How dare he make her feel guilty for leaving them. She felt the anger burn, and let it build. It was illogical and unjust, Olivia knew, but anger was a relief from the pain of loss and agonies of indecision she had suffered all the long afternoon.

They were ill-matched indeed, with less in common than a privet hedge and a wild hawthorn. Her brain accepted that, but her heart didn't. She had fallen in love with a man who was beyond her grasp, and while her heart struggled with her common sense, he had the effrontery to stand there and make her feel guilty about her misgivings. He thought he loved her, but the woman he loved, the woman who'd lived in the mountains with him, was only part of her. He didn't know and couldn't accept the other part. The injustice of it made her even angrier.

"Don't look at me like that!" she snapped.

"Like what?"

"As if you . . . as if you despised me."

He lifted one brow in surprise. "Was I looking like I despise you?" Without warning he took two long steps forward, and suddenly she was in his arms. "Does this look like I despise you?"

His mouth came down heavily on hers. Almost against her will her lips opened. Passions not yet tamed hurtled through the frail barriers she'd tried to erect against them, and her arms wound around his chest. Lost again in their own private world, she couldn't think, couldn't resist.

Finally, he released her, and the cold air of the parlor rushed between them. Shaken, she managed to push herself out of his embrace.

"That's how I feel about you."

"No." She shook her head and denied it to herself as well as him. "You think you love me, Gabriel. But you don't really know me."

"I know you well enough. I know you're quite a woman, Olivia Baron. Maybe the smartest lady I ever met. You're warm, kind, and stubborn as a mule. You have a laugh that reminds me of bells ringing, and you don't laugh enough, and sometimes don't smile enough. Once I thought you had more backbone than any woman I knew. But now I realize you don't have the courage it takes to fall in love."

Olivia clamped her mouth shut on the reply that sprang to her lips. She did love him—so much her heart hurt with it. But she didn't have the courage to stay with him—for so many reasons.

"Perhaps you're right," she said quietly. "Or perhaps I have enough courage to fall in love, but not enough to live with you in your uncivilized world."

His eyes seemed to turn into hard, bright glass. She could read nothing of his feelings in them.

"This is good-bye, then."

"Yes. I suppose this is good-bye." Olivia longed to articulate the emotions flooding through her, but her throat choked closed on the words.

"Olivia!" Sylvester's urgent demand intruded on her agony. "Olivia, come quick! It's Amy, and she's in a bad way!"

Chapter 17

*O*livia's hope that Amy's labor was a false alarm faded as she examined her patient. The contractions were real, and Amy was frantic with panic, not so much from the onset of pain as the fear she would lose this child as she had lost the others.

"Calm down, Amy. You have a long task in front of you to bring your babe into the world."

"No, Olivia!" Amy's face was ashen. "Don't coddle me. Tell me the truth. I'm losing the baby, aren't I? It's too early! Much too early! Oh God help me! I thought this one . . ."

"Amy, calm down! You're no help to yourself or to the child if you give in to hysteria. It's early, but I think not too early. We may have been a week or two off in estimating the birth date, and in any case, you're over eight months. Your baby might very well be fine and healthy, but we must get it delivered before we will know."

Sylvester was no help. He sat beside the bed, clutching Amy's hand and whispering his wife's name in dolorous tones while Olivia instructed Mrs. Grisolm to gather clean sheets.

"And put on some comfrey tea, if you please, Mrs. Grisolm. A big pot. We may be at this quite a while. Is there someone you can send for the midwife?"

"I'll go myself, Dr. Baron."

Amy cried out, and Sylvester moaned with her. Olivia put her hands on Amy's stomach and judged the contractions to still be very weak. Amy panted with fear rather than pain.

"That wasn't so very bad, was it, Amy?"

"N-n-no."

"For this early in a labor, everything seems very normal, dear. Try not to worry."

Sylvester had his head in his hands and looked ready to cry. Olivia took his arm and led him away from the bed. "Sylvester," she said softly, "you're feeding Amy's fear and making this much harder for her."

"My God, Olivia!" he whispered vehemently. "Tell me she's not going to die! Please! I couldn't live without her! Oh God, this is all my fault!"

Olivia patted his arm. "Why don't you just wait downstairs?"

"No. I have to be with her. These may be the last hours I'm with her. . . ."

"Oh no, Sylvester. One patient at a time is all I can handle. Come with me."

Olivia was surprised to see that Gabriel was still in the parlor. She had assumed he'd left when she had dashed out of the room to care for Amy. Seeing him still standing in the middle of the parlor rattled her composure; she had pushed her heartache into a separate compartment of her mind, to be taken out and tended when Amy's crisis was past, but now it threatened to swell past the barriers she had set.

"Gabriel."

"How is Mrs. Talbot?"

"She's having her baby."

"I thought you said it wasn't due until February."

"It isn't. Babies sometimes have minds of their own."

A little cry came from the upstairs bedroom. Olivia reached out and grabbed Sylvester as he turned to go back up the stairs. "I'm glad you're still here, Gabriel. Would you please do something with him?" She pushed Sylvester forward.

Gabriel raised one brow. "Just what do you want done with him?"

"I don't know. Take him somewhere. Tie him up if you have to. Just keep him out of the bedroom upstairs. He's more scared than Amy, and they're just goading each other to new heights of anxiety."

"I'll take care of him," Gabriel said with a devilish grin. "Any liquor in the house?"

"Look in the library. Through there."

"Come on, Talbot." Gabriel took Sylvester's shoulder and propelled him in the direction Olivia had indicated. "You look like you need a shot of whiskey."

Mrs. Grisolm put clean linen and a rubber pad on Amy's bed while Olivia helped Amy into a clean nightgown and walked with her slowly around the bedroom.

"All that water," Amy said with a grimace. "Such a mess."

"Childbirth is an untidy process, dear, but it's worth it." Olivia smiled. "Or so I've been told by those who've been through it."

"Olivia, do you really think the babe will be all right?"

"I think everything will be fine, Amy. But you must resolve to keep heart. Sometimes I think state of mind has much to do with making a delivery difficult or easy."

"Where's Sylvester?"

"Oh, he's in good hands. I gave him over into Mr. Danaher's care."

"Oh my!" An impish smile flitted momentarily across Amy's face. "That should be interesting."

"The teakettle's whistling," Mrs. Grisolm said. "I'll fix the tea and then go for the midwife, if you like, Dr. Baron."

"Yes, please, Mrs. Grisolm. Two sets of hands are always better than one."

The midwife was nowhere to be found. Her sister thought she was attending a birth at the Chalmers' farm five miles down the road, but she wasn't sure. She'd also been aiming to look at a buggy horse over in Boulder, and if that was the case, Meg Grisolm reported, then she wouldn't be back for a day or two, because her current buggy horse was as slow as a three-legged turtle.

So she and Mrs. Grisolm were on their own, Olivia reflected. Standing in the upstairs hallway, with only the housekeeper to see, Olivia didn't bother to hide her frown. In the hours Mrs. Grisolm had been looking for the midwife, Amy's labor had progressed rapidly. The labor pains had steadily become harder and closer together, but with no progress of the child down the birth canal. Olivia didn't like what she felt through Amy's distended abdomen. The child was not prepared for this premature birth. It had not turned into the proper position nor dropped down in readiness for its journey through the birth canal. She had tried a few times to manipulate the fetus into the proper position, with no success.

"It's bad luck that Mrs. Grover is away." Olivia sighed. "But I'm sure the two of us will manage."

Olivia thought Mrs. Grisolm looked a bit pale at that observation.

"Heat a tub of water for washing, please, Mrs. Grisolm. Then get someone to bring up more firewood. I don't want Amy getting chilled."

"Toby has the day off, and Mr. Talbot's dead drunk, ma'am."

"Is Mr. Danaher still here?"

"Yes'm. He's with Mr. Talbot, but he don't look quite so drunk."

"Then ask him to bring up the wood."

Gabriel was not in the least drunk, though there was a smell of alcohol about him.

"I hear you found a way to keep Sylvester out of my hair," Olivia said with a smile.

"At your service, Doc. That man sure can talk when he drinks. I've heard his whole family history back to when his eight times great-grandaddy sailed over from England."

He glanced at Amy, who had fallen into a troubled sleep. "Anything else I can do to help?"

"I don't suppose you've ever delivered a baby?" she asked facetiously.

"Nope. When the twins were born, the women chased me out of the tipi. Said I'd already done my part. I thought you were the expert on babies."

"I've delivered my share, in the charity clinics and at the hospital for women in New York. It generally goes easier if one has help, but, of course, I have Mrs. Grisolm."

"Is everything all right?"

"I don't know yet. Just keep Sylvester from stumbling up the stairs and barging in at an inopportune time."

"He'll be passed out before long."

"Good."

As day turned into night, night passed into day, and daylight faded yet again, Olivia hoped that Sylvester had indeed passed out from drink and stayed unconscious, for Amy's screams rang throughout the house. The birth pains were hard upon her, but the child wouldn't come. Time and time again Olivia tried to turn the fetus, but it was stubborn in its refusal to cooperate. Amy's hair was soaked with sweat, her face pale as the bleached white sheets beneath her. Every contraction eroded the little strength left to her. She couldn't resist the instinct to push so that Olivia could turn the child, but her pushing was not strong enough to advance the birth.

Mrs. Grisolm was little help. Twice since hard labor had begun, she'd had to leave the room to be ill. When she had started to turn green a third time, Olivia had excused her. The woman was so frightened, she was more trouble than she was worth.

"Olivia," Amy whispered hoarsely in one of the brief respites from the contractions.

Olivia took her hand. The wrist was raw where Amy had braced herself with the rope loops tied to the bedpost.

"How long have we been at this?"

Olivia counted the hours in her mind. More than thirty now. "A very long time, my love."

"I'm going to die."

"Not if I can help it." Olivia checked Amy's pulse. It was weak.

"Can't you please save the baby?"

"It would be better to save you both, don't you think?"

Another pain hit her. Amy arched and grabbed for the ropes. Olivia pressed down on the abdomen. "Don't push yet, Amy. Please. Just hold off."

"I can't!" Amy screamed.

Olivia could feel the fetus under her hands. She applied pressure to work it around. The little one began to rotate when Amy shrieked and bore down, pushing the fetus back into its original position. Her screams went on and on, and then finally faded into sobs.

"I'm sorry! I'm sorry!" Amy wept.

"It's all right, Amy. It isn't your fault."

"Please save my baby."

"What's a baby without a mother?" She took Amy's hand and gently squeezed it. "Amy, listen to me. . . ."

Quickly and bluntly Olivia explained what had to be done. She had seen a cesarean performed when she was a medical student. Both mother and babe had died within forty-eight hours, but she'd heard of other such surgical births that had been successful, though they were rare. It was Amy's only chance.

"Do it, Olivia," Amy whispered tearfully. "Just do it." She squeezed Olivia's hand. "If it doesn't work, my dearest friend—my very dearest friend—promise me that you won't blame yourself. Promise me."

"I promise," Olivia said, not at all sure it was a promise she could keep.

"If I don't survive and the baby does, take care of it for me, Olivia. Please."

"You're both going to survive. I'll see to it."

Another contraction built, and Olivia let Amy crush her fingers in her hand while the pain racked her. When Amy had quieted once again, she went into the hall and wiped the tears from her eyes.

And then she called for Gabriel.

*   *   *

Jebediah Crowe took a long swig of tanglefoot and wiped his mouth in satisfaction. The stuff was good; it warmed him all the way to his toes, and on a night like this one, a man needed all the warming he could get. Of course, there were more exciting ways of heating a body up, though the tanglefoot was a good start. He spied Light-hand Sally working the tables by the bar and smiled. Tonight he had coin enough to have her for the whole night—thanks to a couple of mill workers who thought they could out cardsharp ol' Jeb. He'd made up all he'd lost in the last week, and then some. Ol' Sally was in for a high time tonight. But first another load of tanglefoot would feel just right in his gullet. Fleecing those mill men had made him mighty dry.

He signaled Sally to his table, but every time he beckoned, her head turned the other way. Finally he bellowed for service. Damned whore would learn a thing or two about manners before the night was through, he told to himself.

Sally still didn't come. Swearing aloud, Jeb stomped up to the bar and slammed his mug down.

"What's your drink?" the bartender asked.

"Tanglefoot. Gimme another. Can't a man get served at a table around here?"

The bartender shrugged indifferently.

While the man filled his glass, Jeb spied a creased and crumpled hand-bill an arm's length down the bar from where he stood. He knew the face in the drawing, he suddenly realized.

"What's this say?" He turned the handbill toward the bartender.

"It's a wanted poster," said the bartender. "Man named Will O'Connell. Wanted for murder."

"O'Connell?" Jeb chuckled as he examined the fair likeness of Gabriel Danaher. "I knew I'd seen his face on a poster somewhere. Murder, is it?"

"Fella named Rodgers dropped those handbills off a couple of days ago. Said he'd pay good to anyone who would tell him where this O'Connell is holed up. Thought maybe the face looked familiar, but I couldn't place him."

"Where's this fella Rodgers?"

"Said he'd be back in town Tuesday morning."

"You tell him to come see me—Jebediah Crowe's my name, and I'm staying up the street at the Grand. You tell him as soon as you see him, and I'll see it's worth your while."

"Will do. Fixin' to collect a reward, eh?"

"Hellfire. I jest wanna see justice done. Cain't have murderers runnin' around loose."

Jeb grinned as he took his tanglefoot back to the table. Tonight was a jackpot night, all right. Will O'Connell, alias Gabriel Danaher, was going to be sorry he got on the bad side of Jeb Crowe, and Jeb Crowe wasn't going to have to bust his butt looking for a good silver lode anymore. He was just going to step in and inherit one.

Olivia leaned wearily against a pillar of the Talbots' front porch and released the tears she had held back so long. She had taken a terrible chance, a horrific chance, but what choice had there been? The fact that Amy and her baby daughter were both doing well was something she attributed to a miracle rather than her medical skill.

A miracle and a little human help, for she couldn't have performed the operation without Gabriel's steady assistance. He'd followed her instructions precisely in dripping chloroform in just the right amount to keep Amy senseless. He'd fished her instruments in and out of the carbolic bath when she'd needed them, he'd mopped up blood, wiped her sweating brow, and kept an eagle eye on Amy for any signs of distress. Then he'd washed the tiny babe and wrapped it in warm blankets while Olivia closed her incision. All through the procedure, Olivia remembered with a smile, he'd been silent and rather green. Only after the baby girl was snug and secure by Amy's side did he leave the room to be ill. Then he'd come back in, pale and rather shamefaced, to help Olivia clean up.

God bless him, Olivia prayed as she leaned her forehead against the post. *And God guard Amy and her child.* From childbed fever, from suppuration of the incision, from the host of things that could kill mother and child. The babe was so tiny. Everything was in its place as it should be, though, and the little girl had given a lusty and indignant wail upon entering the world. Her first few weeks were going to be very critical. God grant that the child had the strength to suck and Amy had rich milk, for the tiny infant surely needed to grow.

The pale-gray sky to the east hailed a new day about to be born. Amy and her baby were under Mrs. Grisolm's watchful eye—the housekeeper was only too eager to make up for her squeamishness during Amy's travail by helping now, and Olivia was willing to let her. More than anything she needed a few breaths of fresh air, a bath, and sleep.

A shadow detached itself from a huge pine that stood like a sentinel in front of the house.

"Gabriel! I thought you'd either be getting some well-earned sleep or be on the trail up the mountain by now."

"I'm on my way out. But I have a thing or two to say before I leave."

Olivia sat down heavily on the porch steps. She didn't have the strength to endure another good-bye. Not right now. "I'm grateful for your help with Amy, Gabriel. More than grateful. You were a godsend."

Gabriel dropped down beside her and stared out into the street. "I was sick and shaking the entire time."

"I know, and that makes what you did all the more gallant."

"There's a word that's never been used to describe me."

"Only because people don't know you the way I do."

"And what words would you use to describe yourself?"

Olivia blinked. "What?"

"Right before Amy went into labor, you said I didn't really know you. You said the woman I got to know at the cabin wasn't the real you, and you were right. I didn't even know half of you, did I?"

"No. You didn't. I don't know who that woman up there was. Baking bread, sewing, chopping firewood . . ."

"Rescuing a trapped miner from an early grave," he added.

"That too." She smiled wearily. "Playing with a wolf cub, chopping firewood . . . and everything else. Years from now when I'm a sedate little old lady, I'm going to look back at my time with you and think it was all a fantasy I concocted in my overactive imagination."

"I'll be reduced to a fantasy, eh?"

She looked down at her hands, which were reddened from the numerous scrubbings of the last hours.

"I'll admit I thought this medicine thing was kind of a hobby," Gabriel said, "but it's your whole life, isn't it? It's what you live for, and you're damned good at it. I knew that when I watched you save Katy from choking to death, but I became so wrapped up in the woman part of you that I forgot you were special in ways that had nothing to do with being a woman. You are special, Doc. The other quacks in this one-horse town wouldn't have done for Amy. You were something else."

"Medicine has been my passion since I was Katy and Ellen's age."

He was silent for a moment, then smiled slightly. "You have other passions, too, Doc."

"So I discovered."

"You know, I said some things that I have to take back. I said you didn't have the guts to fall in love—mostly because I was mad that I was losing you."

"I fell in love," Olivia said quietly. "I just don't have the courage to turn my life upside down for the sake of that love."

"I don't believe that. After seeing you last night, I think you have the courage to do whatever it is you want to do, if you want it enough."

She was so tired she couldn't think, only feel. What she felt was that she didn't want him to leave.

"Olivia, I love you. I'm willing to share you with medicine."

When she looked up at him, she was sure her heart was in her eyes.

His mouth twitched in a weary smile. "Think about it, Olivia. Don't go back to New York without thinking about it, and this."

He drew her to him for a kiss. His lips brushed across hers, playing, tasting, then possessing. Olivia had no strength to resist the warmth that flooded her as he urged her mouth open. Gently but relentlessly he branded her with his need and took possession of her soul. She had no will to fight him and the urgent demand of her own heart.

"Think about it, Olivia."

Her head and heart were still spinning as he walked away into the gray, cold dawn.

Olivia had never realized how much joy could be in a family. Her own family had placed more value upon dignity and reserve than love. Affection had been understood between her parents and herself, but seldom overtly shown. She wondered if they had ever been as proud and delighted in her as the Talbots were with their little Jennifer.

On the morning a week after surgery had delivered Amy of her baby, the threesome of mother, father, and child seemed to generate more warmth than the fire they sat beside. This was Amy's first venture out of bed, and Sylvester bustled around her chair like a fretful mother hen, adjusting pillows, tucking blankets, and generally making a nuisance of himself. He had suffered from an excess of helpfulness ever since he had recovered from the massive hangover that resulted from his part in the birth. At least once every hour he declared that the child's safe delivery was a miracle, Olivia was a saint, and even Gabriel Danaher was a fine fellow after all. Out west, he'd informed Olivia when he'd heard of Gabriel's part in Amy's delivery, men weren't judged on their pasts. What a man had been didn't signify, only what he was, and the shared hours and shared bottles with Gabriel Danaher had proved Danaher's mettle as far as Sylvester was concerned. What's more, he owed the man a debt that no amount of money could repay.

At Sylvester's repeated dissertations on the subject, Amy would nod her head in agreement and smile, her eyes twinkling in amusement.

Amy shifted uncomfortably in her chair in front of the fire. "Oh, how I ache. It must be time for Jennifer to nurse."

Sylvester grew red at the prospect. "I'll just leave you three ladies alone, then, my dear. Is there anything you need before I go?"

"No, Sylvester. Thank you."

Amy unbuttoned her nightgown and put the babe to her full breast. Jennifer sucked greedily, and bluish-white milk dribbled down her tiny chin to splotch Amy's gown. Olivia smiled at the baby's voraciousness. She had gained weight and bloomed over the last week, changing from a red and wrinkled little monkey to a pink, healthy baby. Amy also had bloomed. The smile on her face and light in her eyes seemed to be permanent fixtures. Her milk had come in sweet, rich, and full, and so far no sign of festering or childbed fever marred her recovery. It seemed that after robbing her of two children, Mother Nature had decided to smile upon Amy Talbot.

As for herself, Olivia hadn't yet gotten over being tired. Sporadically during the week she'd thought about making plans to return home. Amy wouldn't need her much longer—not more than a few weeks at the rate she was recovering, and the life Olivia had built for herself waited in New York. In New York there were friends and family, an appointment to the New England Hospital for Women and Children, sophisticated shops, theaters, restaurants, crowded streets and fetid alleys. There would be no wind in the pines to wake her to fresh-scented mornings, no sharp, clean Montana sky so bright it hurt the eyes. The rattle of carriages and clamor of a million people would fill the night air instead of the songs of wolves, and she would sleep alone on her feather bed, in her room at her parents' big house, alone with only pillows to hug.

He could share her with medicine, Gabriel had said. She had the courage to do whatever it was she wanted to do. Did she? Did she really? Could she change her life so radically for a man she knew so little of, merely because she loved him?

Olivia felt as though she walked the knife edge of Thunder Ridge. A step in one direction would send her plummeting into a future dull with predictability and loneliness—things she hadn't minded before she met Gabriel Danaher; in the other direction lay a future so crowded with possibilities and uncertainties that it frightened her.

"You seem tired, Olivia dear." Amy looked up from her suckling baby with a smile. She'd been smiling since she first woke from the chloroform and heard she had a baby girl. "I've been selfish, keeping you by my side all this week. Why don't you go out and get some fresh air? The sun looks very inviting out there."

"It does, doesn't it? Who would think that a January day could be so bright, though it's almost February, isn't it? Maybe I will take a walk. Lack of exercise has always put me in the doldrums."

"If you're going to walk toward town, would you stop by the jewelry store next to Shriner's and ask if that stickpin I ordered for Sylvester is in yet? They promised me it would be here by Christmas."

"Disgraceful that they've taken this long."

"Well, dear, this isn't New York."

"No. It isn't, is it?"

The brisk January air revived Olivia's spirits somewhat. The tang of wood smoke scented the air, and in the distance, snow-covered peaks glinted in the pale winter sunlight.

Mrs. Covey at the tiny jewelry shop next to Shriner's apologized that Sylvester's stickpin had still not been delivered. Not yet ready to return to the house, Olivia wandered into Ford's Candy Store and bought some peppermints. Then she went into Shriner's. The hat that Gabriel thought was suitable only for a prospector's mule was still on display. Olivia had to smile at the memories it evoked.

"That's a lovely bonnet, isn't it, Miss Baron?" Henry Shriner's wife Penelope smiled at Olivia from across the aisle. "It would look very nice on you, don't you think? Try it on if you like."

"No, thank you, Mrs. Shriner. Today I'm simply window-shopping. Passing some time."

"Yes, my dear. The men simply don't understand what fun that can be, do they? My, but you do look a bit peaked. You must be ever so grateful to have escaped your adventure in good form. Especially now."

"Now?"

"Now with the news about Mr. Danaher, or I suppose I should say Mr. O'Connell. Surely you've heard, dear. It's all about town."

"I've been in with Mrs. Talbot all week." Olivia's heart hammered. "What about Mr. Danaher?"

"Why, he's a wanted man!" She raised her brows knowingly. "Not that half the men in this town aren't wanted somewhere for something, I suspect, but murder really does get one's attention."

"Murder?" Olivia drew in a sharp, painful breath. "Where did you hear this?"

"A bounty hunter—or at least that's what Henry thought he was, though he claimed to be employed by some notable down in Virginia City."

Virginia City—Gabriel had owned a ranch near Virginia City.

"He spread handbills all about the town, but, of course, you know the men in this town don't like to get mixed up in chasing a man down for his past. Too many of them have pasts of their own. But some very unpleas-ant-looking fellow told the bounty hunter he could take him up to Mr. Danaher's cabin. They were in only an hour ago getting supplies to ride up there—buying more ammunition than beans, they were."

"Oh, my dear, you're white as a sheet. This must come as a shock to know you were in the hands of a murderer for all that time." Her voice lowered in horror. "And a woman-killer, no less. The man killed the Indian woman who lived with him. Of course, they're really after him for killing the man along with her."

Olivia felt as though she'd been hit on the head with a sledgehammer. Gabriel murdered his beloved Minnie? Impossible. Ridiculous. He had loved the woman, had children by her. He would never commit such a horrendous crime.

And yet he had been remarkably cryptic about why he had left his ranch in Virginia City. And he could be roused to violence at times.

No! Impossible! And yet there was a bounty hunter out to collect a reward by chasing Gabriel down, and someone who knew the way up Thunder Creek rode with him. She thought of their riding into that peaceful little clearing with all that ammunition they'd just bought at Shriner's. They would take Gabriel by surprise. Katy would try to help and might well get hurt. Ellen also.

She had to do something.

"Have they left already?" Olivia demanded of Mrs. Shriner.

"Who, dear?"

"This bountry hunter? Has he left to go after Mr. Danaher?"

"Why, I don't believe so. Mr. Rodgers—he's the fellow with the hand-bills—mentioned that his horse had gone lame and asked where he could get a good mount. I sent him over to the livery, and Gregg Smoot will probably haggle over the price until the sun's down."

"Maybe they won't leave until tomorrow morning."

"I wouldn't know about that, dear. Mr. Rodgers seemed anxious to be on his way. But I imagine Mr. Danaher will be there, whenever they go. The man only comes to town three or four times a year. I always thought he looked like a man a woman would do well to avoid. You must have been terrified the whole time you were at that place of his."

Olivia gathered her composure and smiled blandly. "It seems I should have been more terrified than I was. Thank you, Mrs. Shriner."

"Not at all, dear. You say hello to Mrs. Talbot for me, bless her."

"I will."

Olivia nearly ran up the street toward the Talbot house, heedless of the curious looks she drew. She knew what she had to do, and she had to do it fast.

Chapter 18

The ride up the mountain seemed interminable. When Olivia had first come up this trail, she'd had other things on her mind than paying attention to the route, and now she found that tracks forked off every which way. These mountains had been mined extensively, and every wagon rut seemed to be preserved for the sole purpose of confusing her. All she could do was follow the trail that looked right, and when more than one looked right, simply hope that good fortune was with her. If there was any justice in the world, the two men after Gabe's hide would be as confused as Olivia was.

Being atop Amy's frisky saddle mare didn't help matters any. The horse had been exercised only sparsely over the months of Amy's pregnancy, and now she wanted to jump at every sound and movement. Olivia's horsemanship hadn't improved much over the past weeks. If she lost her seat, the mare would likely leave her behind on the ground with a flick of her tail for good riddance.

The trail became easier to follow once Olivia reached Thunder Creek, for then all she had to do was follow the creek up to the high meadows below Thunder Ridge. That was all, Olivia told herself, trying not to think about the snowdrifts that were tiring her mount, the sun rapidly sinking behind the mountains, the treacherous debris slide that she would have to cross in the dark, and the wolves that had serenaded the mountains almost every night that she'd been in Gabe's cabin.

Amy had warned her that a New York greenhorn was not up to riding alone in the Montana wilds. Her romantic notions about Olivia and Gabriel Danaher had evaporated abruptly when Olivia mentioned murder.

"Killed his wife?" Amy had gasped. "Olivia! And to think you spent all that time alone with him!"

"He couldn't have killed his wife."

"But if the law—"

"I have great respect for the law, Amy, but this was a bounty hunter or some such person. If Gabriel has been tried and convicted, why isn't a marshal or some other real lawman on his trail?"

"Maybe because lawmen are few and far between out here," Amy said sensibly. "Olivia, stay out of this. You'd be aiding a criminal, and how would that look to the board of that hospital where you're going to work? Your future, everything you've worked so hard to achieve—Olivia, think!"

Olivia had thought, but she hadn't been able to think of anything but Gabriel. Strange that the accusations against him convinced Amy of the impossibility of the match between them while they made Olivia realize that she couldn't leave him. She didn't know the man's history, but she knew *him*. Mind and soul were the measure of a man, and Gabriel's mind and soul were a part of her. If she left him now, she would never again be whole. And, God forbid, if Gabriel were hung, shot, drawn, and quartered, or whatever the law did to criminals in this still-uncivilized land, a big piece of Olivia would suffer and die along with him.

It was almost noon the next day when a cold, hungry, bedraggled, and saddle-sore Olivia rode up to the cabin. Ellen greeted her at the door, bouncing up and down with joy. "You've come back! I told them you would come back! I told them you wouldn't leave us!"

"Ellen, where's your father?"

"Pa and Katy are in the mine. They found a new vein that—"

"You must go in and warn your father that a bounty hunter is headed up here to take him away on some charge that—!"

Ellen's jaw had dropped open, and her face turned ashy pale. Olivia realized she couldn't give voice to the awful charge in front of Gabriel's daughter.

"There's no time to explain, Ellen. Get me a lantern. Quickly! I'll go in. If by any chance someone rides in here and asks for your father, tell them he's gone. You haven't seen him in days."

Two minutes later Olivia stumbled up to the mine entrance, her legs so stiff from the long ride that she could scarcely walk. She called Gabriel's name into the tunnel, but there was no answer. She would have to go in.

"I've done it before," she said to herself. "I can do it again."

Jaw clenched, she strode into the tunnel before she could lose her courage, shouting Gabriel's name as she went. He met her halfway to the end.

"Olivia!" His white teeth flashed in the lantern light as he took her by the arms. "You came!"

Before she could say anything, he kissed her. She allowed herself to melt against him for a moment only, then pushed him away. Katy was grinning at them from the edge of the lantern light.

"Gabriel! There are men coming up here to get you. They think you're wanted for . . . for murder. You have to run. They could be right behind me."

His grip on her shoulder tightened along with the expression on his face. "Who was it? A man named Candliss? Tall? Sandy hair? Probably has a limp?"

"No. A bounty hunter named Rodgers, and someone who offered to guide him to the cabin."

The grim set of his features relaxed just a bit. Katy moved up to take his arm. "You ride out fast, Pa. Ellen and me'll be all right till you can find a new place and send for us."

From the look on Katy's face, Olivia guessed that the accusations against her father weren't news.

"Katy," Gabriel said. "You go on ahead, saddle Longshot, and get some gear together for me. I need to talk to Olivia."

Olivia objected. "No time to talk, Gabriel. Those men will be here—!"

"Hush," he said gently as Katy disappeared. "You rode up here all alone to warn me?"

"Yes. Of course."

He grinned. "You do love me, don't you?"

"Yes."

"You haven't asked me if I really am a murderer."

"I don't have to. I know you're not."

He kissed her again, long and hard, then set her back from him, gripping her shoulders tightly and drinking her in with his eyes. A wry smile twisted his mouth. "Just my luck to find you right before I have to light out again. But I'm not going to give you up."

"Gabriel . . ."

He shook his head and released her. "I'll explain the mess to you someday, Doc. I swear I will. But like you said, there's no time right now." He hesitated for a moment, then asked: "Will you take care of the girls for me?"

"As if they were my own daughters."

A quick grin transformed the grim lines of his face. "They will be, as soon as I can get this straightened out and drag you to a preacher." He kissed her again, briefly but thoroughly. "I love you, Olivia."

"I love you, too."

They almost made it. Katy had Longshot saddled and waiting at the mouth of the tunnel, a bedroll and provisions tied to the back of the saddle. Gabe had kissed the twins good-bye and was ready to mount when Hunter's growl and raised ruff warned of strangers riding in.

The two men appeared suddenly at the edge of the trees fifty feet away. Olivia saw the moment of indecision in Gabriel's eyes. His foot was in the stirrup, his hand on the saddle horn. He could swing onto the horse's back to run for it. His eyes flicked to the rifles the two held ready, rifles that were pointed in his direction, which meant they were pointed at the twins and Olivia as well. His hand tightened on the saddle horn until the knuckles were white. Then he let it go and took his foot out of the stirrup.

"It's just not worth it," he said softly to Olivia.

"Pa!" Katy pleaded. "You can make it! Run!"

"Simmer down, Katy, my girl. This time we'll have none of your heroics."

Katy muttered a soft curse. Olivia threw Gabriel a questioning look, but he just shook his head. "I'll have to tell you about that someday, too."

"Well, if it ain't Mister Will O'Connell." Cal Rodgers chuckled. "Last time I saw you was with a rope around your neck." He glanced at Katy and spat. "Mebbe I should haul in the little spitfire, too."

"You've got me," Gabriel said with quiet intensity. "Touch any of the others and you're a dead man. I guarantee it."

"Just a thought."

"Jeb?" Olivia said as the second man rode closer. "Jebediah Crowe, is that you? *You* brought this man up here?"

Jeb touched his hat. "Howdy do, ma'am. 'Pears you're gonna be without a man now."

"Why, you . . . you . . ." She couldn't think of a word scathing enough.

Katy was not hampered by inhibitions. "You low-down, slimy, crap-eating piece of scum."

"Snake!" Ellen added.

"You better get on your horse, O'Connell," Jeb warned, "before I'm tempted to teach these little gals a lesson they won't forget."

Rodgers motioned with his rifle to Gabe's horse. "Ma'am. You get that rifle off the saddle and bring it to me real easy."

Olivia looked at Gabriel, who nodded.

When Rodgers had stowed the rifle on his own saddle, he had Jeb search Gabriel for a pistol or any other weapon he might carry. Then he ordered Gabe to mount and tied his hands behind him.

"Cain't take no chances," Rodgers explained with a grin. "This here's a slippery one, and Ace Candliss wants him delivered whole so he can watch his face while he hangs."

Jeb chuckled. "We're doin' you a favor, ma'am. This here's a bad 'un— a woman-killer, so's I hear." He grinned at Gabe. "Too bad there's no man here to please your woman and mine your silver, now, ain't it?"

"Shit, Crowe," Rodgers said with a laugh. "I doubt you're man enough to do either."

Gabriel's face was hard as stone. A slight jerk of his head brought Olivia to his side. He leaned down to kiss her while Jeb and Rodgers crowed out scathing advice.

"Make it a good one, man. It'll be your last."

"Make it one to remember when you're wearin' that noose, boy."

Gabe said quietly against her lips, "There's money. Ask the girls where. Take it and get out of here."

"Gabriel!"

"This isn't the end. Leave word with the Talbots where you are," he whispered, "and I'll find you."

Olivia put an arm around each girl as they watched the three men start down the trail. "You can be sure this isn't the end," she said quietly. "It's a long way from the end if I have anything to say about it."

The jail cell was dirty. It stank of rotten food, vomit, urine, and fear, but it was preferable to a grave. Gabe had halfway expected Candliss to hang him without the formalities. Two years ago, with the marshal in his pocket, he hadn't bothered with a trial. Maybe now that Montana was a state he was treading a bit more carefully. After all, a prospective senator couldn't have a lynching in his past.

Gabe had hoped to escape on the long ride from Elkhorn to Virginia City. Cal Rodgers was just one man, after all—he had paid Jeb Crowe off in Elkhorn and sent him about his business. Like any man, Rodgers had to sleep, he had to relieve himself at least once or twice a day, and he had to have some moments when his mind wasn't quite on his job. Gabe had been prepared to take advantage of anything he could. But Rodgers was a crafty sonofabitch—Gabe had to give him credit for that. He'd kept Gabe tied up tighter than a turkey trussed for roasting.

"It don't matter none if yer hands turn black and fall off," he'd said. "Don't need hands to git hanged, and that's fer sure where you're headed."

His hands hadn't turned black, but after two days in jail, Gabe was just beginning to get feeling back in his fingers. Candliss had stopped by both days to gloat, to brag about his bright and powerful future, and Gabe's lack of one. Gabe was glad to see his bullet had left Candliss with a bad limp. He hoped the bastard was in pain every day of his life.

Ace Candliss didn't completely dominate Gabe's thoughts, however. Olivia was the one who did that. Gabe spent his days fretting and his nights worrying. He hoped to hell she'd had the sense to get herself and the twins away from the mine and the cabin before Jeb returned, for the dumb bastard had made his intentions clear enough. He hoped she'd remembered about the money; when he'd told her about it she'd been upset and scarcely listening. The sheen in her eyes had threatened to dribble over into real tears. She'd ridden all the way up to Thunder Ridge—much of the ride at night—to try to save him from Candliss. The thought always made him smile when it came—until he remembered where he was, and the near hopelessness of ever seeing Olivia or his daughters again.

"Wake up, O'Connell! Breakfast!"

Deputy Roscoe slammed the door behind him as he came in with the tray. "Looks like cornmeal mush this mornin', and Miz Eloise makes mush like no other woman, I tell ya."

Deputy Roscoe liked more about Mrs. Eloise Crabtree than her mush. He'd spent several hours in friendly conversation with his prisoner detailing the virtues of the young widow who ran the boardinghouse across the street and provided meals for prisoners in the town jail. Deputy Roscoe, an affable young man with a ready laugh that bobbed his prominent Adam's apple up and down, seemed happy to have a captive audience to regale with his lady's excellence.

"Sausage, too," the deputy announced. He opened the cell and handed Gabe the tray. "Mind you don't dig your way out with that fork," he said with a laugh.

"That would take a year or so. Do I have that long before the judge comes around?"

"Never can tell."

Deputy Roscoe was getting a bit careless, Gabe noted as the young man went back into the marshal's office—opening the cell door a second longer than he had to, a bit wider than necessary, getting a fraction too close to the bars. It might be the death of him someday when he had a prisoner less gentlemanly than Gabe.

An hour later Deputy Roscoe came back into the cell area with a big grin on his face. "You got a visitor," he announced. "An' this time it ain't Ace." He called out the door: "Come on back, ma'am. He's fit fer company."

Gabe's heart almost hammered right through his chest when Olivia walked through the door. She was the most welcome sight he'd ever seen, in a fancy Back East dress that was the same blue as her eyes. A soft-looking pile of dark hair at the crown of her head had replaced the scraped-back bun, and tilted forward at a jaunty angle atop the pile was one of the most ridiculous little straw hats he'd ever seen.

His Olivia and her stupid hats. Gabe wanted to reach through the bars and pull her to him for a kiss, and to strangle her in the same instant. She should be anywhere but in Virginia City, damn her!

"Thank you, Marshal Roscoe."

"Jest Deputy Roscoe, ma'am."

Olivia gave the boy a smile that would melt granite. "Deputy, then. I appreciate your letting me see your prisoner. You won't mind if we have a few moments of privacy, will you?"

"Well . . ."

"Come on, Deputy. Do I look the sort of person to engineer a jailbreak?"

"No, ma'am. I guess it'd be all right. You give a shout if O'Connell gives you any trouble."

"You can be sure I will."

As soon as the deputy left, Gabe exploded. "*What* are you doing here?"

"Visiting you," she said calmly.

"Where are the girls?"

"They're with me, of course. Well, not with me. They're at the Fairview Inn. I didn't want them visiting you before I saw what kind of conditions these people were holding you in. I practically had to tie Katy to the bedpost." She smiled. "One of your tricks."

"I don't want them coming to the jailhouse. You shouldn't be here either."

"Why not? You need someone on your side—Mr. O'Connell. Will O'Connell?"

He caught the question in her raised brows. "Uh . . . William Gabriel Danaher O'Connell. Danaher is my mother's maiden name."

"So Katy told me on the trip down here."

"What else did she tell you?"

Olivia grinned. "She told me a grand story about how she rescued you from a lynch mob here in Virginia City. She said you killed the fellow who killed their mother."

Gabe's stomach still turned to a ball of ice when he thought about that day.

"You don't have to tell me about it, Gabriel. Whatever you did, I know it wasn't murder."

"Guess it depends on how you define murder," he said quietly. "Minnie and I had a ranch a few miles west of town. For nine years we lived there, raised horses and cattle for the army, and minded our own business. People hereabouts aren't real fond of Indians, and they gave Minnie the cold shoulder, but that didn't bother us much. We had us, and the girls, and the ranch.

"Then I came home one day from town and walked in on two men who had Minnie down on the floor." Gabe could feel his stomach twist as he spoke of it. "They'd taken turns with her, then when they were tired of that they beat her just for the fun of it—because she was an Indian, I guess, and she'd had the cheek to fight them. I went for my gun. Buck Candliss had dragged Minnie up from the floor and had her by the throat. When he saw me, he tossed her away to get to his gun. She hit her head on one of the stones of the fireplace. Split it open, scalp and skull too. I killed Buck. His brother Ace got away with just a bullet in the leg."

Olivia bit her lip. "Where were the girls?"

"Katy gave one of the men some lip when they first broke in. He knocked her clean out. Ellen dragged her into the bedroom and hid under the bed with her."

"Oh my dear Lord."

"I shoulda lit out with the girls the minute Ace rode off, but I was out of my mind. I hardly remember anything until Ace came back with Marshal Kale and a posse. I was still trying to wake Minnie up when they got there. The judge wasn't due in town for a couple of weeks, and Candliss wanted to get me strung up fast, so he convinced the marshal to go along with an old-style vigilante hanging."

"You didn't even get a trial?"

"Candliss is a big name in these parts, and Ace is the top dog in the pack. Can't say I blame the marshal for not standing up to him."

"Well, I blame him! Gabriel, they can't hang you for defending your wife and your home!"

"Sure they can, Doc. If you and the girls don't get out of town quick, you'll get to watch them do exactly that."

"They have to at least give you a trial!"

"Yeah. They'll do that. Candliss has ambitions that go beyond Virginia City now that Montana's a state. He'll want this to be nice and legal."

"Well, they absolutely cannot convict you! It would be a gross miscarriage of justice."

"Doc, you're as innocent as a babe if you believe that."

"I'll hire you a lawyer."

"You'd have to go a long way to find a lawyer with guts enough to stand up against Candliss. Besides, I've got nothing but my word to defend me. My word against Ace Candliss. A 'squaw man' against the town's leading citizen."

"You can't just give up!"

"Olivia," he said gently. "It's not your fight."

"It is my fight! I love you!"

He reached through the bars and took her hand. "Doc, the thought of you and the girls safe and happy is just about the only thing that's going to get me through this."

"There must be something we can do!"

"There is. You can take the girls and go back to Elkhorn. Stay with the Talbots, or someplace where you'll all be safe and away from this."

"I can't just leave you."

"Leave me, Olivia. If I can find a way out of this, it's not going to be by legal means, and I don't want to be worrying about you and the girls if I have to knock a few heads together."

Her lips tightened to stop the hint of a quiver.

"Did you get the money?"

"Yes. You're quite a well-off gentleman."

"I was saving to give the girls some kind of future, and some of it was to hire some men to help me go after Candliss. Thought maybe if I had a gun barrel stuck up his nose he might admit the truth in front of witnesses. I'd get everything I wanted—revenge and freedom, too." He grinned wryly. "Then I started wanting you worse than revenge. Hoped maybe I could run away and forget the whole thing. Too bad the law didn't see fit to forget as well."

"I used a bit of the money to hire two men to look after the mine, Ted Brown and Rufus Hollins. I was afraid Jeb might try to jump your claim. He showed up the day before we left, but Rufus and Ted backed him down."

"Just so he doesn't jump my claim on you."

She laughed. "Jeb isn't nearly as interested in me as in the mine, and Ted and Rufus guard it like it was their own."

"They can have it. I got what I wanted out of it. Use the money to get the girls away from here to someplace where people won't care that they're half Blackfoot. And use it for yourself, too. It doesn't matter that there's been no words said over us, my lass. You're my wife in every way that matters."

She ducked her head, hiding her eyes from his view, and her hands clenched at her sides. When she looked up, however, her eyes were dry. "I'll take care of Katy and Ellen until you can come back to be with us. You don't need to worry about them."

Gabe felt as though the moment of their final parting was rushing toward them like a wall of floodwater. He wanted desperately to push it back, to fight like crazy to prevent it from sweeping them up and casting them both to separate fates—his most probably a hangman's noose. Olivia was losing her battle for control; he could see the sheen of tears in her eyes. She was stubborn enough not to let them flow, innocent enough to believe there was still hope. Perhaps it was kindest to let her believe.

"Leave word with the Talbots where you are. I'll find you."

She pressed her lips hard together and bit down on them with her teeth. He could see the struggle in her face not to give in to weeping.

"I'll do that," she finally said.

"Come here." The bars weren't wide enough to allow a kiss. All they could do was hold hands and touch noses.

"Tell the twins . . . tell them I love them."

"I will."

"Good-bye."

"Good-bye, Gabriel. Until—until later. Be careful."

Gabe watched her go out the door and felt that he didn't have to wait for a noose to end his life. It was over now.

"I don't know, Ace. I know how you feel, my friend. If my brother had been the one shot down, I'd feel the same way. I wish I could tell you it's a sure thing, but it plain and simple isn't."

Dennis Walters looked at Ace Candliss from across the expanse of a desk littered with case files, wanted posters, legal briefs, and the remains of his lunch. He was glad the desk was between them, because he could see the anger seething inside the man. Ace Candliss was a man of deep emotion and explosive temper. His younger brother had been all the family left to him when Old Man Candliss got killed. The brothers had been close. They'd worked hard to expand the Candliss empire, and sometimes played rougher than a man ought to—but always together. When Buck had been shot by Will O'Connell, Ace had nearly gone crazy with grief.

"Hell, Dennis! Are you telling me the jury might let that bastard off without hanging him?"

"Juries are hard to predict, and it's only your word against his. He tells a different story about what happened than you do."

"Well, who are you going to believe—a no-good Irish squaw man or a man who's been a leader in this town for years, whose family was one of those with guts enough to first settle this area? Who's the jury going to believe?"

"Like I said, Ace, juries are unpredictable." Walters himself didn't know quite what to believe. Ace's version of what had happened out on that ranch two years ago rang with conviction, but a man could convince himself of his own version of the truth. In the nine years Will O'Connell had ranched his stretch of land outside Virginia City, he had been friendly enough, but a loner. Walters hadn't known him well enough to say what he was likely to do at finding his woman bedding down with two other men. And O'Connell claimed the Candliss brothers had raped the woman. That would certainly be enough reason to start many men shooting. "Everyone around here's real conscious of being a state now, Ace. Folks want Montana to look like a civilized part of the Union. Could be they'll send him to the pen instead of hanging him."

"I want to see that sonofabitch swing! Hell, if I'd of known there was any doubt about it, I wouldn't have brought him in."

"If you're wanting that seat in the Senate, my friend, you'd better give up the idea of taking the law into your own hands."

"Well, the law's hands aren't very capable sometimes, are they? The law didn't bring O'Connell in—I did! Hell, Dennis! The law wasn't even working at finding him. I put out the handbills on the man. I put up the reward to find him."

"Maybe if you'd waited for a trial to convict him the first time around instead of trying to lynch the man, the law would have been more interested."

"Bullshit! All I can say is the law better do what's right. My brother's dead, and I'm crippled because of that sonofabitch."

Walters shook his head. "I'll present the best case I can to get the maximum penalty, Ace. I just wish you had a witness besides yourself. Oh, by the way, did I tell you that O'Connell has a lawyer now?"

"What?"

"A lady came by about three days ago and informed me that she'd retained Douglas Berman to defend him."

"The Jew? That's a laugh."

"He's a competent lawyer."

"People don't like him." His eyes narrowed. "Who's this woman?"

"Olivia Baron's her name. She was staying at the Fairview Inn with a couple of kids that looked like they could have been O'Connell's daughters."

"Is she still in town?"

"The afternoon that she talked to me, she and the two kids took the stage. They bought tickets to Boulder. I checked."

"You should have told me."

"Why? The man has a right to a defense, and if O'Connell's got a lady, it's not really your business. Your beef is with him."

"You were curious enough about her to check where she was headed."

"I'm in charge of prosecuting this case. I like to keep tabs on anything that has something to do with the prisoner."

Ace smiled, and Walters wasn't sure he trusted that smile. "The same way I feel, Dennis. Exactly the same way."

One day later Ace walked into the marshal's office for his daily look at the prisoner. Some days he just sat and stared at the man, as if his hatred could drain the life away from the arrogant Irish Indian-loving bastard. Sometimes he gloated, talking to O'Connell about hangings he'd seen, about men jerking on the end of the rope while the noose slowly strangled, about black protruding tongues, popping eyes, and men emptying their bowels into their trousers as the life was choked out of them. He had spent two years imagining O'Connell's hanging; he wanted O'Connell to imagine it too—in rich, vivid detail.

Today, however, he would talk about something else. Dennis Walters had been kind enough to warn him about the way things stood, and Ace Candliss wasn't one to sit calmly by for such a miscarriage of justice. The law owed him a hanging—or at least a death—for his brother Buck's murder and for the bullet that had left him a damned cripple for life.

"Hello there, O'Connell. Lodging up to your standards?"

The prisoner merely stared at him like some brute too dumb to answer. Hatred gleamed in his eyes. Candliss hoped the sonofabitch was burning with it, that it ate at him as it ate at Ace. Soon, Ace's hatred would be satisfied; O'Connell would die with the venom still eating at him, and Candliss intended to make it even worse.

"Hear tell you had a lady in town asking after you. The sweet thing even hired you a lawyer, much good it'll do you. Had a couple of kids with her. Pretty little girls, I hear, in spite of being 'breeds." He smiled. "Of course, I always did like a taste of Injun now and then."

Candliss was gratified to see the fire flare in his victim's eyes.

"How old are those little girls now? Twelve, thirteen? A bit young, but old enough."

"Your fight is with me, Candliss."

"Yes it is, isn't it? You killed my brother, O'Connell. My brother was the only family I had. Sometimes I think it hurts more to see your family die than to die yourself."

"The only one listening here is me, so you don't need to play the innocent injured victim with me. Your brother got what was coming to him, and if my aim had been better, you would have gotten the same. You raped my wife, beat her, killed her."

"An Indian!" Candliss raged. "You killed my brother over a damned Indian squaw!"

"My wife! Mother of my children."

"A squaw, goddammit! We were just having some fun, and if she hadn't sassed us, we wouldn't have had to rough her up. Killing her was an accident. It was as much your fault as ours."

O'Connell just looked at him with eyes that could have done murder.

"My brother. My only family. Just as those half-breed daughters are your only family. I want you to think about how helpless they'll be after your neck is stretched."

"They're far from helpless, Candliss."

"I might even get the state to give me custody of the little dears. A magnanimous gesture, don't you think—caring for the daughters of my enemy. Should get me some votes."

The prisoner's face was etched in stone, but deep in the eyes Candliss could see a desperation building.

"I know where your cabin is, O'Connell. And I know the name of the woman you sent them off with. Even if they don't go back to your cabin, I'll find them. I'm a powerful man. No one can hide from me for very long."

He chuckled as he saw the barb strike home.

"Think about it. Think what I'm going to do to those girls after you're gone—maybe even before, since there's not much you can do to stop me. Young girls are such tender things. They break so easily."

As Candliss turned to go, he saw O'Connell grip the iron bars that held him prisoner. His knuckles were white, his face set and grim.

"Just keep thinking about it, you bastard. Maybe it'll keep your mind off the hanging."

                              *   *   *

An hour later a drumbeat of hooves thudded past the jailhouse. A rock shattered the barred window and wedged itself between two of the bars. Gabe pried it loose just before Deputy Roscoe stuck his head through the door from the office and looked around.

"What was that?"

Gabe jerked his head toward the broken window. "Someone threw a rock."

"Damned hooligans. You're gonna have a cold night, O'Connell. I won't be able to get that fixed till morning."

Gabe shrugged. "Maybe I'll crawl out between the bars."

Roscoe regarded him suspiciously, as though Gabe might actually be able to squeeze himself through the three inches between the window bars. "Maybe I can at least get it boarded up. I'll go talk to Jake Miller when I can find someone to watch the office."

"You do that."

Once Roscoe was gone, Gabe examined the item that had been tied to the rock. Unless he was mistaken, it was a key to the door of his cell. He smiled. Candliss was an efficient fellow. When he wanted something to happen, he made sure it happened.

The trap was obvious enough to be laughable, but then, there was no need for subtlety between William Gabriel O'Connell and Ace Candliss. They both knew what they wanted, and only one of them was going to get it.

Chapter 19

*T*he night was black and thick with moisture. Clouds hid the moon and stars, and a few tentative snowflakes drifted from the sky. Just outside the door of the jailhouse, Gabe squeezed himself against the brick wall, blending with the night shadows. He'd left Deputy Roscoe slumped over his desk, felled by a coffee mug applied to the back of his head. The heedless young fool hadn't heard the door to the cell room open behind him or Gabe's soft footfalls across the plank floor. No doubt his attention had been diverted by Widow Crabtree's excellent supper on the desk in front of him. Perhaps that worthy woman would patch up his head and give the boy a much-needed lecture on paying attention to one's work.

Virginia City's saloons and gambling houses were in full swing, splashes of light and tinny piano music spilling from their windows and doors. Shops and places of business were locked and dark. A couple of men walked purposefully along the boardwalk on the other side of the street toward the saloons. Other than those two, no one was on the street. Marshal Kale was probably up to his nose in whiskey by now, as he was on most nights. There was no sign of Candliss or his men, but they would be somewhere close. Ace hadn't provided him with the key to his jail cell to let him leave in one piece.

Gabe pulled his hat low over his face and walked toward the livery as though he had every right to be out on the street. This was going too smoothly. Somewhere Ace Candliss and his men were waiting—they had to be. Candliss had given him an engraved invitation to escape, and with his taunts about the twins he had made sure Gabe would accept the invitation. He wanted the pleasure of shooting him down rather than waiting on the decision of a judge. That was fine with Gabe; he was glad to let him try.

Not that Gabe believed for a moment that Candliss hadn't meant every word of his threat to the girls. He had to escape the trap that waited somewhere ahead, if only to make sure Katy and Ellen were safe.

The livery was dark, and Gabe didn't dare light a lantern. He found Longshot near the back. In less than a minute Gabe was mounted. A rifle from the marshal's gun cabinet nestled in the saddle boot and a brace of holstered pistols was belted around his hips.

When Gabe emerged onto the street, the night was still calm. The two men who had been on the street had found a saloon. The pianos tinkled away. Snow was beginning to fall in earnest. A furtive movement in the alley next to the livery caught Gabe's attention. There they were, no doubt planning to stage a grand chase through the street to establish a justification for shooting him down. He could feel Candliss's presence in the darkness. Time for an old-time Irish fox hunt, with himself as the fox.

"Tallyho!" Gabe muttered, and spurred Longshot. The mare sprang forward into an instant gallop. No need for stealth now. He heard a victorious whoop as hoofbeats drummed behind him, trampling the night's peace. A bullet plowed the dirt beside him. A hundred feet ahead, where the main street turned to go into the hills, the road was barricaded by three men with rifles in their hands. The trap was sprung. Between the hammer and the anvil, Gabe was bound to get pounded.

A fierce exultation flooded through Gabe's veins. If he was in Ace Candliss's gun sights, Candliss could just as easily be in his. With a savage yell, he wheeled the mare around and charged toward his pursuers, firing a spray of bullets before him, every one of them aimed toward Ace Candliss. He saw the men's mouths drop open with astonishment. They milled in confusion, horses dancing and backing into each other, anxious to flee from the barrage. Then Candliss shouted and brought his rifle to bear. The others raised their weapons. Gabe was almost on them when flame spouted from their guns, each flash of hellish orange sending a bullet into the night. He heard nothing but the pounding of blood through his body and the thunder of Longshot's hooves, felt nothing other than the need to see Candliss fall.

Both pistols empty, Gabe crashed through the barrier of men and horses. Candliss was still aboard his horse, more's the pity, but Gabe had no time to get his rifle from the boot. Longshot saw the empty street ahead of her and sprang for freedom. Shots thundered behind him, and pain erupted in his left thigh. For a moment Gabe thought he would lose his seat in the saddle, but he managed to hold on in spite of the nauseating shock of impact. More men appeared suddenly ahead of him.

He hauled Longshot to the right and plunged into the dark alley between two buildings. At the rear of the buildings, a ravine paved with rocks and ice forced him to slow the mare to a trot. In the shouts of confusion behind him, Candliss's voice roared out.

"Find him, dammit!"

They found his escape route, but by then Gabe was well on his way into the night-cloaked hills. Longshot stretched her legs in a mile-eating gallop. The saddle beneath him slick with his blood, Gabe held on and let Longshot take him where she would. Slowly the sounds of pursuit grew more distant.

"I ain't gonna stay with the Talbots!" Katy took her father's rifle down from its pegs above the fireplace and wiped the barrel with a rag. "Sylvester Talbot is a dandified turd."

Olivia looked up from where she was packing the tinware and dishes into boxes. "Katy, that's rude—and wrong. Mr. Talbot is a good man and a fine gentleman. Your sulking and cursing isn't going to help your father."

"Neither is piddling around up here at the cabin. We should be in Virginia City, where I could do something."

"*You* are not going to do anything, young lady. Your father doesn't want us there—any of us."

"Well," Ellen said. "We *have* to do something!"

"I hired him the best lawyer I could find."

Katy snorted. "Lawyer!"

"I don't understand how a jury could even think of convicting him for defending his own home and family."

"They'll do whatever Ace Candliss wants them to do," Katy scoffed. "Everybody else does."

Hunter whined and looked from Katy to Ellen to Olivia, no doubt trying to make some sort of wolfish sense out of the confusion of the last days. Olivia absently scratched his head. She felt a hundred years old. She almost wished she could say yes to Katy, who had taken to wearing trousers and a flannel shirt once again. Like the twins, Olivia longed to purge some of her frustration in planning an escape, or a heroic rescue— to do anything that would keep her from feeling so helpless.

Keeping Gabriel's daughters safe was more important than her frustration, however. This was what he had asked of her, and this was what she would do, even if the girls themselves might not understand. Some things had to be faced alone, without the encumbrance of having those you loved watch.

Katy stomped around the cabin, snatching up items that still had to be packed and throwing Olivia sour looks.

"We've been over this time and time again, girls, all the way back to Elkhorn and then all the way up here to pack your things."

Ellen sniffed. Katy glared. Hunter's ears flattened in uncertainty.

"Don't you realize your being in Virginia City to witness what happens would only make things harder on your father? And God forbid you should do something crazy like trying to break him out of jail. He'd be so busy trying to save you that he wouldn't have time to think about saving himself."

Both girls scowled at the floor.

"I know this is difficult to understand, but sometimes the most loving thing you can do for someone is to stay away when he wants you gone. The most loving thing, and the hardest thing."

Tears dribbled down Ellen's cheeks. Katy's eyes burned a hole in the floor.

"Did Mr. Berman say anything about Pa's chances?"

"The letter I got in Elkhorn simply said that the judge would be in town starting the twentieth of February."

Still a week away—time enough for Olivia to get the twins temporarily situated and get to Virginia City for the trial, for despite her lecture to the girls, she couldn't stay away. Gabriel needn't see her, but she needed to see what happened.

"Take this box out to the wagon, will you, Ellen? Katy, check the loft to make sure you haven't left anything behind that you want to take. Rufus and Ted will be moving in here, and they'll likely use anything you leave."

"They can have it!" The fact that the two strangers would be living in her home didn't seem to bother Katy. Her grief was all for her father.

"Are you sure you can handle those mules pulling this heavy load down the trail? You said yourself the track's worse than you've ever seen it."

"This stuff ain't that heavy, and I've done it plenty of times before. I'm gonna bring in the harnesses so I can check 'em over tonight. Don't want a strap giving way."

Ellen gave Olivia a sad look as Katy went out the door. "You're right,

Olivia. Pa wouldn't want us there. Katy would get us all in trouble, and then Pa would have to try to get us out."

Katy's frantic shout interrupted Olivia's reply.

Gabe had been riding for an eternity, it seemed. Riding where, he wasn't quite sure. Riding and hurting, struggling to stay in the saddle. Passing out, sometimes. Always hurting. Always moving.

Now Longshot had stopped, and he couldn't get her to budge from the place she'd chosen. He was too tired to try again. Voices echoed in his head—or were they real? He didn't know.

"Pa! What happened? Pa? He's hurt! There's blood everywhere!" That was Katy, and the high-pitched fear in her voice almost jarred him enough to speak.

Ellen's voice: "He's tied himself to the saddle. Pa? Pa?"

"Gabriel! My God! Look at you!" That was the voice he had imagined all through the long ride. "Girls, help me cut him down!"

The ropes that cut into him eased. They were his strength, the only thing that had kept him on his horse. He felt himself sliding from the saddle. Darkness claimed him before he hit the ground.

Olivia watched him wake, his eyes cloudy with confusion, his face so pale that the sheets on the bed looked more healthy than he did.

"Gabriel? Can you hear me?"

His lips moved. At first no sound escaped. Then he whispered. "Olivia?"

"Well, I see you have your senses about you again."

"Where am I?"

"In your own bed at the cabin."

"What the hell am I doing here?"

"You rode in about two hours ago."

He tried to rise but fell back to the mattress. "Damn horse! I must have passed out before I got to Elkhorn. She took me right on through." He frowned at her, his eyes still muddy. "The cabin? What are you doing at the cabin? I told you to get away."

"We came to pack some of the girls' things. We were perfectly safe. The men I hired to work the mine were here, but I sent them on errands to Elkhorn before they could discover you'd come back."

"We have to get away from here!"

"You're not going anywhere, Gabriel. You've lost so much blood, I'm surprised you haven't collapsed like a deflated balloon."

"Candliss could be right on my tail. He can't find the girls. Didn't mean to come here. Only meant to go to Elkhorn to warn . . ."

Olivia pushed him back down as he attempted to rise again. "Lie still or I'll tie you to the bed." She grinned sadistically. "I've seen it done before."

He caught her wrist as she held him down.

"Relax, Gabriel. Mr. Candliss won't be coming up that trail tonight. With all the ice and snow on the track, Katy practically had to tie me to my horse to get me over it, even in the daylight. If your Mr. Candliss followed you to Elkhorn, he won't be able to start for the cabin until morning—not if he doesn't want to slide down a mountainside between here and there. That should give us time to think of something." She gently touched his freshly bandaged leg. "Was this his parting gift?"

Gabe closed his eyes wearily. "Yeah. You might say that. Candliss said he was coming after the girls, then he set me up for an escape. Mostly he aimed to gun me down, but he wants the girls, too. He hates me that much."

Olivia couldn't imagine what kind of monster would do harm to children just because he hated the father. "Are you sure he'll come here?"

"This is the first place he'll come."

She took his hand and entwined their fingers, white and slender interlaced with brown and blunt. "Longshot brought you back to me. What would I have done, Gabriel, not knowing if you were alive or where you were? What would Katy and Ellen have done? Speaking of your daughters . . ."

Two identical frowns stared down at them from the loft.

"You can come down and say hello to your father now, girls. He's awake."

They tumbled down the ladder, then abruptly slowed and practically tiptoed to the bed. "Are you all right, Pa?" Ellen asked in a hushed tone.

"You sound like you're at my funeral, lass. Don't give up on me yet."

"Takes more than a bullet in the leg to stop our pa!" Katy declared.

"I see you've taken to wearing trousers again."

"It's needful. This ain't no time for bein' a woman."

Gabe sighed. "You may be right. Do you think you can get Olivia and Ellen down the trail tonight?"

"If I had to, maybe."

"Gabriel!"

He raised a hand to shush Olivia. "Candliss will be here tomorrow, Katy. I'm pretty sure of it. He can't find you and Ellen here, or Olivia either. You'd be safe at Talbot's place."

Katy looked thoughtful.

"Gabriel, you are the stubbornest man alive. You are in no shape to go anywhere, and we're not leaving you. Mr. Candliss wouldn't dare hurt these girls with me as a witness."

"You don't know Candliss, Olivia. He's gotten the idea that he's such a big man in the state that he can do whatever he wants."

"I know what we can do," Katy said with a smile.

Gabriel objected loudly to Katy's plan, but flat on his back and practically helpless, he was in no position to enforce his objections. With a great amount of energy, the twins fashioned a travois while Olivia gathered blankets, matches, lanterns, water, and food. Then they piled Gabriel and the supplies on the travois and all three dragged it into the mine.

The entrance to the new tunnel Gabe had opened behind the cave-in was almost impossible to see unless one knew where to look, and several boulders rolled into place by Katy and Ellen made it even harder to find. They made Gabriel as comfortable as possible in the little underground room, then Katy and Ellen scampered away like conspiring squirrels to erase the travois tracks from the cabin to the mine.

"If I ever get out of this," Gabriel told Olivia from his bed of blankets, "I'm going to turn you over my knee and make you sorry you're such a stubborn, disobedient female."

She touched his cheek and smiled. "You must be rubbing off on me. I knew no good would come of sleeping with an Irishman."

"You're playing with fire, Olivia."

"Ever since I met you and those daughters of yours, it seems."

"Be serious."

"I am being serious." She leaned down and touched her lips to his. His arm came up to trap her, and he hungrily claimed her mouth in much more of a kiss than she had intended.

"I thought I'd never taste you again, Doc."

She kissed him once more, savoring the hardness of his lips against hers, the roughness of his several days' growth of beard against her cheeks. "Promise me you'll stay in here—for all our sakes."

The eyes that locked on to hers were no longer muddy with confusion; they were vivid with anxiety. "The girls . . ."

"We'll be prepared, I promise. Those girls are something to contend with, as you ought to know. Mr. Candliss won't get close to them. I'll shoot him myself if I have to."

He touched her lips with one finger. "You should have been Irish."

More than anything in the world she wanted to stay with him. In the lantern light his face was so pale against the inky black of his hair, the lines of pain so deeply etched in his expression. She forced herself to smile. "I'll be back tomorrow with fresh water and more food."

"What happened to your fear of closed places?"

Olivia smiled. "I'm cured, I guess."

She'd found more important things to be afraid of.

Morning came, bringing with it flurries of snow. Katy checked and rechecked the shotgun, rifle, and two pistols she had cleaned and loaded the night before. Ellen sat silently in front of the fire, every now and again getting up to look out the window down the valley, and Olivia paced and worried, hoping against all reason that Candliss would not come to the cabin—and that Crooked Stick had seen the lantern Katy had hung in the pine the night before and would arrive in time to spirit Gabriel away.

Candliss did come, however. In the gray late afternoon, four men rode into the clearing. Forewarned by Ellen, who had been watching down the valley, Olivia met them with the shotgun in her hands. In the cabin, Katy stood at the window with her rifle trained on the quartet.

The horseman in the lead was tall and sandy-haired. With a square, freckled face and wide mouth, he didn't look like a villain, but a flicker of something dark in his eyes as he glanced around the clearing made a chill ripple down Olivia's spine. Finally his gaze settled on Olivia and the shotgun in her hands.

He touched the brim of his hat. "Ma'am. I take it you are Miss Olivia Baron."

"I am."

"No need to be alarmed. We mean no harm."

She recognized one of the men behind Candliss as the bounty hunter who'd taken Gabriel before. He grinned at her and tipped his hat in mock courtesy.

"My name's Ace Candliss, from Virginia City. We're looking for Will O'Connell—also known as Gabe Danaher."

"If you're from Virginia City, then you should know that Mr. O'Connell is in jail there. The gentleman in the black hat was the one who escorted him there."

"Well, Miss Baron. That's just the problem. O'Connell made a jail-break."

"He didn't come here."

Candliss glanced around the place, his eyes sweeping over the cabin, corral, and sheds. "I find that hard to believe."

"What you believe is irrelevant, Mr. Candliss. He's not here."

"Now, I hate to imply that a lady's a liar, but I think we'll just have a look around for ourselves."

"Look anywhere you want."

Olivia followed them into the cabin, where Katy glared at them from behind her rifle. Hunter crouched in his box. A low growl rumbled in his throat.

"Let them pass, Katy. And take hold of Hunter."

Candliss eyed the twins in a way that convinced Olivia that he looked like a villain after all. One of the men shouldered Ellen aside to get to the loft ladder.

"Outta my way, girlie."

Katy and Olivia raised their weapons at the same time. "I said you could look around," Olivia said. "I didn't say you could bulldoze your way through the cabin like Sherman marching through Georgia. If you don't have the decency to show civilized manners, you can go."

Candliss grinned. "Mind your manners, boys. Miss Baron is apparently a lady of sensitivity, and we wouldn't want to upset her."

They searched the cabin, the outhouse, the sheds, and even the henhouse.

"Mr. Candliss," one of the men reported, "there's a horse in the shed that looks like the one O'Connell was riding."

Candliss raised a brow in Olivia's direction. Her heart beat crazily in her chest—they'd completely forgotten about the damned horse! "If it's the bay mare you mean, that's my horse."

Candliss looked at her thoughtfully, his eyes unreadable. "Does it look like it's been ridden hard?" he asked his man.

"Nah. Not really."

"You sure it's his horse?"

"It's a bay mare, about the same size. Looks like it, but I can't say for sure."

"Keep looking."

When Candliss and his men entered the mine, Olivia tried her best to look unconcerned. She shooed the girls back to the cabin so their transparent faces wouldn't give their father away. Then she prayed.

The searchers came out dusty and empty-handed. Candliss met Olivia at the door of the cabin. "I know he's here."

"Indeed?" Olivia asked smoothly.

"That's his horse in the shed. I'd bet on it. He's here, unless he bled to death and you buried him already."

"You shot my pa?" Katy demanded, looking innocently surprised.

"He won't come back here," Olivia said. "He knows this is the first place you'll look."

"Yes'm. That might be true. But there's something here he's mighty concerned about." He nodded toward the cabin. "I think those little girls had better come with me."

Olivia felt ice water flood her veins. Suddenly she knew that she was capable of killing a man.

"Those girls haven't broken the law, Mr. Candliss. You have no right to take them anywhere."

"Well, now, that's not strictly true. They helped their daddy escape a hanging a couple of years ago."

"The way I heard, it was a lynching, not a legal hanging. Do you have a badge?"

"No, ma'am."

"Do any of the men with you have badges, Mr. Candliss? It seems to me that you're a lot more interested in Mr. O'Connell than the law is."

"The law will be happy enough when I bring him back, and they won't quibble about using a couple of no-account half-breed brats for bait."

"Then you send an officer of the law for them, Mr. Candliss. I won't give them over to you."

"I wasn't asking, Miss Baron. I was telling. Be careful or I might decide that you need to come along as well."

Olivia blocked his way into the cabin, shoving the shotgun against his chest. He started to slap it away, but froze when she pulled back the hammer. "Back off, Mr. Candliss. Right now it wouldn't bother me a bit to blow a hole through you."

The grins on the three men behind him faded into confusion. She guessed they weren't used to thinking of a woman as anything other than something to be pushed around.

"Katy. Bring that rifle out here."

Katy appeared in an instant and took up a position where she had a clear shot at the three men behind Candliss.

"Now." Olivia struggled to sound calm in spite of the blood rushing through her veins. "Since you gentlemen have forgotten your manners, you can drop your guns before you leave here."

"Like hell!" one of the men muttered.

Katy's mouth lifted in a smile that shouldn't have been on a young girl's face. The three men hastily unbuckled their holsters.

"You also, Mr. Candliss." Olivia prodded him with the shotgun.

Lips tight with frustration, he took his pistol from its holster and dropped it. "You're obstructing justice, Miss Baron."

"I don't see any justice here. I fully intend to write Mr. O'Connell's lawyer and see that he brings your little private war on children to the attention of the authorities. Even Montana couldn't be so uncivilized as to condone such a thing."

They mounted up, and Candliss shot her a look that let Olivia know he had just added one more target to his private war. "You're becoming a nuisance, Miss Baron. If you know what's good for you, you'll keep your nose out of this business."

"Good-bye, Mr. Candliss." She smiled sweetly. "If I see Gabriel, I'll be sure to tell him you're looking for him."

Candliss spat, leaving an unpleasant pockmark in the clean snow. Then they were gone.

Or so Olivia thought. Katy assured her that the men were not gone, however, when she came back from following their tracks for a ways down the trail. They had forked off the trail and scattered toward the ridges that surrounded the valley. Like coyotes poised at a mouse hole, Candliss and his men waited for Gabe to appear so they could snap him up. They played a waiting game that they, like the coyotes, were likely to win.

"He didn't believe me about the horse," Olivia concluded with a sigh.

"I shoulda thought to stake her out in the woods somewhere."

"It's not your fault, Katy. They probably would have found her anyway." She sighed. "I wish I'd thought to get the rifles from their saddles as well as their pistols. I guess I'm just not cut out to be a gunslinger in the Danaher—pardon me—O'Connell gang."

An arm around each disheartened girl, Olivia led them back into the cabin.

Next morning, Ellen served biscuits and gravy without bacon for breakfast. "We can't stay here very long," she told Olivia. "There's no food to speak of."

"I'll hunt," Katy said.

"You will not!" Olivia ordered. "Candliss would love to catch you alone out there."

"What're we gonna eat?" Katy demanded. "Wood chips?"

"If we must have food, we'll all go together."

"Oh, that'll be somethin'!" Katy declared. "You two are about as quiet in the woods as a moose crashin' through a dry thicket."

They managed to bag three squirrels and two rabbits without going far from the cabin, in spite of Olivia's and Ellen's ineptness at silence and Hunter's jumping on anything that moved. Candliss and his men didn't show themselves, and Olivia dared to hope that Katy was wrong about them staying to watch. Her hopes were dashed when they returned to the cabin to find their belongings ransacked.

Olivia sighed at the mess. "No doubt they were looking for a clue to where Gabriel is. Inconsiderate ruffians! They found their pistols and took them, I see."

"Maybe Rufus and Ted will come back and help us," Ellen said hopefully.

Katy snorted. "They'd shoot their own toes off. Rufus cain't lift a shovel but what he hits his ownself in the head." She threw her catch onto the table. "I'm going after Crooked Stick. He's the only one who can help Pa. I'll slip out tonight."

"No you won't," Olivia said sternly. "Those men out there are more than a match for you, Katy. You'll help your father the most by staying safe."

"They won't get me. I'm quick as a weasel and slippery as a snake, and I'll twist Ace Candliss's tail around his backbone till he don't know whether he's comin' or goin'."

"No, Katy! That's final!"

Olivia was at wit's end scraping for ideas to get them all out of this mess. She refused to let Katy risk herself to fetch help, and aid was not likely to stumble by on its own. Her only hope was that Candliss would grow tired of the game and look elsewhere for his prey.

A false peace settled over the cabin below Thunder Ridge as one day followed another in seeming tranquility. There was no further sign of Candliss or his men, but Katy, who apparently had the eyes of an eagle, reported seeing flashes of sunlight glinting off a rifle barrel.

Night was the only time that they could visit Gabriel—when their watchers couldn't see them slip into the tunnel. The girls bubbled over with the tale of how Olivia had faced down Candliss, and Katy begged her father for permission to find Crooked Stick.

"No," he told her in a tone that permitted no argument. "We don't even know where he is."

"I could find him. He might still be at Buffalo Hump's camp."

"That could be anywhere on the reservation."

"I could find it."

"You'll stay here and do what Olivia tells you to do."

"Oh, Pa!"

Olivia always stayed in the tunnel long after the twins left. In those hours she didn't want to think about what had been or what was to come. She couldn't help but believe these hours would be the last they would spend together.

They spent their time planning for a future they both knew wouldn't happen, and by mutual consent neither mentioned how far their plans were from reality. Gabe would use the money from the mine to buy land and stock a ranch in one of the grassy valleys of western Montana. Olivia would start a medical practice in Bozeman or Great Falls or whatever town was closest to the ranch. They would be a family, the four of them, and maybe add two or three down the road.

All of it was fantasy. They both knew it, but it brought comfort just the same.

Every day in the tunnel, however, made Gabriel a bit more restless. Olivia could see the itch to fight grow along with his returning strength. It was against his nature to hide like a rabbit crouched in its burrow

"You heal faster than anyone I've ever treated," she told him on the sixth night. "The swelling in your leg is down, your color is healthy, there's no fever." She laid a hand on the bare, iron-thewed thigh above where she had just changed his dressing. "No heat here." She felt his brow. "None here."

He took her hand and guided it to a very different spot on his anatomy. "How about here?"

"Gabriel! Behave yourself."

"Why? I do have a fever, Doc. It's been growing ever since the last time I made love to you."

He kept her hand where it was, and she didn't pull away. Her blood began to heat with the same fever he complained of.

He grinned, his eyes reflecting the lantern light in green fire. "Do you think it's contagious, Doc?"

"You're injured . . ."

"Like you said, I heal fast." He pulled her down beside him.

"Gabriel, you're going to hurt yourself."

"I hurt now, but it's got nothing to do with that bullet hole. You just keep that hand where it is, sweet lass."

He rucked up her skirts and worked his hand up her leg until he was exploring the hot, ready moistness between her thighs. He chuckled in satisfaction. "Just as I thought. Contagious." His finger slipped through the open seam of her pantalets and thrust inside her, moving in a gentle rhythm that made her gasp with pleasure. He buried his face in her hair, his breath warm in her ear. "Sweet lass. My sweet, sweet lass."

Chapter 20

*O*livia didn't know quite when she abandoned her physician's caution and surrendered to her woman's desire. If Gabriel was strong enough to seduce her, then she would permit herself the luxury of being seduced. Need pounded through her like thunder. It seemed like forever that she had lived with the grief of losing him, of steeling herself to be strong in the face of his loss. They deserved this moment of passion. God only knew if they would get another.

She helped him remove her clothes. There in the dim, flickering light of the lantern, his warm hands worshiped her body as though he'd never touched her before, as though their loving were the first time instead of the last. They wandered in a leisurely but thorough exploration of her breasts, fanned out over her ribs and belly, curled in adoration around her buttocks, glided down her legs and in a slow, tantalizing path up the insides of her thighs. She gasped in pleasure as his fingers forged a path through the silky curls that protected her sex. He urged her legs apart, his fingers teasing, taunting, brushing that most sensitive flesh and delving inside only deep enough to drive her to frenzy.

"You're the devil himself." Olivia moaned her frustration as he dangled her over the cutting edge of passion.

"Paradise is that much sweeter when the journey there is slow."

In the darkness, she could feel his grin more than see it. His thumb found the center of her physical universe and circled there in gentle, loving caress until she could scarcely breathe. Her body, taut as a bow-string, arched toward him in silent supplication. With a sudden thrust of his fingers he sent her soaring like a bird released from a cage.

She half-sobbed his name before he possessed her mouth and de-voured her like a man starved. Pinned savagely to the floor by his strength, she didn't feel the hard rock grinding into her back through the blanket, only the warmth of his body as it lay along hers, touching every inch of her, only the joy of his possession, the fire of his passion, the warmth of his soul.

"I love you," he murmured into her mouth.

Her hands caressed the lean planes of his face. "I love you, too, Ga-briel. You know I do."

"Marry me."

"Yes."

"You'll be the best doctor the West has ever seen, and I'll get rich selling cattle and horses to the Army."

"Yes."

He kissed her again. His legs slipped between hers, the iron muscles of his thighs pressing against her and eliciting a little squeak of pleasure. She could feel him grimace at the effort to prop himself above her, though.

"You're hurting yourself!"

He fell back, carrying her with him. "Like I said, there's other places I hurt more. We'll just have to expand your education about relieving this particular pain."

Flat on his back on the blanket, he drew her across him until she lay on his chest, her legs straddling his hips.

"I'm crushing you."

"You're light as a flower petal." He ran his hands down her back and over her buttocks, brushing the soft, sensitive folds of flesh between. "I could be at death's door and I'd still get hot for you, sweet lass."

Hands on either side of her hips, he positioned her over him and thrust. Her breath whooshed out in a sigh of pleasure at the sudden and complete impalement. She moved, fitting herself to him more completely as he arched beneath her. In four powerful thrusts he brought them to the peak of passion and catapulted them to release. His arms gathered her in as she collapsed upon his chest in limp satisfaction.

Inhaling the intoxicating scent of musky satisfaction, secure in Ga-briel's strong arms, Olivia surrendered to sleep before reality could once again overtake her.

A sense of reality had never left Gabe, however. Even in the heat of passion, he had known full well that all their talk of marriage and ranches was a fantasy. His future stretched before him as a set of grim choices. He could leave the mine and face Candliss's guns—he had no doubt his pursuers would be on him like flies on a dead cow before he'd gotten a mile from the cabin. Or he could try to sneak out by the dark of night and worry about what Candliss would do to the twins and Olivia if they discovered he'd slipped away. Either choice had him damned.

Gabe stayed awake as Olivia slept. He refused to waste the little time he had left to hold her, to smell her warm woman's scent, to feel her silky flesh beneath his hands. That she loved him was a miracle. She'd drained the bitterness from him as she might lance a boil on one of her patients. He'd given her only trouble, yet she gave him love in return. Softhearted Olivia. She couldn't help but love an injured or needy creature that needed her help—lame Murdoch, a broken-legged marmot, bloodied little Hunter, and William Gabriel Danaher O'Connell.

Olivia sighed and stirred. Her fingers moved against his chest, making him desperately long for some kind of magic spell to make the night last forever. He wanted to make love to her again, but the night was slipping away from them. He satisfied himself with a kiss instead.

Her mouth met his eagerly, and her arms wrapped around him. "Did I fall asleep?"

"Like a baby."

"I wish I could stay the night," she murmured into his chest.

"I think you almost have."

"Oh no!" She grabbed at her scattered clothes. "I don't want them to see me leave the mine. They'd guess you were in here."

Gabe didn't bother to tell her that they probably had a pretty good idea he was in here anyway, or they wouldn't have stuck around this long.

"I'll see you tonight." In the lantern's dim glow, Olivia looked forlorn.

He brushed her cheek with his finger. "Cheer up, my lass. This will be over soon."

"Do you think so?"

"Yes."

She didn't believe him, Gabe saw, but she smiled anyway. "I'll be back tonight," she said, and kissed him quickly, pulling away before either one of them could succumb to temptation.

He watched the glow of her lantern disappear down the dark tunnel, then lit his own and began to stretch the stiff muscles in his leg. Pacing the short length of the little spur tunnel where he hid still made him tired. It would be days before his full strength returned, but he didn't have the patience to wait for days, hiding like a rat in a hole as the ratters yipped around the entrance to his lair. It was high time he saw the sunlight again and ended this thing with Ace Candliss.

Sunlight was not what Gabe saw that morning when he limped from the tunnel; the sky was appropriately ominous for what he figured might well be the last day of his life. The fresh dressing that Olivia had applied to his wound the night before was spotted with blood, but that didn't concern him. It was a mere drop in the bucket of blood that no doubt would be spilled today. He only hoped that some of that blood would belong to Candliss.

The morning was still peaceful when he came in sight of the cabin. Ellen chopped wood, her breath frosting in the cold air as she swung the ax. Her eyes grew big when she saw him.

"Ellen, saddle Longshot. Quickly, my girl."

"Pa! What are you doing?"

"Leaving. Now, go! I don't have much time."

As she ran to do his bidding, Olivia came around the corner of the cabin.

"What do you think you're doing?" she demanded in the tone she no doubt used with the unruliest of her patients.

Gabe had to smile. Last night she'd been soft as warm honey; this morning she was tempered steel. "Today's as good a day as any to fight this out. I'd like to pick my own place, though, and that isn't here."

"Gabriel Danaher O'Connell! You're in no shape for this."

"Sure I am. Where's Katy?"

Olivia's disgusted sigh froze to a cloud in the cold air. "Last night Katy took Murdoch and rode to Elkhorn for the marshal. I'd mentioned to her earlier that if you could ever have a fair trial, you'd probably go free, so she took it upon herself to fetch the law. I guess she'd waited just about as long as her patience could bear."

"Shit!"

Ellen trotted up with Longshot in tow. He took the reins from her and painfully swung aboard. "Let's just hope Candliss comes after me instead of after her—or better still, he didn't see her leave."

"He didn't, Pa," Ellen said hopefully. "You know how sneaky Katy can be."

"Yeah. I do at that. This is the first time I've been grateful for it."

"Gabriel, don't. Please don't. Go back into the mine. Maybe they didn't see you come out."

He merely shook his head.

"You're the stubbornest, orneriest, stupidest man alive."

"Comes from being Irish." He drank in the sight of her standing there glaring at him. Even mad she was still beautiful. How had he ever believed her plain? Ellen regarded him with solemn eyes. He branded both their faces on his memory, then begged one more favor of Saint Patrick —the last ever, he promised. If that good saint would keep Katy, Ellen, and Olivia safe, Gabe swore to become saintly himself for the rest of his life, right after he killed Ace Candliss. The promise didn't cost much, since the rest of his life could most likely be measured in hours, but he hoped good old Patrick would overlook that detail.

"You two stay in the cabin. Keep a gun nearby—both of you—just in case I don't get Candliss and he decides to come back here and get nasty. Ellen, from now on, I expect you and Katy to take care of Olivia. You hear?"

"We will, Pa." Ellen's voice trembled.

He heard Olivia curse as he wheeled Longshot and pointed the mare down the trail. "Gabriel, damn you, if you let yourself get killed, I'll—"

Her threat was drowned by the sharp whine of a bullet that plowed the ground a foot in front of Gabe's horse. The good-byes had lasted a moment too long.

"Get inside! Now!" he ordered Olivia and Ellen.

Another bullet dug into the tall pine that was their message pole to Crooked Stick. Gabe swung off Longshot and gave the mare a slap to send her in the direction of the horse shed. He was grateful to see Olivia and Ellen scramble through the large back window of the cabin rather than run around front to the door. They appeared a moment later brandishing weapons, a shotgun for Olivia and a pistol for Ellen—and expressions fierce enough to be lethal in themselves.

Gabe ran for the spruce thicket at the edge of the clearing just as a volley of shots kicked up dust in a killing arc through the spot he'd just stood. He wanted Candliss shooting anywhere but toward the cabin. Not shooting at all would be even better.

"Candliss, you yellow sonofabitch. Come down here and fight me without hiding behind the rocks."

Another volley answered his challenge.

"How many of there are you out there? Three? Four? You need that much help to bring in one shot-up Irishman, Candliss? Come down and fight me hand to hand. Just you and me, like it should be. I kill you or you kill me, without messing things up with outsiders."

For a moment silence stretched over the ridge and valley.

"You afraid to get a little blood on your hands, Candliss? I'd have thought you'd like to feel my blood on your hands. It's so much more personal than a bullet."

The trees themselves seemed to hold their breath. Then came the answer Gabriel had prayed for. Saint Patrick, it seemed, was on the job.

"I'm not afraid to fight you, O'Connell. We're coming down. Don't try anything funny."

The curtain of silence fell once again, as if a scene in a play had ended and the next had not yet begun. Olivia's heart hammered in her chest until she thought some vein or artery must burst with the strain. It had been hammering since she had gotten back to the cabin before dawn and discovered that Katy had left during the night to fetch the law from Elkhorn.

"I tried to stop her!" Ellen had cried. "But she wouldn't listen. She said that you told her Pa had a better chance with the law than with Ace Candliss."

Olivia had said that. She'd also told Katy that she was not to go wandering off under any circumstances for fear that Candliss or his men would nab her.

"She is *so* stubborn!" Ellen had rolled her eyes dramatically. "But if anyone can sneak by Candliss, she can. She's like a snake in tall weeds."

There had been nothing Olivia could do other than wait and pray, and then Gabriel had limped up to the cabin with his wild idea that the time for a showdown had come. Men! Stubborn, impatient, listening to their animal instincts rather than their heads!

She could see him crouched in the thicket, rifle held ready, scanning the valley walls and concealing trees. If he expected Ace Candliss to fight him fairly, then he certainly had no business calling *her* naive.

"Ellen, I want you to slip out the front and hide in the woods until this is over."

"But, Olivia—!"

"No argument. Go. Take Hunter with you, and one of those pistols. Don't come back until your father or I call out that it's safe."

"But—"

"Go."

She went. When Ellen was safely away, Olivia clutched the shotgun to her like a baby and swung her legs over the low, wide sill of the back window.

Gabriel wasn't pleased. "Get back in the cabin, Olivia."

"No. Candliss has three men with him. You need someone on your side."

"You're worth more to me in the cabin, where I don't have to worry about you."

She shook her head.

Before Gabriel could protest again, the crash of brush signaled Candliss's arrival. Four horses broke through the spruce trees at the edge of the clearing. In the lead was Candliss, and in his hands was a rifle trained on Gabriel. Ranged behind him, his men regarded Gabe contemptuously. Olivia didn't like their looks now any more than she had when they were at the cabin before.

"Get in the cabin, Olivia."

"I will not." Olivia hefted the shotgun to a more comfortable position. "You can trust in your man-to-man fight if you want, but I'm going to keep an eye on Mr. Candliss's helpers."

"Get in the cabin."

"No." She ignored the thunderous look he sent her way. "I have a right to be a fool every bit as much as you do."

"No funny business, O'Connell." Candliss rode into the clearing, the muzzle of his rifle remaining steadily pointed at Gabriel. "Throw down your rifle. The pistols too."

"We'll throw down our weapons together, Candliss. You, your men, and me. At the same time. That's only fair."

"What about her?"

"Her too." Gabriel shot a stern look her way. "But it's me who's going to kill you, Candliss. You don't need to worry about her."

"Somehow I don't see it that way." He leveled a look toward Olivia. "Put the shotgun down, Miss Baron, or I'll blow a hole through O'Connell right where he stands. And if he gets me first, my friends here will shoot him. What do you say?"

"Do as he says, Olivia." Gabriel's tone was forged in iron.

Put that way, Olivia considered it was wise to obey. She carefully laid down the shotgun.

"Now get away from it," Candliss ordered.

She backed toward the cabin window.

Candliss grinned. "At least you got yourself a white woman this time, O'Connell."

Gabriel's eyes narrowed. Olivia realized at that moment that both men would gladly give up their lives just to feel the blood of the other wash over their hands. The feral light in both their eyes said that guns and bullets just weren't personal enough.

Candliss dismounted and threw his rifle beside the shotgun. "Get rid of your iron, boys, or the little lady will cry foul."

44

The men threw pistols and two rifles near the other weapons, tipping their hats mockingly in Olivia's direction as they did so. Gabriel's pistols and rifle completed the pile of discarded weapons well out of anyone's reach.

"Now we see what you're made of, O'Connell."

As Olivia and the Candliss men looked on, Gabriel and Ace circled each other, both grinning at the prospect of killing the other. Olivia hugged herself against the chill of their expressions.

Candliss was the first to lunge. Cripple that he was, his attack was awkward, but Gabriel with his wounded leg was in no better fighting shape. They grappled, both striving for a hold on the other's throat. Candliss succeeded. Olivia gasped as Gabriel's face turned red, but he wedged his hands beneath Candliss's and broke the hold. They both stumbled back. Gabriel panted: "You've been spending too much time behind a desk, Candliss."

"I'm still fast enough and strong enough to lay you in a grave, you bastard. This shouldn't take long."

Candliss swung with a vicious right. Gabriel ducked and brought an iron fist up to plow into Candliss's gut. His other fist connected with Ace's chin. Candliss flew backward and sprawled on the ground; Gabriel launched himself on top of him. For a moment the two pummeled each other, rolling on the ground like a pair of brawling boys and grunting in what sounded like obscene enjoyment. Somehow they rolled onto their feet, still pummeling. Both faces were streaked with blood and dirt.

Time seemed suspended, and the whole universe seemed focused on the pair who punched, stumbled, lurched, kicked, and buffeted their way around the clearing. Olivia could hear the labored whistling of their breathing. The bandage around Gabriel's leg was dark with blood. A cut over his brow spilled crimson down the side of his face and neck. Candliss looked no better.

Ace swung, seeming to put all his might behind the blow. Gabriel ducked and gave Candliss a shove that drove him headfirst into a tree at the edge of the clearing. He hit the tree with a thunk that sounded like Katy's ax cutting into a block of firewood. His legs folded under him, and he slowly slid down the trunk. Before he could regain his senses, Gabriel was straddling him, hands around his neck and squeezing. Candliss's face grew red. Then purple.

Alarmed by the savagery of what she witnessed, Olivia started forward, but Gabriel was not completely lost to the lust of killing. His hands eased a bit around Candliss's neck.

"Give up, you sonofabitch?"

Candliss's arm thumped the ground in assent.

"You going to tell the law what really happened when my wife died?" The arm thumped again, desperately.

Gabriel's eyes narrowed, two embers of green fire looked out from a mask of dirt and blood. "I ought to kill you anyway, and to hell with it all. It might be worth a noose to know you're roasting in hell."

"Gabriel." Olivia spoke softly, and the inferno in Gabriel's eyes dimmed a bit.

Suddenly Olivia was roughly shouldered aside. Before she could grasp what happened, one of Candliss's men clouted Gabriel over the head with the butt of a rifle. He dropped without a sound.

Ace Candliss groaned, rubbed his bruised throat, and staggered to his feet. "About time, you idiot. What the hell were you waiting for?"

Olivia ran to Gabriel and knelt beside him, but another of Candliss's men grabbed her by the arms and propelled her toward the cabin. "Stay out of the way, girlie, or you're gonna get hurt."

"You gave your promise!" Olivia felt idiotic even as she hurled the words at Candliss. Damn Gabriel for believing Candliss's men would stay out of the fight!

Candliss chuckled hoarsely. "I'm not that stupid, Miss Baron. Rodgers, put the bastard on your horse and get a rope around his neck. I swore two years ago I'd watch O'Connell hang, and I mean to have that pleasure. Get a bucket of water to throw on him. I want him awake to feel the rope tighten around his neck."

Olivia watched helplessly as Gabriel was doused with freezing water and hefted aboard a rangy sorrel mare. He sputtered and blinked as his hands were tied behind his back and a crude noose looped around his neck.

"You can't do this!" Olivia declared. "You can't hang him without a trial! The law—"

"Shut her up," Candliss told one of his men. "I'm getting tired of her whining."

"Ace, she's gonna make trouble about this."

"Just shut her up. No one's going to take the word of an outlaw's whore against mine."

Rodgers grabbed her. Another of the men drew back his fist, but Olivia scrambled out of Rodgers's grasp. The blow landed on Rodgers's shoulder instead of her jaw. Both men cursed.

"Olivia, get back to the cabin and stay there." Gabriel's voice was hoarse as if the rope already choked him, but firm. His face was bruised, one eye swollen, but the gaze he fixed on her was level and calm. "Go back to the cabin. Candliss, she won't make any trouble for you."

Candliss grinned up at Gabriel, taunting. "Maybe I'll just make sure she doesn't miss your attention too much when you're gone, O'Connell. Then . . ." He chuckled. "The perfect solution. After all, you're known as a woman-killer. What better justification for me to hang you out of hand than to find you've gone and done in another one, eh? After all, Montana's a state now. We can't tolerate such things now that we're a civilized part of the Union."

Candliss continued his taunt, crowing to Gabriel about Olivia's fate, enjoyment and triumph swelling his voice. Trapped between Candliss's men and the cabin, Olivia spied her shotgun lying where she'd earlier dropped it. The weapons that had been piled on top of it had all been retrieved by the men while she had been concentrating on the fight, and the shotgun lay alone, temptingly near. She lunged for it and swung it to point toward the nearest enemy.

"Don't come any closer or I'll shoot."

The man guffawed. She pulled back the hammer, and he fell silent.

"Oh, Miss Baron," Candliss called. He smiled at her and leveled his rifle. "Drop the shotgun."

"Not before I shoot one or two of you. Any volunteers to be first?"

Candliss still smiled, but his men looked uneasily at the shotgun she held so steadily.

"Your boss is going to get some of you killed," Olivia told them, playing upon the doubt she perceived in their faces. "Is his revenge worth your dying?"

Despite the cold, her hands sweated, making the shotgun slick. She prayed she would have the nerve to fire if necessary.

She pushed further. "You're insane, Candliss, lynching a man who has yet to be tried and planning to murder an innocent woman. These men of yours aren't going to stand by and let you do that, especially since one or two of them are going to get shot in the process. Just cut Gabriel down and take him back to the law in Elkhorn. That way you get your chance to see him punished, and no one gets shot."

The men eyed Candliss uncertainly.

"You going to listen to a woman?" Candliss raised his rifle and took aim. The skin over Olivia's left breast tingled, as if she could feel the rifle sights home in on her heart. Her senses sharpened to an unnatural acuity. She smelled the sharp scent of pines and spruce, felt the moist cold of the breeze against her face. Gabriel's gaze rested on her like fire, and Candliss's like ice. In her hands, the shotgun was heavy and slippery with sweat. The blood thundered noisily through her veins, and her breath was a quiet hurricane moving in and out of her lungs.

She was eerily unafraid as she swung the shotgun toward Candliss. "My thumb is holding back the hammer, Mr. Candliss. If you shoot me, you're going to get shot yourself."

Candliss's rifle didn't waver.

"For God's sake, man, let her go. Send her down the trail. She's not a part of this."

Candliss seemed to enjoy Gabriel's plea. He smiled and opened his mouth to answer, just as a shot rang out. His smile twisted into a grimace as he dropped the rifle and folded onto the ground, clutching his leg.

Olivia dashed toward Gabriel and jerked the hanging rope free from the tree branch.

"Pa!" Katy shouted as she rode into the clearing. At her back was Crooked Stick and a number of Blackfeet that Olivia didn't bother to count. They looked as numerous as the trees, each face with eyes like black marble and expressions grim as death.

Rodgers cursed and froze. His comrades looked into the hungry black muzzles of the Indians' rifles and didn't move.

"Pa! Are you all right?"

Gabriel slid down from the horse into Olivia's arms.

"I found Crooked Stick coming up the trail, Pa. He'd heard you got out of jail and was coming to help."

"Well, he sure helped," Gabriel said, rubbing his throat.

Crooked Stick rode up to where Candliss was trying to rise and nudged him with his rifle. "This is the one who killed Many Horses Woman?"

"His brother killed Many Horses," Gabriel said. "But this one stole Many Horses' honor, tried to hang me—twice—and threatened the twins and Olivia."

Crooked Stick nudged Candliss hard enough so that he toppled back onto the ground. "He dies."

"No!" Candliss whined. "Don't let this savage have me, O'Connell. You're a white man, for God's sake. Do you know what he'll do to me?"

Crooked Stick grinned a death's-head grin.

"Many Horses was my favorite sister, white man. I have waited a long time for Horse Stalker to point the finger so I know who you are."

Candliss turned a pleading face to Gabriel. "Do something!"

"Why should I?" Gabriel wrapped an arm around both Katy and Olivia. "Why the hell should I?"

"Because you're a white man, goddammit!"

"No particular honor in that."

"If you let those red bastards have me, I won't be able to tell the judge in Virginia City what really happened the day you shot Buck."

Gabriel's arm squeezed Olivia tighter. He hesitated, then said: "That's true. But then, after what you did, I might just take my chances with the law and find out what sort of inventive death Crooked Stick might think of for you."

Candliss turned paler than he already was. Olivia almost felt sorry for him.

"Then again, maybe not." Gabriel looked solemnly at Crooked Stick. "If you kill Candliss, my brother, then the white men will still think I killed your sister."

Crooked Stick's face was impassive. The rifle pointed at Candliss didn't waver.

"He'll be tried and punished for his crimes, Crooked Stick."

"The white men will not punish him for what he did to Many Horses Woman. They will not care, because she was one of the *Kainah.*"

"If they don't punish him, then we will—you and I."

The sound that rumbled in Crooked Stick's throat sounded remarkably like a growl. He dismounted, drew a knife, and before anyone could move, sliced it three times across Candliss's cheek. Candliss yowled.

"That is my mark," Crooked Stick said. "You belong to me, white man. I give you for now to my brother, but you belong to me. May the Earth and the Sun hear me when I say you will die."

He wiped his bloody knife on his leggings and vaulted into his saddle. "We go with you back to Virginia City, Horse Stalker, so this one cannot escape."

"I'm grateful, my brother. Take him now, and the others too. We'll meet you down the trail."

Crooked Stick and his little band efficiently tied Candliss and his men together in a line and herded them toward the trail. When they had disappeared, Olivia turned her face into Gabe's shoulder. "I thought we were both dead."

His hand moved up to lightly massage her neck. "So did I, sweet lass. So did I."

For a moment the three of them stood and savored the peace of the empty clearing. Then Katy's voice piped a question. "Is everything all right now, Pa?"

"It's going to be, Katy girl. I swear it's going to be." He delivered a gentle swat to her trouser-clad rear. "You go find your sister."

"Where is she?"

"Hiding in the woods," Olivia said.

"Figures," Katy chortled.

As Katy loped off in search of Ellen, Gabriel turned Olivia so that she fitted into his embrace, her head tucked neatly beneath his chin. "I hope you meant it when you said you'd marry me, Doc, because it looks like we might have a future ahead of us after all."

She tilted her head back to look up at him. "Do you really want to marry someone who smells more often of carbolic than cologne?"

The corner of his mouth twitched upward. "It would be a sacrifice, I grant you."

She laughed and aimed a blow at his ear. He dodged, grabbed her arm, and brought her firmly against him for a kiss that made her knees wobble and her head swim.

"I think I can put up with carbolic," he said with a grin, "if you can put up with an Irish oaf and his two demon daughters."

"Just kiss me like that every day, and I'll manage."

"Good thing. The way my life's been going, I need a doctor in the family."

He dodged another blow and gave her a quick kiss. "Come on, my love. Let's find our girls and be on our way to Virginia City."